The Compromise

Zoë Miller

HACHETTE
BOOKS
IRELAND

First published in Ireland in 2013 by Hachette Books Ireland
First published in paperback in 2013 by Hachette Books Ireland

1

Cataloguing in Publication Data is available from the British Library.

ISBN 978 1 444 743 180

Typeset in AGaramond and Sakkal Majalla by Bookends Publishing Services
Printed and bound in Great Britain by Clays Ltd, St Ives plc.

Hachette Books Ireland policy is to use papers that are natural, renewable
and recyclable products and made from wood grown in sustainable forests.
The logging and manufacturing processes are expected to conform to the
environmental regulations of the country of origin.

Hachette Books Ireland
8 Castlecourt Centre
Castleknock
Dublin 15, Ireland

A division of Hachette UK Ltd
338 Euston Road, London NW1 3BH

www.hachette.ie

This book is dedicated with lots of love and thanks
to my family and friends

Acknowledgements

I'd like to express huge thanks and appreciation to all those who have helped my dream become a reality:

The brilliant team at Hachette Ireland, who constantly pull out all the stops and work so hard behind the scenes, in particular Ciara Doorley, for her fantastic, insightful editing, Joanna Smyth, for her patient and endless assistance, also Breda, Jim, Margaret, Ruth, Bernard, and Siobhán. And Hazel Orme, for her superb copy-editing skills.

My wonderful agent, Sheila Crowley, for her warm encouragement and constant belief in me, and the marvellous support from Becky, Laura and the Curtis Brown team.

I truly appreciate the privilege of working with you all.

This book is dedicated to my circle of family and friends, who all deserve tremendous thanks for amazing encouragement and stellar support: in particular Derek, Michelle, Declan, Barbara, Dara, Colm and the especially precious Cruz. I love you all so much and thank you from the bottom of my heart for always being there for me. Also my extended family, who still talk to me and keep me on their invitation lists even if I don't see them half as often as I would like: Margaret and Pat, Peter and Margaret, David and Denise, Kevin and Hazel, Clare and Patricia, Rita and Pat, and Denis and Mary.

One of the themes of *The Compromise* is the value of female friendship, and I would like to take this opportunity to express heartfelt thanks and appreciation to some lovely ladies for being in my life and for laughter, fun, and wonderful support: Angela, Mary and Kate; Eileen, Mary and Anne; Kathleen and Alice; Majella; Geraldine and Joan; Bríd, Margaret and Pauline T.

Thanks also to my work colleagues and circle of writer friends – you know who you are!

And lastly but by no means least, a big thank you to all my lovely readers for trusting enough in me to buy my books, and for all the wonderful messages that come via Twitter and Facebook and through www.zoemillerauthor.com. It means everything to me. I really hope you enjoy *The Compromise*.

Zoë xxx

Prologue

Dublin, Saturday, 17 March, 7.15 a.m.

It is one of those pristine, pearly mornings when the world is hushed, the opalescent sky goes on for ever, everything seems sparkling and brand new, and you don't expect anything bad to happen. Even the sea is calm, from the far-off horizon where it hazes into the sky, right up to where the incoming tide foams lightly against the pewter cliffs.

As he jogs around the headland track, the whole day lies ahead of him, waiting to be lived and filled with possibilities. He will shower when he gets home, and bring his pregnant wife a cup of tea. Later, he might paint the nursery. They might go shopping for a Moses basket. Or out to dinner. But for now there is just this: the cool, early-morning breeze on his face, the salt-scented air filling his lungs, the sound of his footfall on the earth, and then the glimmering sun, breaking free of a hazy cloud to send bright yellow flurries across the rippling expanse of water. The vital energy of it all surges through his veins and he feels he could run on for ever.

Then, out of the corner of his eye, he sees something odd, something out of place, an aberration in this calm, still morning. His stride falters. He stops. He hears his breathing, loud in his ears. His heart skips a beat.

It is far down, near the base of the cliffs. It looks like a heap of dark clothes, but the sudden chill running up his spine tells him it is something else. He reaches for his mobile, with him at all times, powered up and switched on in case his wife goes into early labour. A call to the emergency services will put him through to the coastguards: the area officer's pager will go off, and he will raise the cliff rescue team, maybe the helicopter.

He dials, knowing that that is only the beginning. Other calls will be made, shattering peaceful lives, like boulders crashing into a pond. His wife will still be sleeping, so he decides to keep a vigil, on the headland, until the person is safely rescued.

He hopes he or she is still alive and hasn't been lying there all night, alone. He sits down and waits, a light sweat cooling his skin, and all about him the morning unfolds, the gulls stretch their wings as they wheel into the breeze, and the sun floods the sea with bright light. He thinks of his unborn child, waiting to join the world, innocent and new, and his heart turns over. As soon as he is home, he will tell his wife he loves her very much.

Part One

Juliet

ONE

Dublin, Friday, 16 March, 7.30 p.m.

In the beginning there is nothing at all. It's like the moment I wake up and everything is a blank sheet. Then I taste fear in my mouth.

The tail end of a nightmare?

I struggle into wakefulness. I hear the slap of waves beating against the rocks and the hiss of shooting spray. It's the sound of the sea and the familiar backdrop to my evening stroll around the cliff top. There's no need to be fearful because, any minute now, I'll wake up under my duvet.

Something cool puffs against my face and my skin tautens. It shimmies up from my chin. It flows over my nose and cheeks, and across my forehead. It's like a breath and it carries the damp, briny scent of the sea. A breeze. A *breeze*? My eyelids flutter, heavy and sluggish. With an effort, I prise them open. But instead of my shadowy bedroom ceiling, I'm staring up at the night sky.

I *am* dreaming. That's how it feels. I see the stars, sprinkled like fairy glitter across the heavens. A crescent moon gleams, suspended in the sky like a sail on the high seas.

How beautiful it is.

The dream suddenly alters and shifts to another night, a night buried so deeply in my heart that I never venture there. But now the gateway is unlocked and I'm free-falling into it. I'm there again, lying on my back and looking up at a star-studded sky. Music, laughter and the click of castanets float across the distance and mingle with the hiss of waves on a sloping beach. This time the breeze is warm and sweet-scented, and it flutters up from my toes to my scalp. Sand grains rasp against my back and hips. Hard, unfamiliar skin slides against mine. My fingernails skid across the planes of his powerful body and I look over his shoulders to where palm trees are blackly silhouetted against the sky.

So this is what it's like … I cling to him and let desire take over as we mesh together, time and time again. Then comes a sparkling moment when everything swells inside me until it reaches a perfect peak and I'm spinning freely over the edge of the universe.

Little did I know that that was the start of my downfall and the end of my freedom.

That long-ago night fades. In my dream the breeze is coming in flurries, a little stronger, more insistent. Once again I'm staring up at the night sky while the incessant sea shifts and murmurs in the foreground, as though it's alive and breathing and whispering its secrets to me. There is a rapping noise, like seawater spattering off the jagged rocks that jut out from the base of the cliffs. And then the unmistakable sucking sound as the pull of the moon draws out the tide from hidden nooks and crannies.

How come it sounds so close? Usually I'm hearing it at a distance, the clamour muffled by the long drop that plummets from the walking trail at the top of the cliffs to the sea. And why is this dream so real? I should be awake by now, stretching in my bed, not feeling a chilly breeze on my face.

And feeling nothing else at all …

Not even my heart jumping into my throat, as it surely should be, because this is one hell of a bad dream …

And then, a thought so terrible I can't go there: *If it is a dream* …

TWO

The night was thick with long shadows, and a cool breeze snatched at Rebecca Ryan's hair as she wove through the silent car park towards the Seagrass Hotel.

Glass doors to the lobby glided apart at her approach, and when they closed behind her, she might have been in another world. The warm air that wafted about her and the dazzle of chandeliers bouncing off pale marble walls was so much at odds with the dark, chilly night outside that she felt momentarily disoriented.

She took a breath, ignored the butterflies in her stomach, and told herself she could do this.

As she stepped across the lobby, traces of expensive scent lingered in the air. She glanced to the long table at the side. It was cleared of everything except a white tablecloth and empty champagne buckets. She tightened her grip on her overnight bag as her ears were assaulted by the sound of popping corks, the laughter and buzz of a wedding party. She was glad that the lobby was quiet, with just a low hum of conversation from a handful of guests scattered on big squashy couches, the rest still in the banqueting room, having dinner.

She had timed it perfectly.

'Good evening, Madam,' the receptionist said. Her uniform

was pristine, and Rebecca felt tatty in her jeans, furry boots and leather jacket, even though the latter had been an expensive gift to herself during a trip to New York back in the Celtic Tiger days. When she saw her reflection in the long mirror behind the reception desk, she winced. With warm blonde hair – thanks to her hairdresser – good cheekbones and expressive eyes, she'd sometimes been likened to a younger version of Joanna Lumley. However, this evening, her face pale and tight, she didn't look remotely like the sparky actress. She forced a smile, smoothed her hair, straightened her shoulders, and looked a hundred times better.

'Have you a reservation?' The receptionist exuded a brightly glossed confidence in the way only a twenty-something could. Rebecca fumbled with her bag and produced her confirmation email. She'd never had such confidence at that age. Few of her generation had.

Except, of course, Juliet.

The receptionist slid a registration form across the polished marble and went through the usual patter. 'Can I confirm that it's single occupancy, Mrs Ryan?'

'It's Ms Ryan and, yes, that's correct.'

'My apologies. It's just that you ticked Mrs on the registration form.'

Mrs. For a moment Harry is standing by the reception desk in a far-off holiday hotel, organising their passports and key cards, smiling as he begins to propel her case. 'Let's be having you, Mrs Ryan.'

A fresh crump in her stomach. Harry had been gone six years already. He had been fifty-three. Sometimes it felt like six days or six weeks. Other times it felt like six decades. Almost as though he had never been. And there were times, like tonight, when she missed him so much and would have given anything to have him there, at her back. She kept her expression neutral as she said, 'Old habits.'

The receptionist gave her a bland smile. 'The Seagrass has a special rate for those attending the Johnson-Maguire wedding. You're here for the evening reception?'

'That's right.'

'The wedding party is in the Blue Water salon on the first floor. The dinner will be over shortly and then they'll be welcoming the evening guests.'

'Perfect,' Rebecca said.

It had been a last-minute decision to accept the invitation from an old friend of Harry's to join the celebrations for his son's wedding in the north County Dublin hotel. At first Rebecca had had no intention of being there: if things had been different, her family and friends would have been gathering in the south of France, where Danielle, her daughter, had planned to get married. Then she'd decided it would be better to mingle with old acquaintances than sit at home trying to keep her mind off a cream shot-silk wedding dress, muffled in layers of tissue, Danielle's stifled sobs, and the flight tickets to a honeymoon in the Maldives, which she guessed hadn't been cancelled.

Not to mention the other curve balls that life was throwing at her.

Rebecca tucked her key card into her bag, followed the directions to her ground-floor room, and told herself she could handle it. She'd even timed it so that she could shower, change, put on a happy face and look as though she hadn't a care in the world when she joined the party.

She still found it hard to believe that, less than three months ago, life had been almost perfect as she'd sat at the table in

Verbena View, Juliet's home, for a pre-Christmas gathering. She had been with the people who were closest in the world to her: darling Danielle and her fiancé Conor, Rebecca's older sister Rose and husband Matthew, with their son James, and Juliet, her best friend, whom she'd known for most of her life. Her twin sons, Kevin and Mark, who both worked abroad, were missing, and of course, Harry, who had practically grown up with her, Rose and Matthew in the rough-and-tumble of Lower Ballymalin Gardens. Her heart had swelled as she looked around the table and counted her blessings.

Juliet's table had been simply but festively dressed in red and silver, with candlelight casting a subtle glow over arrangements of fat red berries and crystal glasses. Best of all was the banter and laughter that flowed between them all, lifting Rebecca's heart.

'You must be counting the weeks now,' Rose had said to Danielle. Rose! She might be a far cry from the Rose of yesteryear, elegant now in black velvet and Cartier diamonds, as though she'd just stepped out of a *Tatler* society page, but to Rebecca she still bore traces of the quiet ten-year-old girl who had felt their parents' tragic death more keenly than the younger Rebecca. Rose had gone on to become a self-effacing teenager, and equally modest adult, afraid to expect too much from life, lest it be taken away from her.

'Yes, the wedding's less than three months away.' Danielle, beautiful in silver Ben de Lisi, blonde hair shimmering in the muted light, diamond engagement ring glittering, exchanged a smile with Conor.

'Three months?' said Rose's son, James, in mock dismay. 'I guess the band better get in some practice.'

James had joined Juliet's annual Christmas bash for the first time in quite a while. Rebecca wondered if that was why Rose was slightly flushed. Her son was bass guitarist in The Name, a globally successful rock band and, beside his tall, rather rakish figure, she was bursting with pride and adoration. Even Matthew, who had recently featured on a short list of Ireland's most influential businessmen, seemed happy enough to take a back seat to his mega-successful son. The Name would be playing at Danielle's wedding in the south of France on St Patrick's Day.

'Too right you'd better,' Rebecca said. 'Especially for the first dance. I can't imagine The Name do much romantic stuff.'

'You won't hear any bum notes, Rebecca.' James flashed his aunt a grin. 'We can do a rather good "Wind Beneath My Wings".'

'Is that the best you can think of?' Danielle said, exaggerating her horror.

'Hmm. What about "Always And Forever"?' James suggested. 'Or what's that one from *The Bodyguard*?'

'Yeah, right.' Danielle sniffed. 'Conor and I will pick something suitable.'

'Whatever you choose, I don't think James will let you down,' said Matthew.

'You heard the man, little cuz.' James smiled. 'Whatever you want, we'll deliver.'

'I fervently hope you do. Danielle deserves nothing but the best. Now who's for more bubbly?' This was from Juliet, oozing warmth as they lingered at the table long after the meal was over.

Juliet, unlike Rebecca and Rose and their husbands, had been born into a life of power and privilege. She made light of this, letting it roll off her back. She'd thrown all her vibrant energy into her colourful career and had never married, despite a constant string of admirers, some of whom Rebecca had been aware of and others whom Juliet had kept discreetly under wraps. Juliet had a brother in Florida, whom she rarely saw, and had come to regard Rebecca and Rose and their families as her own. Tonight she was a sparkling hostess as she joked and laughed, refreshing wine glasses and passing *petits fours*. The deepening twilight pressed against the wide patio doors and now and again, when Rebecca looked down the table, she saw them all reflected in the glass, the people she loved so much, their faces superimposed on the dark mauve sky.

Now Rebecca reached her room and rummaged for her key card. If only she could have held all the people she loved in a protective bubble of happiness. But time had ticked by. James was the first to rise to his feet and break up the party, and then everything had changed.

Soon after Christmas, Danielle's wedding was off.

'I don't want to talk about it, Mum,' Danielle had said, her blue eyes hard and dark-shadowed, when she'd shown up at home unexpectedly on a cold January evening, announced that she and Conor had split up and asked to stay for a couple of nights. 'It's not up for discussion. Not now, not ever.'

Rebecca had clutched at her throat. 'Oh, Danielle! Darling! How terrible. Did you? Or was it Conor?' Then words had failed her.

Danielle had merely shaken her head, ignored her embrace, and begun to climb the stairs to her old bedroom.

'Darling, talk to me! Surely it's better to share it,' Rebecca had said desperately, glancing at Danielle's ringless finger as if for proof. 'At least let me know if there's anything I can do.'

'How could you do anything?' Danielle had snapped, in an unusually sharp tone, which had betrayed the depth of her pain. 'Sorry, Mum. I just can't talk about it right now. You'd be a lot better off living your own life and leaving me to look after mine.

I can handle it. And if Conor calls, looking for me, I'm not here. Right?'

'Understood.' Rebecca had been devastated by the stony look on her daughter's face and deeply hurt that Danielle hadn't confided in her.

A couple of days later, Danielle had bolted to Rome with her broken heart, and even though they had stayed in regular contact, Rebecca was none the wiser about what had gone wrong. She just hoped Danielle wasn't holed up alone in her apartment tonight, drowning her sorrows on what would have been the eve of her wedding.

That had been the first shock, and Rebecca would have coped with it: life had dealt her far crueller blows. Then, in the last couple of weeks, Rose and Matthew had embarked on a challenging campaign that had the power to shatter their hard-won comfortable lifestyle. Rebecca feared for their happiness.

As if all that wasn't fraught enough, the previous weekend Juliet …

Rebecca closed her bedroom door and leaned against it, fighting a stab of anxiety. Out of nowhere, her friend had begun to talk about setting herself on a collision course with Matthew and Rose. It would leave Rebecca tiptoeing through a minefield and perhaps, eventually, having to choose between her family and her friend.

THREE

Friday, 16 March, 8.00 p.m.

I'm coming back from somewhere dark and heavy, as though I've been asleep. There is the cold of hard stone against the back of my head, and something sharp, like a flint, is pinching the top of my skull.

I've been here already, staring at the night sky from this position, with the hiss of the sea, perilously close, and the salt-laden breeze riffling my face. Can you dream the same dream twice? For this has to be a dream. Or, rather, a nightmare.

Soon I will wake up, laughing with relief, in my bed. Bring it on, I urge. I've had enough of this stupid nightmare. My face is cold and it's getting a bit boring.

For a long time, nothing happens. There is just the spatter of water on the rocks, the plaintive call of a sea bird, and the breeze on my face. A drift of shredded cloud wafts across the face of the moon and I am spellbound once more by the perfect beauty of the night.

Then a solid wall of panic slams into my head. My eyes have adjusted to the night and I can make out something dark and solid rising on my left, blocking out a segment of the starry sky.

It looks exactly like the angle of a steep cliff face.

Oh, God. Oh, dear God.

If my heart is pumping in blind terror, I can't feel it. Neither can I feel my legs. Or my arms. Or anything below my face. I open my mouth to scream but no sound comes out. I feel detached, though, as if the nightmare is happening to someone else. I pounce on this and will myself to believe it.

It has to be a nightmare. A nightmare in which I'm imagining myself lying far too close to the sea, by the base of the cliffs, staring up at the night sky, unable to move or feel anything below my head.

It can't be real.

For these are my cliffs and my sea. No harm should come to me here. This is the breeze I feel most evenings as I stroll around the headland track, looking out across the vast expanse of the bay. I close my eyes and see the way the light falls across the surface of the sea. It looks fresh and vibrant in the early morning, sleepy and tranquil in the late evening. I often wonder at the secrets it holds. Some days the water is the clearest aquamarine; on others it is a stony grey ripple, but it is always beautiful.

I see a photograph of it, enlarged and framed, on a wall somewhere. I know that wall: it's in my office at the university. *What university?* I see, like translucent ghosts, the blurry shadows and shapes of people who stop to admire it, and hear their muffled voices as though I'm listening to them from under water.

'It must be the Seychelles …'

'Nah, it has to be Thailand. When were you in Thailand?'

'Look at the luminosity of those colours – almost like a painting!'

'It's the Irish Sea off Howth, where I live.' That's my voice. I hear the note of pride even at this remove.

'You lucky thing.'

'Yes, I walk there most evenings. There's a great track that goes all around the headland.'

'Oh, wow. That's cool.'

'Yes, it's so invigorating … better than a week in a five-star hotel.'

'Wish I had that on my doorstep.'

'You can join me any evening.'

Laughter. The clip of heels. The sound receding. A door closing.

The image fades. I'm thrust back into the grip of the cold, hard, inky black nightmare. Soon I'll wake up in my bedroom, surrounded by my things.

My bedroom: ivory sheets, plump pillows, a deep pile chocolate-brown carpet that feels like marshmallow under my bare feet. A stand-alone dressing-table, with crystal atomisers of my favourite perfumes. A walk-in wardrobe in which all my clothes are neatly arranged. Draped gowns and tailored suits, figure-hugging jeans and casual tracksuits. Shelves of shoes, boots and high-heeled sandals. A multitude of bags and cases. The wardrobe of a busy person leading a full, active life.

I will slip out of bed and stand under the shower, then put on my cream towelling wrap. I will go into the kitchen for breakfast – on one wall, big patio doors look out to sea. On fine days you can fold them back and soak up the warmth. I will make porridge, then a poached egg on toast. The taste is almost in my mouth. I deserve it after this horrendous nightmare.

The image shatters as hard reality crashes into my head. Why can't I feel my legs?

Where are they? *My* legs.

It's not only my legs I can't feel, it's my arms. Why can't I feel them?

Voices float out across the cold air above my head. A dog barks and from the yipping sound it makes, the owner is dragging it along against its will. I hear the tinny clink-clink-clink of an empty can, as though it's bouncing off a series of rocky outcrops. It comes closer and closer until it clatters past within a few feet of me. I hear a splash. Then silence.

Perhaps it fell down the cliff face and landed in the sea.

Did that happen to me? Did I lose my footing and bounce down the cliff face to where I'm lying helpless now, staring up at the indigo sky?

It's not just a dream or a nightmare. It's going on too long. I should have woken up by now. I can't figure out how long I've been here, how I got here, what day it is, what time, how this happened, or how I'm going to get back up that cliff to my life …

Help will come. It *has* to. Someone must know I'm here.

What's the last thing I can remember? The *very* last thing?

FOUR

In their four-bedroom red-brick period house, set in landscaped gardens on Belgrave Park, Matthew Moore strode ahead of Rose to the front door. 'I don't know how you managed to arrive home late tonight of all nights,' he flung over his shoulder. 'You know how important it is for me.'

She almost laughed at the way he had assumed she'd be following in his wake. Which, of course, she was. As she had done for most of their marriage. Rose had long ago accepted she hadn't a rebellious bone in her body. 'You've a lot more balls than I have,' she'd once said to Rebecca.

Rebecca had responded with a sympathetic look.

Matthew activated the security system, his fingers stabbing the wrong buttons so that he had to start again. 'Bloody hell, what's *wrong* with it?' he fumed.

Rose watched the grim set of his jaw and remained silent as he finally keyed in the correct code and she found herself propelled outside. Standing in the porch, as Matthew turned the key in the complicated lock, she glanced back through the leaded-glass panel into the hallway where she'd left on a lamp. Every instinct urged her to crawl back into the house, go straight up the stairs to bed and blank out the world with a sleeping pill. But there was no escape from the reception being hosted by the CEO of the American Ireland Youth Association on the eve of St Patrick's Day, so she followed him down the granite steps to the driveway.

She hated these functions. Matthew loved them. He revelled in the undercurrents of power and one-upmanship that ricocheted around such a gathering under the cover of bonhomie. They made her nervous and edgy. Especially tonight, with so much at stake.

She'd have to get used to these occasions, she told herself. There'd be a lot more high-level socialising and strategic shoulder-slapping in the coming weeks. Recently their lives had taken a surprising turn, the shock waves of which she was still struggling to absorb.

'Why are you so tetchy?' she said, as they took the flagstone path beside the drive to his car. 'The invite was eight for half past so we're okay. And,' she looked at him, 'I'm not the only one who arrived home late. You were so late you barely had time to jump into the shower. What kept you?'

'I had to go back to the office to finish a report,' Matthew said brusquely, as he opened the passenger door of the Mercedes. 'So, you see, I was working. I wasn't out dining and whining with the ladies who lunch. And neither will I be drinking tonight as I need a very clear head.'

Before she stepped into the car, she glanced up at him. The front garden, surrounded by mature trees and shrubs, was alive with night-time shadows. For a moment, framed in the wash of the garden lamplight, her husband seemed like a tall, dark stranger, and Rose shivered, despite the *faux*-fur stole she was wearing over her Helen McAlinden taffeta gown.

'You're very bold,' she said, her tone deliberately light. 'What you've just said wouldn't go down too well with the ladies in question. Never mind me.'

'Ah, Rose, sorry about that and thanks for your concern,' he said, in his warm, public voice, the one that had been labelled beguiling and charismatic. 'Don't worry your pretty little head – I can take care of the ladies. You just smile and look good.'

'I always do,' she said. She'd spent years perfecting the art of smiling and looking good, which, tonight, was a definite advantage.

She slid into the passenger seat and the door clunked shut.

'Off we go,' he said, looking suddenly youthful.

Rose was reminded of the young John F. Kennedy lookalike she'd first seen lugging a heavy schoolbag up the mean streets of Lower Ballymalin Gardens in another lifetime. The couple in the plush Mercedes purring through the tree-lined avenues in one of south Dublin's most exclusive neighbourhoods bore no resemblance to the young Rose and Matthew: they'd got together as teenagers on cobbled streets where small terraced houses had no gardens and pavements were narrow, where the lucky few found work in the nearby upmarket village of Howth. Matthew's parents had eked out a living on his father's disability pension, but his mother had decided her only child was bound for better things: she had taken on a cleaning job to pay for extra tuition over and above the basic education offered in the local vocational school. Quiet, anxious-to-please Rose was only too happy to hang around windy street corners listening to the boy with the dreams.

Sometimes the teenagers got together to spend summer Sundays on the beach at Howth, or took the bus to the summit to picnic and play spin-the-bottle on the grassy slopes. And while Rebecca played hard to get in her romance with Harry, Rose and Matthew had always been together, bound by his ambitions to take on the world.

When Matthew landed a job at the bank, justifying his parents' sacrifices and faith in him, he said it was only the beginning.

They married in their early twenties on a tiny budget, had a week's honeymoon in Donegal, then set up home in a little house on the edge of Dublin; the deposit had devoured most of their savings. It had been a dream come true for Rose: she couldn't quite believe Matthew loved her enough to *marry* her.

Sometimes she still found it hard to believe. Now, almost a lifetime later, she could hardly remember the wedding, or the small reception. She had James, their son, but the journey from penny-pinching suburbia to affluent Belgrave Park had been full of dark twists and turns.

Matthew had long left the bank behind him. By degrees, he had become a charming, confident and hugely successful businessman. With hard work and ruthless focus, he had confidently embraced the growing opportunities in new technology as Ireland had slowly emerged from the recession of the 1980s. He'd founded Tory Technologies in the early 1990s and the company was still showing a healthy profit in spite of the current recession, as was his portfolio of investments, wisely diversified to include commercial investment property in Switzerland, as well as vineyards in Spain and stud farms in Argentina.

Matthew had also scaled the social ladder and was quite at home in the corridors of power, thanks to his judicious networking, his courting of senior politicians, and his state agency membership. His profile had gone into orbit, and Rose wondered what he continued to see in her, his quiet, unassuming wife. Was he still happy with her ... or were some of his needs being met elsewhere?

She'd been a stay-at-home wife and mother, keeping house

and ironing shirts, going to cookery and flower arranging classes, and helping with community activities. When Matthew had insisted they get a part-time housekeeper on their move to Belgrave Park, and Mrs Barry had arrived, Rose had volunteered at the Children's Hospital.

Now, thanks to Matthew's drive and ambition, there were more rollercoaster rides to come: he was planning to campaign as an independent candidate in the forthcoming presidential election. The prospect filled Matthew with elation and Rose with alarm.

'So the campaign starts in earnest tonight,' Rose said.

'I've learned a lot from following last year's contest,' he replied, as the car halted at a pedestrian crossing. 'I'm a good candidate, and I've got the right men to advise me.'

The previous year Ireland had been plunged into a hotly fought contest, which resulted in the surprise election of David Doolin, a forty-something television broadcaster, whose Saturday-night show was a constant winner in the ratings war. A household name, he had swept to a landslide victory. A celebrity president, some had said. He hadn't lasted long: just as he was becoming disenchanted with presidential protocol, American television moguls had asked him to front a prime-time weekend show.

Suddenly a fresh election campaign was on the agenda, and Matthew was running as an independent. The last thing Rose wanted was the spotlight that a career in politics would shine on their lives. At first she'd thought it would blow over, that he didn't really mean it. But it had taken on a life of its own. She did her utmost to rein in her anxiety, to conceal it beneath the smiling mask she wore in front of everyone, even Rebecca.

'Besides, we've no skeletons in the cupboard,' Matthew said.

'Haven't we?' she said, her breath faltering in her throat.

Without hesitation, he met her eyes. 'No, we haven't,' he said firmly. His were clear and steady, warm with reassurance. Matthew's face was a little craggier with the passage of time and it suited him. Tonight he was wearing his navy Paul Smith coat over his suit with a careless ease that belied his humble origins; it set off his short, silvering hair attractively. 'Look, Rose, I want this opportunity more than anything else in the world. This is my ultimate dream.'

'I want you to have it but—'

'No buts.' He smiled. 'We can do it, us, together. Trust me.'

He looked the part, she thought, swallowing. He looked every inch the perfect candidate. He looked like someone you could trust with your life.

At least for the moment she could be sure Matthew wasn't having an affair, despite his late nights at the office, sudden trips abroad, and the mobile phone that was never out of his sight. He wouldn't risk it now, when he had so much to lose, would he?

They joined the stream of traffic surging around Ballsbridge, Rose feeling as though she was snagged in a swiftly moving current. She remembered the packet of pills concealed in her silk clutch. They'd saved her from many a bad moment, but no way could they blot out the feeling of impending doom clawing at her chest. In spite of their success, or maybe because of it, Rose lived with constant dread: the fear of being found out.

She also felt torn in two. While she wanted Matthew to have his dream, she wanted her life to stay as it was. Surely he had achieved more than enough already, she fretted, as they swept in through the entrance of the Four Seasons Hotel, slightly late. How far did he need to go to prove himself to himself?

'Do you think Juliet might be here?' she asked, a little breathless, as she watched his face carefully.

There was a short, tense silence.

'I've no idea,' Matthew said. 'Did she tell you she was coming?'

'I thought she might have been invited,' Rose said. 'I thought all the presidential hopefuls were coming tonight and that it would be a sort of informal get-together ...'

Matthew gave a short laugh. 'Ah, Rose, you're so funny. It'll be more like an ambush, with the opponents circling each other like gladiators in the arena. Some of my rivals will be here but my guess is Juliet will stay away because she'll want to avoid me.'

'Really?'

'I might have known she'd put her name in the hat once she heard I was interested in the race. I'm still trying to figure out if she's serious about running or just trying to rattle me.'

'And why would she do that?' Rose asked, her grip tightening on her clutch. She wondered if it had been the other way around. Had Matthew entered when he'd heard Juliet had been approached?

'She's always enjoyed challenging me,' Matthew said.

Surely he meant that *he* enjoyed challenging *her*, Rose thought, remembering some of their verbal spats.

A friendly but pointed rivalry had simmered between them, right from the time Juliet had joined their group of Ballymalin friends, changing the comfortable dynamic with her exotic air and sheen of privilege. At the time, Rose had been secretly relieved that her wedding was just weeks away, with no time for Juliet to pose any real threat. Still, Matthew had always been unable to disguise his envy of Juliet's privileged background, and their rivalry set Rose on edge. Tory Technologies had become involved in a charity programme only when Matthew had seen the plaudits Juliet was gathering for hers.

They paused in the line of cars waiting to disgorge their occupants. Up ahead, Rose saw doors opening and closing, designer-clad ladies and men in dress suits stepping out. The wealthy and privileged, with their ultra-perfect lives. Just as they would appear to the people in the queue behind them. She felt Matthew's gaze on her face.

'Juliet knows that I know she'd be a shoo-in,' he went on. 'With her profile, intelligence, and avant-garde, all wrapped up in a beautiful package, she's the one we'd all have to watch. And she ticks most of the boxes of her successful predecessors. Just think,' he laughed, 'we could be going head to head.'

Is that what he really thought of Juliet? A beautiful package? 'I don't think that's remotely funny. And,' she continued, her voice shaking, 'Juliet's hardly squeaky clean either.'

'Either?' Matthew shot her a glance. 'Relax, Rose. There's absolutely nothing to worry about where Juliet's concerned,' he said. 'Or me. It'll all be fine. I promise. Juliet's not going to upset any apple carts. She has too much to lose. Hey, here we go,' he said, excitement in his voice as he spotted the journalists and camera crew gathered outside the hotel entrance. 'And, darling,' he took his hand off the steering wheel long enough to squeeze her arm, 'you look wonderful. As beautiful as ever. I'm so proud of you, and I'm sorry if I was snappy earlier. My nerves got the better of me.'

The car door opened, and Rose put her knees together before she got out. She could almost hear Juliet's voice in her ear, talking about the perils of flashing her thighs or, worse, her knickers as she got out of a car. She stepped out on her diamanté heels and, although she felt like slinking quietly into a corner, she drew herself to her full height and smiled. There was a camera flash, then another. Matthew gave the car keys to the valet and took her arm, angling her towards the cameras and pausing briefly to allow for another couple of photographs.

It was starting. Matthew Moore was suddenly front-page news, and the idea chilled her to the bone. Life as they knew it would soon be turned on its head.

Oh, God, take this cup away.

FIVE

Friday, 16 March, 8.10 p.m.

A filament of memory detaches itself from the thick shadows in my head. 'I'll leave them until later,' I say, looking at the wine glasses on the counter.

Two empty glasses, red wine staining them. Surely it was this evening if I can see it so clearly. I'd had a visitor. Someone who knows where I am. Because if the glasses were on the counter, not even rinsed, they had just been used, and I had left the house in too much of a hurry to put them in the dishwasher.

'Let's get going before the light fades too much. Otherwise we could walk off the edge of the cliff ...' There is laughter in my voice as I pick up my key.

Everything else is a blank.

Nonetheless, relief floods through my head. Whoever I was with has gone to get help. Soon I'll be out of here and back in the familiar routine of my life. Okay, I've had some kind of accident. I missed my footing and tripped over the edge, perhaps where it was crumbling away. I wonder if I broke any limbs in my fall.

This will make a right mess of things. I haven't got time to be laid up with broken legs or fractured arms. Worst-case scenario,

I might have injured my spine, and that's why I can't feel my limbs. Right now I can't remember my name but I know, with a deep-felt certainty, that I'm a busy person with a packed diary.

I have a sudden image of the calendar pinned to the corkboard in the kitchen. It's a daily appointment calendar, specially designed for me, with personal photographs adorning each month, birthdays already printed in their respective boxes. Out of nowhere comes the knowledge that somebody gave it to me last Christmas.

'So you won't have to worry about forgetting your important dates, like my birthday, for instance.' I hear a girl laugh, as I unwrap the ruby foil while twinkling lights from a nearby Christmas tree glint on the shimmering paper.

Did I worry about forgetting? Who is the girl? I sense she means a lot to me.

'I know you put reminders into your phone,' she says, 'but this will show what's coming up in advance. Especially the wedding of the year.'

Wedding? Whose? I struggle to recall the details but they're elusive, and then to remember who was with me, drinking wine. I wonder how long I'll have to wait for help to come.

The breeze ruffles my hair – it'll be ruined. My *hair*? Why does it matter if it's ruined? Something tells me I had it done today. Or was it the day before?

Highlights and a trim. Make me gorgeous. Make me sexy. Out of nowhere memory flashes and I hear my careless laughter. I see myself staring into a brightly lit mirror, an enormous black gown swathing me, my face pale, white plastic parcels clinging to my head in carefully aligned tiers.

Suddenly I see his reflection sitting beside me, a greying-white wig curling around his head and falling to the gathers of his black gown. The judge, against whom no sin may be committed because … because …

Because he loves me so much.

He dissolves as someone moves in and peels off my black gown to reveal me sitting with my hands neatly folded, in a cherry-red shirt that sets off my hair. Funny, I'd expected to see myself with the jet-black urchin crop I'd worn for years. But the image I'm staring at is pale blonde tints washed with pink, which adds a touch of sexiness to my short, jazzy style.

'There you are, Juliet, all done.'

Juliet. My name. I clasp it to me as though the knowledge will make up for the cold of the stone at the back of my head and the absence of light, heat, shelter, arms and legs.

Juliet Jordan. Daughter of the late Mr Justice Henry Jordan.

Part of the fog blanking out swathes of my memory lifts away and pictures of my life are dancing in front of me, not linear, in date order, but rather like a film jerking from forward into rewind.

I stride along the cliff top. My hair is damp with sweat as I reach the finish line of a mini-marathon; I spring out of a limousine, dashing into a building to avoid the rain; I march down a grey tunnel to the interior of a plane – I'm pulling a small case, laughing at the tell-tale clink of my duty free. I feel water slide off my skin as I swim with a dolphin in the blue ocean. My eyes adjust to a blindingly white ski slope that rushes to meet me. I drive along a motorway with the top down on a sunny day, singing along with Rihanna.

I mount a wooden podium. Rows of upturned faces look at me with interest. There is an expectant hush. Who are these people? I must have something to say that interests them. As I speak, a ripple of laughter runs around the room and there is a burst of applause.

My arms shrug into red shirts and cashmere jumpers. They embrace friends. My hands light candles, arrange flowers, toss a cloud of flour into a mixing bowl, and raise a glass of wine to my lips; I have nimble fingers that fly across a keyboard, call up a friend on my mobile, switch on a microphone and angle it towards my mouth.

My mind races and I grasp at floating tendrils of my life. I see my home as though I'm looking through a mist. Verbena View. I've known it all my life and I especially love the kitchen. I would give everything I have to be there right now, warm, the scent of herbs mingling with that of the freshly baked scones on the cooling rack, and the view of Dublin Bay through the patio doors.

When I get home, I will never complain again of not having enough time for a decent holiday. I will quite happily spend the rest of my days there, for it is the most beautiful spot in the world. I will never complain about anything ever again. Or be short with Rose. Or not have enough time for Rebecca.

Rose and Rebecca? My surging thoughts halt and backtrack … My friends. Rebecca more so than Rose, who was always a little wary of me, and still is on account of Matthew … Who's Matthew? The name makes me feel uneasy but I can't think who he is.

Suddenly I see Rose standing primly by the sewing box, as her sparrow-like, grey-haired grandmother pins up the hem of my mother's ivory ballgown in my parents' bedroom at Verbena View. She stares at me with solemn eyes that are too big for her thin, pale face. Now Rebecca sidles into the room. She has been in the kitchen, where the housekeeper has given her a glass of milk and some soda bread. Rebecca is younger, nearer to my age, seven, but bigger than me, and her hair is in tight plaits. It's the first time they've come to our home with Mrs O'Malley, the dressmaker my mother occasionally uses. Their shoes are a little worn and their clothes look like they've been washed too often, but they're spotlessly clean.

I smile at Rebecca, and my face freezes: I've just remembered that their parents died in a train crash and they are newly orphaned – my mother must have told me – and they are now living with their grandparents. I can't imagine how horrible it must be to lose both parents and it makes me feel all heavy inside.

My father comes in, his bulk and sheer vitality reassuring. He offers them a lift home but Mrs O'Malley shakes her head. When I watch them marching proudly down the garden path, and Rebecca puts her arm through Rose's, I wish I had a sister. Or a best friend who would put her arm through mine. I feel ashamed of my thoughts, because I have so much and I still want more. I turn away from the window and run into my father's study.

All these fractured glimpses of my life flash around me with lightning speed, yet so real that I want to reach out, catch one and bring it close so that I can somehow slot myself back in there. *Be* there, in my life.

How did I get here? Although some fragments of my life gleam crystal clear, others are smudged. I try to think back to earlier this evening and what might have happened to me.

Let's get going before the light fades too much. Otherwise we could walk off the edge of the cliff . . .

Something's floating at the back of my mind, just out of reach. I know it's significant but it slides away from me every time I try to fasten on it. It's something I said, words coming out of my mouth that shouldn't have. Was I goaded into saying them? Pushed into a corner where I dropped my habitual guard?

Pushed.

Pushed?

I thought I was already cold, but now an icicle of terror spears through my forehead. How come that word resonates with me? Was I pushed? Over the edge of the cliff? Or is my muddled mind playing tricks on me?

But how else did I get here? I'm usually careful, and I know the track around the top of the cliffs like I know the back of my hand. Could a sudden gust have caught me unawares? Am I imagining it or was there pressure on my shoulders? I have a fleeting recall of shock as I slewed off balance. Then I'm plummeting into empty space …

Noooo …

SIX

Feeling as though she was observing it from a distance, Rebecca smiled brightly as she circulated through the stylish gathering in the Blue Water salon, catching up with old friends and acquaintances of Harry, grateful that air kisses, compliments and chit-chat distracted her a little from the concerns that teemed in her head.

'Rebecca! You look amazing! It's lovely to see you.'

'Rebecca Ryan, it *is* you. We weren't sure you'd make it.'

'Neither was I,' she admitted.

Then Paul Johnson, Harry's friend. 'Thanks so much for coming, Rebecca. Let me introduce you to our son and his beautiful bride.'

The bride was indeed beautiful. Rebecca thought of Danielle, her broken dreams, and her heart squeezed. Still, she managed to put that to one side as she laughed and chatted and glided between people, glad that she'd dressed to the hilt in her curve-skimming, cobalt blue Louise Kennedy gown. The party, with the excited buzz, the beautiful people under the ornate ceiling and the cleverly diffuse lighting, was a perfect diversion.

Not all her worries were swept away. As she mingled and sipped wine, she kept wondering how Rose was getting on at her celebrity function. It would be a taste of what was to come, a challenge for the self-effacing Rose. Slavishly loyal to her husband, Rose would never admit, even to her sister, that she was unhappy with Matthew's plans.

And then there was Juliet, throwing the equivalent of a stick of gelignite into her life, whose fallout could affect them all. No wonder Rebecca had had cross words with her just the previous Sunday.

The best man asked for some hush as they were about to show a short montage compiled by the newly married couple, a collation of photographs and video clips, charting the milestones of their lives and accompanied by the music that had formed the background to their romance. Rebecca accepted a glass of champagne and sat with a group of Harry's friends, heedless of the images rolling across the screen, seeing instead the events of the previous Sunday.

☜☞

It had all been so totally unexpected.

When Rebecca dropped into Verbena View, Juliet had greeted her with a hug. 'Rebecca, it's great to see you. I want to talk to you. In fact …' Juliet hesitated '… I was just about to go for my power walk if you want to join me? I've been glued to the computer all day, and I could do with some fresh air.'

'Sure, I could do with some of that myself,' Rebecca said. She'd often walked the cliffs with Juliet. 'And it's gorgeous out, like summer. Shame you were cooped up all day.'

'Busy, busy.' Juliet smiled, then nipped to her bedroom. She came back moments later, her slight figure in a navy tracksuit, smiling as she ran her fingers through her hair. 'Just caught a glimpse of my hair in the mirror. God – I didn't know my roots were that bad! I'll have to squeeze in the hairdresser before next weekend.' She ducked into the closet and reappeared wearing a pink baseball cap. 'That's better. Now, where did I leave my key?'

'Here.' Rebecca grinned, picking it up off the hall table.

They took the track that looped up around the headland. The evening breeze was light and tangy, and in the calm hiatus between the busy day and the onset of evening, sea and sky blended into a grey-blue haze. As she looked out to the shimmering horizon, Rebecca drew a deep breath and felt as though she was walking on the edge of infinity.

'First,' Juliet said, 'how's Danielle?'

'So-so, I guess. I'm afraid to go near her, and she still won't talk to me about what went wrong.'

'Poor darling. I might pop over to visit her in Rome. Phone calls and emails aren't the same.'

'Whatever about me, I know she'd love to see you.'

'I'll tell her I need to replenish my wardrobe on the Via Condotti, so she doesn't think I'm playing agony aunt.'

'She'll see through that one straight away. She's always admired the way you fly the flag for our Irish designers.'

''Suppose. And how are you? Oh, hell, I forgot …'

'Forgot what?' Rebecca asked, instinct telling her just what Juliet was about to say.

'It would have been this coming weekend, the wedding, wouldn't it?'

A silence.

Juliet went on, 'God, I feel really bad about this, but I'm tied up for most of the weekend, so I won't be around much, in case you need a shoulder to lean on.'

'I'll be fine,' Rebecca insisted stoutly, even though she'd half expected Juliet to be around for her. However, Juliet was busy, she knew, and naturally she'd be in demand on the national holiday. 'I was only going to be mother-of-the-bride,' she said. 'It's Danielle who'll want to block it out.'

'Still, I wanted to be there for you, I know it'll be rough, but I need the whole of Friday to complete some urgent paperwork, even it if takes until midnight. I'll be working from home and locking myself away in the study. I have a lunch engagement on Paddy's Day plus a couple of evening receptions. And it's all in the course of duty. Hey, why don't you come along with me to the receptions? I'm going to drinks at the university, but I'll be sticking to water as I'm going on to a charity bash where I'm the keynote speaker.'

'No, thanks. I'd only be in the way,' Rebecca said. Sometimes she found it impossible not to feel a trace of jealousy at Juliet's rather glamorous life. She was always in demand, as vice chancellor of the Institute of Dublin University, and had a string of letters after her name, various fellowships and non-executive directorships. She was also the founder and patron of the Children's Dream Holiday charity.

'It would be great to have you along,' Juliet said. 'We could have a blast.'

'It's fine. I won't be in the mood to socialise next weekend.'

'Well, if you change your mind, just text me.'

They hadn't ventured much further along the headland when Rebecca said, 'You've heard about Matthew's latest quest?'

'The presidential race? No surprises there, given his boundless ambition.'

'It's Rose I'm worried about,' Rebecca admitted. 'She says she's happy for Matthew to follow his dream, but I don't think she'd be able to cope with the kind of intrusion it would bring.

She'd never survive it. And God knows what would happen if the media started to sniff too deeply.'

Juliet said nothing, and Rebecca went on, 'The last time I was talking to her, she sounded so positive that I don't know if she was trying to pretend it wasn't happening or already acting the part and practising her lines. Oh, Juliet, I don't know why they can't just be happy with what they have. Rose fell apart before, remember? Now her peace of mind could be shattered.'

Juliet was unusually quiet and Rebecca sensed that she was turning something over in her mind.

Eventually she said, 'You might as well know – I'm surprised you haven't heard the rumours by now. Approaches have been made to me from one of our main political parties about going forward as a candidate and I'm seriously considering it.'

Taken by surprise, Rebecca blurted the first thing that popped into her head. 'You're joking. You're not trying to compete with Matthew, are you?'

A cloud of annoyance darkened Juliet's face. 'Of course not. It's an honour to be asked.'

'Even though you'd be pitched against Matthew? And the last election was nothing short of a mud-slinging bloodbath?' Rebecca said, consternation rising inside her.

'I've probably a few enemies lying in wait,' Juliet said. 'I've trodden on a few toes in my time. But I'll cope with that.'

'Jesus, you do realise the enormity of what you're taking on? Have you thought this through? I'm sure you'd be brilliant in the role, but don't you think … God, it's bad enough that the media will be hounding Matthew and Rose, but you too? Everything you've ever done will go under the microscope.'

They strode on around the track. Down below, jagged cliffs

plummeted to a silky grey sea and cawing gulls wheeled lazily on the thermals.

'Maybe that doesn't bother me too much,' Juliet said tightly. 'Maybe it's time a few things were out in the open.'

'I can't believe I'm hearing this.' Rebecca was weak with dismay. 'You can't mean that. Especially after all this time. You have a fabulous life with everything going for you. I don't understand why you can't just leave things the way they are, any more than Matthew and Rose. You really can't afford to have your private life hung out to dry. God only knows what would come crawling out of the woodwork.'

'Maybe I'm willing to take my chances,' Juliet said. 'See what Fate has in store …'

'This is madness.' Rebecca's mind spiralled back to the time, years ago, when Juliet's world had collapsed. Rebecca had been instrumental in putting the pieces back together. It was something they never spoke about, as though it had never happened.

'Thing is, Rebecca, you don't know what it's been like to live with the deceit all these years,' Juliet said. 'It's niggled at me for a long time, but lately I've started to wake up at four in the morning, wondering if I could quietly atone for it in some way. Sometimes I wonder how on earth I could have done what I did … and how I could have covered it up.'

'You did it with my help, remember,' Rebecca said. 'I aided and abetted you, so to speak. Are you regretting that now?'

'Hey, no.' Juliet put a hand on her arm. 'Your support was invaluable. Any regrets are mine. You did nothing wrong. I'm the one with the stain on my conscience and the sore heart. And it's troubling me so much that maybe I'd like to have it in the open.'

'And maybe wreck your life, never mind others'?' Rebecca said.

Juliet was unusually quiet as they turned down from the summit and headed towards Verbena View, which told Rebecca how deeply she was thinking.

'Look,' Juliet said, reached the bungalow, 'it's probably best if you stay out of it.'

Rebecca felt stung. Danielle's refusal to talk had been a hurtful snub that lingered. Now Juliet, her best friend, was talking about pulling the pin on a hand grenade.

'How can I stay out of it? I was involved. I was there with you, all the way. Are you sorry about that now?'

What stunned Rebecca even more was the small, tight smile Juliet gave her as she said, 'Involved? My dear Rebecca, it's probably just as well you knew only half the story.'

What the hell did Juliet mean? 'Well, that puts me in my place,' Rebecca huffed, reeling with disbelief at her friend's words.

'Hey, look, I'm sorry,' Juliet said. 'I didn't mean to be short with you. I'm not myself at the minute. Too many sleepless nights.'

'Well, I'm not myself either after hearing that,' Rebecca said. 'I can't believe you're so heedless to the Pandora's box you might be opening, never mind putting yourself on a collision course with Matthew – *and* Rose. It's going to be great fun keeping the peace between you.'

'Then, all things considered, it's really best if you stay out of it.'

When they got back to Verbena View, Rebecca declined her friend's offer of coffee and left, barely saying goodbye, her hands shaking as she fumbled with the ignition key and accelerated out of the driveway.

❧⁓❧

Someone topped up her glass and she looked at the final scenes of the newly wed couple's photo montage. Then the lights were dimmed and the band came on. She watched the happy couple circle the floor to 'Flying Without Wings', and couldn't help recalling the Christmas table at Verbena View when James had teased Danielle and Conor about their first dance as a married couple. Life had been almost perfect. Suddenly she needed a break from the merry-making. She'd go back to her room for a while.

She left the first-floor salon, and when she reached the top of the staircase, she glanced down towards the foyer, and was flustered to see a tall man going into the bar. Liam Corrigan. Obviously back in Dublin.

He was an old-friend-turned-foe of Juliet's, someone whose toes she had totally flattened. Rebecca hadn't noticed him in the crowded reception room, but he might be there for the wedding. Liam had grown up in a modest cottage near the harbour in Howth, and had cycled to Lower Ballymalin vocational school. He'd hung around the edges of the group of friends from the Gardens, often playing football with Harry and the other lads. He'd known Juliet, too, and Rebecca had bumped into him at Verbena View over the years.

Then, during the boom time, when his construction business had taken off, he'd transformed his life, becoming one of Dublin's most flamboyant developers. Long separated from his American wife, he'd begun to live an extravagant lifestyle that gave the gossip journalists palpitations as they filed last-minute copy recounting his exploits.

Occasionally Juliet and Rebecca had been invited to champagne-fuelled parties at his County Dublin estate, just a couple of miles north of the Seagrass Hotel. Rebecca knew about the chauffeured Bentley that had whisked him in and out of the city, and the private jet that took his inner circle to his south of France villa. Then it had all imploded and he had fled Ireland four years ago when Corrigan Holdings had gone bust, leaving his life in tatters.

And partly on account of Juliet.

SEVEN

Friday, 16 March, 8.45 p.m.

My face feels stiff. I can't remember how it feels to be warm. The darkness is like oily black soup. The stillness is broken by the murmuring sea, and some kind of raging noise in my head. When will help arrive?

How long have I been like this? How did I end up here, like a trashed rag doll, with just the moon and the stars gleaming above me, the sheer side of the cliff looming beside me, with the murmuring sea for company. Surely my friends will notice I'm missing.

Rose and Rebecca. Rebecca and Rose.

They slide through my head, Rebecca laughing, Rose more reserved. Sometimes, if it's not a school day, they come to Verbena View with their grandmother. My mother is petite, and the hems of almost all her gowns need to be altered. Eventually the girls stop coming, and when I ask Mrs O'Malley why, she says they're at home as they're big enough to mind themselves.

Then Mrs O'Malley stops coming. My mother tells me she has passed away.

Yet Rebecca and Rose still drift on the sidelines of my life. I see them on the beach at Howth, teenagers now, with a big group of friends, too busy playing tennis or beach football to notice me walking with my father. Until Rebecca turns her head and, across the distance, I see recognition, then the flash of her smile.

They pile off the bus, jostling their way towards the summit of Howth Head as I cruise by in my father's car. They're laughing and joking far too much to notice me. A couple of the guys are tall and attractive, and I can't help feeling envious of their camaraderie, but our lives are so dissimilar there may as well be a six-foot wall between us.

Rebecca and Rose might have stayed for ever on the sidelines of my early years. And everything would have been so different. But, as my grandmother said, life can turn on a sixpence.

My beloved Granny Jordan, with her baby-soft skin, lavender powder, and smiling brown eyes in her creased face, my father alarming me as he cried at her funeral: he told me later it had been the worst moment of his life.

Now I know exactly what Granny Jordan meant.

Pure chance has shaped a lot of my life. One seemingly inconsequential moment can lead you down a certain path and, before you know it, you've drifted off your track and ended up in a place you'd never imagined you'd be.

Like me, here, now …

Who was with me? *Was* someone with me? Did he or she join me on my walk round the cliff? All I can recall is a feeling of menace … my arms flapping uselessly, my body free-falling backwards, as if in slow motion … a scream forming but never voiced …

Menace? I'm surely imagining it. I've spent too much time lying here waiting for help and I'm going crazy. And yet … there is something dark at the corner of my mind. But it slips away before I can grasp it.

Think, Juliet. *Think*. Who'd want me out of the way?

I see the empty wine glasses in my kitchen and—

It's possible no one has gone for help. Whoever shared my wine might have come with me for my usual evening stroll and witnessed my fall. Or even made it happen. Helpless rage bubbles at the back of my throat. Could I really be that much of a threat to anyone?

Oh, God.

I wonder if I'll be saved from an appalling fate. Anything else is unthinkable. I know, instinctively, that I've too much to sort out in my life ... and left important things unsaid.

Help. Help. I hear the scream building, louder and louder, until my head is fit to burst, but nothing comes out of my mouth.

EIGHT

'Rose! How are you? If you don't mind me saying, you look a little frazzled around the gills. What's up?'

'I'm fine, Liz, couldn't be better! A lovely gathering, isn't it?' Rose's face felt stiff with the effort of smiling as she moved through the chattering throng only to come face to face with the one woman she'd been desperate to avoid.

But there was no escape.

Liz Monaghan detached herself from the group she'd been with and swooped on Rose, drawing her in to kiss the air near her cheeks. She stood back and Rose saw her feline eyes flick over her as the younger woman swiftly appraised her, taking in everything about her from her carefully styled dark hair to her diamanté shoes. She felt as though she'd been flayed with the thinnest scalpel.

A former model, Liz was originally from Ballymalin, but the choice, semi-detached houses on Upper Ballymalin Grove, where her doctor father had lived and practised, had been a world away from Granddad Paddy's humble abode tucked in the maze of Lower Ballymalin Gardens. Liz was in her late thirties, with a failed marriage behind her, and was now a gossip columnist renowned for her sharp tongue and outrageous comments. Her weekend diary page struck delight, fear or disappointment into the hearts of Dublin's socialites.

'Lovely?' Liz's laughter pealed. 'Only you would come out with something polite like that, Rose! I think it's a minefield.' Her voice lowered conspiratorially. 'Tons of juicy material for next week's column. Can't you sense the hostilities? Can't you smell the battle for power? I can practically see the drawn knives. Intoxicating. I love it! *Love* it.'

Rose backed away. Liz was almost feverish in her glee. Her eyes glittered with an expression that made Rose fear for anyone who got in her way.

'I can't believe we're in the thick of another pre-election skirmish,' Liz went on. 'It's the most fantastic fodder. Some of the sitting ducks are even here tonight, poor innocents!'

'Really?' Rose wondered if the woman slotted her into that category.

'Yes, I've already spotted Des Thornton, the former MEP, and Senator Colin Redmond, both pressing as much flesh as they can. And where is your eminent husband? He may be a little outside the political fold at the minute but that won't last.' Her sparkling eyes scanned the throng with a laser-like focus.

'Oh, he's around somewhere,' Rose said, waving her hand dismissively.

The room was so hot and crowded, so full of bright, shiny people, dressed to impress, that it hurt her head. Disoriented, she knew she had had too many glasses of champagne, despite her best intentions, but the silver trays revolved around her far too often for her shaky willpower. Still, it was time to call a halt. God knew who had been counting the number of drinks she had had. She was grateful for the cache of tranquillisers in her bag: when she felt the urge to blank out her jangled nerves and detach from everything, she could disappear into the Ladies and swallow a couple.

As soon as they had set foot in the ballroom, Matthew had been whisked away by some of his cohorts. He had glanced back at her with a satisfied smile, as though to say, 'I can't help it if I'm in demand. Look happy for me, please.'

She had tried. She had drifted from group to group, wearing a forced smile, not getting drawn into any conversation until Liz had snagged her attention.

'I was sorry to hear about your father,' Rose said, relieved to have stumbled on a different topic. 'I saw the piece you wrote about him. Please accept both Matthew's and my condolences.' Liz's father had died just after Christmas, having spent his final years in a nursing home after a severe stroke had robbed him of speech and left him confined to bed.

Liz's eyes were suddenly blank. 'It was a release,' she said. 'In reality he went a long time ago. It was painful to have to visit him in that nursing home. I'm glad it's over.'

'I'd say it was difficult all right,' Rose said.

'I was in Ballymalin for the funeral services,' Liz went on, her attention once more focused on Rose. 'It was strange being back in the family home. Dad's surgery was cleared out years ago, when he retired, but the house needs to be emptied before I put it on the market. I'd no idea there was so much clutter and lots of …' She paused, staring into space.

'Lots of what?' Rose prompted.

'Memories,' Liz said.

Rose shivered at the stony look in her eyes. 'So you're not going to hang on to it as a second home?' She could have bitten her tongue when Liz gave her a wintry smile.

'Mine wasn't exactly a happy home,' she said. 'The memories are tarnished and rather painful. I want to be shot of it. The sooner the better.'

Rose recalled that Liz's mother had been an alcoholic and had taken her own life many years ago. It had been rumoured at the time that the then teenage Liz had found her. Her father's death had no doubt brought it all back, making the last couple of months very difficult for her, especially as she had been an only child, coming along after her parents had almost given up hope.

'Anyway, it looks like both you and Matthew are set for the big time!' Liz said, back to her normal self, her eyes flashing with naked curiosity. 'I've been following all the coverage. You could be Ireland's next First Lady. If you play your cards right, of course.'

'I'm not so sure about that. There's still a long road to go.'

Liz studied her so keenly that Rose felt like the proverbial rabbit caught in the headlights. 'And an even longer road behind you,' she said, 'if some of Matthew's more, ah … ambitious business ventures are to be believed. I can't wait to sit him down and have a decent in-depth interview with him. I'm keen to prove myself as a bona-fide journalist, not just a social diarist. I'm sure he'd be glad of the exposure. But do you have doubts about your husband's ability to succeed?' She had slotted in the leading question so expertly that Rose was caught off guard.

She felt herself flush. This was what she hated and feared: feeling flummoxed and anxious, having to watch every word that came out of her mouth, especially in front of someone she was no match for, like pit-bull terrier Liz, who was on top form tonight.

'I never said that,' she protested. 'You know yourself it's still early days and there are a lot of hoops to jump through. Even the best-placed person has to be careful of snakes in the long grass.'

'I hope you don't mean me,' Liz laughed. 'I presume you're talking about Juliet Jordan.'

'Juliet?' Rose looked suitably wide-eyed, she hoped.

Liz raised supercilious eyebrows. 'Didn't you hear she's been approached to stand by one of our main political parties? It's the latest gossip to hit the wires. And if anyone could give his male hotness, ahem, Matthew, a run for his money, it's Juliet. They both have connections in the right places and their Photoshopped posters would look equally attractive, hanging side by side on the lampposts of Ireland. Ah ...' her eyes roved over the top of Rose's head and halted, as if fastening on her next target '... I see someone arriving that I want to talk to. But you've no worries, Rose.' Her thin hand clutched Rose's arm, and Rose just about prevented herself from flinching. 'If it comes to pistols at dawn, or domination of the great live televised debate, I'm on your side. And I'd never be able to dig any skeletons out of your cupboard. After all, we both hail from the same little village in Dublin. So if you'd anything at all to hide, I'd have found out by now, wouldn't I?'

Rose felt faint and tried to move her rubbery mouth into the semblance of a smile while Liz studied her with hawk eyes and grinned, showing big white teeth that suddenly resembled fangs. Then she was gone, slithering through the crowd, the feel of her claw-like grip lingering on Rose's forearm.

NINE

Friday, 16 March, 9.00 p.m.

I'm so cold now that the inside of my head feels totally frozen. Even my terror is contained inside a solid block of ice. It's a terror like I've never known before, mixed with alarm and outrage and incredible fury, but it seems disconnected from me somehow, as though that side of my brain has become numb with overload. Or profound shock.

I stare into the dark abyss of the horror I'm in, while significant fragments of my life are stirred up around me, etched against the moon, the stars and the backdrop of the cliff.

22 May 1971
I'm making my way along the swaying railway carriage, gripping the top of a seat for balance as the floor shifts beneath me, and the Belfast to Dublin train rattles across the grey, glinting ripple of the Malahide estuary en route to Amiens Street station. Aged eighteen and I think I know it all.

I almost pass the two girls. They are undeniably sisters, with light brown wavy hair and darkly lashed blue-green eyes, but I pause and give them a second glance, and in that moment my life swerves direction, like a train rattling over points to a different track and destination.

'Hey, Rose and Rebecca? It *is* you, isn't it?'

Startled, they look up at me. They're grown-up now. Rose has a fine-boned face. She is neat and prim and beautiful. At first her eyes are suspicious, as if nervous of my intrusion.

Then Rebecca, taller and broader, slightly more relaxed, recognises me and smiles. 'Juliet! I don't believe it! We haven't seen you in years!'

'I've seen you on and off,' I tell her, 'hanging around Howth with your friends.'

The seat opposite them is empty so I slide into it. Over a few minutes we catch up with our lives. Rebecca is eighteen now, the same age as me, but whereas I'm just coming to the end of my first year at university as a law student, Rebecca has almost a year's work under her belt in the typing pool of an insurance company. Rose is a clerical assistant in the Civil Service.

'I was sorry to hear about your grandmother,' I say.

Their faces cloud.

'We're still living in Lower Ballymalin with Granddad Paddy,' Rebecca says. 'Although Rose won't be there for much longer.' She grins.

'Rose?' I prompt.

Rose finally smiles at me and extends her left hand. 'Yes, I'm engaged to be married. The wedding is at the end of July.'

I admire her ring. 'Congratulations. Anyone I know?'

'I hope not,' Rebecca jokes. 'Rose and Matthew were childhood sweethearts.'

'Matthew?'

'Matthew Moore. I'll soon be Mrs Rose Moore.'

I wonder why she's so keen to lose her identity, but now is not the time to debate it with her.

'We've been in Belfast, shopping for the day,' Rebecca says, with enthusiasm. 'Rose picked up a lovely going-away suit and we both got some summer outfits.' Her eyes twinkle. 'Mind you, we're wearing half the clothes under our coats to get through Customs.'

They do look a bit puffy under their belted raincoats.

'So you're not part of the movement?' I ask.

'What movement?' Rose looks at me cagily.

'The women's movement.'

Rose sniffs and twists her ring around her finger. 'Don't remind me about those women's libbers. Taking over almost two carriages. Passing out leaflets and God only knows what. We don't want to get mixed up in all that stuff, isn't that right, Rebecca?' She gives her sister a meaningful stare.

But interest flashes across Rebecca's face. She realises I may belong to the group her sister has disparaged. I wink at her, and Rebecca's face breaks into a wide grin, showing her dimples. The smile reaches her eyes, making them appear bigger and brighter.

'I dunno,' Rebecca says. 'It all depends.'

'Rebecca!'

She makes a face at her sister. 'No need to be so square. I'm not about to pull my bra off and start burning it, but they have some good things to say. Like equal pay for starters. I'd like some of that.'

'Thing is, I have a bit of a problem,' I admit. 'When we reach Amiens Street station, I need to – ah – borrow your scarf,' I tell Rose.

Rose flushes and fingers the grey scarf knotted loosely around her neck. 'My *scarf*? What for?'

'I'm not supposed to be on this train,' I tell them, with a laugh. 'I've done my best to dodge the photographers and reporters in the carriages, that was a bit of fun, but it'll be difficult to smuggle myself through the exit barriers at Amiens Street, never mind going through Customs, without running the risk of being caught on the television cameras. If I could borrow your scarf it would hide my face.'

'Oh, gosh, why do you need to hide it?' Rebecca leans across the table, alive with curiosity.

'What have you done wrong?' Rose interrupts.

'I haven't done anything wrong. I've bought some condoms but, as far as I'm concerned, I was well within my rights to do so.'

Rose draws back.

Rebecca's eyes are shining with a mixture of excitement and adoration. 'You mean you're really one of *them*? And you went up to Belfast to buy condoms today?'

'We're not a different species. A lot of the women sitting in the carriage back there are ordinary students, wives and mothers, shop assistants and typists. Unfortunately, thanks to the ridiculous laws in this country, we're treated like second-class citizens.'

'I wish I had your nerve!' Rebecca says. 'Have you got them there? Can I see one?'

'Rebecca!' Rose says. 'I can't believe I'm hearing this.'

'Why not?' Rebecca rounds on her sister. 'Don't be so stuffy. Have you never seen one before?'

Rose's cheeks are pink. 'Don't tell me you have!'

'Hey, girls,' I put in, before a row breaks out. 'Sorry to say I'm not that brave. I daren't arrive at the station with my stash or be caught with it coming through.'

'You scarcely want us to help you out there,' Rose says stiffly. 'I'm not putting my finger on one.'

'They're not for your finger.' Rebecca giggles. There is a gleam of mischief in her eyes as she says to me, 'I don't mind smuggling some through for you. I'll put them down my bra. How many would I fit?'

'I wish I'd known that,' I laugh with her. 'But I've got rid of them already. Whatever I picked up in Belfast I dumped in the bin in the toilets.'

'You didn't!'

'Look, don't get me wrong. I really believe in the movement. It's so important to shift this backward country out of the dark ages. We women have been downtrodden for far too long, and it's crazy what's going on, but I shouldn't be on this train.'

'Why not?' Rose asks. 'And why didn't you just ask one of your feminist friends to take your …'

'Condoms,' Rebecca prompts.

Rose grimaces.

'They're not really my friends, and they don't know that I tagged along with them today. It was my private rebellion.'

There is a silence.

I tell them. 'If I was arrested under the Criminal Justice Act of 1935, which, in case you didn't know, forbids the import or sale of contraceptives, my life wouldn't be worth living, because my father would go nuts if he found out I was on this train, let alone in contact with some condoms. It was hard to dodge the reporters on the train, but there'll be television cameras at the station and I can't be seen. No way. My father's a judge, you see. So I'd really be in trouble.'

'That's different. Why didn't you tell us that in the first place?' Rose says, taking off her scarf and handing it straight to me.

When we get off the train the station platform is bedlam. Customs officers are out in force. Behind them, a phalanx of placard-waving supporters waits for the members of the Irish Women's Liberation Movement to come through. Railway officials are doing their best to block the television cameras by holding up big boards in front of them.

But the Customs men are no match for the large procession of victorious women who surge down the platform, brazenly shaking their contraband. Condoms, packets of pills and spermicidal jelly are scattered across the ground and hurled over the heads of the officers to the waiting supporters. I find the euphoria contagious, especially when I realise that the Customs people know it's going to be impossible to arrest all the militant women. And the packets of pills are ordinary aspirin, as it was impossible to get a contraceptive pill without a doctor's prescription, something the movement hadn't factored in. They eventually give up their searches and stand back to allow everyone through. Some of the more rebellious women inflate their condoms and bounce them like balloons.

Rose averts her eyes.

I want to give her a shake and tell her that these courageous women are breaking tightly controlled boundaries imposed by the Catholic Church and our male-dominated society. In years to come she'll thank them for having the guts to act on their beliefs and break through the ridiculous restrictions imposed on women. But the words stick in my chest. I feel ashamed of myself, slinking through the barrier on the coat-tails of those women instead of alongside them, hiding between Rose and Rebecca, with Rose's grey scarf swathing my cropped black hair and half covering my face.

We stand at the top of Talbot Street, unsure what to do next, and a little at a loss after the adrenalin of our march through Customs.

'Will we go for a drink?' I suggest. 'I want to thank you for getting me out of a tight spot.'

'A *drink*? I'm going home,' Rose says, clutching her shopping bags like a shield, ready to flee from any threat I may pose.

'There's no rush. You're not seeing Matthew this evening, are you?' Rebecca says.

'No, but I'd rather go home.'

'Right so. I'll go for a drink with Juliet and catch a later bus,' Rebecca says.

Rose's surprise at her sister's defection flits across her face as she weighs up leaving her to the mercy of my influence against her desire to go home. Then she says, a little grudgingly, 'Well, okay, just one.'

I'm tempted to order three pints of beer, knowing we'll be refused by the barman, but I don't want to scare away Rebecca or Rose. So, over a glass of Harp for me and Rebecca, Britvic orange for Rose, and a round of toasted-cheese sandwiches in a pub on Abbey Street, I hear all about Rose's forthcoming wedding and her fiancé. Matthew is a junior bank clerk. I might have guessed her job and her fiancé would be ultra-conservative, safe and predictable. She looks uneasily round the pub, as though someone is going to pounce on her. But, given her childhood, I don't need to look too far to see why Rose is the responsible, cautious one.

A local dressmaker is making her dress, Rebecca will be her bridesmaid, and they'll have fifty guests in total. After the wedding reception, they'll spend their first night in a Dublin hotel before catching the morning bus to Donegal.

'I wish you all the best,' I say, 'but don't you think it's unfair that you'll have to leave your job as soon as you get married?'

'No. I love Matthew and I'll enjoy making a home for him.' Rose jumps to her own defence.

'That's great if you're happy,' I say, 'but I think it's wrong that clever women are expected to give up their careers as soon as there's a wedding band on their finger. What will you do all day? Polish the brasses? Wipe specks of dust off the gleaming crystal? Iron his Y-fronts?'

Rose flushes. 'We're hoping to get the key of our new house at the end of next month, so I'll be busy with making a home for us, and we'll be starting a family soon.'

Her life is all mapped out. Safe. No surprises.

'Still, housework has its limits,' I say. 'I'd be bored out of my tree polishing and cleaning.'

'Is that why you joined the women's lib movement?' Rebecca asks.

I have to laugh. 'I'm not actually a paid-up member, much as I'd love to be. It's hard to believe how unfairly women are treated in this country. We're second-class citizens, in a country where power is held by men and the Catholic Church. So it's men all the way. And they make the rules to suit themselves …'

Rebecca is clearly intrigued. Even Rose is beginning to look at me with a glimmer of respect, as though I'm finally making some sense. By the time we part on the corner of Abbey Street, Rebecca has invited me to join her group of friends for drinks the following weekend and, just like that, the six-foot wall between us has fallen down and I have stepped through the gap.

TEN

After she moved away from Rose, Liz sidled through the crowd as best she could on her vertiginous heels. The room was too hot. When she reached the bar at the back, she sank gratefully on to a stool.

'A double vodka, please, no ice, and just a splash of soda water,' she ordered. When her drink was passed to her, she sipped it greedily.

There had been no one arriving that she'd wanted to talk to and there was no one whom she was remotely interested in right now, for all her talk to Rose.

She sipped her drink and pretended to be engrossed in her mobile, staring fixedly at her old text messages. She shouldn't have come tonight. Not after the rotten few days she'd just endured, between pacing around the empty rooms in Ballymalin, with ghosts for company, and picking through the sad debris of her parents' lives.

Then there had been the shocking documents hidden in an envelope at the back of a sideboard. No wonder she felt so cut adrift from reality. The room spun again, even though she was sitting down. She tried to take a few deep breaths, then ordered another double vodka, which she drank far too quickly.

Thankfully, there was no one to lecture her if she got home pissed. Which also meant there was no one to care. She could do pretty much what she liked now that Gavin, her ex-husband, was out of her hair.

Their marriage had lasted barely a year, and had been a mistake from the very beginning. The give and take involved in marriage wasn't for her, a lesson she had learned the hard way, after many rows over silly things. It was a pattern she'd recognised, emerging from the legacy of her parents' unhappy union. She would be forty next year and more than likely still unattached, which meant she would probably never have children. And surely that was for the best.

Nonetheless, Gavin had been a great support at her father's funeral, and he'd phoned her several times afterwards, even offering to help her clear the house. She had been too caught up in herself to figure out whether he was being genuine or scenting money. Not that the sale of the house would fetch anything like it would have done a few years ago. Mind you, she'd been tempted to accept his unspoken offer to go to bed with him, and take her mind off everything. One of her colleagues swore by sex with her ex. Guilt-free, uncomplicated sex. And Gavin had seemed to be offering it on a plate. For a moment she weighed her mobile in her hand and flicked to her contacts. A quick call was all it would take. She sighed and ordered another drink instead.

After a while she felt numb enough to forget about the trauma of the last few days and the envelope she'd found. Instead she focused on Rose and the look in her eyes when she'd mentioned skeletons in the cupboard. It had been a throwaway, meaningless remark, directed to the most mousy, deferential person she knew, but it had found an unexpected target. Liz had recognised that look. It had told her that, for all her demure, ladylike airs and graces, Rose Moore was afraid of something.

Liz felt a kick of excitement in her gut as her mouth curved in a smile.

ELEVEN

22 May 1971

That night, in the sitting room of the family home, Verbena View, the judge stands up and marches across to the black and white television set, snapping it off midway through the programme.

'There. I don't know what's happening to this country. Teilifís Éireann is an absolute disgrace. How can they give those immoral women any kind of air time? Before we know it they'll be demanding divorce. *Divorce!* Can you imagine it, Kitty? This country has gone to the dogs.'

Mr Justice Henry Jordan is so incensed that minuscule flecks of spray shoot from his mouth. The Saturday-evening talk show has raised the thorny subject of what is already being labelled the 'contraceptive train'. Some of the women from the train are in the audience, and naturally the judge has objected. I can see a pulse beating at the side of his face.

I meet my mother's eyes across the room, as if searching for some feminine complicity, but none is forthcoming. I think she would have preferred me to be pink-cheeked and blonde, soft and compliant, rather than awkward around the edges with unruly black hair. As though she senses the rebellious ideas boiling beneath my calm surface, she deliberately looks away and picks up her embroidery ring.

Mr Justice Henry Jordan is a tall, well-built man with a heightened complexion, a man's man, as they say, fond of his evening whiskey, the undisputed king of his home and hearth. My mother flutters obediently behind the immense bulk of his powerful persona. I sometimes wonder if she minds her own life being submerged, sacrificed and meaningless, in the shadow of his. Sometimes I see her looking at my father in admiration and helpless wonder, as though she's trying to figure out how a lowly shop girl from Mullingar landed such a magnificent specimen. Apart from visits to her sister in Dun Laoghaire, attending morning mass and the ladies' sodality in the local church, helping with the garden fête and fundraising cake sales, my mother doesn't socialise without him. An occasional Babycham at Christmas is as far as her alcohol indulgence goes.

I have sucked mints all the way home on the bus to disguise the smell of my breath. Because, for all his intransigence, and a sternness that borders on forbidding, Mr Justice Henry Jordan has an Achilles heel: his eldest child. Me.

My father loved me. Loves me. Will always love me. I could describe it by the way he looks at me, talks to me and moves around me, as though I'm a priceless gift. It is painted across his face, in the way his gaze immediately alights on me when I come into the kitchen in the mornings. As though I'm the most beautiful princess in the whole world, rather than the spiky ugly sister, the only daughter ever to grace the face of this earth.

Sometimes my younger brother Robert doesn't get a look in. Problem is, I know my father would be hugely disappointed with many of the ideas floating around in my head. Bold and dangerous ideas that would anger and shock him.

For somewhere deep inside me a different Juliet is struggling to get out. A Juliet who feels that the sky is the limit, that she is equal to any man, marriage should be on equal terms, and that a woman should be allowed access to contraception *and* divorce. The last thing I want to see is disappointment clouding my father's face and dulling the beam in his eyes as he gazes at me. Or my mother unhappy in the face of his upset. But how long can you try to be a person you're not in order to keep your parents happy?

He thinks I've spent today in the college library, poring over my books. My father has absolute trust in me. He'd never believe that I'd travelled to Belfast on the infamous contraceptive train, let alone purchased some condoms.

So is it any wonder that I find myself sitting on the edge of my seat, my heart thumping in case I look guilty?

'I'm sorry you had to hear that trash, Juliet,' my father says, as he splashes whiskey into a crystal tumbler from the decanter on the sideboard. 'I'd no idea it was going to be broadcast into the homes of Catholic Ireland. This is a new low. Decent, God-fearing people shouldn't be subject to such rubbish. It's sacrilege. Your mother and I are so thankful that you have the sense to ignore all that wickedness. Isn't that right, Kitty?'

From across the room my mother sends me a tight smile.

❧

The following weekend, I meet Rebecca in town. I can't believe how much this means to me, as I don't have many friends. I was top of the class consistently, then gained a scholarship to university, which didn't endear me to my schoolmates. And I'm still finding my feet in college, trying to strike a balance between my studies and the exciting talks and rallies that are constantly happening around the campus, nervous of taking too much interest in case word gets back to my father. But there's something genuine about Rebecca that warms me and I feel as though I've been invited to join a magic circle.

Tonight we're meeting Rose and Matthew for a meal in the grill bar beside the Gresham Hotel before going on for drinks.

I recognise Matthew immediately as one of the tall, attractive guys I've seen with Rose and Rebecca's group of friends. But we don't get off to the best of starts.

'So this is the famous, or should I say infamous, crusading Juliet!' Matthew stands up as Rebecca and I approach the table. 'I hear you're responsible for inciting all sorts of rebellious ideas in my wife-to-be.'

I'm tempted to respond with a smart comment about our male-dominated society but manners prevail. 'I'm pleased to meet you, too, Matthew,' I say, feeling I've somehow scored a point by not rising to his bait.

He gives me a puzzled, head-to-toe sweep, as though he's trying to figure out why Rose and Rebecca have befriended a rather ordinary-looking, average-height girl, with short black hair and mischievous ideas. Up close, he's even better-looking, and I can see why Rose is staring at him with adoring eyes. Her knight in shining armour, who will whisk her out of the boring, dusty office to a new life. A new life where she will have the luxury of a Formica kitchen, a plumbed-in washing-machine and back-boiler central heating, where they will be able to have legitimate sex and he can demand his conjugal rights at any time, thanks to a ring on her finger. He wears, like a suit, the pride his parents wrapped around him when he'd landed the fabulous, permanent and pensionable bank job. He has the eager, slightly cocky air of someone who fully expects to go all the way to the top, and I sense straight away that he feels in competition with me because of my privileged background and university education.

'Rose tells me you're studying law,' he says, challenge in his eyes.

'That's right,' I say evenly, determined to stay cool.

'Isn't it a bit of a waste? What good will that do when you're married with a family?'

I'm conscious of Rose watching me. 'Who knows?' I shrug. 'Do you think I'd be better off in the bank counting other people's money instead of my own?' I smile as pleasantly as I can.

Matthew laughs. 'Fair play. I was just seeing what you're made of, Juliet. You might come in handy when I need some advice.'

'Advice?'

'I don't intend being a bank clerk for ever,' he says, with such dogged conviction that I believe him.

Rose gives me a nervous smile and I wonder how she'll keep him tethered.

July 1971

My mother invites Rose and Rebecca to lunch at Verbena View, to celebrate Rose's forthcoming wedding.

'I've never forgotten how lovely your home is,' Rebecca says, as she comes into my bedroom, admiring the bathroom off it and the walk-in wardrobe. 'Our house in Lower Ballymalin Gardens would fit into a corner of this.'

I take it for granted, the spacious, rambling, white-fronted bungalow surrounded by landscaped grounds, with splendid views of the sea from the south- and south-west-facing rooms.

It's been in the family for years. My father grew up here, and when his father died and Granny Jordan's health began to fail, he had it renovated and extended and moved back in with his wife and baby daughter – me.

The judge remembers them and has them eating out of his hands. He is full of warm old-fashioned gentlemanly courtesy when I bring them into his untidy study, a room with huge squishy armchairs set round an open fire, one wall lined with brimming bookshelves, an alcove decorated with framed certificates, including every single school certificate I've ever been awarded, and another fantastic view of the sea.

My mother has put out fresh flowers, and she fusses around, trailing after our housekeeper, ensuring the table is properly set and the lamb slow-roasted to perfection. She gives Rose a wedding present of crystal glasses and Rose turns scarlet with pleasure.

Afterwards, we go for coffee down by the harbour.

'Rose, I wish you the very best of luck,' I tell her. 'I hope they give you a good send-off from the office next week.'

'I can't believe I'm leaving,' Rose says. 'No more Monday mornings and no more gossipy coffee breaks. Even if I wanted to stay on, I can't. But I'll be married to Matthew and I'm looking forward to moving into our new home.'

We both know that the family home will belong to Matthew. If anything goes wrong, he can sell it over her head.

'I'm sure you'll be very happy, Rose,' I say to her. 'But unfair and unequal laws will change, and women will start to have choices. Clever women are speaking up at last, determined to fight for proper justice and get rid of ancient regulations.'

'And your father would agree with all of this,' Rebecca says, with a teasing glint in her eye.

'What do you think?' I hold my breath.

'That you're the apple of his eye, his golden princess, and more.' She gives me a puzzled look. 'You have so much, I don't understand why …'

I can see she's not quite sure how to put it. 'You're surprised I'm such a rebel. I should be happy with my lot instead of engaging in militant behaviour.'

'Well, yes. If I had what you had, I'd be pinching myself.'

I stir my coffee with a heavy hand. I hear the clink-clink of the boats bobbing about their moorings and the cries of the gulls wheeling above the rippling grey sea. The salty breeze flickers like a feather on my skin, playful and carefree.

After a while I say, 'We won't know ourselves in ten years' time. The sky will be the limit. Women will be able to have it all and do whatever they want to do. Hey, sisters, we'll be totally invincible.'

∂∽∽

Invincible. Now, as the shadowy night presses on top of me, the memory of that long-ago day suddenly fades and my words, uttered so confidently, trail into the dark horizon. Ah, the blind, trusting innocence! I know now, only too well, that neither women nor men will ever have it all: life is full of compromise and sacrifice; rules and regulations don't matter a jot when it comes to the complexities of people, let alone the depths of the human heart.

And no one is invincible once they love somebody. That changes everything. And likewise if they are loved – even that brings burdens.

The darkness seeps into my face and slithers through my hair.

Yet even in the oily black depths, there is life. I feel it all around me, as you would another presence, as though the world is taking slow breaths in tempo with the murmuring sea while it waits for the night to pass.

I wonder how injured I am, if I'll have to wait for the night to pass before I'm found. It can't end like this. It *won't* end like this. I want to walk up Grafton Street in warm summer sunshine and listen to the buskers. Pause by the flower sellers at the corner of Duke Street, and inhale the vibrant scents. Mingle with the lunchtime crowds strolling across a sun-dappled St Stephen's Green. Taste the breeze coming off the Liffey. Visit Paris again and sip hot chocolate on the Champs-Elysées. Go shopping in New York. Visit Rome and enjoy a bowl of pasta in a quaint corner of Trastevere.

Rome? That strikes a bell somewhere.

I want to have friends around for spag Bol and a few bottles of good wine, turn up the music, and sit on my patio overlooking the sea as day blends into a lingering twilight, where on calm days the sky is a vast canvas and you can see across the bay to the blue-grey ridges of the Wicklow mountains.

And I have unfinished business and important things to say.

Most of all, flashing like a beacon through the murky grey clouds in my head, are the words I've left unsaid and the need to tell someone I love him very much, no matter what it costs.

The need that might, just might, have brought me here …

TWELVE

Rebecca was delayed at the top of the staircase by an old colleague of Harry's, who insisted on regaling her with funny anecdotes of Harry and himself on the golf course, telling her how wonderful her husband had been.

By the time she reached the foyer and glanced into the bar, there was no sign of Liam Corrigan, but the television screen on the wall stopped her in her tracks. The nine o'clock news was still on, and she saw Rose, caught in a blaze of flashbulbs with Matthew as they stepped out of his car and paused at the entrance to the Four Seasons Hotel, en route to their drinks reception.

Already the media were zoning in on possible contenders for the presidential race. Rose had a smile pinned to her face, but Rebecca could see that it was a little too bright. She's not as happy about this as she makes out, Rebecca thought, despite what she'd said when the sisters had met for lunch in Harvey Nichols earlier that week.

'Are you and Matthew really serious?' Rebecca had said.

'Yes, and why not?'

'Because … Oh, come on, you know,' Rebecca said. 'I don't have to spell it out. Are you able for all the hassle this will bring?'

'That's a lovely way to talk to your sister, I don't think,' Rose said huffily.

'Anything you've done in the past, no matter how small, will be held up for all to see. It's bad enough that Juliet's taking such a risk, but I'm surprised that Matthew ...' Rebecca couldn't bring herself to say any more.

Her sister looked beautiful and was elegantly dressed. But she was well able to don a pair of heels, skinny jeans and a cotton top and hang out backstage at one of The Name's gigs. Or get her casual clothes full of sticky fingers and puke when she helped out in the children's hospital.

'I'd do anything for Matthew,' Rose said. 'Years ago he made all my dreams come true. Now I want to help him have his. I hope you're giving Juliet some of this advice.'

Rebecca shook her head. 'I tried. She told me she didn't care if her life was upended. She thinks it's time a few things were out in the open. I don't know what's got into her.'

'Well, that's a first. I've never heard you criticise her before,' Rose said.

'I can't understand why you're both happy to lob ginormous sticks of dynamite into your lives. Everything's fine as it is. Why look for trouble?'

Rose stared out of the window to where Wednesday-morning shoppers strolled around the Pembroke District of Dundrum Town Centre. Then she met Rebecca's eyes, and said, 'There's no need to concern yourself with me and Matthew. We'll be fine.'

'The Moores make a nice, respectable-looking couple, don't they?' a man's voice said. 'Lambs to the slaughter, methinks. You can't afford to be nice any more. And certainly not in that battlefield.'

Rebecca swung around and stared at the man standing behind her. It *was* him. Larger than life, undeniably attractive but dangerous as hell, given his history.

'Liam!' Rebecca said, her chest tight. He was wearing a grey suit and a white shirt open at the neck. He had always been handsome, and his red hair was as thick as ever, but shot through with silver. His face was tauter than she remembered, which made his blue eyes more vibrant. Late fifties by now, she guessed, and leaner all over. His expression was easy and friendly, totally at odds with how it had seemed the last time she'd seen him. As Rebecca regarded him, the years rolled away and she saw Liam leaning over a table at the Shelbourne Hotel, where she and Juliet had been having dinner before going to the theatre.

His face had been stiff with rage, fists clenched till the knuckles showed white. From what he'd said to Juliet, in a terse voice, Rebecca had gathered that his construction empire, Corrigan Holdings, which he'd built from nothing, was imploding and he blamed her. He'd bought a pocket of land adjacent to Verbena View at an eye-watering price, but to develop it he had needed right of way along the side of her garden and to install piping beneath her property. She'd refused.

'You got yourself into this mess, Liam,' she'd said, in a perfectly calm voice. 'This time you overstretched yourself and signed on far too many dotted lines without checking the small print, including the plans for that land. It's not my fault that the property bubble has burst or that the banks are knocking down your door.'

'You were the one who stood in my way when I could have made a fortune,' he'd hissed. 'I wouldn't be in this mess today but for you. You've put the final nail in my coffin and ruined me. *Ruined* me!'

'You ruined yourself,' Juliet had said, as though she didn't really give a damn. 'Maybe if you'd spent less time strutting your stuff in the city's celebrity restaurants and clubs and more time listening to your solicitor and accountant, you wouldn't be in this mess.'

Liam had glared at her. 'You'll pay for this,' he said. Then he had picked up her glass of red wine, chucked the contents into her face and stormed out. Rebecca had been furious, and even more upset when a couple of weekend tabloids had recounted the incident in lurid detail, but Juliet had laughed it off.

'Rise above it, Rebecca,' she'd said calmly. 'Why should I let Liam Corrigan push my buttons? Obviously he's upset, and I'm sorry he's got himself into such a mess, but even if I'd allowed him right of way through part of my property, it wouldn't have made any difference. He'd already over-extended and is in deep trouble with the banks. And that's without factoring in the value of the site tumbling to rock bottom just after he bought it.'

A couple of weeks later, Rebecca had heard that Liam had fled to Spain, his legendary lifestyle in ashes at his feet. Since then, she hadn't seen or heard of him until now.

He smiled. 'Rebecca Ryan. I'm glad I haven't changed beyond all recognition.'

'It's only been a couple of years,' she said, a little haughtily.

'Four, actually.'

'So you kept count?'

'Each and every one, unfortunately,' he said, his glance full of wry humour as it rested on her, as though she'd caught him out in some misdemeanour.

'Don't tell me you're here for the wedding?' she said.

He gave her a look as though he was debating whether to take her into his confidence. 'I could say I'm supposed to be enjoying an illicit rendezvous with my secret lover, only now I see my cover is blown.'

This was accompanied by such a comical, self-deprecating smile that Rebecca was almost amused, but she recalled the last time they'd met and looked at him coldly. 'Very funny,' she said.

He recoiled. 'Nothing so torrid or interesting,' he said. 'Paul Johnson is an old friend of mine as well as Harry's – but the band's come on and it's a while since I've had the ears blown off me.'

'So Golden Boy Liam came home for a wedding?' Rebecca was surprised he'd bothered to interrupt his exile to Spain for that.

'Not just the wedding,' he said pleasantly. 'And I'm no longer a golden boy. I have some unfinished business that I need to straighten out, and the two dovetailed nicely, but it's rather a long, dull story.'

'Yeah, sure,' Rebecca laughed. 'You dull, Liam? That's a contradiction in itself.'

'You might be surprised to hear that a few things have changed since the last time we met.' He looked at her steadily and she was surprised to see honesty in his eyes. Whatever had happened to him in the intervening years, he seemed a different man from the one who had insulted her friend before hotfooting it out of Dublin with his construction business in ruins: he'd risked storm clouds in venturing back to the scene of his crimes just to be here for the wedding of an old friend's son.

'So you remember the last time we met?' she said, deciding that she was going to remind him if he'd forgotten.

He smiled ruefully. 'Of course. I was horribly rude to Juliet and I bet you haven't forgiven me.'

'No, I haven't,' she said. 'Rude, Liam?' Rebecca echoed his

words. 'You were totally intimidating. See you around.' She headed for the corridor by the side of the hotel lobby, her head high.

'Rebecca – wait.'

She wheeled around. 'I've nothing to say to you, Liam.' She was wary of the way he was looking at her, as though he liked what he saw and was happy to have bumped into her, in spite of the way she was dismissing him.

'Juliet's forgiven me,' he said, his hands open in a conciliatory gesture.

'What?' It was impossible to hide her surprise.

'You didn't know? I thought she would have told you straight away on account of you two being such close pals.'

'No, she didn't,' Rebecca said. 'I'd have thought she was the one person you'd want to avoid.'

'Ah, you know Juliet. I couldn't stay angry with her indefinitely. Four years in Spanish exile gave me plenty of time to think. And we go back a long way, me and her.'

'That's putting it rather mildly,' Rebecca said, a little acerbically. 'So when did this great act of forgiveness happen?'

'Just today.'

'*Today?*' She couldn't keep the surprise out of her voice.

'Yeah. Juliet was part of my unfinished business. I owed her a bottle of wine and a grovelling apology, to say the least, so I dropped in to see her late this afternoon, before I came here.'

'Was she expecting you?'

'Of course. I emailed her during the week. Even I had more sense than to turn up unannounced, given our history.'

Rebecca was taken aback. Naturally, Juliet didn't tell her everything that was going on in her life, but Rebecca had witnessed their row and her friend should have mentioned that

Liam was on the scene again. Then again, she and Juliet hadn't exactly been on speaking terms when they'd parted.

Liam was still talking. 'I was relieved to have the chance to put things right between us,' he said. 'I told her I was really sorry I'd lost the head with her that time. She accepted my peace offering of a rather good French reserve, and we chatted for a bit before I left. I think she was expecting someone else so it was all very short and sweet.'

'Who was it?' Rebecca asked.

I need the whole of Friday to lock myself away and complete some urgent paperwork, even if it takes until midnight …

'Dunno,' he said. 'I'm just glad to have squared things with her. Water under the bridge, or almost … I still have to make my peace with you.'

'Consider it done,' Rebecca said, edging away, glancing down the corridor to her room. She wished she was there already, away from this man. He put her on her guard.

'I'd love to buy you a drink,' he said, in such a circumspect tone that it would have been difficult to refuse without sounding churlish. 'I also owe you a glass of wine for any upset I caused. Although maybe you'd rather get back to the wedding …'

She hesitated. 'Liam, I've only your word that you called to Juliet and she's accepted your apology.'

There was a flicker of disappointment in his eyes. 'Do you think I'd make that up?' He didn't look as if he had. 'Give her a call if it makes you feel better. It's just a friendly drink. I promise I won't chuck it over you,' he said. 'I'd like a chance to talk, and draw a line under the past.'

There was a shriek as the bride, in swathes of white silk, appeared in the lobby to greet some late arrivals. A pink bridesmaid appeared to join in the fanfare. She was in her bare feet, having abandoned her heels. They ran into a group hug with the newcomers, talking and laughing at the top of their voices.

Among them Rebecca saw another old golfing friend of Harry's, who threw her an interested glance. She turned back to Liam. 'I need to pop back to my room for ten minutes or so. Let's not meet in the bar,' she said. 'Somewhere away from the wedding.'

THIRTEEN

Friday, 16 March, 9.40 p.m.

Above me, one of the stars gleaming in the night sky swells so that it's bigger and brighter than any other. It frees itself from the cluster and, winking brightly, cuts a brave, independent trail of its own through the heavens.

Bravo, I silently applaud, feeling a swell of recognition. I was like that, once upon a time. Just for a short while. Until my wings were clipped.

But as it comes closer, I realise it's not a freedom-fighting star after all. In the same moment that I spot tiny red lights blinking beside it, I hear the unmistakable whine of an aircraft coming in to land, the high-pitched drone that had accompanied it across the Irish Sea changing key.

From my vantage point it doesn't look much bigger than a toy, and I picture miniature people sitting in miniature seats in the brightly lit cabin, talking and chatting and wondering how quickly they'll be able to disembark, then if they'll be delayed at Baggage Reclaim or by a long queue at the taxi rank. Thoughts that usually preoccupy me whenever I approach the end of a flight.

Oh, the luxury of having that concern at the forefront of your mind.

Help. Help. Who will see me in the dark? How long must I wait before someone notices I'm missing? Why can't I feel my legs and arms?

My mind slews away from something too terrifying to contemplate. Instead I latch on to the whisper of a memory, of another time when I lay on my back and watched planes pass overhead. As the breeze stirs, cold and moist, I grasp it before it fades, and even though it was almost a lifetime ago, I'm there again, and it's as clear as though it was yesterday.

August 1971

The sun is beating down from an azure sky, and it's warm. We've picked the most comfortable spot for some sunbathing and the ground is soft with bracken and fern. I've taken off my cork-soled platform sandals and pushed up the legs of my bell-bottomed trousers as far as they'll go. At eighteen years of age, a sun tan is a major fashion accessory. Rebecca's A-line skirt is tucked up around her thighs and even Rose has taken off her nylons, baring her legs. So far we have counted five planes droning into Dublin airport. I have brought along my tape recorder and we've been listening to Jimi Hendrix. Then, to satisfy Rose, we play Cat Stevens.

'Do you ever wonder where everyone's coming from?' I ask, lying between Rose and Rebecca. A welcome breeze flutters across the headland, refreshing our slowly burning limbs.

'What do you mean?' Rebecca says.

'All those people flying in from other parts of the world … London, Paris – I'd love to go to Paris some time, maybe even America.'

'It would be very expensive to fly to America,' Rose points out, in her usual cagey manner. Sometimes I wonder what she would have been like had her parents not died when she was at such a critical age.

'It's very expensive to fly, full stop,' Rebecca says. 'You could become an air hostess, Juliet, and get to all those places for free. Think of the glamour and excitement! Never mind rubbing shoulders with all those good-looking pilots.'

'I've no intention of getting a job based solely on my face,' I say stubbornly.

'No, I guess that wouldn't suit a women's libber like you,' Rose says.

'And why are you assuming all the pilots are men?'

'Because they are.' Rebecca laughs.

A short silence.

Then I say cheerfully, 'When that stupid marriage bar is removed, the world will be our oyster. We can be anything we want to be. Maybe, who knows, president of Ireland?'

'President!' Rose scoffs. 'We'll never have a female president.'

'We will.' I'm full of conviction. 'If you talked to the women I meet, or heard them speak, you'd have no doubt about that. It might take twenty years but we'll get there.'

'Maybe you could become the first Irish woman pilot, Juliet, instead of an air hostess,' Rebecca says. 'They'd have to come up with a woman's uniform, though.'

'It's a bit late now,' I say. 'You need honours maths, which my school didn't think was a suitable subject for genteel ladies.'

'We had to do domestic science. It was compulsory,' Rebecca says wistfully.

'I enjoyed that,' Rose says.

'I didn't.' Rebecca snorts.

'I didn't have the option of domestic science,' I say. 'My school's view was that we'd have cooks and maids to do what had to be done while we sat back and looked pretty for our husbands.'

'I'm quite happy doing the cooking and cleaning in my home.' Rose is on the defensive. 'As soon as we start a family I'll be the happiest person on earth.'

'Yes, I'm sure you will be, but you don't actually own your home, do you?' I point out. 'It belongs to Matthew, not you. Legally, it's not even shared between you, and I bet you used your lump sum from your job when you had to leave as part of the down-payment.'

There is another silence. I didn't mean to score a point off Rose. I know it must be tough for her having to sit at home twiddling her thumbs all day and depend solely on Matthew's wages to pay the bills, the mortgage, her knickers, her sanitary pads and everything else. Sometimes I wish she wasn't so sweet-natured and reserved. She has never smoked, and rarely drinks, only when we goad her into it. But surely there's a limit to the number of Britvic oranges you can consume. And all her skirts go to her knee. A perfect model of Irish Catholic womanhood. I can imagine her baking a load of apple tarts for rosy-cheeked children and making sure they go to mass on Sundays with shiny shoes. I see her looking at Matthew the way my mother looks at my father. And Matthew, to give him his due, seems very protective towards her.

'Stop it, you two,' Rebecca says. 'We're supposed to be having a relaxing afternoon and making the most of the sunshine. I didn't bunk off work to listen to you bickering. Not much use wearing a symbol of peace, Juliet, if you're squabbling with Rose.'

I touch the pendant that hangs around my neck on its leather thong. 'I'm not squabbling,' I say. 'Rose knows how I feel by now, don't you, Rose? No hard feelings between us. I'm glad you're very happy in wedded bliss. It just wouldn't suit me. No one's going to chain me down or tie me to a kitchen sink. I'll be fancy-free, like that butterfly, flitting wherever I choose.'

'I'm fancy-free this afternoon,' Rebecca says, 'but I'll have hell to pay with Moany Mullen in the morning so you don't always get away scot-free. And yesterday I spilt a whole bottle of Tipp-Ex across the carriage of my typewriter so I'm already in the doghouse.'

'And I skipped another lecture,' I tell them. 'I'll have to beg very nicely to borrow someone else's notes. Again. Just tell Miss Mullen you were in bed with your monthlies. That'll shut her up. Here, pass over that bottle of oil so I can I sizzle some more and get a tan.'

❧

I can still smell the coconut scent of the sun-tan oil as I smeared it on my legs, but I can't remember who first brought up the subject of going to Spain the following year. I think it was Rose, boasting that Matthew was going to whisk her away on a sort of second honeymoon. Somewhere exotic, with blue skies and palm trees, like Benidorm. They hadn't even got passports and would have to save like mad.

Or was it Rebecca, talking about sun tans and romantic foreign men?

Or me, talking about freedom such as we'd never tasted?

I remember thinking that anything Rose and Matthew could do, I could do better.

❧

'I've already saved some money from my summer job in the solicitors' office,' I say. 'I can do the same next year, so if we plan our hols for late August I should be okay. What do you think, Rebecca?'

'Foreign men! Cheap vodka in a long glass! I can't believe it could happen to me.' Rebecca sighs. 'It's like a fabulous dream. It would be tough to save enough on seven pounds a week, though. Maybe I could take an evening job as well. I could get thirty shillings in the local fish-and-chipper on a Saturday night. Oh, I'm getting all excited just thinking about it.'

Cat Stevens finally ends so I switch to the radio and Mungo Jerry's 'In The Summertime' floats across the air.

'And what about Harry?' I ask her.

'We're just good friends,' Rebecca says, in a nonchalant tone that reflects the way she continues to play it cool with him, unlike Rose, who clung to Matthew like a limpet.

'That's not what he'd like to hear,' I say, thinking of the way Harry Ryan's eyes follow her whenever we're out as a group.

'He wouldn't stand in my way,' Rebecca says. 'I haven't even been on a plane yet – it's so exciting! Hey, Rose, we'd get it cheaper if we went as a foursome. So long as Matthew wouldn't mind being blessed among women.'

'I don't know.' Rose is hesitant. 'I'd have to make sure we stayed away from you two as much as possible.'

'Don't worry, we wouldn't dream of butting in on you love birds. We could pretend we didn't know you,' I say. With long strokes, I slather more sun-tan oil over my legs. 'I'm a bright shade of pink already, girls.'

'Ooh, great,' Rebecca says. 'It might peel but then it'll turn a lovely golden brown. And I know it'll feel like we're waiting for ever but roll on next year. I can't wait …'

❦

Darkness presses around me and I'm frozen to the bone. *Roll on next year.*

I can still see Rebecca and me sitting in that cabin, surrounded by a planeload of excited holidaymakers as we hurtle across the skies above the Irish Sea, over England and down across France on the way to Spain. Rebecca and I, our shiny new cases full of light summer clothes and colourful bikinis. Our heads full of anticipation for the holiday ahead. Sun, sea, sangria, and maybe a little romance. Totally innocent of life and its vagaries.

Untried, untested. Unblemished.

FOURTEEN

It was late when Matthew returned to the reception, throwing smiles and greetings in all directions, as though he was already practising his walkabout. He came up to Rose and kissed her cheek.

'All good so far and thanks for being so patient,' he murmured. Then he took her hand. 'I have to introduce you to people.'

Rose made a huge effort to smile and chat, even though her head was whirling. She was still off balance after her encounter with Liz and the naked, almost feverish excitement in the woman's eyes. The fact that they were from the same small village in Dublin wouldn't cut any ice with Liz if it came to a scoop. Besides, Rose had married and moved out of Ballymalin before Liz had been born, so there would be no loyalty there. Liz would be on just one side: her own. An only child, she had always got whatever she wanted, boasting about this on her diary page as she fired warning shots at recalcitrant celebrities who refused to talk to her.

Eventually, Rose escaped up the wide staircase to the Ladies, but found no respite there. Three women were gathered in front of the mirrors: Celia Coffey, with Rachel and Megan, her cronies. And as Celia's voice floated to her, Rose hesitated in the doorway.

'It's only a matter of time before he's found out,' Celia was saying, as she leaned in close to apply her lipstick, her loud voice carrying clearly. Celia owned a chain of beauty salons that had

narrowly survived the recession, thanks to her sheer hard work
and rigorous cost adjustments. She plucked a tissue from the
marble container on the counter and patted her red mouth.
Then she scrunched it into a ball and lobbed it into the bin.

'You don't know for sure,' Rachel said, leaning into the
adjacent mirror. 'It could all be perfectly innocent.'

'Yes, and babies are born under cabbage leaves.' Celia snorted.
'Wait and see. He won't be able to keep that a secret for long, not
with the spotlight turned on him, and then the shit will hit the
fan.'

'It's his wife I feel sorry for,' Megan said. 'They're always the
last to know.'

'Oh, *hello*, Rose,' Celia said, finally spotting her. 'Do come in
and join us. Don't be shy. We were just talking about Brendan
and Lorna. It seems their marriage is about to hit the rocks.'

'Dreadfully sad,' Rachel said. 'Lorna will be heartbroken.'

'And, as usual, if they break up she'll be left with the main
responsibility for bringing up the kiddies.'

'While he's out gadding, wherever his fancy takes him.'

'Or wherever his mickey takes him!'

'Nothing much has changed for women, has it? We're still the
main caregivers.'

'Don't let Rose's friend Juliet hear you say that!' Celia beamed
at Rose.

The trio seemed to be talking all at once and far too brightly.
Rose hoped her voice didn't sound too flat. 'Sorry, I don't know
who you're talking about, apart from Juliet.'

'Brendan and Lorna? Really? He's behind one of those banking
scandals.' Celia flapped a hand in the air, as though everybody
should be privy to that vital information. 'He's coming before
some tribunal or other shortly – God knows what they'll discover.

But it looks as though you'll soon have a different kind of fight on your hands, Rose!'

'What do you mean?' Even though Celia's friends had turned back to their respective mirrors and seemed absorbed in fixing their already perfect makeup, she was conscious that they were hanging on every word.

'You're going to have a hard time keeping the lines drawn between your husband and your friend!' Celia said.

'So you've heard the rumour as well?'

'Duh! As my teenage daughter would say! I think it's gone beyond the rumour stage. Everyone will know soon enough. Juliet's profile is about to go viral, to borrow my teenage son's expression.' Celia laughed as if she was extremely proud of herself for keeping up with her children. 'I'd say Professor Jordan will be a tough nut to crack, so Matthew will have his work cut out. But, Rose dear, aren't you a little concerned about the battle that lies ahead? You're far too nice for that kind of heat.'

'Why should I be worried?' Rose forced a smile. 'I'm sure Matthew and I will be able to handle anything that's thrown at us, and if I'm that nice it shouldn't affect me at all, but thanks for your concern.'

'Well, don't say I didn't warn you. Liz Monaghan's prowling around tonight, and I've never seen her so fanatical about digging for dirt. And she's nothing compared to the big guns you'll have on your back.'

Rose composed her face as she moved past them on rubbery legs and went to the line of cubicles. She rummaged in her bag for her tablets, pressed one out of the foil, and swallowed it whole. It wouldn't take too long, she hoped, for mind-numbing relief to soothe her jangling nerves.

FIFTEEN

Friday, 16 March, 10.00 p.m.

August 1972

I stare at the destination over the check-in desk.

Benidorm.

Rebecca's excitement dips momentarily when she meets people she knows in the queue and she's no choice but to introduce us.

'I'm keeping away from them,' she says afterwards. 'I don't want to speak to a single Irish person for the next two weeks. Not even Rose or Matthew.'

'We won't,' I assure her.

Rose and Matthew are flying out to Benidorm next week, but staying in a different hotel, and we've agreed to avoid them as much as possible. Rose has said we might meet for drinks on our last night, but that's all. Rebecca has privately told me that Rose hopes the romance of it all will result in a baby.

Rebecca's excitement mounts again when we're finally airborne. She unscrews the top of her vodka and tips the liquid into a glass. 'I can't believe we're here at last, up in the sky, looking down on puffy clouds instead of up at them! In two hours' time we'll be landing in Spain. *Spain!*'

'Neither can I believe it,' I say. 'I was so glad to walk out of that solicitors' office for the last time. They didn't think I was entitled to go on holidays, seeing as I was supposed to be covering for their staff. All I was doing was filing, answering the phone and making tea. They didn't take me seriously because I was a woman.'

'I'm sure you weren't long in demanding your rights. They didn't know who they were taking on in Juliet Jordan.'

'Too right. Let's order another drink and practise some Spanish phrases. How does "You look very sexy" go?'

Rebecca laughs.

I want to touch the wing tip and alter the flight path, changing my destiny. But it's impossible to change the course of a life, and I see the inexorable hand of Fate playing out as the plane screeches to a halt on the foreign tarmac. Rebecca and I feel heat stifling our breath as we carry our cases out to the sun-drenched car park, where a coach, engine thrumming, waits to deliver us to our fate.

A fate in which we're captivated by clear skies and blinding sunshine, the blue sea, evenings when trellises bursting with blossom infuse the air with scent. Night-time warmth, when you need nothing more than a light lace stole over a sleeveless top and feel exotic and beautiful and far too ready to listen to sweet nothings …

❧❦

Images of our holiday flick through my head like a series of glossy photographs: Rebecca lying on a sun lounger with the sea in the near distance, me lying on a sun lounger, while past the row of oiled bodies, someone is half sitting, watching us. There is Rebecca sitting on the tiny balcony of our hotel, raising a glass of vodka and orange, wearing a garish embroidered blouse she'd bought from a market stall without haggling.

Then one photo of me, close to the camera, wearing cheap yellow sunglasses and a wide grin. (Afterwards I'd stared at the photograph for ages, heart thumping, wondering if the ephemeral reflection of the man who had taken it had been captured in my shades. But there was no sign of him.)

❦

'You're so luscious, Juliet.'

I've never been called that before. Luscious. It makes me feel womanly, curvy and desirable. I've never in my wildest dreams thought I could be that kind of girl, but here, in the scented heat and heady romance of foreign soil, I feel different and it's all too easy.

'You've bewitched me.'

'Have I?' I ask, in a voice that isn't mine, all sexy and flirtatious. A sultry, bad-girl voice, fuelled by cheap vodka, a romantic atmosphere and a sense of breaking away from other people's expectations. I'd sensed him watching me from a distance over the last couple of days as I'd moved from the beach to the promenade restaurant, from scanty bikini to floaty kaftan.

Some Scottish guy had been eyeing up Rebecca all evening and I'd encouraged her to go to a cocktail bar with him. As soon as they were out of sight and the coast was clear, I knew he'd come looking for me.

His wife has gone to bed. She has nothing to do with the urgent need that ripples between us. It holds us in thrall, and shuts her out as though she doesn't exist. We talk for a while and then I let his hands slip beneath my kaftan to my bare breasts, teasing the nipples, sending a hot flood of want through me. Confident, assured hands that know what they're doing and how to bring me to fever-pitch excitement. Not like the hesitant fumblings of my college peers. The scent of his strong body is all around me in the warm, humid night. It's heady and musky and sharply male. I feel alive like never before.

'Have you ever …?' His hand slides slowly down to the warm valley between my thighs and I gasp. My panties drop to my ankles. I step out of them.

I part my legs slightly. He knows exactly what to do with his sensitive fingers. My heart is galloping. 'No … not yet.'

An indrawn breath, a glitter of triumph in his eyes. Excitement crackles all around me. A sense that I am stepping out of my own skin, leaving aside the restricting ties of family love. Because I want to prove to myself that I'm not a flawless princess, but flesh and blood. Faint with giddiness, I slide down onto the night-time sand and he is kneeling over me, wrenching off his shirt. I hear the clink of his belt buckle as he opens it, and the rasp of his zip. I reach down to the hem of my kaftan and slowly bring it up as far as my waist. Then, emboldened, I sit up for a minute and pull it over my head, then lie down on the sand, part my legs and open my body to him.

Luscious …

The taste of forbidden fruit and the start of my private downfall. For what begins on the warm sands in Benidorm doesn't end there. One night isn't enough: it barely satiates me, never mind him, and to my shame, there is more, later, back in Dublin.

September 1972
It wasn't planned. It should never have happened. A month later, when I meet him by chance on Grafton Street in Dublin, we look so different against a light September rain and the grey

afternoon that we almost pass each other by. My kaftan has been replaced by denim jeans and I'm wearing a checked jacket with a big collar turned up against the rain and hugging a briefcase to my chest. I see him first, coming towards me. He's wearing a dark trench coat and carrying a large black umbrella, and for an instant I hesitate, torn between slipping past anonymously and stopping to say hello …

If I could go back, would I have done it differently? Would I have scurried past on the other side of the street? But I've hesitated too long. He sees me out of the corner of his eye. And it's too late.

'Juliet!'

'Hi.'

There is a taut moment of awkwardness, both of us unsure of this new landscape, which is electrified by the desire we shared on a shadowy beach. We are aware that the right thing to do is to nod politely and go our separate ways. The moment stretches out and already we are falling into a new, forbidden space. He tilts his umbrella towards me so that we are both tucked under its shelter. We're alone together, marooned in a world of slow caresses, intertwined limbs and cries of delight, a million miles removed from the mundane reality of rain pattering on the umbrella and dripping slowly off the spokes, the legs of shoppers surging around us, and the line of cars swishing slowly up the street. Under the umbrella, the air is so heavy with possibility that it's hard to breathe and my throat closes. He lifts his hand and curves it around my face.

He smiles. 'Luscious.'

Three months. We have three months of snatched moments, time stolen from his life and mine, the lovemaking between us all the more intoxicating for its urgency. I move through lectures and reading rooms, slip into and out of anonymous country-hotel lobbies and have breakfast with my father, wondering why no one notices that all the cells in my body are glowing. I don't think about his wife as my mouth tastes the delicate hollow of his neck or my teeth nip the skin of his inner thighs, or as I move on top of him and sink down, feeling him inside me. She doesn't suspect anything, he says. She has no place in the hot, sharp current surging between us. I am amazed at my capacity to blot out everything in my need for him.

Then one Friday evening before Christmas I meet him after lectures. I haven't seen him for two weeks and he is more urgent than ever, almost rough, clinging to me with all his strength as he comes immediately. He apologises for his haste when he tears his mouth away from mine, but his wife is beginning to ask questions. Also, she thinks she might be pregnant …

Although he begs me to continue, and promises to be extra discreet, he knows me well enough by now to understand that, no matter how I feel about him, this will end everything between us.

But it wasn't the end of my downfall. It was only the beginning.

SIXTEEN

'We probably shouldn't be here,' Rebecca said, her voice lowered to a whisper.

'So? We'll wait until we're thrown out. In the meantime, everywhere is locked up, so we can't do any harm, and it's perfect.'

'How did you manage to find this spot?'

'I know the hotel because once upon a time I used to live just a couple of miles up the road.'

Rebecca sipped her wine. She didn't know what had happened to the huge mansion in the parkland setting where Liam had once held court. She was afraid to ask.

'You said to find somewhere quiet, didn't you?' Liam went on.

They were sitting in the spa reception area, on velvet-covered armchairs that backed on to a bank of leafy potted plants. Rebecca breathed in the scent of bergamot and geranium, courtesy of the adjacent spa. To one side, large picture windows faced out on to a small courtyard where spotlights illuminated water features and miniature shrubbery. In front of her, and behind a sheet of glass, lay the swimming-pool, and in the dim lighting, the surface of the water shimmered. The low table in front of them held their glasses and a bottle of white wine in a cooler. They were just down the corridor from the hotel lobby and through another set of sliding doors, but might as well have been in a different world.

'It's a far cry from Lower Ballymalin Gardens,' Rebecca said.

'That brings me back,' Liam said. 'Although I only went to school there.'

'I'd forgotten you hung around with Harry and the others. You were the posh one.'

'Living over a vegetable shop on the edge of Howth? You're joking. Juliet was the posh one.'

Liam had been more on the outside, looking in, Rebecca recalled. Self-possessed, tall and lean, with a hungry determination to make his mark on the world.

'They were the good old days,' he said. 'Being a teenager in the summer of 'sixty-nine ... Who can forget the first time they saw *Easy Rider*? Or heard Bob Dylan? Or got drunk? We had some laughs. Harry was great. You must still miss him. How long now?'

'Six years.' She bit her lip. Sometimes it felt as though he had never been: she couldn't remember the sound of his voice and needed a photograph to conjure up his face. 'I keep busy,' she said. 'It's the only way. But it was tough. Still is, sometimes. Mostly I glide along fine, and then something happens that reminds me ... or something goes wrong and Harry's not there to share it.'

'You kept him guessing, you know,' Liam said. 'He thought he'd never get you up the aisle. Everyone else was a little in love with Juliet.'

'Were you?'

'We all were, except Harry. Juliet was different, with that mixture of seduction and feistiness, but way off limits, living in that house on the hill. Sparky, too, when it came to cutting us down to size and letting us know who was boss. She turned into one hell of a woman. And from what I've heard she's going all the way to the top.'

'She's talked to you about …?'

He lifted the bottle of wine out of the cooler and topped up their glasses. 'I knew already. It's Dublin's worst-kept secret, and it'll make for some really juicy debates. Juliet will light a fire under everyone else. I wished her the best of luck.'

'Did you?'

'I hope it goes well for her. I'd love to see her sitting in the Park – nothing against Matthew, but Juliet would be perfect.'

She watched his face as she said, 'That's a bit of an about-turn from the last time I saw you two together when you were telling her she'd ruined you.'

'I've had my epiphany,' he said, lines fanning out from his eyes as he smiled wryly. 'And a few sleepless nights. But we'd be here all night if I got started on that.'

He stared out through the darkened glass and she wondered what he was thinking. About the sleepless nights for which Juliet might have been responsible? The lifestyle he'd worked so hard for, built on a bubble? A line of creditors, baying for his blood? She felt a spike of caution. Four years ago, this man had blamed Juliet for his catastrophe. How could he have forgiven and forgotten?

Liam caught her studying him. 'Most of those nights are behind me now. But being back in Dublin, meeting old friends …' He shrugged. 'It's made me realise what a complete arsehole I used to be.'

'I can't believe I'm hearing this from one of Dublin's former hot-shots.'

'I know you might find this hard to believe, but time was, I couldn't even think of Juliet's name without feeling savage. When I'd cooled my jets a little I saw she was right.'

'I guess that could be called an epiphany.'

'I don't know how I got so carried away. When I look back now, though, I was like someone possessed. Christ, I really lost the plot. I can't believe I paid a small fortune for a tiny pocket of land adjoining her house and was arrogant enough to expect her to grant me a right of way through her property. I wasn't the only one, though, caught up a mindless gamble – but, hell,' he gave her a lopsided grin, 'it wasn't the end of the world.'

'Are you sure you weren't holed up in a Zen retreat for the last few years?'

'Not quite. After the crash, it was funny, Rebecca, but I found a strange kind of freedom in having nothing but the basics, and going back to the essentials in life.'

'Definitely a monastic retreat,' she said, a little flippantly. Where had the gilded, charge-it Liam Corrigan gone?

'Thing is, I might have had the flashy lifestyle and the big cars, but it was meaningless. It was an empty power trip. I wasn't happy. I had lots of so-called friends, but no one to love, to share my life with. And you get to know who your friends are pretty quickly when things go bust.'

'You do,' she said. It was amazing the number of 'friends' who had dropped off her radar in the couple of years following Harry's death. She took a few sips of wine.

'Harry and I had to go back to basics once or twice during the eighties,' she admitted. 'It was a struggle to pay the mortgage and raise a young family, but we had each other and were happy. And we came out the other end. What brought you back to Dublin? Apart from settling your differences with Juliet.'

'I'm home to face the music, so to speak,' he said. 'I don't want to be in exile for ever, and I need to sort out my financial affairs but I may be declared bankrupt.'

'Bankrupt? Wow.' She tried to stop the shock flashing across her face. What a tough prospect for the man with the champagne lifestyle.

'I've talked to Juliet about it,' he went on. 'I had to let her know, as there might be a problem with the land I bought behind her house. All my assets are being trawled through. But she was fine about it. It'll soon be common knowledge,' he said, 'and coming to a television screen near you. You'll probably see shots of me emerging from the law courts and trying to hide from the cameras.'

'I'm sorry to hear that. But don't try to dodge the cameras. That looks pathetic and they'll catch you anyway. Just walk tall and pretend they're not there. It's a lot more dignified. Smile at them, if you like.'

'Like this?' He put on a huge wide grin, like a child showing off his teeth, and in spite of herself and her reservations about him, she laughed.

'That's a lot better than trying to skulk behind the scenes.'

'I'll take your advice.'

Rebecca glanced at her watch. 'I'd better go back to the wedding.'

'You go on ahead,' he said. 'I'm going outside for some fresh air.'

'Thanks for the drink,' she said. 'And,' she risked saying, as she slid her feet into her shoes and got up, 'you took me away from a bad place this evening.'

He raised an eyebrow. 'Did I? I can't imagine you having any bad places.'

'You'd be surprised. There are places in my head that I don't want to go right now.'

'And there was me prattling away.'

'I was happy to listen.'

'I was glad to talk to you and maybe have you revise your opinion of me,' he said, seeming oddly vulnerable.

'Ah, but you don't know what my opinion was ...' she said.

'I can guess,' he said ruefully.

They left the spa area and he walked back as far as the lobby with her.

'Will I see you in the morning? At breakfast?' he said.

'Depends. I'm hoping to fit in a walk on the beach before I leave.'

'Would you mind if I tagged along with you?'

'Feel free.' She wondered why he wanted to spend time with her. And if she wanted to spend time with him.

Still, at least it would keep her bad places at bay for a little longer.

SEVENTEEN

Saturday, 17 March, 12.30 a.m.

I wonder if I'm going to die.

The threat circles like a bird of prey in the black space over my head. What would be the language of my death? An accidental fall? Manslaughter? Murder? It seems so absurd that a prism of hope pulls me back from the brink.

I'm being melodramatic. *Of course* I'll be found. *Of course* I'll be rescued. The life of Juliet Jordan is far too precious, busy and full to end in this stupid way. I catch glimpses of myself gliding through a landscape where all is bright and warm, where I walk through open doors and people welcome me ... where I'm full of energy and purpose.

I catch glimpses of myself with my father ...

June 1981

Tall, strong, and puffed with pride, he smiles at me across the table.

We're dining in the restaurant of my father's club in Dublin city centre. We have done this every year, on all the occasions of my excellent academic results, my father bringing me out for a celebratory meal, carefully ushering me to the table as though I'm a piece of fragile, wickedly expensive crystal. When I sit down I allow the waiter to unfold a linen napkin across my lap.

This time, it's my PhD. Next spring, I'll be going to Harvard as a research fellow in international women's rights. I'm using my law degree as a stepping stone to the area of social policy and human rights, so I'm not exactly following in my father's footsteps. Still, I'm not yet thirty and the road to further success and achievement is beckoning. Back home, my mother positively glows in the sparks of delight coming from my father.

He has, as usual, ordered a bottle of Moët. 'And here's to you, Juliet.' He beams, as he touches his glass to mine. 'Well done, darling, although I was never in any doubt as to your success. You've made your mother and me so proud.'

'Thanks, Dad.'

But as I sip my champagne, the liquid catches in my throat. It cuts an abrasive trail as it slips down to my stomach, settling in a sour pool. I should be happy. I should be on top of the world. My father is happy, therefore I am happy, I tell myself. It didn't matter that when I'd dipped my toe into the waters of rebellion, the consequences had been dire, because it is all behind me now.

December 1988

It is incomprehensible that the stalwart, indestructible Mr Justice Henry Jordan has fallen prey to, of all things, double pneumonia. Even though my mother had died three years previously, of a sudden heart attack, I had always considered my father to be immortal.

Surely the doctor is wrong about it being fatal. Surely double pneumonia is fixable, in this day and age. The 1990s are just around the corner, the new millennium just twelve short years

away. The country might be in an economic slump, thanks to
the recession of the eighties, but we're living in modern times
and medicine has made huge advances. Besides, my father will
fight this off, as he has fought against so many things in his life,
with his usual determination.

I'm sitting across the table from the doctor. My hands, in the
lap of my camel cashmere coat, are twisting my brown leather
gloves around and around. I stare at him and wait for this
charade to be over, for him to laugh and tell me it's a bad dream.
I'm there, but not there.

'Your father ignored a persistent cough,' he says.

Yes, well, he's a busy man, I argue silently. He's never caught a
cold in his life. He's an active, vigorous man, who had bounced
back after his wife's death, pouring his energies into his work, as
tireless as ever, even though he's now in his late sixties. Which,
on my return from America, had made it easy for me to live in
my new city-centre apartment and throw myself into my ever-
expanding career.

'He hasn't been looking after himself properly,' the young
doctor continues. 'The cough turned into influenza, which gave
rise to a chest infection. I understand his wife has passed away?'

'Yes. Three years ago. But Dad was never sick with a cold.'

'Hmm. Sometimes it happens that the person left behind
slides into a kind of depression. This can weaken the immune
system.'

I've taken my eye off the ball. I, the – almost – perfect
daughter, have neglected him in my headlong rush for success
and achievement.

'Maybe if he'd seen the doctor in the initial stages and had
adequate rest and fluids …'

Rest? My father had never even had a lie-in, let alone spent a day in bed. Any kind of sickness was for weak people, not strong men like him.

'But the infection that caused the pneumonia has entered the bloodstream and is now affecting other organs …'

'There must be something you can do …' My voice trails away and I bite back my frustration. I want to dive across the table and give the doctor a good shake. Don't you understand that this is my *father*? You have to make him better. It's unthinkable that a cough has led to this.

'I'm sorry but his situation has become complicated. It's all very touch and go.' He looks embarrassed. I realise I'm sitting there with my mouth open, and close it quickly.

He's still talking: 'His lungs have swollen because the disease has filled up the air spaces and his breathing is difficult …' As he continues, his words cut into the space around me: bronchioles, air sacs and alveoli. It's a foreign language, but I try to understand because this may be the absurd language of my father's death. '… so at this stage we can only make every effort to ensure he's comfortable …'

Comfortable? He couldn't be talking about the judge. For the judge didn't – correction, doesn't – do comfortable. Ever.

'I'm sorry …'

I stare past the poster of a chest cavity pinned to the wall and through the window, where the first snow of the winter has appeared and is dusting the top of the Dublin mountains, like icing sugar.

Only yesterday my father helped me to build a snowman in the back garden at Verbena View, his big capable hands rolling the snow with ease, the ends of his long overcoat furred with a snowy white frill, his laughter booming in the still, calm air.

Only yesterday he brought me up into the woods and forests

of those same mountains in search of glossy green holly, a special trip, just the two of us, leaving my young brother at home with my mother. He turned the heat up in the car. He covered my hands with mittens to protect them from the cold and the sharp spikes of the holly.

That holly bush is probably still there, in its quiet corner of the woods, berries glowing, but today my father is thin and shrunken in the hospital bed. Like a magnificent oak felled in error. Even now I'm convinced he'll pull through. Where there's life, there's hope. Sometimes a glimpse of hope can be all that's needed to sustain us. My father's faded eyes light up when he sees me and he tries to talk through the mask, but his words are indistinct.

'Be quiet, Dad,' I say, trying not to look at the frightening jumble of tubes and monitors that are needed to support his life. 'You just have to rest and get better. We'll have you out of here by Christmas.'

Why am I saying 'we'? Robert, my younger brother, is in America, having emigrated three years ago. He's hearing it all second-hand from my regular phone calls, but he's not about to jump on a plane, not for pneumonia or, indeed, for his father. There's not much love lost there: he felt he was always a pale runner-up after me and he'll be enjoying Christmas in Florida with his new wife.

'Besides, you have to bring me out for more champagne,' I tell him.

'Another achievement?'

'More things to celebrate …' I tell him I've been appointed vice-chair to the newly formed Council for Women's Political Equality. My urchin crop has gone and my hair is longer now, styled around my face in a pageboy cut. My tailored clothes, smart court shoes and expensive jewellery reflect my new status.

My father stares at me. 'I need to talk … to tell you …' he wheezes.

'Ssh, it's fine.'

He tries to lift his head from the pillow, neck suddenly scrawny and crêpey, but the effort is too much for him and it flops down again. Even his thick, springy hair has become limp and sparse across his skull. Somehow I find this difficult to look at. It's only hair, after all, but the judge was proud of his thick, wavy hair and now its paucity seems to represent the decline in his body in the most pathetic way.

'You need to know …' he begins again, crooks out a finger for me to come closer. The nurses are keeping him spotlessly clean, but there is sweat on his brow and I can smell a stale scent. I clasp his hand. It feels as soft as velvet, the bones inside disjointed. These hands once hoisted with ease a small girl on to his shoulders, but now if I squeeze them too hard I fear they might shatter. I wonder what gem of advice he's going to give me on the meaning of life.

'… how much I love you …' he says.

'Yes, Dad, I know.' I smile at him.

'You don't.'

Even on his death bed, he is debating with me. But this cannot be his death bed, while there's the tiniest breath of life.

'You don't know how wonderful it is to have a child of your own … a son or a daughter … to see your own flesh and blood created out of nothing but love …' He gathers his strength. 'You don't know the pure joy you've brought me, how perfectly you've made my life complete …'

Another pause.

My head is whirling. *Joy? Perfect? Oh, Dad, please don't say these things. I'm a fraud. You don't know the real me. What I've done.*

'Nothing else matters, Juliet, nothing at all … Success and achievement are good, and you've surpassed any expectations Kitty and I had for you, but love is far more important. Love is all that matters. In the end it's all that counts … I hope you relax long enough to find someone to love and maybe have wonderful children of your own …'

He stops, exhausted, staring over my shoulder into the space beyond me, and I think he has finished until he gathers strength again and goes on, 'I want to tell you that I love you … I want you to know … the joy, the sheer wonder of it all. The circle of life is a wonderful thing …'

He has never spoken to me like this before, and his words gouge a painful trail through my chest. I lock them into a far corner of my mind. I cannot bear to think of the full meaning of what he is saying just yet. Later, perhaps, when I'm away from here, I know they'll crawl out of their dank hiding place and drip through my veins like poison.

Because I don't deserve his love.

'You're not going anywhere, Dad, except home with me for Christmas,' I tell him, using the brisk Ms Jordan tone that warns people I mean business and sends grown men and women rushing to do my bidding.

His eyes are suddenly childlike and contrite as they fasten on mine and wrench at my heart. 'I have to go,' he says, the once-strong voice whispery. 'Kitty's waiting for me. My life hasn't been the same without your mother … I miss her and I want to be with her.'

I've no answer to that. How come the woman who lived in the shadow of her husband, sublimating her own life and potential, yielded so much power that he's prepared to give up his life without a fight to be with her? Perhaps his love for her, and hers for him, which I took for granted, were far greater and more powerful than I ever realised.

A life submerged and sacrificed, I'd thought, thinking I knew it all.

How little I'd known.

'Her whole, unselfish life was all about loving me, you and Robert,' he gasps. 'Nothing more. We were her world, and she was my anchor … I miss her so much …'

Neither do I realise how much of an anchor he has been to my life, how staunchly he has formed its backbone, how much he has coloured the air I breathe, until I see him lying in his coffin, the frilly white lining almost absurd against the cold stiff marble of his patrician face. I feel something collapse inside me, as though a vital part of me has crumbled away, never to be rebuilt.

People file past me at his funeral service. I don't remember any of them or what they mouth to me. Robert struts around, basking in my father's afterglow. Rebecca and Rose are there, and I talk to them, as if through a solid wall. I watch my father's coffin lowered into the cold, muddy ground, where it will stay buried for ever on an incline overlooking the sea, and as they close the gaping hole, something closes in my heart.

He is gone. It is over. As long as I live, I will never see him again.

I am free now to be whoever I want to be. All restrictions have been loosened. All love ties cut. The person I struggled to please has gone, but I don't feel free. It's as though my right arm is missing and all I'm left with is a cold feeling that nothing much matters any more.

For my father will never know just how much I loved him because only yesterday I made the ultimate sacrifice. Only yesterday I turned my back on everything that was real and essential at the core of my life to save his pride.

EIGHTEEN

Saturday, 17 March, 1.00 a.m.

February 1973

Rebecca runs after me.

'Juliet? Are you okay?' she asks, rapping on the cubicle door after I excuse myself from the table in the Chinese restaurant and flee for the Ladies.

It's impossible to answer her with my head stuck in a toilet bowl and everything I have eaten that day projecting itself into the mess below me. When I have a moment's respite I snatch at the loo roll. The tissue is hard and grainy against my sore lips. My stomach convulses and contracts. Then I push the hair out of my face and gingerly raise my head.

'Does it sound like I'm okay?' I ask, my voice so hoarse I scarcely recognise it. The ache in my chest is ten – no, a million times worse than any pain in my stomach.

It's Valentine's evening and I'm out for a meal in a Chinese restaurant on Dame Street with Rebecca and three of her typing-pool workmates, the unattached girls, who have no date for the evening. Rebecca is having an 'off' period with Harry and we are celebrating our date-free status in the true spirit of women's liberation. It was my idea. Why sit at home lamenting the absence of roses or Valentine cards? I'd said to Rebecca. Surely it was better to go out and enjoy ourselves.

I open the door and let her in.

'Ssh,' Rebecca says. 'You'll be fine. Here, I'll rub your back.'

I don't ask her how that's supposed to help, because once more I can't talk and turn back to the bowl just in time. All the same, the light pressure of her hand, stroking, makes me feel human again and, more importantly, brings me back from spiralling into a deep, black void.

Eventually I raise my head and look at her. She's wearing the new cheesecloth top she bought in She Gear, and blue platform shoes. She looks so young and innocent, her twenty-year-old face still showing traces of puppy fat, her skin glowing, her eyes, rimmed with sparkly green Miners eye-shadow, clear and guileless. I know that what I'm about to say is going to take every scrap of innocence out of those eyes.

'Gosh, Juliet, something didn't agree with you, to say the least …'

Her voice trails away in response to my immobile face, which feels so hard and flat that I can't raise even the semblance of a smile. My eyes feel like lead and perspiration prickles my forehead.

I wait. Feeling raw and vulnerable, achy and terrified, I say nothing, can't bring myself to speak, just wait for her to respond to the look on my face.

'It's not just the Chinese food, is it?' she asks.

I know she's unwilling to imagine my upset stomach is due to anything other than food, but I shake my head. I wonder if she'll still be my friend when she finds out what I've gone and done. That I'm that kind of girl. That I've sinned. The unholy mess I've made, the huge shame of which I can't begin to grasp. Disgrace and dishonour. Hellfire and damnation. A living nightmare.

It's not supposed to be like this. Not standing in a messy toilet cubicle where the pungent smell of vomit mixes with cheap cleaning fluid. Not with my tummy churning painfully, my teeth chattering and my heart frozen with fear.

'Juliet! Tell me!'

Somewhere at the back of my mind I'd held a soft-focus image of myself at some future date, dressed in floaty white lace, smiling serenely at a handsome husband, who has just handed me a bouquet of flowers, while the sun shines around us and life stretches ahead, shining and bright, like a new gold coin. My parents, proud, pleased and happy for us. That's the way it's supposed to be for Juliet, née Jordan, beloved daughter of Mr Justice Henry Jordan.

My head spins. My hands tremble as I feebly clutch the top of the cistern for support.

'Juliet!' Her voice is behind me.

Then, 'You're not … Juliet?'

I can't bring myself to look into her eyes.

'Oh, God, you can't be …' Her voice is hushed.

My silence and hunched body are answer enough. There is a long moment during which I can almost hear her thoughts, opinions and ideas about me being hurled into the air until they settle again. Then Rebecca touches my shoulder. Without a word, she begins to rub my back again.

I close my eyes and we stand like that for a long time in the grimy, smelly cubicle.

❧❦

'You have to be certain,' Rebecca says. 'It could be a mistake. You might just have some kind of bug …'

'It's not,' I say flatly. My parents are out for the evening, my father at his club in town, my mother at a Tupperware party, and Robert at a friend's house, supposedly studying. He's studying something all right, but not his textbooks, I guess. My brother and his friend are in the middle of that awkward, pimply adolescent stage and have suddenly discovered that it's okay to talk to girls. It suits me: he's so wrapped up in himself that he wouldn't notice if I dyed my hair flaming red.

Rebecca and I are in my bedroom, able to have a decent, honest-to-God conversation without fear of being overheard. The pink and white curtains are pulled against the dull, wet February evening. I sit cross-legged on the bed, and fidget with fibres from my pink candlewick bedspread. 'I'd been hoping and praying, but I haven't had a period since early December – I've missed two now.'

Rebecca sits in my white wicker chair and fiddles with the pink flouncy material running round my dressing-table. Her face is furrowed with worry and it gives me a sense of relief that she is sharing, talking about and taking seriously the nightmare I'm hiding from everyone else. 'Still … you need to have it confirmed, your date and all that …' she says, saying aloud what I am afraid to face.

I get up and go over to the long white mirror, looking at my now flat tummy. It is incomprehensible to think that it will soon fill with a baby. A *baby*!

'And have you any great ideas as to how I might do that?' I say tartly. 'I can't exactly go to the local doctor, you know. The first thing he'd do is lift the phone to my father. Then he'd call the parish priest.'

'There *is* somewhere you can have it confirmed or not …'

'How would you know?' I'm sharp with her in my abject fear and misery.

Rebecca sighs unhappily. 'I know from girls in the typing pool. You're not the first this has happened to and you won't be the last.'

'What did they end up doing?' I asked, curiosity getting the upper hand. I'm sure there are students in college who have fallen the same way as me, but it's been covered up so discreetly that it's impossible to find out any of the basic practical facts. And I daren't risk asking any of my peers. Word would get back to my father, like wildfire. I'm alone in this, except for Rebecca.

'There's a place in town,' she tells me. 'You hand in a sample and it's anonymous. I think it costs about twenty pounds. So it's very expensive. They give you a number and you phone them a few days later for the result.'

'And if it's positive? What then? The end of my life? Can you just imagine me telling my father?' I close my eyes against the horror of it all. 'Oh, Rebecca, this would kill him. I can't do it.' I feel a lump the size of a football in my throat. I hadn't yet cried. I still can't.

'The girls in the typing pool went to England. They got six months' leave of absence without pay for domestic reasons. I'm not sure what they told their families.'

'What's the odds their families knew and were quite happy to have them out of their hair? You couldn't keep that kind of thing a secret for long.'

'I dunno. There was another girl in the typing pool who didn't know she was pregnant until she was six months gone.'

Pregnant. Even the sound of the word on Rebecca's lips makes me feel sick. It's every Irish Catholic father's worst nightmare for his daughter. How have I allowed this to happen to bright, clever Juliet Jordan? And in the most disgraceful circumstances?

'I think she was afraid to know,' Rebecca says. 'Funny thing, none of us realised either. She didn't show much until then, and next thing she was missing at coffee break. We've been told she's gone to her aunt in Liverpool for a visit. She's still not back in the office.'

I attempt a joke: 'At least nowadays most of us are spared the horrors of the sweaty Magdalene laundries or lifelong incarceration in some mental hospital. The ferry to England will be like a holiday in comparison.'

'First things first,' Rebecca says, showing a solid practicality I cling to and am immensely grateful for. 'You need to know for sure. Only then can you decide what to do.'

∂∾∽

Rebecca comes to my aid again that cold afternoon in February, by accompanying me to the second-floor office off Camden Street where my urine sample will be tested anonymously and my fate revealed.

'What if I bump into someone I know?' I hiss, as we approach the narrow doorway. I stop, terror-stricken.

'Pretend it's for me,' Rebecca says staunchly.

As we stealthily mount a worn wooden staircase to the seedy room on the second floor, where every tread squeaks and loudly announces our presence, she holds out her hand and I silently give her my small container, concealed in an envelope. It takes less than five minutes to hand it over, with the cash, to a receptionist who looks as though she's seen it all before. She glances at us disinterestedly as she passes back a small ticket with a number on it and tells us in a nasal voice to phone in a week's time. Then we're outside again, scarpering, like frightened mice, and I draw in lungfuls of cold air.

I don't need to phone to know the answer. But in case a miracle of some sort has been granted to me, I skip a lecture the following week and go down to the public phone box on the corner of St Stephen's Green. My fingers are shaking as I push two sixpences into the slot and dial. The interval between calling out my assigned number and waiting for the reply is the longest few seconds of my life. I picture the receptionist drawing a bright red fingernail down a long list of anonymous numbers, stopping at the appropriate one, then moving it across to a life-altering result in the safe security of her gloomy room. Has she any idea of the power she wields? I push more coins into the slot while I wait, and I have enough time to wonder if anyone is ever lucky enough to be told their test is negative. Or if the receptionist ever makes a mistake.

But I know it is no mistake when she comes on the line and, in a voice tinged with triumph, tells me my test is positive.

☙❦

I fell into a deep black pit all those years ago, just as I'm doing now, when I allow my eyes to close and blot out the breathing, living, star-spangled universe around me.

Back then, an all-encompassing terror consumed me.

I thought I was doing the right thing. But I know I short-changed Mr Justice Henry Jordan. For I failed him in the most essential way of all: I didn't grant him the opportunity to be bigger than himself, a truly loving, all-forgiving, all-compassionate father. For all I know, a love far greater than his pride might have blossomed if I'd told him I was expecting his grandchild.

Now I'm gripped with a different kind of terror: the prospect of my life ending far too soon, only half lived in spite of my successes, and brimming with regret for the love and happiness that might have been, and all the love I have kept hidden from the world …

NINETEEN

Rose woke with a start. The bedroom was dark, except where the closed door was framed by the landing light. She was glad of those thin lines relieving the solid blackness for she knew, from her racing heart, clammy sweat and the sickening dread swirling in her tummy, that she'd been having a nightmare. Thankfully, the details escaped her. Her mouth was dry and thick, and her head was pounding: the familiar consequences of having had too much to drink on top of a tablet or two.

Matthew's side of the bed was empty. The digital clock told her it was half past two. She'd been asleep for an hour.

She got up, pulled on her dressing-gown and thrust her feet into her slippers. Out on the landing, she paused. Slightly disoriented, she had thought for a moment she was back in their first home, where the landing was narrow and there was only one small white bathroom. Life had been straightforward then, with no room for secrets or shadows lurking in corners. Here, in Belgrave Park, the landing was spacious and elegant, with several doors opening off it, and even though the curved staircase was wide and roomy, it all pressed in on her in a suffocating way. Feeling like a stranger in her own home, she stole down to the vast, state-of-the-art kitchen, with the sandblasted glass and ergonomic Bulthaup units, complete with integrated Miele appliances. She poured a glass of chilled filtered water and helped herself to a couple of extra-strength painkillers.

She padded up the hallway to where pale light was coming through the open door of Matthew's study. He sat in his shirtsleeves in front of his computer, a single lamp burning behind him, absorbed in his task. She watched him for several moments until he sensed her presence: his head snapped up so fast that she jumped. His face was drained of colour, pale and ghostly in the light coming from the screen. 'Rose! What are you doing there? You startled me.'

'And you startled me. What are you up to?'

'Just getting some emails out of the way.' He returned to the keyboard, his fingers flying across it. After a short while he looked up again, his face alight with fervour. 'It's happening now, Rose, it's really gathering pace.'

'So I guessed from tonight.'

'Sorry if you felt abandoned, but it was important for me to touch base with some people.'

'Is this what the next few weeks will be about?'

'Hopefully. I need a dedicated website and a blog, pronto. I also need to get out there and connect with people. I hope that when they think of integrity and honesty, they'll think of me. That could be my sound bite for the campaign.'

Integrity? Honesty? 'Get real, Matthew,' she said.

He held out his hand, 'I *am* real. Rose, come here. The first thing you have to do is wipe that anxious look off your face. The world isn't about to end.'

She ignored his hand and remained in the doorway, hugging herself. 'Isn't it? You know every single part of our lives will be scrutinised.'

Her encounter with Liz Monaghan had been lightweight

and fluffy, compared to what might lie in wait for them. She looked beyond him to the trappings of his hard-won success: the mulberry leather chair, the wide antique desk and book-lined walls, the thick cream curtains pulled across long, elegant windows facing out onto a landscaped back garden. For a moment it swam in front of her. She took a quantum leap in associating the earnest Matthew Moore of Ballymalin with the smooth, confident Matthew Moore sitting in front of her.

Where had their lives gone? How had everything become so complicated in the blink of an eye?

'So?' he said, rising to his feet and coming over to her. He put his arms around her waist and she caught the scent of him as he pulled her close. 'Do you think I'd go ahead with all of this if I thought I was putting us and our comfortable lives in jeopardy? Nobody is going to find any skeletons in our closet. Because there aren't any. Get it?'

She remained silent and avoided his eyes.

They never spoke of the time she'd almost lost it, just four years ago. They never discussed the days and weeks she'd spent struggling through a spiralling blackness, while strange voices had echoed in her head and she'd tried and failed to make sense of a world that had suddenly caved in on her.

It had all come to a head in Dundrum Town Centre one morning, when she'd stood frozen with panic in the House of Fraser cosmetics department, not knowing how she'd got there, unable to move or articulate anything. A kindly shop assistant had spotted her distress and had peeled Rose's clenched fingers off the straps of her bag so that she could reach in for her mobile, scroll through her contacts and call someone to come to her.

'Juliet?' she'd said, her face swimming in front of Rose. 'Will I call Juliet for you?'

'Juliet …' Rose had tried to grasp the name, the fleeting image of a laughing girl flickering for a moment before that, too, slipped away from her. 'No …'

'Rebecca?'

'Yes, please, Rebecca …'

Even now, four years on, Rose was still filling in the blanks of what exactly had taken place during those lost months of her life. Panic attacks, the doctor had said. Anxiety. Depression. Words that were easy to say, but went nowhere near describing the dark pit in which she'd found herself or the months it had taken her to crawl out of its depths.

Depths that might be terrifyingly easy to plunge into once more.

She tried to banish the thought. 'What will happen to Tory Technologies, if you're taken away from it?' she asked.

'I thought you might step into the breach,' Matthew joked. Then he went on, 'I have all that worked out. My team of senior executives is more than capable of holding the fort. I wish I could convince you that everything will be fine. I'll have a good team around me to take care of the campaign details. I've already been pledged lots of support. My job is to talk persuasively to a few county councils. Yours is to go shopping and have facials and stuff with Rebecca. I'll look after the rest. You'll just smile, shake hands, and look like a future president's wife. Life is going to get busy and exciting so the best thing you can do right now is run back upstairs and get a good night's sleep.'

She was still silent, questions and concerns ricocheting in her head.

'Rose, there's no need to be anxious,' he said. He was smiling at her as though she was a child, afraid of a bump in the night. 'I want this opportunity to make my mark. It's a fantastic prospect and far bigger than anything I've ever anticipated. It's more than a dream.'

'Liz Monaghan cornered me tonight. She says you're top of her interview list.'

'That bitch? She'll have to join the queue. Anyhow, I'll be engaging a campaign manager and assistants to organise all that stuff so she might find herself off the list completely.'

'Liz thinks you're hot stuff,' she said, watching his face. '"His male hotness", she called you.'

Matthew laughed. 'Did she really?'

Suddenly he pulled her close and kissed her hard on the mouth. Rose found herself clinging to him for reassurance as he deepened the kiss. He pulled at the sash of her dressing-gown and thrust his hand inside her lace nightgown, clutching at her curves. Rose melted into the familiarity of him and tried to forget her fears.

After a while he drew back. 'I need you with me, Rose, every step of the way.'

'I am, but …' Rose faltered. 'I want you to have your dream, Matthew, but what about Juliet?'

'What about her?'

She plucked at his shirt. 'Liz talked about your posters, hanging together on the lampposts. Juliet could take it all away from you, couldn't she?'

He flicked back her hair. 'I'll just have to work extra hard and make sure she doesn't. Trust me, I know what I'm doing.'

'Do you? Juliet said …' Rose paused.

'Go on,' Matt prompted, his eyes suddenly hard. 'What did Juliet say?'

Rose swallowed, anxious that her mouth was running away with her. 'She just – asked me if you were genuinely passionate about serving our country or if it was more about …' Her voice trailed away.

'More about what?'

She said, very quietly, 'More about feeling important.'

'And when was this?' he asked, equally quietly, gripping her wrists.

'A couple of days ago. I told you what she said to Rebecca,' she babbled. 'Oh, Matthew …' She sighed. 'I said she had no right to speak of you like that.'

He released his hold, almost sending her off balance. 'For God's sake, I'll deal with Juliet. You just keep out of it, right?'

'I was trying to help.'

'Help?' he fumed. 'You're out of your depth. I don't think you fully grasp how big this whole thing is. From now on *I'*ll do the talking. You just have to look good, hang onto my arm and keep smiling. Is that too much to ask?'

'Yes, but Juliet …'

He glared at her. 'I don't give a flying fuck about Juliet Jordan. Get it? There's only one thing I'm interested in right now. This is my moment, my chance to dream the biggest dream and give my life a sense of purpose.'

'*Purpose*, Matthew?' she asked, feeling suddenly cold. 'How could that be missing from your life when we have so much?'

'It's a personal validation,' he said. 'I'm as good as any of the other contenders. Why shouldn't it be me, us?'

'So is that what's really driving you?'

There was a long silence while he looked at her, exasperated. 'Go back to bed, Rose. You'll feel better after a good night's sleep. James will be home soon and has promised to lend his support,' he went on. 'He knows I'm very proud of him. I'd like to make him equally proud of me.'

'You do know the opposite could happen, if things go belly up,' she said, grasping at straws in the face of a gale-force wind.

'They won't, at least not by my doing,' he said. Then he put a finger across her lips and said quietly, 'You're hardly going to rock any boats all by yourself, are you?'

She shook her head.

She went back upstairs to their bedroom, wishing she could take some of his self-belief and wrap it around herself, like a shield. For she needed a shield against the black devils of the night that had once engulfed her, but most of all, against the unspoken treachery that had put them there.

TWENTY

Saturday, 17 March, 3.00 a.m.

I never knew the depths of the night could be so iron-hard cold and bloody lonely, or that the star-filled night sky could be so clear and vast, yet totally serene, and heedless of my terror-filled predicament.

Help. Help.

There is still no sound coming out, only gossamer threads of my life weaving through my head like glittering spider's webs. I need to piece together those threads to figure out how I've ended up here.

But can I go there, to the place I've barely touched, the memory of which has up to now been locked away for fear of the devastating pain it would unleash? Yet there can't be anything more painful than lying here, totally helpless, listening to the whispering sea and wondering if I'll ever see the people I love again ... especially the person I love most ...

I close my eyes and peel back the memory with a gentle hand ...

1973

My God-fearing parents don't suspect. My mother doesn't notice that I've filled out a little around the waist. I had assumed most mothers would sense such things. My father fails to notice that I'm unusually subdued and edge my way guiltily around the house. For that's how I feel: edgy and guilty. Although, to be fair to them, the idea of their darling daughter falling pregnant would never cross their minds, not in a million years.

'I'm due in September,' I tell Rebecca. I calculate the date by reference to a gynaecological book she has bought, in a bookshop at the far end of town, where she was sure of not bumping into anyone she knew.

'September? That's perfect,' she says.

'You have to be joking,' I say, stony-faced. 'How could anything about this be perfect?'

I'm like a mutinous child to her almost motherly patience.

'I'm not joking, Juliet,' she insists. 'You can complete your year in college, then tell your parents you're going to London to find work for the summer and that you'll be back in time for your next college year.'

'Yes, ha!'

'Lots of students do it.'

'Yes, but London!'

'Well, it has to be somewhere like that. If you tell your parents you're going to Cork or Galway, your father will want to visit you and expect you home at the weekends.'

I shudder. 'Yes, you're right.'

'So it has to be somewhere like London, where they'd scarcely visit, or expect you home during the summer.'

'But how – where would I stay? How could I support myself? And my father … he's bound to ask so many questions I'd never get away with it.'

'You will. We'll work it out. I didn't say you actually had to *go* to London …'

I have no alternative. I lie sleepless in bed at night, turning it all over in my mind. Sometimes I look at my father's face at the breakfast table and imagine breaking my news to him. It doesn't bear thinking about. I picture my mother's reaction and visualise her world falling apart. I can't let that happen. And that is all the fright I need to plan my escape, right after my third-year exam at the end of May. It also means I have only three months at home to hide my thickening waist with larger jeans and Rebecca's borrowed cheesecloth tops.

Two of my college mates are off to London for the summer, so of course I'm madly interested in their plans. I make them my own in conversations with my parents, so that places like Oxford Street, King's Road, and offices in Marylebone begin to trip off my tongue. I even compose a letter from a supposed personnel department of a London insurance office, seal it in an envelope and address it to me, and Rebecca sends it to a cousin of hers in London to post back to me, spinning a false romantic yarn about it. I tell them I'll ring home from a local callbox every Sunday, as there is no phone in the flat I'll be sharing with three other Irish Catholic girls. And, for once, my father is distracted by two things: a course of study he will be pursuing during the normally quiet summer months, plus detailed preparation for an important case that is coming up in the autumn.

Which is just as well, because I don't go to London. I spend the whole summer in Galway, hiding away from the world in fear of being found out, as I wait for my baby to be born.

⌘

The months I spend in Galway are a blur, as though there is a filmy veil between me and those lost days. The fear of being found out is so great that it threatens to overwhelm me. My belly swells and I feel the baby move and kick, but I never visualise it as a real, live baby. I never imagine it as *my* baby.

I don't think I fully accept what has happened, not because I don't understand it, but because I still can't believe it has happened to me. At one level it's easier to pretend it's not happening at all.

'What does John think of all this?' Rebecca asks, when she visits me and we talk of the baby being adopted immediately after the birth. 'Surely he has some say.'

I'd been expecting this question, but it doesn't make it any easier for me to answer. Naturally Rebecca has assumed all along that the baby is his. After all, he's my occasional college boyfriend. I find it impossible to look her in the face. 'It's not John's. I've never slept with him, so he's totally in the clear. And I finished with him as soon as I knew.'

'Then who is the father?' Her voice is tentative and she looks at me very closely for quite a long moment.

I continue with my carefully constructed lie. 'The father is a cousin of John's.'

'A cousin of John's,' she repeats.

'He was home from San Francisco for Christmas with his wife …'

'His *wife*?'

I force myself to look at her. 'Yes, I slept with a married man. It was a big mistake.'

She stares at me without saying anything.

'I don't blame you if you never want to talk to me again. I'm already thoroughly ashamed of myself so you don't have to lecture …'

'Have I said anything?' she says sharply, clearly upset at the mess I've brought on myself.

I fill in the gaps. 'We met at a family party and had a short and very stupid fling.' That part was true anyway. It had been short and stupid. And I guess I became pregnant that last time before Christmas, when he'd been so urgent that we'd taken a chance. I can't quite believe how silly I was.

'I don't remember meeting him. Did I?' She wrinkles her brow.

Oh, the innocence of my trusting friend!

I evade her question. Sometimes white lies are important. I can't burden her with the uncomfortable truth. 'He's gone back to San Francisco with his wife, and he'll never know about the baby,' I say. 'Oh, Rebecca, for all my lofty, change-the-world ideas, I'm nothing but a second-rate fraud. I've let every single woman and all my feminist friends down. Never mind my parents. And now I'm denying my baby.' I put my fist to my mouth, still unable to cry.

Rebecca stays silent, but her face shows nothing except compassion. I don't deserve it, any more than I deserve my father's love.

'You're doing what you think is best,' she said eventually. 'Best for everyone concerned. The baby, your parents, you ... The baby will go to a loving home, and it'll never be called illegitimate. You're sparing your parents' heartbreak and disappointment, and after all this, you'll still make a great life for yourself. You're young, Juliet. This time next year you'll be getting ready for your finals and a whole new life. This will be behind you.'

I let her words trickle through the tight ball of frozen nerve endings that are lodged in my chest. It sits there as the weeks roll on, spreading to encompass my neck and head. I dutifully phone home every Sunday evening, pretending I'm calling from London, even buying English newspapers so that I can stay abreast of the news. My due date arrives, slips past, and then, four days later, I wake very early to twinges in my back. I stand by the window of an anonymous bedroom in Galway, watching the dawn unfurl across the September sky, and manage to bury the spark of awe and amazement that courses through me: I have put all my feelings on hold and this is happening to someone else, not Juliet Jordan, most perfect, beloved darling daughter of Mr Justice Henry Jordan.

This . . .

It's not me lying on the hospital bed as my body performs nature's most amazing ritual, nor is it my hands reaching for gas whenever the strong, purposeful pain threatens to overwhelm me; it's not me beginning to think my back is about to break in two and I just can't take any more, when at last they tell me to bear down; and it's not me experiencing that truly miraculous moment when the life that has been nurtured inside me for all those heart-wrenching months finally bursts forth, whole, complete and oh-so-perfect, into the waiting world, on that hushed September evening.

And it's not me who gives away that warm, white-wrapped bundle a few days later.

And arrives back in Dublin to pick up the threads of my life, as though none of it has ever happened. And fraudulently sips champagne with my proud father year on year, toasting each fresh success.

Except the one that truly matters.

TWENTY-ONE

'Liz! What the hell … What's been happening to you?'

The ground swayed in front of her. She caught a glimpse of her shoes before her head snapped back and her face was washed in the glare of an orange street-lamp. She clutched the railings beside her and wheeled around, crashing face first into them, hitting her lip off the cold metal. She felt something swing out and around from her shoulders and realised it was her handbag.

Gavin's anxious face appeared in her vision, blurred and indistinct. 'Liz! Jesus! I'm getting you home.'

She felt his arm anchor itself around her waist, and allowed herself to be shunted down the road. She was vaguely aware of curious glances, the tittering of passers-by, the snarl of traffic, and headlights hurting her eyes.

'Will you be okay in a taxi? Can't have you getting sick.'

Her teeth were chattering so hard she couldn't answer. She moved her head in what she thought was a nod.

'How – how did … you …' She grappled with the words, trying to form them properly, but her mouth and teeth felt as if they were made of sponge.

Gavin knew what she was trying to say. 'Some good Samaritan called me from your mobile,' he said. 'She was concerned when she saw you slumped in a corner of the Ladies at three in the morning. You still have me down as your emergency number. I don't know what you were doing guzzling your brains out in that rip-off nightclub, but you were lucky someone was looking out for you. Otherwise you'd be in A&E right now. Or in the gutter.'

'Thanksh.'

'Can you manage?'

She felt herself being half lifted, half pushed into the back of a taxi, caught the faint smell of leather mingled with that ubiquitous taxi scent, as she relaxed into the seat, and the door closed, shutting out the cold night air. She was dimly aware of Gavin getting in beside her and asking the taxi man to drive to Harold's Cross. She closed her eyes and sank back as they swirled into the stream of traffic.

The next thing she was aware of was Gavin opening the passenger door and half pulling her out. She didn't think she was going to be able to stand on her shaky legs, but somehow she managed it. Then her handbag fell on to the pavement outside her home, scattering most of the contents. Gavin pushed her against the window ledge for support and she looked at the dark blond spikes of his hair as he bobbed around and gathered up her phone, keys and makeup. He opened the hall door, switched off the alarm, and half carried her down the narrow hall to the small kitchen. She blinked in the bright light.

'Water, lots of it,' he said, turning on the cold tap.

'I don't …' Once again she tried and failed to speak coherently.

'You must. Have you any idea how drunk you are? For God's sake, Liz, how did you manage to get into this mess?' He didn't wait for her to answer. He thrust a large glass of water at her, and even pushed it against her mouth as she sipped it, her teeth clinking against the glass. It seemed to take for ever and she gagged a few times, convinced she was drowning. Then, at last, the glass was empty and he put it on the sink.

'Right. Bathroom and bed. I'm staying, but just to make sure you're okay and don't choke on something. Jesus, woman, you had me scared for a moment. I've never seen you like this before.'

He hauled her upstairs, took off some of her clothes, and pushed her into the bathroom. When she held onto the washbasin for balance and looked in the mirror, she saw two sets of red squinty eyes ringed in smudgy kohl staring back at her. Devil eyes.

Oh, God, was she going to pay for this.

Eventually she swayed out into the bedroom. Using her hands to grasp the furniture and help her unsteady legs to negotiate the room, she finally reached the bed and collapsed on to it. He pulled the duvet out from under her inert body, tucking it around her. 'Get some sleep. You'll need all your strength for the hangover you're going to have tomorrow.'

'Mmm.'

'Liz,' he asked, after a beat, 'are you really that cracked up over your father and the house?'

'Mmm.'

'We'll talk tomorrow,' Gavin said, in a kinder voice.

Maybe someone did care about her, after all. She turned on to her side, relieved when he clicked off the lamp. She hadn't the energy to talk. Nor did she want to. How had she gone so totally off the deep end tonight? She tried to piece together what had happened earlier, wondering who might have witnessed her descent into Blotto Land. She vaguely recalled leaving the Ballsbridge Hotel with a couple of other partygoers and hitting a Leeson Street nightclub. Before that, she'd been chatting to Rose Moore.

Liz's head spun as she lay in bed, her body curved into the foetal position.

Definitely something amiss there.

TWENTY-TWO

Saturday, 17 March, 3.45 a.m.

I sense I'm reaching the deep, dark depths of the night. And I'm beginning to think I need a miracle. I haven't been one for prayer in recent years, but maybe I could do with some praying as I stare at the heavens and think of my terrible sin, my disgrace, my downfall.

It took almost four years for the reality of what I had done to hit me.

1977
Rebecca and I are having a rare evening out together as I'm home from Queen's University, Belfast, for a reading week. Rebecca has just turned to me and told me in a rush, as though she'd been holding the words pent up inside her, that she's pregnant and getting married.

Surprise catches me off guard, and sharp, black pain slices through me. It hasn't bothered me that Rose and Matthew now have James, their wonderful son. Still cocooned behind the barricade of the armour plating I built around that episode in my life as a means of saving my sanity. On the odd occasion I am in their company, I watch impassively as he grows from babyhood to toddler, and while each milestone is anticipated and feverishly applauded by his proud and loving parents, it all flows past me as though it is meaningless. Because clever clogs Juliet, expertly schooled in the rationality of law, has taught herself to be emotionally detached.

But Rebecca, my best friend, having a baby … It's the first time I feel a chink in my armour, and I'm not sure I can cope with the eviscerating pain.

Rebecca's eyes are appealing as they watch me. Her circumstances are different from what mine were. She is finally in a committed relationship with Harry. He works in a big accountancy firm and I was with her the night they met unexpectedly in Sloopy's disco in Fleet Street, not having seen each other for three months. He asked her to dance to Queen's 'Bohemian Rhapsody'. She melted into his arms that night and has scarcely left them since.

Even now, things are shifting a little in so-called modern-day Ireland. In the public service and semi-state bodies, women no longer have to resign on marriage – big deal – and it's possible to apply for a period of twelve weeks' maternity leave with pay.

Although Rebecca's will still be called a 'shotgun wedding', and girls are still 'getting into trouble', looking for six months' unpaid leave and quietly getting boats to England, then returning home with broken hearts.

'It'll be a small wedding,' she says, looking nervously at me.

I hug her. 'That's great, Rebecca. I'm really happy for you and Harry, and I know it will all work out.'

'Will you be my bridesmaid? I know you're going back to Queen's next week, but we're getting married at Easter …'

I'm improving myself further by adding a prestigious doctorate to the letters after my name. It's keeping me busy and justifying my parents' flourishing and unabated pride in me. I have given them that much, but their pride lies in tatters inside me.

'No matter. Your wedding is more important. I'll come down from Belfast anytime. And you can come up to visit me and we'll shop together for your going-away clothes.'

When sweet little Danielle is born, I've had time to prepare myself for the sight of the warm bundle in Rebecca's arms and my armour is back in place, putting a thick, hard shield between me and everything I'd felt during that traumatic time in my life. I'm relieved to feel nothing beyond the happiness you'd share with a friend. As well as that, safe behind my armour, I'm free to dote on Danielle, to hug and kiss her, to feel the warmth of her in my empty arms, and give free rein to my suppressed maternal instincts by loving her as though she's my own.

And Rebecca, in her generosity, declares I can be Danielle's honorary mother.

When Rose sees the way I dote on Danielle, as she grows from babyhood to toddler, she says I can be James's honorary aunt.

As I steadily carve out a name for myself in the area of women, gender and equality studies, the thick shield between me and that traumatic time in my life serves me well. It means I can spend the week in the cut-and-thrust of the university and business environs, but now and again indulge my maternal instincts by enjoying time with Danielle and James, taking them to the pantomime, the cinema, the beach, even Verbena View to meet my parents at Christmas, and spoiling them on their birthdays.

The best of both worlds.

Almost.

TWENTY-THREE

Saturday, 17 March, 4.00 a.m.

I know this hour like you would a familiar friend. I've kept watch with it too often. It's the darkest time of the night, impenetrable and still, as though morning is a long way off and every living person is sound asleep, except me. Not much use calling for help, even if I could do so. Right now, I'm totally alone in the world, and apart from the whispering sea, it seems that even the universe is keeping a death-like silence.

Or a vigil.

No matter what age you are, you still think it's going to last for ever, your life. You think there's going to be time for everything. Time to put your world to rights. When I was younger, the years rolled on into an infinite future that bore no relation to how speedily they pass, and how limited they become. Now time seems to have flitted past on wings that beat swifter with each successive year, just as fragmented pictures of my life are whirling into the dark space above me.

The acute loneliness makes me feel I have fallen to the bottom of the void and, surprisingly, lends me strength to watch with an eerie calm as moments that make up my life unspool around me. I try to make sense of what has happened, and figure out exactly how I arrived here …

Who could have pushed me? Why did it happen? Could I have prevented it?

1990

'I'm moving back to Verbena View,' I tell Rebecca one afternoon, about two years after my father's death. We're having a meal in the Trocadero, St Andrew Street, before we go to see Patrick Swayze in *Ghost*, the hottest movie at the moment. By now, Danielle is a shy, smiling thirteen-year-old, on the sweet, tentative edge of adolescence. Rebecca's twin sons are nine and football mad, and she has matured into a warm, loving person whom I feel privileged to call my friend. She's beginning to get back to herself after the busy child-rearing years, and has started to tint her wavy hair with blonde highlights. It suits her.

'It's a fine house,' Rebecca says.

'It'll be perfect. It's about time I got on the property ladder and stopped renting. Robert will be only too happy if I offer to buy him out. He's never going to come back to Ireland to live. The house needs a bit of a makeover, rewiring and an upgrade to the central heating.' My father had let it go a little, which had been another symptom of his loneliness that I'd been too blind to see. 'And I'm going to knock down as many walls as I can to let in the light and fantastic views,' I continue cheerfully, 'especially in the kitchen, so it'll be something to keep me busy.'

'Keep you busy? Juliet, you're the busiest person I know. Between your career, your charity work and your travels, you don't have a spare moment.'

'I'd prefer to have no time to think. This will be something positive … It might help me finally move on after my father …'

'How long now?' Rebecca asked, instantly sympathetic, her hand on my arm, her gaze softened.

God bless Rebecca, one of life's nurturers. Still in mother-mode with me a lot of the time.

'Two years, and I know I should be over it by now.'

'Juliet, you never get over these things, you can only learn to adjust to them.'

'Yes, well …' I fall silent for a moment. 'Verbena View will be big enough for great parties and for everyone to visit. All of you. I can see us sitting on the patio sipping chilled white wine, you and Rose, with Matthew and Harry, and the kids in the TV room that I'm going to kit out. Television, stereo and a computer for games. Your children are the nearest I'll ever have to a family.'

'You don't know that.'

'I do. There's no sniff of romance in my life. I'm not interested either. Besides, I'm too old at thirty-seven to start accommodating a man in my life. And I wouldn't bring a child into the world unless I was in a committed relationship, which I'll never be.'

'You're far too young to be making announcements like that.'

I smile at my friend. 'Rebecca, you should know. I can't be truly honest with any man, therefore I'll never marry.' It was the closest I'd ever come to talking about my colourful history in all the years since I'd given up my baby. Normally it was a closed book between us. I preferred it like that, and I think Rebecca did, too.

'You're being very harsh on yourself.'

'I'm being honest and realistic. Besides, I'm married to my career. Did I tell you I've been invited to Oxford to speak to their women's studies undergraduates? They're examining a paper I wrote.'

'I'm impressed with that, but not impressed with the way you're turning your back on love and motherhood.'

'I don't deserve either, not after what I did.'

'Juliet! You can't condemn yourself like that. You were young, and maybe a little foolish. You did the best you could. That doesn't mean you have to give yourself a life sentence. Do you still have regrets?' Rebecca's blue-green eyes looked worried.

'No.' I hastened to reassure her, perhaps even to reassure myself.

But I had. Of course I had. Especially since my father had died. Two years on, I'm still finding life achingly empty without him and haunted by what I did. Rebecca has no idea how guilty I feel. Or how the ghost of my father still lurks in the corners of my life, never mind the ghost of the baby I gave away, as well as the man I loved just briefly and turned my back on.

My love for Danielle is a reflection of the love my father poured on me, and has helped me to realise that, had they known, my parents would have been far more hurt by my subterfuge and reluctance to trust them than any trouble I might have brought them. Slowly but surely, the magnitude of what I had done to my parents was crawling home to me. I had denied them a grandchild. I had denied them a chance to love me and offer me support at a time when I needed it most. And I had denied myself love. For clever, talented Juliet Jordan had thought she knew it all when she hadn't known anything about courage, or being true to herself, or the redeeming power of love.

෧෨

As I lie caught between heaven and hell, neither of which I believe in, I run through the age-old prayers my father taught me. *Forgive me, Father ...*

Then peace descends. What great wrong had I done, after all? What immoral sin had I committed? I'd brought life into the world. *Life*. Why had I carried that like a blemish for almost forty years and allowed it to colour my life so darkly? And I'd loved somebody who had badly needed my love.

So could I, please, have the chance to put things right?

Dear God, if I could have just *one* more day ... Please? If I could wake up in the morning with a whole glorious day stretching in front of me, enough time to take care of the really important things ...

TWENTY-FOUR

Saturday, 17 March, 4.30 a.m.

Liam. Liam Corrigan.

Out of the dark, grinding depths of this night, the name slides through the back of my head and faint pictures twirl on the edge of my mind. Who is he? Why is the name so familiar, as though I've known it all my life? Was he with me this evening as I fell? I wait to allow the flickering images to make sense. And then they pour through me, clear and distinct and colourful, pictures of the times our lives collided …

1965
We are in the vegetable shop, my mother and I, and he is near the back door, weighing out bags of potatoes on big industrial scales, muffled in a brown overall brushed with potato dust. The air is pungent with the scent of citrus mingling with the deeper, earthy smell of clay.

I've noticed him before, kicking a football with the other boys in the village, and scrubbed up for church on Sundays. I've seen him trekking up and down the hills of Howth while I swished by in my father's car. Taller than the other lads, but skinny, with unruly red hair, he seemed friendly enough. But this time when he shoots glances at me between tipping hessian sacks over the lip of the scales and sending a clatter of potatoes into the bowl, his face is proud and resentful, and I wonder what I've done to deserve it. Then his eyes linger scornfully on my school uniform, the wine-coloured tunic with the crest of the private city-centre school I attend, which tells me everything.

My mother looks overdressed in her costume and pill-box hat. She's particularly choosy in placing her order, breaking off every so often to chat to May, the wife of the owner. She explains that our housekeeper is ill. I wish she'd hurry up because he's making me feel uncomfortable. I move a little closer to her and catch her light, familiar scent. Then May notices that he has slackened off a little.

'Liam, get a move on. I need them potatoes sorted by four o'clock, and you've to start making up the orders for delivery after that. Snap to it.'

He scowls at me one final time before he turns his back. His shoulders are stiff and the tips of his ears burn crimson.

May shakes her head at my mother. 'Kids nowadays. So ungrateful. He should be thankful after all I've done for him.'

'He's a bit young to be working,' I say to my mother, when we're eventually out in the clear bright air. I had put him at around twelve, my age. My mother slides her small hands into soft leather gloves and places one protectively on my arm as we cross the road to the spot where my father will collect us.

'He's lucky he has May looking after him,' she says, when we're on the other side. 'It's only right that he should help her in the shop when he's home from school.'

'Why?'

My mother speaks softly, as though she's imparting highly

sensitive information. 'He's adopted. May took him in when he was a small boy. Otherwise he would have had to go to an industrial school.'

'What's that?'

'It's a place for children who have no parents to look after them. The lucky ones are adopted. So Liam is one of the lucky ones.'

Lucky to be rescued from the grim prospect of an industrial school by being adopted. My mother's tone had seemed to imply that Liam was extra indebted to his adoptive parents, and I wonder how that makes him feel. No wonder he was scowling at me in my private-school uniform.

After that, anytime I bump into him in the village, we eye each other guardedly. When he is a little older, he begins to do the Saturday deliveries and sometimes I'm home when he drives up the hill in a battered van and calls to our house, lugging a box of vegetables and fruit into the larder off the kitchen. His face is shadowed with resentment, especially when my father's big car is slung across the driveway instead of hidden in the garage.

Occasionally I see him hanging around with the same group of friends as Rose and Rebecca. But it's not until I start college that his resentment towards me thaws a little. He works for a builders' supplies company during the week, and we sometimes catch the same bus home.

May 1971

'I'm going to make my fortune by the time I'm thirty,' he boasts, one warm early-summer evening, as the bus crawls along the Howth Road.

Dublin Bay is a swathe of pearly grey silk, the outline of Howth Head at one end and the Pigeon House towers at the other seeming to drift in the heat haze. Everything in life seems possible. Still, I hear a hint of vulnerability in his tone, as though he doesn't quite believe in himself. He's trying to impress me and I'm touched.

'That's very ambitious,' I say. 'How are you going to manage it?'

In his blinkered defensiveness, he misinterprets my words. 'I knew you'd think I'm far too big for my boots,' he says wryly. 'Too presumptuous for someone who left school at sixteen and still has to help May in the greengrocer's on Saturdays. I don't even know who my real ma was. She never bothered with me, so I'm the original cocky bastard.'

'That's not what I meant,' I say evenly. 'How do you plan to make your fortune?'

He gives me a considered look. His need to impress me overcomes his pride. 'Construction. It's doing really well and I want a piece of the action. I want to send my kids to a posh school and live in a big bungalow on a hill with views of the sea, and have a big car in the garage.'

His voice is so thick with hunger that I don't know what to say. 'Will that make you happy?' I ask eventually.

'Too right it will. It'll make me very happy. I bet you're going to run the country.'

'What makes you say that?'

'You're clever and going to college,' he says. 'You could blow the present lot of politicians out of the water.'

He wouldn't be saying that to me if he knew that when the students' union was looking for volunteers to hand out contraceptives I'd balked. When feminist campaign meetings were being held off campus I didn't attend. When huge crowds attended a Women's Liberation meeting in the Mansion House

I stayed away. I couldn't run the risk of word getting back to my father.

But I was going on the train to Belfast in a couple of weeks' time. I could mingle with the regular passengers and hide in the crowd, but at least I'd be part of it, if a little removed. It would be my private rebellion.

'Thanks. I'd love to rule the world, but I think you might have to adjust your expectations,' I say, trying to let him down gently.

'So I'm not good enough to aim high?'

'Of course you are. It's just— Look, we may be in an expanding construction cycle at the moment, but I don't think it'll last long enough for you to make your fortune. So don't put all your eggs in one basket.'

'Don't be such a kill-joy. The seventies is going to be a great decade.'

1985

Liam turns up at my mother's funeral, looking a little older and wiser and wearing a good suit. A far cry from the skinny, resentful adolescent with the freckled face and grubby overall. After a spell of unemployment in the late seventies, he has spent the last few years working in America.

'I know this is a bad day for you,' he says, his eyes warm, 'but can we meet for dinner? Soon? I'm home from the States for three weeks and would love to catch up.'

Funnily enough, caught in an unreal limbo after my mother's passing, there's no one else I'd rather go out with. We meet the following Wednesday night. When we have dispensed with the normal pleasantries and I've once again accepted his condolences, he fidgets with the salt cellar and says, half teasing, 'You were right with your forecast, dammit. My thirtieth birthday was a couple of years ago, and I'm far from my planned millionaire status.'

'Same here,' I say. 'I'm not ruling the world.'

He laughs and goes on to tell me about his project-management job in construction, based in Pittsburgh. 'I'm doing very well, thank you, making contacts and stashing some cash. And I'll be more prepared to jump on the bandwagon the next time the country heads into a roll. Not bad for an illegitimate brat.'

'Stop, Liam. Don't carry that kind of baggage. You're an adult and you're the only person responsible for yourself now.'

After a while he says, 'And what about you? Marriage? Kids?'

I manage to shake my head and smile, even though the baby I gave up lets out the plaintive cry of a newborn at the back of my mind. I give my standard reply. 'Still waiting for Mr Right.'

'I don't suppose I'd be in with a chance?' Then, almost immediately, 'Nah, don't answer that. You were always in a league of your own, Juliet, and far too good for the likes of me. All the guys were a little in love with you, back then.'

I laugh it off, hoping I don't sound too dismissive.

We order dessert and talk about the Live Aid concert that has just taken place in London and Philadelphia. We both agree that Queen and Freddie Mercury stole the show. He walks me back to Verbena View and kisses my cheek at the gate, a little tentatively, as though we're shy teenagers instead of thirty-somethings.

In the numbness of the following months, I adjust to life without my self-effacing mother, who has left a huge vacuum in her quiet wake. I tiptoe around the edge of this gaping hole with my father. Three years later, around the time that my father is dying, an invitation arrives to Liam's wedding in New York. He is to be married to a Rachel Summers. She sounds blonde and beautiful, like someone from *Charlie's Angels*, but I'm caught up in nightmarish hospital visits and ignore it.

Then years later, and out of the blue, Liam turns up at my fortieth birthday party.

As I lie suspended between the dark void surrounding me and an even darker void that is stalking me, I close my eyes and allow myself to sink back into the embrace of that night …

TWENTY-FIVE

Saturday, 17 March, 5.15 a.m.

1993

One minute, it seemed, we were twenty-somethings, the bright young things of the groovy generation. Then, in the next breath, we're forty, Rebecca and I, our birthdays just a couple of months apart.

'Forty! How did that happen?' Rebecca asks, sounding disgruntled.

'Don't ask me, I still feel eighteen.'

'When I was eighteen, people who were forty were old. *Old*.'

'The world's changed since then.'

'Even Ireland's come of age. You were right all along, Juliet. I didn't think we'd see a woman president.'

'The first of many, I hope. But our generation of women is still young and pushing down even more barriers. Didn't you hear that forty is now the new thirty? And by the time we get to sixty, it'll be the new forty?'

'Hmm. I might be able to live with that.'

❧❧

Feeling very extravagant, we head to London for a weekend, and go shopping on Oxford Street. I buy a leather and sheepskin flying jacket, the nearest I'll ever get to a pilot's licence, I joke to Rebecca. She spends ages in Selfridges, picking out tops for Danielle, until I finally persuade her to shop for herself.

Then I throw a party at Verbena View. The renovations are complete and the house has been modernised, while holding on to some comfortable, timeless features of my grandmother's day. Out in the garden the caterers have set up a small marquee where the drink is flowing and the food is plentiful.

These are good days. Ireland has emerged from a long, grey recession and there is light at the end of the tunnel. The mood is buoyant among my friends and acquaintances from the university, as well as Rebecca and Rose, along with their friends and families. We're all glammed up. I'm clad in a Dolce & Gabbana gold dress, with black suede shoes. Rebecca goes all out in a black velvet Richard Lewis dress and a crocheted silver cardigan.

Danielle is sixteen and has turned into a beauty. She has cornflower blue eyes, blonde hair, and Rebecca's soft, warm manner. She's wearing a raspberry taffeta dress that suits her slim figure, along with the silver Tiffany pendant I'd given her. I love her to bits. She's delighted when I press a glass of champagne into her hands. 'Gosh, thanks, Aunt Juliet.'

'Hey,' I laugh, 'I've asked you before to please drop the "Aunt". Besides, I'm not really your aunt. That's reserved for Rose. Don't forget, I'm your honorary mum.'

She looks flustered and I could bite my tongue. 'Yes – sorry – it's just, well, I've never had real champagne before.'

That I could believe, for Harry's income has been fairly average all these years, and he'd had a spell of unemployment in the eighties. Rebecca had stayed at home to raise the family, so there were no luxuries in the household. Now that the twins Kevin and Mark are twelve, Rebecca has returned to work. Just as we'd hoped all those years ago, there are opportunities for her to balance work with her home life that didn't exist for our mothers. Discrimination based on age, gender, marital status and other grounds is now illegal. This year the legislation that outlawed homosexual acts was repealed. I can't help wondering if Mr Justice Henry Jordan has turned in his grave at all these changes. Perhaps he turned in it long ago over the shadowed life of his precious, dutiful daughter.

Something that still haunts me, even at forty.

Still, he would have liked the fact that I'm living here, using his study as my own, sitting in his chair, even adding to the framed certificates on the wall. I'm sure he would have been happy, too, with the party I'm throwing, and the beautiful young people milling about, Danielle, Kevin, Mark, and Rose's son, James.

I've seen a lot of my friends' children over the years, mostly Danielle and James. They've sometimes stayed at Verbena View, in my parents' old bedroom, which I turned into a guest room with en-suite bathroom. I taught James and Danielle how to swim on the beach at Howth, I brought Danielle shopping for her first makeup kit, and I taught James to drive on the quiet roads around Howth in my trusty red Triumph, which Matthew wasn't all that pleased about. I think he wanted that milestone to be reserved for himself.

'You'll be having lots of lovely champagne in the years to come, Danielle. Your life is all ahead of you, and it'll be brilliant.' I give her a hug, and her cheeks redden with pleasure.

'Thanks, Juliet. I love coming here,' she says. 'I love the comfy feel of your house. It's so relaxing, even the study with the shelves full of books. And the big leather chair in front of a log fire on a winter's afternoon is perfect for curling up in. But the kitchen is something else. Wow.'

'Yes, isn't it?' I tuck my hand in her arm and we walk into the room that runs right across the back of the house.

I have knocked out one wall, and replaced it with glass doors that fold back on each other, and tonight they are open to the sea and sky, with friends and colleagues laughing and chatting, drifting between the kitchen, the patio and the marquee. 'You know my door is always open, don't you? And bring your friends. I've plenty of room.'

'Thanks, Juliet.'

'Where are the guys?' I ask, looking around.

'They're in the television room playing computer games. They've been holed up there most of the evening,' Danielle says. 'I think James …' She hesitates, colours a little. 'No, forget it,' she says, smiling in such an embarrassed way that I'm loath to question her.

It's not long, however, before I discover what was most likely bothering her. Shortly after that I walk in on Rose and Matthew having an argument about James in my bedroom. And some of my pleasure in the night evaporates. I was trying to get away from the noise and bustle of the party to touch up my makeup and have five minutes to myself, but as I open the bedroom door I catch Matthew's heated words.

'I'm not having it, do you hear me?'

'I hear you loud and clear, Matthew,' Rose says, in a tone I have rarely heard from her, a voice I scarcely recognise. Confident, authoritative. 'I'm also listening to what James has to say,' she continues, and I realise she sounds so assertive because she is defending James. Like a lioness defending her cub.

'Why don't you listen to his side of the story?' Again, a strong, direct tone, most unlike Rose. She falters when she sees me on the threshold, and Matthew, who has had his back to me so far, wheels around and glares at me.

He hates me catching him on the back foot. We are both ambitious people and have always sparked off each other, the rivalry between us thinly veiled in our debates. In front of me, Matthew likes to act as if all is perfect in his carefully controlled life, so now he is annoyed that I have seen him with his guard down.

'Sorry, Juliet,' Rose says, her face a little pale against the black lace of her dress. 'We needed a word in private and found ourselves in here.'

'No worries,' I say. I stand my ground, unwilling to back out. 'But if you want to have a row about James, this party is the last place for it.'

'We have a bit of a crisis on our hands,' Matthew says, struggling to keep his voice even.

'Crisis?' I echo, and raise my eyebrows, even though I'm unwilling to be drawn into the conflict between them.

'I don't think we should be having this conversation.' Rose shakes her head.

'And when were you going to tell me?' Matthew snaps. 'Or were you going to let me find out for myself?'

I raise my hands in surrender. 'Hey, look—'

'I know, I know,' Matthew says impatiently. 'Wrong time, wrong place.'

'We're in the middle of a party. Maybe you could have this conversation tomorrow.'

'Tomorrow?' Matthew shakes his head. 'How am I supposed to wait until then to put some sense into his head?'

'Matthew! For God's sake, it's not the end of the world,' Rose says. She darts a worried glance at me and, for the first time, her composure seems ruffled.

By now I've ruled out an incurable illness, which would be the end of the world for both doting Rose *and* Matthew. Pregnant girlfriend springs to mind, or caught rolling a joint in college rooms. Neither of which is the end of the world. Nowadays.

Rose turns to me. 'Thing is, Juliet, James has decided he's dropping out of his course in college. Like now.'

For a long time, I say nothing. Then, mildly, 'Is that it?'

'Matthew's not happy with him.'

'Would you be, Juliet, if you were in my shoes?' Matthew's eyes gleam, as though he's daring me to come down on one side or the other.

It's easy to sidestep his challenge. 'I'm not in your shoes, Matthew,' I say smoothly, 'so it's none of my business. Though James could probably have picked a better time to make his announcement, rather than tonight.'

'It's all happened very suddenly.' Once again Rose jumps to defend him. 'James has been offered a place in a rock band after their bass guitarist had a car accident. But they need him immediately because they've been offered a support spot in U2's European tour. It's a fantastic opportunity, with lots of European dates, plus London and Dublin.'

'A rock band?' I try to keep the surprise out of my voice, although I should have guessed: James spent his adolescence superglued to his guitar.

Matthew interjects: 'I never heard of The Name, did you? And after everything we've—'

'Careful, Matthew,' Rose says. 'We're not having a row about this here.'

'Too right you're not,' I say. 'At this party, I want to see happy faces.'

For a moment I'm tempted to urge them to allow their son to follow his heart, not the path they'd prefer for him, but I won't challenge Matthew about it. We're interrupted by Harry putting his head round the door. He's been looking for me.

'Juliet,' he smiles in a way that tells me he knows I've landed in the middle of a heated exchange between Rose and Matthew and that he's about to rescue me, 'there's someone at the door who wants to talk to you. I think he's a bit reluctant to come in.'

'Okay, I'll be there now,' I say to him, relieved to have an excuse to get away from Rose and Matthew.

I walk up the hallway to find Liam Corrigan standing in the porch.

If, in his heart, he still carried any remaining trace of the resentful adolescent there is no sign of it in the self-assured tilt of his chin and the ease with which he squares his shoulders in his beautifully cut suit. Confidence oozes around him, like an aura.

'Juliet, I'm here to complain about the awful racket coming from this house. You can be heard all the way down in the village.'

I laugh and, delighted to have been delivered from a rather fraught scene with my dignity intact, throw my arms around him, then invite him in rather more warmly than I otherwise might have.

He mingles easily, drawing quite a crowd. He looks at home in Verbena View as he relaxes in a patio chair, chatting with Harry and flirting unashamedly with Rebecca. It's not the first time he's flirted with her in my home, but Rebecca stays cool, and Harry curves his arm around her shoulders, marking his territory. Danielle blushes crimson when Liam tells her she's a fabulous young woman, beautiful enough to rival any New York model.

Rose and Matthew have effected some kind of truce: they stroll back out on to the patio, holding hands, as if they've stepped out for a photo call. I wonder how often they have posed like that for the sake of appearances and it bothers me. Even though they haven't met in years, Matthew and Liam still don't quite hit it off, both of them eyeing the other, like circling dogs trying to establish which is superior. And when James stalks out of the TV room, sensing the storm has abated, it is clear that Matthew is the winner.

If Danielle, at sixteen, is dazzling enough to outshine a New York model, then James, at twenty, might have stepped out of a Hollywood movie. Tall and lean, with messy dark hair, he's not conventionally handsome, but he has a sensitive, caring face and the kind of smiling, darkly lashed blue eyes that could hold an audience. I manage to wink at him and give him a thumbs-up out of Matthew's view, then follow it with a grin as I strum an air guitar. He flashes me an answering smile.

'Your son, all grown-up?' Liam asks, in a voice tinged with envy.

Matthew positively swells, any grievance with James swiftly smoothed over in the interests of impressing Liam. 'Yes,' he says.

'Lucky man,' Liam concedes. 'I don't have family.'

He looks at me as he says this and I wonder what has happened to his marriage.

ᐇᐁ

'I can't believe I've hit the grand old age of forty and still haven't made my fortune,' Liam says later, as we sit at the kitchen table after everyone has left.

'Life doesn't always turn out the way we expect it to,' I say, marvelling at my understatement as I crumple a pile of discarded paper napkins together.

'I'll give you a hand clearing up,' he says, half rising to his feet.

'No need. The caterers are sending people tomorrow to put the place to rights. Here.' I hand him a bottle of wine. 'Pour some more and tell me what happened with your wife.'

Liam refills our glasses and gives me a sad summary of his failed marriage. 'Unfortunately Rachel and I have irreconcilable differences,' he says. 'We rushed into things far too soon and I'm filing for divorce.'

'Sorry to hear that.'

'It's fine. She doesn't mean anything to me any more.'

'Hmm. I thought I saw you giving Rebecca a few interested glances tonight. What's that about?'

'Ah, you were the sparkling unattainable one we drooled over, Juliet,' he grins, 'up there, in a league of your own. But Rebecca's the warm, reliable girl next door. She's turned into a very attractive lady and Harry's a lucky man. Then again, it was always Rebecca for him. I think he was the only one of us who didn't lust secretly after you in the days of our youth.'

'You're making me out to be a right schoolboy's crush, and if you say it once more, I'll make you clean up.' I laugh, lobbing a tinfoil tray at him. 'When are you heading back to the States?'

'Next week, but just to tie up the red tape on the divorce, and then, well, I have some big plans.'

'I'm glad your dreams haven't been crushed.'

'Anything but,' he says, sitting up a little straighter. 'I'm coming back to Dublin permanently, and setting up my own construction business. This little country of ours is ripe for economic expansion and I want to get in at the start. I have some investors lined up, and I'm about to launch Corrigan Holdings.'

'Corrigan Holdings? Sounds impressive.'

'Doesn't it? I'm getting there at last, Juliet. My time is finally coming. When we hit the new millennium, I reckon I'll have a few million turned over and then some. Not bad for someone whose ma didn't want to know him.'

❧❦

This time Liam is right. Corrigan Holdings rides the wave of the building boom. Then, years later, it judders to a halt before plummeting in spectacular free-fall.

Just as I have, now. Although I don't believe in karma.

Let's get going before the light fades too much. Otherwise we could walk off the edge of the cliff … I hear laughter in my voice as I pick up my key. Then, nothing.

Liam? Didn't he threaten to make me pay for ruining him?

I've a feeling he's not the only one who would sleep better in his bed at night if I weren't around. Have I really that many enemies? But whatever happened earlier this evening, and whatever transpired at the top of the cliff, is still a blank. I know that shock can partially wipe out memory for a short while. So can concussion.

Still, other fractured images of my life drift through my mind's eye, and while cold rage at my helplessness burns inside me, I watch them slide past, wondering if there will be any clues, any pointers, as to how I ended up here …

New Year's Eve, 1999

'Is Liam not coming tonight?' Rebecca asks. 'I thought he might have dropped in for the great occasion. It's not every New Year's Eve we turn a century.'

She pops the cork on yet more Veuve Clicquot in the kitchen at Verbena View. The room is decorated with swirling streamers and drifting balloons bearing the legend of the new century. Rebecca and I are wearing matching silver tiaras in the shape of '2000' and sipping champagne from similarly emblazoned glasses. I don't know what we're expecting at the dawn of a new century, and neither of us has bothered to dress up for the occasion – I'm wearing my grey silk shirt over black Zara jeans bought in Madrid – but we're having a small party anyway, a girly night, as Rose and Rebecca's husbands are caught in their respective offices. Chilling in the fridge, I have a vintage Bollinger someone gave me, ready for the midnight chime.

'I haven't seen Liam in a couple of years,' I say. 'I expect he's celebrating in Barbados or somewhere exotic like that. Or else he's buying up half the Maldives. From what I'm reading in the papers and hearing on the grapevine, his empire's growing by the day and shows no sign of letting up.'

'Same with Matthew.'

Rebecca tops up my champagne, judging it perfectly, as though she's been pouring it all her life. 'One last blast,' she says, 'before everything goes belly-up on the stroke of midnight. Although I hope, for Harry's sake, it doesn't. I'm sorry he's stuck in the office tonight, in case the dreaded millennium bug strikes and the accounts files fall through the cracks.'

'And what about Matthew?' I ask her, with a teasing glint in my eye. 'He's on call tonight as well. God forbid his business goes down the tubes.'

Rebecca glances around. 'What's taking Rose so long? Did she lose her way back from the bathroom?'

'She went into my study to phone James and wish him a happy millennium.'

'Between you and me,' Rebecca eyes are dancing, 'I'd love to tell the millennium bug to jump up and take a lump out of Matthew's arse.'

'Ah, Rebecca! You don't mean that!'

'Bloody sure I do. I can't forget all that carry-on about him being the first of us to get a mobile phone and an email address. It did my head in. Fair play to him that his business has taken off like a rocket, but I'm sick of hearing about his personal tailor. And all that name-dropping! So what if he's in with a few politicians? And suddenly he's an expert on fine wines and food. It's far from Leinster House or duck confit he was reared.'

'Careful you don't sound jealous. Matthew is doing his very best to make up for his humble beginnings. Still, who'd have thought he had the balls, never mind the vision, to expand his business so successfully? Fair dues to him. And, like Liam, there's no sign of him resting on his laurels.'

'He was always very ambitious, but he seems almost, I dunno, blinkered in his quest to be bigger and better. God knows where it will end.' Rebecca sighs. 'I get the feeling he's still dissatisfied and always searching for fulfilment of some kind.'

I help myself to some nibbles on cocktail sticks and ask, 'Do you think he's making up for something missing in his life?'

'Could be.' Rebecca shrugs. 'Still, Rose is doing well out of it, between her beautiful jewellery, designer clothes and gorgeous home. And now Matthew's talking about having a Dublin 4 address, so I reckon they'll be on the move again to even bigger and better in a year or two. She told me one night after a glass of wine too many that if Matthew floated his company they could live off the fortune for the rest of their lives. But I don't always think she's happy.'

'I never thought I'd see the day when Rose would have a glass of wine too many, and a couple of charge accounts, never mind getting glammed up to the hilt.'

'Same here. I get the feeling she's doing her best to keep up with Matthew and be the kind of wife he needs. She loves him, warts and all.'

'What do you think is making her unhappy?'

'She's never come right out and said it …' Rebecca paused '… but, between you and me, I think she suspects that Matthew has played away now and then.'

Then Rose walks into the room, preventing me from responding. I don't think she heard what Rebecca said as she's all talk about James and his band's sell-out tour of west-coast America. Unlike us, Rose has dressed up for the night in her Vivienne Westwood olive green dress. We forgot to tell her we were staying strictly casual. 'He won't be back in Dublin until February,' she says.

Rebecca thrusts a glass of champagne at her sister. 'Drink up, Rose, before the millennium bug bites!'

I know, from her slightly shadowed face, that she's missing her son a lot, even though he moved out of home soon after he joined the rock band. I wonder what it's like rattling around in her house with just Matthew for company, wondering if he's playing away. For the first time ever I feel as though I'm getting into her shoes.

And they're not very comfortable.

TWENTY-SIX

Saturday, 17 March, 5.45 a.m.

More of my life is speeding past me, like a movie on double fast-forward. My rage at my helplessness has been overtaken by a blank weariness. It steals across me slowly, and all the fight and feistiness I ever had is beginning to drain away. It's easy to drop into the slipstream of images and wonder if it will jog a more recent memory ... tonight, for example, and who might have pushed me off the cliff ...

2003
Then we are fifty.

Rebecca and I celebrate our half-century with a luxury break at the Mandarin Oriental in Barcelona.

'I'm being spoiled,' Rebecca says, as we sit on sunny Las Ramblas, sipping expensively hiked-up cocktails, our senses filling with the heat and noise of the colourful city as it parades by.

'It's about time you did some self-spoiling. You always seem to run after everyone else.'

Rebecca slips her feet out of her jewelled sandals and stretches out her sun-tinted legs. 'Life definitely gets better.'

'So, you enjoyed your Caribbean cruise?'

'Harry and I had a ball. I could easily get used to this way of life. Here's to the next fifty years. We'll make a pact to celebrate together, even if we're on Zimmer frames and have lost all our teeth.'

'Hey, it'll be more like face-lifts and titanium hips, thank you. Still, I can't imagine us growing old,' I say. 'Even now I get a terrible shock when I look in the mirror some mornings. In a funny way I still expect to see my nineteen-year-old reflection.'

'It'll be fun.' She laughs. 'We'll only be interested in enjoying ourselves and it'll be to hell with everything else. I can't wait to get to the stage when I can tell people exactly what I think and not worry about the consequences.'

I don't think she realises quite what she's said until I tell her, 'You can do that any time. You don't have to wait until you're old.'

She's silent for a while, then forces a short, careless laugh. 'That depends on what I'm telling them.'

I take off my sunglasses, lean forward, and ask, 'What exactly are you afraid to say? And to whom?'

Once again, Rebecca is silent and I sense she's chasing around in her head to form the right context for her words. I wonder if it has anything to do with me.

Then she says, 'I'd like to be able to tell Rose to relax. She's too – anxious, I guess, a lot of the time. She worries about every little thing. What has happened, what's going to happen and what may happen in the future.'

Her eyes are hidden behind her glasses so I can't see their expression, but her voice is sombre.

'Has this anything to do with Matthew?'

Rebecca sighs. 'Let's just say I'd kill anybody who hurts

her. Even Matthew. Anyway, forget it, we're on holidays.' She straightens and summons the waiter from the nearby bar, her cheap bracelets jangling and glinting in the sunlight as she raises her arm.

Afterwards I wonder if it was just Matthew that both of us meant, or if we were speaking a silent language of our own.

2006

There is another funeral.

This time it's Harry's. Rebecca, Danielle and the twins are inconsolable. It's a mournful day, freezing January rain sleeting down, all of us garbed in black, clustered beneath the undertakers' giant umbrellas as the remorseless rituals of death and burial are carried out. Now I know how it feels to be helpless in the face of your friend's distress. I wonder if this is how Rebecca sometimes feels when she's faced with Rose's insecurities: powerless, useless, nothing to say but trite, meaningless words. At the graveyard, Rose is huddled between Matthew and James.

James flew back that morning from a tour in Germany, and squealed to a halt outside the church in a car a lot flashier than his father's, jumping out in full leather regalia and causing an excited wave of interest to ripple around the mourners gathered at the gate. They parted like the Red Sea to watch him stalk up the steps into the church. Matthew, standing by the door, waiting to escort Rose and Rebecca inside, had witnessed it. Now he catches me looking at the three of them, and we stare at each other for a long moment before he looks away.

Matthew!

Then, 'You're not just trying to compete with Matthew, are you?'

My mind slews forwards again. Yesterday? Last week? Rebecca is talking to me with a worried frown. Snatches of our conversation come back to me against a backdrop of charcoal grey cliffs and a murmuring sea. 'The last election was nothing short of a mud-slinging bloodbath,' she is saying, her voice distorted by the breeze and the white noise in my head. 'It's bad enough that the media will be hounding Matthew and Rose, but you, too? You know that everything you've ever done will be put under the microscope?'

And me, dismissive of her worries: 'Maybe I'm willing to take my chances …'

Matthew is someone else who may not sleep too easily from time to time, thanks to me. He may well be responsible for where I am now. Then, again, so may Rose.

Or even, for that matter, Rebecca.

Rebecca. My true friend. Loyal. Always there when I need her. But always there for Rose. A loyal sister. *I would kill anybody who hurts her.*

Blood, they say, is thicker than water. Family will always come first with Rebecca.

Let's get going before the light fades too much. Otherwise we could walk off the edge of the cliff …

Oh, God, how have I ended up here? When will help arrive? There is so much I still want to do and see that I could weep from frustration and aching loss. Will I ever again marvel at a tree in summer or a winter sunset? I couldn't bear not to see Danielle having a baby … or his face ever again …

I'm suddenly saved from falling into the blackest pit of

despair when memories of my golden holiday in Australia hang suspended above me like a jewelled ball, spiralling around like an ornament on a Christmas tree.

2010

'The sun shines almost every day, Juliet, you won't believe it,' Danielle twists around from the front passenger seat to talk to me as we leave the airport terminal behind and Conor takes the slip-road for the motorway into the city. The car roof is down and her blonde hair whips in the breeze. I haven't seen her for nine months, except for photographs she's emailed, and now her eyes are sparkling. She's beautiful. 'And the beaches,' she rolls her eyes, 'wait till you see them! Gosh, I love it here!'

'How long is left on your visa?'

She pulls a face. 'Just three months. I don't know where the time's gone.'

'You're only allowed to use that expression when you get to my age,' I tell her.

'Age? It's just a number with you, Juliet. Anyway, I've arranged to take some time off work to show you around. James will be here later this week and has emailed to say he'll be free some days. We're all going to his concert in the ANZ Stadium. So you planned it well.'

'Didn't I just – thanks to you!'

Rebecca had already been to visit Danielle and Conor, and urged me to go. It was almost the only country in the world I hadn't yet been to. Then we heard that James and the band would be on tour for a couple of months, including Australia and New Zealand, so Danielle suggested I time my visit to Sydney to coincide with him. Both Rose and Rebecca said they'd love to be in my shoes. I had asked Rose if she wanted to come with me, but she'd refused. I wondered if she was afraid to leave Matthew alone for a couple of weeks. It would have done her the world of good after the way she'd been 'under the weather' the year before last. That had been Rebecca's way of describing the sudden panic attacks and depression that had gripped Rose, and the months it had taken her to recover.

This holiday would have restored Rose's faith and hope, I decide, looking out of my hotel-room window. I had seen it plenty of times, in the movies and on postcards, but the real-life tableau of the opera house, the iconic bridge and the wide, majestic harbour is one of incredible, uplifting beauty.

'Fantastic!' I say.

Danielle has been waiting for my reaction, holding her breath. She smiles with almost childish delight. 'You like?'

'I love, love, love!' I sweep her into my arms and catch her light, clean scent as excitement lifts me. 'Thank you so much for dragging me over to this side of the world.' Then I hold her at arm's length. 'Do you feel you were right to give up your job and follow Conor out here?'

Conor is the latest in her long line of boyfriends, but she seems serious about him. They've been together for four years, and when he was transferred out here by his software firm to manage a twelve-month project, Danielle handed in her notice and came with him.

'I know it was a big step to chuck it in, when jobs are so thin on the ground,' Danielle says, 'but I needed to see what Conor and I would be like together, away from family and friends. Just the two of us.'

'And? Are you happy?'

'So far, so good,' Danielle says. 'We're still together. Besides, Juliet, I was sick of what I was doing. Marketing and research have become hugely competitive and such a painful treadmill that I was beginning to stress out.'

Time flows by, no matter how hard I try to hold it back: a blur of days spent on long golden strands, Danielle running through the surf, blonde hair flying, seawater glistening on her tanned, slim body. She is a more confident version of her mother. Her youthful bloom is palpable and intoxicating to be around. She laughs a lot, as does Conor, when we get together for barbecues in the evenings, sometimes sitting long into the twilight on the small balcony outside their apartment. I listen to their laughter and look up at a sky crowded with stars. I bring them to a restaurant overlooking the harbour, where we watch the ripple and swell of the water as the ferries and boats cut across the expanse.

James arrives, with the juggernaut of the band, fresh from sell-out dates in Melbourne. The Name cause a major sensation when they walk in to join Danielle, Conor and me for a meal in a restaurant overlooking Darling Harbour. It's fun, and Danielle glows.

One afternoon when James is free, he arranges a car and driver to take Danielle, me and him to the Blue Mountains. It's a special afternoon and every moment is ingrained on my memory. I know that Rose and Rebecca would give anything to swap places with me as we explore the spine-tingling, hand-of-God terrain on the sunny afternoon and have our photographs taken against the blue-haze backdrop of the Three Sisters in Katoomba.

I have always thought that the sunsets off the west of Ireland are among the most spectacular in the world, until we are coming home along the motorway, all of us quiet and reflective after the day we've just had, and Danielle tells me to look behind. She is sitting in the back seat with James and, rather than twist in the front passenger seat, I lower the sun visor and look in the mirror, where the view through the back window is reflected.

For long minutes I soak it up. The car radio is on low, an Alicia Keys ballad. Danielle and James, the family I never had, are silhouetted against the back window and a sky that defies description, such is the bold luminosity of the yellows and tangerines shooting through a violet haze. I feel a rush of contentment and know that this is a moment of perfect happiness. I fix it in my mind, like a freeze frame, so that I can take it out and relive these moments whenever I need to.

We are VIP guests, naturally, in the ANZ Stadium, for The Name concert. The pure energy and excitement of the night make me feel young again. Then, barely giving themselves time to come down after a sensational night, James and the band are gone, off to another sell-out gig in Perth, and the days I have left begin to slip through my fingers like grains of sand, and there is nothing I can do to slow them.

Then I'm down to counting the precious hours. We're out in Watsons Bay, Danielle and I, eating melt-in-the-mouth fish and chips from paper containers, and on the horizon the gap-toothed skyline of Sydney's steel and glass skyscrapers is like a misty mirage, floating across the bay.

Later Danielle and I climb to the top of the hill behind us. We lean against a wall and stare out to sea. There's something in the atmosphere of that golden, sunshiny afternoon that saddens me. I look at the blue swell of the Pacific Ocean below us, feel the gentle heat caressing our limbs, and the knowledge hits me that I'm off tomorrow and this won't ever come again – although, when I see the glint of tiny planes in the sky above us, I can't picture myself leaving.

'Have you had a good time?' Danielle is a little subdued, as though she senses my mood.

'It was magic,' I tell her. 'The best. And you're magic,' I say, 'both you and Conor.'

'Do you think so, Juliet?' She looks uncertain.

I want to squeeze her tight and tell her how beautiful she is. I want to pour the best of my good wishes for her directly into her veins so that she'll never doubt herself for a single moment. 'Danielle, of course you are. You're special. You're beautiful, intelligent and talented. Never underrate yourself. And I'm sorry if this sounds like a lecture, but I mean every word. Never sell yourself short. Make every minute of your precious life count. And always ...'

'Always what?' She smiles at me.

'Above all else, no matter what kind of storm is raging about you, listen to your heart.'

I feel choked as I utter those words. It's far too late for me to take my own advice, and sometimes when I wake at four in the morning I can't help wondering where I'd be today if I'd had the guts to listen to my heart.

Danielle puts her hand on my arm and kisses my cheek. 'Is that what you did, Juliet?' she asks. 'Mum always said you were a trail-blazer and she found it hard to follow in your slipstream in those stuffy, olden days. And you're still blazing a trail. But me and my friends, we take all that hard-won equality and freedom for granted.'

'Which is exactly how it should be. Things were ... a lot different in Ireland not so long ago. It's still hard to think how repressed we all were.'

She looks at my face for a long time with her observant blue eyes. Can she see through the shutter over my guilt to the sadness that is normally hidden?

I blink and the connection is broken. I talk to her about the importance of being her real self, rather than fitting in to please others. 'I keep telling Rebecca she should be busy blazing a trail of her own and not bothering about me. And, Danielle, unfortunately I didn't have the courage to listen to my heart at one very important time in my life. I took the easy option instead of standing my ground, and it's something I've lived to regret.'

'I can't imagine you having any regrets, Juliet.'

'Oh, believe me, I do. And I know they're a pure waste of time, and I can't change anything in the past, but it doesn't stop me having them. There's someone … Well, I love someone very much but, thanks to the situation I'm in, I can't speak of it. So take heed of my words and always listen to your heart. Sometimes we have to adjust our sails, but whatever you do, don't compromise the essence of who you are.'

I turn away in case she sees my loneliness in my eyes. She puts her arm around me, rather awkwardly, but I don't shrug it off. I let it rest there peacefully and we stand like that for a while, looking out across the sparkling Pacific Ocean.

TWENTY-SEVEN

Even though Rose had slept fitfully, and had been disturbed by Matthew coming to bed at an unearthly hour of the morning, she still woke up just before six. She eased herself above the warmth of the duvet, feeling a slight chill on her bare shoulders. She was far too wound up to settle back to sleep.

She went downstairs, pausing outside Matthew's study. Once again she stood in the doorway and looked into the shadowy room, at the mounds of papers on his desk, and wondered if there was anything she could do to stop this dangerous circus invading their lives. All was quiet, the room itself and his desk cloaked in semi-darkness, looking perfectly peaceful and friendly in the shadowy pre-dawn. She went across and pulled back the curtains.

It was only when she turned that she saw Matthew's mobile on the desk. She jumped as though she'd come face to face with a dangerous animal. Her head told her to keep on walking, go out into the kitchen and make some coffee. Forget it was there.

But the mobile was difficult to ignore. It seemed to pulsate as though it had a life of its own. She drew level with the desk and tried to move on.

Impossible.

Feeling as though she was putting her hand into a blazing

fire, she reached out and touched it with her finger. Nothing happened. The house alarm didn't shriek. Neither did the roof cave in. She reached out again, but this time she lifted it and felt the weight of it in her palm. Then she put it back on the desk and told herself to move away before she was tempted to do anything silly.

She was about to leave his office when, on impulse, she snatched it up again and feverishly keyed in his password, wondering as she entered the final digit if he had changed it.

He hadn't.

She didn't know what she had expected to find: the screen sprang to life, she brought up his text messages and, sure enough, there was a line of new ones, messages she dare not allow her finger to linger on lest they open. She scrolled down, very carefully, very lightly, past the unopened messages, but there was nothing very alarming until she came to his recently sent and received messages. A name jumped out at her.

Juliet.

Juliet? What had Matthew got to say to Juliet? Or she to him? She could already see the first few words of the message, which danced in front of her eyes until she took a deep breath and steadied her vision: *We need to talk asap. Your place. Call me. M.*

Her hands shook as she switched off the phone and, very carefully, placed it back on the table, struggling to recall the exact position she had found it in. Had they met? And, if so, when? And what was so secret about it that he hadn't told her?

Something heavy thudded into her stomach.

TWENTY-EIGHT

Saturday, 17 March, 6.25 a.m.

I'm feeling very tired. Funny, really, to feel tired when I'm lying stuck like this. And there's a strange kind of calm stealing over me. It wouldn't bother me to close my eyes and drift off in an instant. Just let go of everything and float quietly away. Rise out of my broken body to be carried away on a magic carpet, as though I'm as light as fairy dust.

It must be close to dawn because the sky has lightened against the dark shape of the cliff and the stars have faded. There's no sign of the moon, which has sailed away from my line of vision. Morning will soon be breaking, and I've been here all night so no wonder I'm having silly delusions about who might or might not have pushed me.

'Your laugh. It hasn't changed at all. Neither has your sense of humour,' Rebecca says. Her face is floating in front of me, mouth curved in a half-smile, hair tossed in the breeze. Far below her, the sea boils against the cliffs, and ahead, the track veers around a corner of the headland where, for several metres, the grass verge has crumbled away.

The image fades. When was that? Last night? Did I stumble and fall where it's all too easy to slip and slide down the steep embankment? Or was I pushed?

Not Rebecca, surely. Giver of life and love?

I can't think much more. White noise is filling my head. My eyes are now half closed. The sheer effort of keeping them open is too much. Even so, I see that the sky is lightening further: bands of night-time inky blackness are separating. There is a rift in the darkness, a soft chink, where a thin pink streak is outlining the rim of the billowing clouds. Pink. Danielle's favourite colour. When she was a young girl.

There's something about Danielle …

We're together around the table at Verbena View. It's Christmas because I have red berries decorating the table in memory of my father. I glance out of the patio door at the purple twilight and, for a nanosecond, I catch her reflection in the glass. The look on her face before she senses my eyes on her stills my heart.

Ah. I'm glad I remember that.

There are sounds of a new day burgeoning all about me. I never realised how musical it is, the early-morning call of the birds against the dawn hush. Close to me, the sea is a gentle, rhythmic whisper, as though it is breathing deeply, slowly, in and out. I know that at this hour it resembles crumpled dark grey silk. Soon the sun will rise and I could paint it from memory, from the first band of fiery red on the horizon, until the rift in the clouds stretches and widens, the sky turning orange and gold. The sea will run a trail of scarlet, until the crumpled silk reflects the apricot sky. Then it will fall into the palest duck-egg blue. The whole show will remind me of an artist having fun with a palette.

I'd love to see it, really see it, and soak it up just one more time.

The start of a new day can be impossibly beautiful, especially along the Dublin coastline. No matter where you are, and no matter your circumstances, the sight of it can seep into every cell in your body – if you let it – and fill you with hope.

It's a pity so many people are still asleep and miss this daily miracle. What could I do if I had the gift of today ahead of me? If I was waking up as usual in my bed, putting my feet to the floor and going into the bathroom to look at my face in the mirror before I shower. If I was living and breathing, like the sea, and able to do things.

What would I do if I had so much precious time? I'd love to see his face once more. I wouldn't waste a single minute in telling him I love him very much. Then I realise that that, too, doesn't matter. I only want to see him and voice my love from the selfish point of view.

Sometimes love means letting go. Maybe, if I slip away on that magic carpet, some truths will come out into the open. If so, it will have been worth it, and how I got here will be totally irrelevant in the grand scheme of things. It doesn't matter if I can't say goodbye. I have lived, I have loved and been loved. He is also loved, and that comforts me. In the end, when life is distilled to the crucial essence, that's all that matters.

It is there now, the beginning of the sunrise, a single brilliant speck so low on the horizon that I can see it through my half-closed eyes. But it is a glimmer of a morning sunrise, so bright and warm and beautiful that I just want to float into it and let it flood through me, like breath itself.

Part Two

Danielle

TWENTY-NINE

Rome, Saturday, 17 March

The loud blare of a scooter horn caught me by surprise and caused me to jump back from the kerb, almost tripping over it in my haste.

'*Scusi*—' I began.

The young motorcyclist gave me a black scowl and shook his fist before he buzzed off into the traffic.

I shook my fist back even though I'd deserved it. I'd stepped out on to the road without paying attention. I'd been too occupied with looking ahead and spotting that the Campo de' Fiori was already clogged with a slow-moving mass of early-morning people, inhabitants of Rome as well as tourists. I was also too occupied with asking myself if this had been such a good idea after all. When I was almost dragged under the scooter's wheel, I was tempted to take it as a sign to turn back the way I'd come, forget about the day ahead and the prospect of drowning my sorrows in the company of friends.

Still, it was far better than sitting at home, where I'd spent more than enough time staring at the walls of my rented apartment, feeling sorry for myself and closing my ears to the shouts of carefree children playing in the courtyard below.

So, I stepped out of the cool, shadowy side-street into the riot of colour, noise and the scents of coffee, fruit and vegetables, the fragrance drifting from the flower sellers that typified this piazza in Rome on a spring Saturday morning. I moved through the rise and fall of conversation and laughter, the shouts of stall-holders plying their trade. Up through the cobblestoned square, past the fountain, the medley of open-air markets, the restaurants and cafés, where staff had already opened shutters, set out tables and chairs and unfurled awnings as they got ready for the first of their Saturday customers, the coffee-and-croissants brigade.

I reached the Irish bar, sidled past people sitting at pavement tables, and went inside. Naturally it was open. Today, of all days, it would be open all hours to help the bemused tourists and dedicated Irish expats celebrate our national feast day in style. I had to press through shouts of '*Viva Irlanda*' and '*Buona festa*', a wall of noisy, green-clad bodies, and a forest of shamrock-shaped balloons and shamrock-decorated banners. A huge television screen to the side of the bar was showing the opening credits of *The Quiet Man*. Then, in a corner, I saw Erin waving, then Gemma, and the stool camouflaged under their coats.

A small rush of gratitude that they were here, waiting for me, even at this early hour on a Saturday. It brought a little warmth fluttering across the empty space where my heart had once glowed.

'Hi, Danielle! Thought you'd changed your mind,' Erin said. She was wearing a hairband decorated with a row of spring-loaded plastic shamrocks that bobbed wildly on their moorings every time she moved her head. Matching earrings danced at each side of her face. The effect was ridiculous but engaging. She gave me a big bright smile that told me she was glad I'd come. It gave me another little lift.

'I didn't think you'd pass up the chance to drown the shamrock,' Gemma said. 'Even if we are a little early, we're not the only ones. I think the Irish celebrations will go on the whole day and well into the night. We'd awful trouble hanging on to this stool. So lucky you,' she said, swiping off the coats and tossing them behind her on to the back of the banquette. 'Give me yours.'

I sat down and handed my jacket to Gemma. I waved at a bar girl, who smiled and shrugged to indicate she had no chance of making it across to us through the throng. 'Thanks. I felt so lazy this morning I almost had second thoughts,' I said.

Second thoughts. It was one way to describe the near panic attack that had momentarily convulsed me. The feeling that everything was pressing down on me, fluttery sparks of anxiety mixed with a sense of desolation. On impulse I'd called home, even though it was an hour earlier in Dublin, for my mother, Rebecca Ryan, could be relied upon to chat away about family gossip or the goings-on back home for long enough to give me something solid to latch on to.

But the call had gone to voicemail. And then I remembered she was at the afters of a wedding in a north County Dublin hotel.

My voice had felt strained as I left a message on the landline, and I didn't bother calling her mobile: the small act of speaking out loud, in response to the greeting of my mother's voicemail, had broken the worst of my panic. I felt calm enough to catch my hair back in a scrunchie, put on my Hilfiger jeans and canvas jacket, then move beyond the four walls of the apartment, where I'd been holed up since leaving work the previous evening, and meet my friends.

In that Irish bar, on the fringe of the Campo de' Fiori, the national party was kicking off with a special breakfast screening of *The Quiet Man*, followed by the RBS Six Nations rugby live from the Stadio Olimpico in Rome, where Scotland were taking on Italy, and the crowd were wasting no time in getting revved up.

'I hope he was worth it,' Gemma said. She dunked her spoon in her cappuccino, breaking up the foam, and looked at me, raising her eyebrows coquettishly.

'He?' I asked, feigning a casualness I didn't feel. In the last couple of weeks Gemma had seemed to be on a mission to discover the finer points of my love life or, more to the point, the lack thereof, almost as though she sensed there was a story to be told.

Which there was, and I wondered what kind of radioactive vibe I was sending out. The woman who had loved and lost? Who had given it all away? Although that wasn't quite true. More like the woman who had loved unwisely ... and still lived to regret it.

It would always be there, running through my veins. It would always have the power to come back and bite me at any given moment. Even in a noisy, crowded Irish bar on a Saturday morning. Especially in a noisy bar: there was nothing like feeling raw and isolated in the midst of jollity. But I was expecting far too much of myself, I thought, this weekend of all weekends. I needed to cut myself some slack. Be kind to myself. Be my own best friend instead of my own worst enemy.

'I assume it was a man who encouraged those second thoughts,' Gemma said, her voice questioning.

I couldn't blame her for being curious. I'd been in Rome for two months, working alongside her, partying most weekends with her, listening to her mojito-fuelled, full-on confessions, yet I hadn't shared with her so much as a titbit of my rather sad and inglorious history. Given that I would be thirty-five next birthday, I knew it must be obvious to Gemma that I'd been around the block more than once. And by now she was surely a little aggrieved that she had been so forthcoming in the face of my reticence.

'I wish,' I said, putting on my usual nonchalant act. The one I sensed Gemma was beginning to see through. 'If only I could conjure up a hot-blooded, well-packed, sexy alpha male, who's brilliant and generous in bed. I'm beginning to think it's a contradiction in itself. But I promise you'll be the first to know as soon as I have any action between the sheets.'

My eyes met Erin's. She gave me a brief sympathetic smile, picked up her bag and rummaged for her purse. 'Danielle, let's get you a coffee. They're doing Irish breakfasts as well, if you're peckish. Or how about a Buck's Fizz? I know it's early but we need to wet the shamrock properly.' With a rush of gratitude I saw she was smiling casually, as though she didn't know anything about my messed-up life, as though a Buck's Fizz at just after nine o'clock on a Saturday morning was compulsory because it was a regular St Patrick's celebration, and not because she knew, as Gemma didn't, that I might feel the need to lose myself behind a fog of alcohol that day.

But even Erin, good friend as she was, only knew the half of it.

I watched two plates of the traditional full Irish breakfast being passed across the counter and knew I had no appetite. 'Just coffee for now,' I told her. 'And maybe a muffin. I couldn't manage anything more.'

'Gemma?'

'Nothing yet, thanks. I'll have a Buck's Fizz soon, if you insist,' Gemma said, in the kind of voice that suggested she was allowing herself to be persuaded against her better judgement.

'I'll go,' Erin said. 'I need a coffee refill.'

'No, let me,' I insisted, knowing it would be much easier to brave the crowded throng and return with the drinks than be left to fend off Gemma's unbridled curiosity.

'Will you manage?' Erin asked, frowning. 'I think I stand a better chance than you of getting through that crowd.'

I stood up and straightened my shoulders. 'I'm not as delicate as I look.'

Erin flashed me a smile that said, 'Good for you.'

I was glad that by the time I returned with the coffees they had increased the volume on the sound system and the three of us began to watch the film. It was the sort of distraction I welcomed.

'I never imagined myself watching this in an early-morning Irish bar on a Paddy's Day in Rome,' Erin laughed.

I felt like saying I'd never imagined lots of things happening, things that filled me with the greatest joy at the same time as the greatest fear and trembling. Things, also, that filled me with heartbreak and left me with an empty space where my heart should have been.

But right now, this minute, I was among friends, doing nothing more demanding than sipping coffee, nibbling a chocolate muffin and watching a film in which a horse and cart trundled across the magnificent sweep of the Irish countryside. As I relaxed a little on the stool, Erin met my eye. 'Hope you're up for the rest of today, Ryan!' She winked at me and gave my hand a quick squeeze.

'I'll try.' I smiled.

'Try? Not good enough.'

We had the whole day planned. Erin had already generously offered to forgo a precious Saturday at home with her Italian husband and little daughter to keep me company. When Gemma had heard us making tentative plans, during lunch break in the office, and assumed we were merely celebrating the feast day of the patron saint of Ireland, she came up with an idea from when she'd been at home last, not knowing I had a hidden agenda. 'We should do the twelve pubs of Christmas,' she'd said.

'The what?'

'I went out with my cousins one night before Christmas, and we dropped into a total of twelve pubs. It was a mad dash around the city centre but great fun.'

'And all the funnier as it went along because you must have been getting more and more maggoty.' Erin had gazed at her sceptically.

'And what's that got to do with Paddy's Day?' I'd asked. I'd already planned to erase the date from my calendar, but Erin wasn't having that. Better to face up to it, but keep myself extra busy – she had volunteered to make sure I did just that. And now Gemma wanted to join in.

'We could do the twelve pubs of Paddy's Day on Paddy's Day,' Gemma had suggested. 'That's if we find enough pubs in Rome, although we could always call back to some of them twice.'

'Gosh. Sounds like you'd need some stomach.'

'I'm sure the day doesn't have to revolve completely around alcohol consumption,' Erin said. 'I'm not in my twenties and able for those mad days any more. We could go for food in between, have plenty of water, and take in some of the sights. Maybe fit in a beauty parlour. A girls' day out.'

And so it was agreed. I went along with it because of the effort Erin was putting in on my behalf but mostly because it promised to stop me thinking too much.

From thinking about anything at all.

Especially what I should have been doing that day.

Getting married.

⤞⤝

Erin had met me at the airport when I arrived in Rome in January, broken and bloodied, too exhausted to cry. She was waiting in Arrivals, a welcoming smile plastered to her face, her right hand on a buggy in which her small, pink-cheeked daughter sat.

She let go of it long enough to throw both arms around my neck and give me a hug. 'Danielle! Lovely to see you.' She held me at arm's length and studied me critically in the manner of a true friend. 'You look good,' she said. 'Considering.' She was trying her best to be positive and upbeat.

She was the only one allowed to speak to me like that. I hadn't talked to my mother, beyond giving her the bare facts – my engagement was off, my wedding cancelled, and I didn't want to discuss it. I knew I'd hurt her with my refusal to confide but I just couldn't take that on board right then. I was far too raw and couldn't bear to sift through the burning embers of my life, even for Mum.

'Do you reckon?' I said to Erin, with a faint smile.

I knew I didn't look so good. I'd popped into the Ladies en route to Baggage Reclaim and had been shocked at the sight of myself in the mirror. I looked exactly how I felt on the inside: wretched, raw, my eyes flat, expressionless and ringed with shadows.

'Has it been desperate?' Erin asked.

I nodded.

'Sorry I had to bring Aimee,' she said, giving the buggy a push. 'I couldn't arrange for anyone to mind her …'

I could have finished the sentence for her: '… at this short notice.'

Following a long phone call with Erin – who'd sent me a lifeline to help me get away from Dublin and my imploded love life – I'd applied for the English-speaking temporary job covering maternity leave in the sales and marketing division of the computer software company where she worked, starting in mid-January. Early in the new year, I'd emailed my CV across to their human resources division and they'd conducted a phone interview with me.

My escape to Rome had been confirmed just two nights ago, and I was starting next week. Luckily, I'd had no notice to serve in my Dublin job as, thanks to the economic downturn, I'd only managed to secure employment on a six-month contract after my stint in Australia; the last had expired at the end of December.

I got down on my hunkers and smiled at nine-month-old Aimee. 'It's lovely to see her – she's fab.' Her blue eyes were solemn as she looked back at me. I stroked her cheek gently and she gave me a wide smile, showing tiny pearly teeth, followed by a heart-warming gurgle. It made me feel I was good for something, if only for making a baby smile. And at least Aimee had no idea of the sad basket case I'd become. She was totally neutral.

Erin pushed the buggy and I wheeled my case across the concourse and out into the raw afternoon, feeling almost as though I was sleepwalking through an unfamiliar landscape. I watched as she strapped Aimee into her car seat and stowed the buggy in the boot, along with my case.

We'd been friends since our first day in college, meeting in the lecture hall when my papers had slewed out of my hand, across the tiled floor. Erin had immediately bent down to help me pick them up. We were from opposite sides of the city centre, and neither of us knew anyone else in our business-science year, but as soon as we went for coffee something clicked between us, a warmth, a friendship. I wondered if this was the kind of female kinship that my mother often banged on about, the kind she shared with Juliet and her sister Rose, so close for so long that they almost talked in shorthand.

'Your friends are so important, Danielle,' she'd said to me, more than once. 'Always make time for them, no matter what. Good friendships can last a lifetime if they're nurtured properly.'

Like me, Erin had no sisters. During our summer vacations as students, we'd gone to America together on J1 visas. Then we'd taken a year out to travel the world, and started our careers in the same marketing company, where we'd worked together until our lives had diverged. While I was still based in Dublin, between jobs right now and with a jettisoned romance weighing heavily on my shoulders, Erin had married an Italian pilot and settled in Rome.

'Lorenzo is away for the next couple of nights so it'll just be us,' she said, as she navigated the airport environs and headed out on to the motorway.

Although he was lovely, and I knew he wouldn't pry, his absence meant I didn't have to put up any kind of a front for those first two nights. 'Great,' I said.

'You can stay with us as long as you like,' she said.

'Thanks, but I'll get a place of my own as soon as I can. I presume it's easy enough to rent for six months?'

'Yes, there are plenty of places within easy commute of the job. It'll be fine, Danielle. You'll fit in well and I'll introduce you to Gemma and Paola, a couple of friends of mine who are single and fancy free, and have a far better social life than I have.'

'Once they don't know why I'm here ...'

She shot me a glance, as though to say, 'Who do you think I am?'

❦

Now, just over two months later, nothing much had changed since I'd arrived in Rome. There were times when I still felt as though I was moving mechanically in a strange vacuum. At others I allowed the mental shutter I'd brought down across the mess of my life to lift a little, but the turmoil in my head still raged so intensely that I quickly closed it again.

Erin, the one person in Rome in whom I'd confided, didn't yet know the details, and hadn't dared ask me. And I was still maintaining radio silence with Conor Kennedy, the man I had known for almost six years, had lived with for two, and should have been marrying later today in the south of France.

THIRTY

Rebecca half opened one eye to the opaque, early-morning light. Snatches of the night before floated back to her and all of a sudden she was wide awake. Without allowing herself any more time to think, she got out of bed and went into the shower.

She was putting on her grey Nike tracksuit when she remembered that Liam had talked of joining her for breakfast and debated whether to slink off to the beach first or brave the dining room. Chances were, he was still sleeping off the indulgence of his mini-bar.

But when she reached the lobby, he was there already, sitting on a sofa, reading the morning paper. A ridiculous wave of uncertainty washed over her, but she strolled across to him with as much nonchalance as she could muster.

'You came prepared,' she said, noting he was wearing the same clothes as the night before.

'Unfortunately I don't keep a sports bag, never mind gym clothes, in the boot of the car,' he said, eyeing her tracksuit. 'Where to first? Breakfast or the beach?'

'Breakfast,' she said, 'while the restaurant's quiet.'

'Agreed. Better than coming back from a bracing walk to find it overrun with hung-over wedding guests.'

'I guess you passed on joining them in the residents' bar?' she said, as he fell into step beside her.

'Didn't you hear us partying all night long?' he joked.

'So that's why you're still wearing yesterday's clothes ...'

There was a moment's confusion when the breakfast manager assumed they were sharing the same room, and Rebecca felt embarrassed. The dining room was on the first floor, facing the beach, and she gazed out of the big plate-glass windows to the long, sandy dunes, and beyond to the pale grey sea. On the horizon, the sky was tranquil and swathes of blue were overlaid with streaks of thin grey cloud. It was all incredibly calm.

Liam broke a bread roll with his long fingers and opened a small, foil-covered container of butter. Then he gave her an interested glance. 'I did all the talking last night. Now it's your turn. How are your family?'

She gave him a wry smile. 'My daughter, Danielle, should have been getting married this weekend.' The words came out of her mouth before she could stop them. 'Today, in fact, in the south of France. But just after Christmas everything went belly-up and now she's in Rome. She had to get away for a while.'

'Sorry to hear that. Was she ... or did ... Sorry, I don't mean to pry.'

'It's okay. You mean was she dumped or did she call off the wedding herself? That's the thing. I don't know,' Rebecca said. She sipped more orange juice, finding relief in unburdening herself. 'Danielle won't talk about it and I won't force her. If she did call it off, I could take crumbs of comfort from the fact that she should know her own mind by now – she's almost thirty-five. Then I reason that if Conor called it off, and was capable of inflicting that much hurt, she's better off without him.'

'Either way, it's difficult. It must make you feel helpless.'

'It does.' She flashed him a grateful smile.

'Yet you had the guts to turn up at another wedding yesterday evening, looking extremely glamorous and in party mode.'

'It's how I cope,' she said smoothly. 'Keep busy. What would have been the point in sitting at home alone?'

'That takes some spirit.'

'Spirit?' She laughed. 'It's more about not giving yourself time to think. Because deep down you're afraid of wallowing in black thoughts. Especially when there's nothing you can do to change things. Same after Harry died.'

He gave her a thoughtful look. 'Yes, you weren't long widowed when you arrived at one of my mad parties along with Juliet. Both of you were half cut and looked like you'd been having a good night. It must have been difficult for you.'

'Again, better than sitting at home moping. If you're going through hell, keep going – isn't that what they say? My parents died when I was seven. It was a shock, and Rose did enough crying for both of us. I blocked it out because it was too horrific to contemplate. I learned to keep going even then.'

'I see.' He smiled at her as though she was still seven.

'And with Danielle,' she went on, trying to ignore that smile, 'it's out of my hands, even though I'd do anything I could to make it better for her.'

'I know you would, if you're still the soft-hearted woman I remember under that practical shell.'

She stared at him and his gaze held hers. Then she broke the connection. She forced a laugh. '*Soft*-hearted? I don't believe in mollycoddling myself, but my family mean everything to me and I'd do whatever was in my power to ensure their happiness.'

'Like a lioness with her cubs?'

'Exactly.'

'And your sons?'

'Kevin is working in Japan, and Mark is in Dubai with his girlfriend, so I don't see much of them.' She began to spear some of the fruit in her bowl, paying a lot of attention to it rather than to the little ache she felt whenever she thought of her scattered family.

'So they're all around the world.'

'Yep. Gone to the corners of the globe. They're healthy, solvent and working,' she said, counting her blessings.

'So how do you keep busy, Rebecca?'

'Hill walking, Pilates, a book club with Rose, and my job.'

'Is the village bijou boutique still going strong?'

Rebecca hadn't expected him to remember. After Harry had died, she'd decided life was too short to spend any more time in her boring office job. She'd heard about a new boutique opening nearby and knew it was the perfect solution to get her out of the house.

'Olivia Jayne? Yes, I'm still there, doing three or four days a week.'

'Good. Although with your get-up-and-go, you could have opened a string of boutiques.'

'So I've been told,' Rebecca said. 'But I'm quite happy working for Amanda. I help to manage the day-to-day stuff, but I don't have any other headaches. Amanda might have a few glam trips here and there to fashion shows, but she has all the business end to look after and the tough decisions to make. All I have to do is turn up looking my usual fabulous self, and I get to spend the day around beautiful clothes, fabulous bags and killer heels, as well as friendly, chatty customers, who are dressing up for parties or weddings. The important thing is, I enjoy it, and I'm quite happy not to have the ultimate responsibility. There are fewer sleepless nights that way.'

'There's a lot to be said for that,' he agreed. 'Far too many people are scrambling up the wrong ladder against the wrong wall in search of the wrong kind of satisfaction. Like me, once upon a time. I've had more than enough dark nights of the soul to last me a lifetime.'

Rebecca felt a sharp jolt. She'd forgotten about his crashed dreams. 'And how are you managing now?'

'I'm not destitute. I have enough to get by. And some of my friends have been great – one's given me the key of a small apartment near the canal in Rathmines that's between lettings, and another has lent me his son's car as he's away in Australia for a while.' He caught her looking at him. 'It's okay, I'm fine with it. I had too much time to think about things when I was living in Spain on a shoestring but I've come through to the other end.'

&<&

Twenty minutes later they were out on the beach, picking their way through tracts of briny seaweed to the hard, compact strand where it was easy to walk. The sea hissed back and forth, like a flirtatious dance, furling and unfurling a creamy lace foam with the pull of the tide, leaving wet slicked sand in its wake. Other people were dotted about, strolling, jogging or walking a dog.

'I don't think we realise how lucky we are that this is on our doorstep,' she said, needing to break the silence, suddenly conscious of him matching her strides as they walked along. Liam Corrigan, the almost boy next door and an old history that had connected them at intervals.

'That's what I love about Dublin,' he said. 'Ten or fifteen

minutes in either direction and you're by the sea. Or the mountains.'

Rebecca was enjoying the spread of the bay, shimmering in the pale morning sun, when they heard the whine of a helicopter in the far distance, shattering the calm of the morning.

'Some guest arriving in style,' she said.

'It's not, actually,' Liam said. The dot in the sky grew bigger until Rebecca saw that it was red and white. 'Search and rescue,' Liam added, shaking his head. 'Some poor bugger ...' He left the rest of his sentence unsaid.

They stalled for a moment, watching as the helicopter veered out to sea, before banking and returning towards land. Then it hugged the coastline as it travelled south, the noise gradually receding. Rebecca shivered. The beautiful sea had its dark underbelly as well, and the crisp morning air seemed suddenly chilly. 'Someone's in trouble, God help them.'

They walked in silence for a while, and as they turned back towards the hotel, Liam said, 'Do you suppose, if I called you, you might come out for a drink some time? Just to chat?' His voice was ultra-casual and she knew he was afraid he might be treading on thin ice.

'I dunno. I haven't really ... since ...' Her voice trailed away.

She hadn't been out with a man since Harry had died. Liam was an old friend, and he looked so attractive when he smiled, his face relaxed and his eyes kind, that she wondered what he'd be like if she got to know him better. Still, she didn't need an added complication in her life right now.

'I can't compete with tycoons or toyboys, so the odds are stacked against me,' he said. 'I can only offer a fish-and-chips supper and a bottle of supermarket wine. Maybe stretch to an Indian takeout and the odd movie.'

'It's not that …'

'So I'm not totally ruled out,' he said, giving her a long, appreciative look that surprised her.

'Look, Liam, I think it's too late for me,' she said.

He insisted on walking her down the corridor to her room, even though she told him there was no need. He was leaving shortly to spend the day sorting through his accounts.

'Maybe you should give yourself permission to unblock stuff and wallow in the darkness for a while,' he said, as he leaned against her door. 'When you come out the other end, the light may surprise you.' He took out his mobile. 'Can I at least have your phone number?'

She gave it to him, wondering how she might react if her phone rang and he was at the other end.

'We'll talk soon,' he said. 'And mind that soft heart of yours.' Then he gave her a quick hug before he loped back down the corridor.

THIRTY-ONE

His voice came from very far away.

'Liz, are you okay?' Then, 'Liz, wake up and let me know you're still alive … You need more water … Here, open your mouth.'

She didn't want to wake up, to face the day. She wanted to stay as she was, disconnected from everything, thanks to her shattering hangover. But she felt her head being lifted off the pillow, causing fresh aches to ricochet around her shaking body. Her teeth clinked against the glass, as cool water seeped into her parched throat and dribbled down her chin. If hell was every cell in your body racked with pain, and a heart scalded to unbearable torment, then this was it.

The acute throbbing behind her eyes stopped her opening them. Turned inwards, her gaze flicked back jerkily over the last twenty-four hours, until she was there again, sitting on the floor in Ballymalin, picking through the wreckage of her parents' lives. Oh, to have everything back to the way it used to be before her life had slipped off its axis, to have those hours wiped away and her heart scoured clean of everything so that it was blank and untroubled. Then again, her heart had never been untroubled.

Her sore head was lowered to the yielding softness of her pillow and the duvet tucked around her limbs.

'You didn't have to stay,' her voice came out hoarse and croaky, 'but thanks anyway.'

'There was no way I could have left you on your own, the state you were in,' Gavin said. 'And still are. I've never seen you as bad as this, Liz. And your face … Jesus … hold on a mo …'

The bed shifted as he got up, and shortly afterwards she felt her hair being smoothed back and the refreshing sweep of a warm flannel across her forehead and cheeks. A soft towel was gently pressed to her damp skin.

'Why are you doing this?' she asked, her throat hurting with the effort.

'Never mind.'

'I thought you never wanted to see me again.'

'Stop asking questions and just relax.'

'We're supposed to be separated.'

'We still are. But even you would put your differences to one side to rescue a drowning kitten.'

'A drowning kitten?' she squeaked.

She heard him give a long sigh. 'Well, you weren't far off it. Drowning in alcohol. Like a helpless kitten.'

'Thanks a bunch.'

He was silent for a while, but it was a relaxed kind of silence, and she was oddly grateful for his calming presence. The small house in Harold's Cross had resounded with emptiness after he'd gone: he'd stormed out after a particularly bad row, during which he'd blamed her for pushing him away. She couldn't remember what the row had been about, something silly about food or a bottle of wine, like many of their rows had been. She had instigated them, as though she was testing him to the limit, deliberately provoking him to see how far she could push him. Childish and irrational, she knew, and Liz had been horrified, more than once, to hear herself arguing over trivialities.

'It's as if you don't want to be married to me,' Gavin had snapped. 'In which case you've got your wish, for our marriage is over, *finito*, *kaput*. I've tried, really I have, but I'm beginning to think nothing will make you happy, Liz.'

She'd been beginning to think that her marriage had been a battlefield of her own making, and at first it was a relief that he was gone and she didn't have to accommodate him in her life. Neither did she have to question his love for her, as though she didn't quite believe somebody could value her enough to want her to be such an intimate part of his life.

After all, Annie Monaghan hadn't wanted to be part of her life, showing her in the worst possible way that Liz had meant nothing to her and that she couldn't bear to live, not even for her daughter.

'Just because we've separated, it doesn't mean I've switched off all my feelings for you,' Gavin said. 'They're still there.'

She didn't believe what she was hearing – he couldn't mean it – but she was too drained to rebuff him with a smart comment. Instead she allowed his words to trickle into her sore head.

And then, 'I still care for you, Liz,' he said.

'What?' she croaked.

'You drive me mad. You test every ounce of my patience. You're the most awkward, belligerent and vulnerable woman I know, but—'

'Vulnerable?'

'You hide it well,' he said, 'with those razor-sharp eyes and that caustic tongue. But I've seen it in your face when you look at me ... that little-girl-lost look.'

'Stop.' She couldn't bear to hear any more. She couldn't bear him to be nice to her. And she couldn't figure out how they were having this conversation in the first place, the kind that was normally reserved for late-night, wine-induced honesty, when this was the morning after the wretched night before, with the light of day pressing against the bedroom curtains.

And she couldn't bear his kindness now, especially, when nothing mattered any more. Neither secrets nor stories.

'Well, you do, and I have …' he said.

He had to be joking. Still, though, he hadn't gone too far away. He hadn't slipped off or disappeared out of her life when she'd least expected it. The kind of behaviour she had learned to deal with. He was still there. And now she hadn't the energy to push him away.

'You look at me … sometimes … with your big, innocent eyes as though you're lost,' he said. Then he gave a soft laugh. 'I always thought I'd save you, Liz, but I think you need to save yourself. And whatever you did last night, mixing your drinks or going on a bender, isn't going to help.'

'Save me from what?'

'Sometimes you're your own worst enemy. It's as though you scuppered our marriage with silly rows because you feel you don't deserve any happiness – not because you're so spoiled that nothing will make you happy. Big difference.'

'Since when did you come up with that fantastic notion?'

'Over the last few months, while I've had space away from you and time to think.'

At last she opened her eyes, painful though it was. He was sitting by the bed, still wearing his clothes from the night before. He looked tense, as though he hadn't slept very well, and he needed a shave, but his hazel eyes were gentle and concerned. For a moment she wanted to reach up and pull his face down to hers, to hold him tight and lose herself in their warm lovemaking. The echo of many, many nights when they'd made love into the small hours came back to her. It seemed like a life belonging to someone else, not the altered existence that had stared Liz Monaghan in the face less than twenty-four hours ago.

She summoned words, knowing that what she was going to say would drive him away from her, but it had to be done. Deep inside, she felt so wretched that she couldn't bear anyone's tenderness. Least of all Gavin's.

'You could be wrong,' she said tiredly. 'They might have been silly rows to you, but perhaps they were important to me. Look, Gavin,' she went on, 'you've been more than kind, and thanks again for coming to get me last night, but I'd rather you left me in peace for now.'

He sat up straighter. 'You're sure this is what you want?'

'Perfectly sure. I just want to be on my own.'

She saw the hurt in his eyes as he got to his feet and, to her shame, it gave her a vicarious thrill.

She might be weak and defenceless now, but Liz Monaghan, social diarist, hadn't gone away. As soon as she got rid of this crippling hangover, and put the previous twenty-four hours behind her, she'd be back.

She had lots of secrets to uncover …

THIRTY-TWO

'Smile, ladies!' Gemma ordered.

Sitting on the low wall surrounding the Trevi fountain, I did as I was told and smiled for the camera as Erin put her head close to mine and Gemma pointed her mobile at us. Beside us, young children scampered about under the watchful eyes of their parents, and my ears rang with their excited shrieks above the splash of the water.

I had a sudden memory of Juliet trying to take photos of us all on the beach at Howth. Mum had been there, and James. The twins were still quite young. Juliet had had a very elaborate camera, and as she fiddled with its buttons, Kevin grew impatient and began to run in and out of the water, splashing at the spray. Mum had got cross with him, but Juliet just smiled.

It would have been one of our earlier summers there, when I still saw life as an exciting adventure.

'That's one for Facebook,' Gemma said, coming back to join us at the edge of the fountain. 'We'll show them how we celebrate Paddy's Day in Rome.'

'Don't tag me,' I asked, forgetting to be discreet. Not that I imagined for one minute that Conor would be checking my Facebook page: he had a horror of it as a form of social media and thought it ridiculously intrusive, but his sisters or some of our mutual friends – if they were still my friends – might see it and tell him. I didn't want to look as though I was having the time of my life on the day we should have been getting married. I hadn't gone near Facebook since Christmas. Not even to update my status. Every part of my life in Dublin had been locked away in cold storage.

I could see Gemma was bursting with curiosity. 'I've had my account hacked,' I fibbed, 'and I'm not updating anything for now.'

'Fine by me,' she said, sounding unconvinced.

'Are we making a wish?' Erin asked, her hand delving into her bag.

'I thought you could only wish to return to Rome,' I said, immediately regretting my cynical words. Erin had been trying to distract Gemma's attention.

'You can make any kind of wish,' Erin said evenly, handing me some coins.

For me, the Trevi fountain symbolises the heart of Rome. No matter when you visit, the area around it is always teeming with life, from babies to lovestruck teenagers to great-grandparents, as well as foraging sparrows, and you have to angle for space on the seating.

Rome was crazy, with its higgledy-piggledy energy, nightmare traffic, narrow streets, ancient buildings and historic monuments almost subsumed by the modern city springing up willy-nilly around its ancient heritage. You never knew what jewel you were going to discover when you turned a corner, a monument, church or fountain. The fact that an ancient church was often cheek by jowl with a graffiti-covered wall didn't lessen the city's quirky charm. Even the wonderful Trevi fountain was surrounded on three sides by drab-looking apartment blocks.

I viewed the jumble from the safety of my dislocated status, the chaos and disorder somehow blending with my mood, mirroring the chaos and disorder boiling in my head behind the shutters.

'Just don't tell us what you wish for,' Erin said, as I lifted my hand.

'There's no fear of that,' I said.

I flung the coins into the air, one by one, and watched them glint in the sunlight before they plopped on to the surface of the enclosed basin in front of the fountain to disappear beneath the pale green water. I had just the one wish.

That I could set my heart free from loving the man I couldn't have.

෴

It was late in the afternoon when Rebecca swung her BMW into the driveway of her south Dublin home. She'd driven from the Seagrass Hotel via the M50, but instead of taking her usual exit, she'd stayed on the motorway and headed for Dundrum Town Centre.

She'd gone shopping, splurging a little on cosmetics and shoes in House of Fraser, then picking up two dresses in Harvey Nichols. She was able to buy a lot of her clothes at cost in Olivia Jayne, but now and again she liked to shop elsewhere. Today it had been more to delay her return to the empty house. She'd even stopped for lunch in Harvey Nichols.

But when she stepped on to the parquet floor in the hall, she felt suddenly relieved to be in her own familiar surroundings, the family home she and Harry, Danielle and the twins had moved into fifteen years ago. Tucked into the far end of a quiet cul-de-sac, it was spacious and comfortable, rather than elegant, decorated in cool, neutral tones, with a bay window in the sitting room, looking out over a well-kept front garden, and a conservatory giving on to the good-sized mature garden that was her pride and joy.

She was up in her bedroom at the front of the house, unwrapping a cashmere jumper from soft tissue paper when she glanced out of the window. A police car cruised down the road. It slowed to a crawl as though it was picking off house numbers. And then it stopped. Right outside her garden.

Her scalp prickled and her heart flew into her throat. Don't panic, she ordered herself. She blinked, steadied herself, and watched a man and a woman get out. The man was looking at her door and talking into a mobile, as though he was checking he had the right house. He opened the gate, and bent his head to confer with his female colleague. As though to check who was going to say what.

The pressure in her throat was so tight she could barely breathe.

If she could just stay like this, in her bedroom, her hand clutching pink tissue paper, if she didn't go down to answer the door, didn't listen to their words, she'd be safe from knowing whatever disaster had obviously happened.

The doorbell shattered the peace, like a signal dividing her old, familiar life and the new knowledge she wanted to avoid. There was the Rebecca in her bedroom, staring at her new outfits, who wanted to know nothing. Then there was the Rebecca who walked stiffly downstairs, to the hallway she'd recently passed through, the familiarity that had wrapped round her now part of a different life.

For a moment she felt a pang of sympathy for the people

visible through the opaque glass of the door, waiting to deliver their news. She felt a pang of sympathy for the Rebecca she'd left in the bedroom, clutching the filmy tissue paper that had been wrapped around a dress. But that vanished when she opened the door to their sombre faces.

'Mrs Ryan?' the man said, very deferentially.

It was bad.

Even though her head felt stiff with tension and pain, she made what must have seemed like a nod, because his female colleague gave her a look of sympathy. They introduced themselves, and she understood that they were part of the police force but their names and rankings floated over her head. They produced identity badges that swam in front of her and asked if they could come in.

Wordlessly, she stood back and let them invade her home. Not the conservatory, though. Whatever she was to hear, whatever she was about to bear, it would begin in her front room, not the oasis of the conservatory.

The young policewoman fiddled with her notebook.

'Sorry to disturb your evening,' the policeman began, 'but we've been asked to contact you by a Robert Jordan.'

She couldn't think who he was. 'Who?'

The policewoman said, 'Robert Jordan, from Florida, has asked us to contact you. It's about his sister, Juliet.'

'Juliet?'

Rebecca stared into the policewoman's eyes and felt chilled by her expression. Her heart dropped like a stone, down and down, as though there was a cavity all the way through her body from her chest to her toes. She fell forward, the centre of her gravity shifting. The policewoman caught her before she fell too far, easing her on to the sofa. She sat down beside her, and told her to breathe slowly. Rebecca didn't think she'd be able to get oxygen into her lungs as her chest was so tight, but after a minute she inhaled a thin stream of air, and then took a stronger breath. The policewoman began to talk to her, words that Rebecca at first found impossible to follow.

She shook her head. 'Sorry, you're not making sense. Could you start again?'

The policewoman spoke very slowly: 'Earlier this morning, a woman was found close to the bottom of the cliffs at Howth. Initially there were signs of a faint pulse, but she was pronounced dead on arrival at the hospital. We've reason to believe it's the body of Juliet Jordan …'

Rebecca shook her head. 'It can't be.'

'A member of the Coastguard team involved in the rescue believes the body to be that of Juliet.'

'You don't understand. Juliet told me she wasn't going out anywhere last night.' What silly words, but she clung to them, as if to deny this new, shocking reality.

'The member of the rescue team wouldn't have volunteered the information unless he was fairly certain. We've checked her house and she's not there. Her car is in the garage and there's no reply from her mobile, but the last signal was traced to the cliffs, late yesterday evening.'

Rebecca shook her head, which felt heavy. 'Sorry, I just think – no, this can't be. Not Juliet.'

The policewoman checked her notebook, as discreetly as possible. 'The woman is average height and was wearing a navy tracksuit.'

A navy tracksuit.

'Her hair might have been dark originally, but it appears to have blonde highlights and pink tones …'

Rebecca stared at her. 'Please tell me this is some kind of a joke.'

'I'm afraid it's not, Mrs Ryan.'

The room spun. Shock made her light-headed. 'You said she was ... unconscious. Had she been ... like that for long?'

In other words, had she known what was happening? Had she felt lonely and terrified? Or in some dreadful pain?

'We don't know the full circumstances yet. We traced Ms Jordan's brother in Florida, and he asked us to talk to you. He said you were very close to Ms Jordan, that you knew her very well, and he hoped ...' She hesitated.

'He hoped what?' Rebecca balled her fists, so tightly that they hurt, but it was impossible to stop herself trembling.

'He hoped you might be able to help,' the policewoman said gently, 'in giving a formal identification. Of the body. Just to be sure. He said he'd really appreciate it. He's on stand-by for a flight home. I have his number if you'd like to talk to him.'

The body. Not Juliet any more, her funny, laughing, clever, beautiful friend. This wasn't happening. A terrible mistake had been made.

She stood up, feeling she was being sucked into a long, dark tunnel from which there was no escape.

THIRTY-THREE

When I was growing up I remember my mother and Juliet saying more than once that they'd never forget where they were the night they heard the news about John F. Kennedy being assassinated. Childishly, and thinking I sounded very clever, I had once said their lives must have been very boring, and both of them rushed to explain what an unprecedented shock it had been, as though all the pillars that present-day society rested upon had been breached and nothing would ever be the same. I wondered what it must have been like to witness such a defining moment in history.

I witnessed my own when the Twin Towers in New York were attacked, another unprecedented atrocity, which had me gasping with disbelief and sadness. I had been working in London for the summer, and wanted to hop on a plane and come home to see my family and friends, reassure myself that everyone was alive and well. Of course, the airports were in chaos and flights were all over the place, so a quick trip home was out of the question.

Then there was the shock of my father's death, still too raw to remember at times.

And now it seemed that history was repeating itself.

Because, for the rest of my life, I'll never forget where I was when I heard that Juliet was dead.

For most of Saturday my mobile had remained switched off at the bottom of my bag, as Erin, Gemma and I had continued our eating and drinking fest all around Rome. That night I had fallen into a deep, alcohol-induced sleep, when I should have been bedding down with Conor Kennedy as his wife, instead of sleeping alone in my small Rome apartment. It was late the following morning when I woke up and switched it on.

It beeped straight away, and my mother's text, which she'd sent a couple of hours earlier, didn't alarm me: *Give me a call when u get a chance and can talk*, she'd said. She wanted to find out how I was after yesterday, I thought. Knowing Mum, she'd been tying herself in knots, reliving every moment as it should have happened, maybe shedding a few silent tears. That was another reason my phone had stayed at the bottom of my bag. I'd wanted no sympathy texts. However, from the timing of this one, she'd waited until she'd thought the worst of the proverbial storm had passed. It sounded as though there was no particular rush so I had a long, lazy shower with my favourite L'Occitane shower gel and sipped a big mug of milky coffee while I relaxed on the sofa, flicking through a three-day-old magazine. When I felt more alive, I called her.

What she had to say didn't make sense. She might as well have been speaking to me in a foreign language. I felt as though I had been sliced into two halves, the slightly hung-over me who'd faffed about in the shower, wasting time, and the me who knew that something truly terrible had happened, the full enormity of which my mind couldn't absorb just yet.

'Are you talking about *our* Juliet?' I said, my voice somehow continuing to function, even though the rest of me felt freeze-framed, stalled, stuck in limbo. I was convinced I was talking about a person who was still alive, not someone who, according to my mother, seemed to have lost her footing and stumbled down the treacherous cliff face, close to where she lived.

'Yes, darling, I'm afraid so.' My mother's voice was hoarse and sympathetic, her concern at that moment for me, not for herself, even though she'd just lost her lifelong friend. Typical Mum. Always looking out for someone else. Especially me. Sometimes I felt like giving her a shake and telling her to be more selfish.

'But I was only talking to her on Thursday night,' I said, foolishly thinking she might say she'd made a terrible mistake.

'*Last* Thursday night?'

'Yes. She called to say she might be over in Rome soon and we ended up having a great chat. Are you *sure* it's Juliet?'

'I am. I saw her myself.'

'*What?* When?'

Then she told me, in brief, about the police calling to the house the previous evening, and escorting her to a hospital morgue, and, yes, she went on in a small voice, so hard to believe, *impossible* to believe, and a terrible shock, but it was Juliet all right. She'd waited until this morning to tell me: she hadn't seen the point in phoning me last night to deliver such bad news, especially when I was on my own in Rome. 'I thought you might as well get your night's sleep,' she said.

My mind slewed away from the terrible image of Juliet lying dead in a hospital morgue. 'Were you on your own when all this happened? Didn't Rose or someone go with you?'

My mother sighed. 'I couldn't get Rose on her mobile until afterwards – she and Matthew were at a St Patrick's Day dinner. The guards had contacted Juliet's brother in Florida and he was waiting to know if … and he asked if I'd …'

There was a silence.

I could guess the rest. Robert Jordan probably hadn't wanted to come all the way home from Florida unless he was sure it was his sister. From the little I'd known of him, there wasn't much love lost between him and Juliet. Then again, it would have been harrowing to make that journey home without knowing for sure.

'And why you?' I asked. I couldn't imagine how desperate it must have been for her. I thought my mother had been remarkably brave and my heart swelled with love and pride. I wanted to give her a big hug. She'd been through so much, holding us all together after my father had died, more concerned about our grief than hers.

'They don't have much family,' Mum said. 'Some cousins, I think, on Juliet's mother's side, but no one that Juliet keeps in close contact with. And she has plenty of colleagues and acquaintances, and some good friends in that circle, but I suppose I'm the closest to her.'

She was talking as though her friend was still alive. 'There's something about it in the newspapers this morning, but they're not releasing the name until Robert is home and has notified all the relatives. He's expected this evening.'

As she spoke, I stared around the rented apartment at the yellow walls, the small spindle table with the jug of dried lavender, the thin-cushioned sofa, and hated it. I hated it for not being home, for not being my space, the Dundrum apartment with the view of the mountains where I'd lived before moving in with Conor. Most of all, though, I hated it for being the strange place where I'd heard that Juliet had died.

'I don't suppose there'll be any word on the funeral arrangements for another day or two,' Mum said. 'It will depend on when they release the body. There has to be a post-mortem.'

Her words thudded into my head and I badly needed to

breathe fresh air. I went across the living area, phone in one hand, opened a glass door and stepped outside to a tiny balcony that could barely hold one person standing. Down below me in a small cobbled courtyard, children were playing, their voices echoing. Beyond the terracotta roofs on the opposite side, I could make out the grey sprawl of the city stretching into the distance. Above that, puffy clouds floated serenely in a pristine blue sky. From the near distance came the muted roar of traffic and the chime of a church bell. The scent of a spicy tomato sauce drifted out of an open courtyard window along with the staccato Italian of someone having a row. Life going on as normal. As though nothing dreadful had happened. I wanted to scream at everyone to shut up. I wanted to be back in my normal life. Whatever that was. I didn't bother reminding myself that life hadn't been normal for a long time.

'It's just unthinkable,' I said. 'I can't believe we're having this conversation.'

'Neither can I, love. It hasn't sunk in yet.'

She sounded so incredibly sad that I wanted to be there with her, right now.

'I'll be home as soon as I can,' I said.

'And, darling, how are you, after yesterday?'

'I went out for the day with friends. We did a sort of pub crawl around Rome.'

'One way of passing a few hours.'

'Did you say Juliet was found yesterday morning? So that all the time I was out, she was already …' I couldn't say the word. It didn't belong in the same sentence as my mother's warm, sparkling friend.

'Danielle, don't let that get to you. What could you have done differently? And you weren't the only one who was busy living your life. We were all getting on with things. I was even—' She broke off and gave a short, harsh laugh.

'You were even what?'

'I was drinking wine and going for walk with an old enemy of Juliet's.'

'Oh, gosh.'

'Yes. Liam Corrigan. Do you remember him? Supposedly he's turned over a new leaf. We were even talking about Juliet' – another harsh laugh – 'and I can't contact him because although I gave him my mobile number he didn't give me his.'

There was the sound of my mother choking back tears and once again I longed to be with her.

'I'll be home tomorrow evening,' I said. 'Can I stay with you?' I had nowhere else to go.

'Of course, darling. I'd love that. I'll have your old room ready.'

'I'll have to go into the office in the morning and do a quick handover. Then it'll be straight to the airport for the next available flight.'

'I suppose you mean you're just coming home for the funeral? Not for good?'

'Yeah, I'm not ready for that just yet, Mum.'

'Okay, love, just asking.'

She still didn't know why my wedding had been cancelled, and she was puzzled by that. But I couldn't take her into my confidence. I just hoped I could cope with the emotional ghosts of being back in Dublin, as well as the funeral of the woman who had been a second mother to me. The beautiful, kind woman, whose unconditional love had always burned brightly in my life and whose advice I'd eventually followed: she'd told me to listen to my heart.

I can see her still: Watsons Bay, Sydney, the sun in her eyes when she turns towards me – and she shades them with her hand while she reaches for her sunglasses.

'Let go of who you think you should be,' she said. 'Just be who you are in this world, your real self.' Something passed between us, I dunno, a message from woman to woman.

Surely if anyone had been their real self, it was Juliet.

There was more.

'Make every minute of your precious life count, Danielle,' she'd said. For a long, charged moment, her eyes were sad, and her message was that she didn't want me to have similar regrets. I wondered what had happened to make her feel sad, in a life so full of achievement and success. I hadn't asked Mum – I couldn't bring myself to pose the question – if Juliet had died instantly, or if she'd been lying there on the rocks, thinking of her regrets as her life ebbed away.

It didn't bear thinking about.

After I'd ended the call, I stood for ages on that tiny balcony, feeling icy cold inside, unable to work out what had to be done next, recalling the similar shock that had numbed me when I'd heard about my father's death. That time, I'd thought my broken heart would never repair itself. Now, it was as though a particularly bright light had been extinguished so everything seemed drab and grey.

And I had to return to Dublin, quite possibly face the man I loved but couldn't have.

THIRTY-FOUR

'Do you want some coffee?' Matthew asked.

'Coffee?' Rose said, heedless of her scathing tone, which implied he'd suggested a trip to the moon. 'I don't feel like anything. I don't even know why I got up and I'm sitting at the table.'

He busied himself with the cafetière and took a mug out of the press. 'You have to have something. You need to keep your energy up. It'll be a long week. And a busy one.'

'Oh, yes, I should have known that's exactly what you'd think,' she snapped. 'A long week with more public appearances, but now it's a funeral instead of a drinks reception. And there'll be people there, important people, wanting a piece of Juliet. Politicians, scholars and dignitaries. People to impress. Never mind the television cameras. I bet you've already planned your wardrobe. I bet you began to work that out as soon as Rebecca phoned yesterday evening,' she ended savagely.

'Rose! For Christ's sake! I think you do need that coffee.'

'I don't want coffee,' she shouted.

'Jesus, what's wrong with you?'

'This is!' She stabbed at the newspaper. 'Look! Look at that picture and tell me you feel like coffee.' She pushed the page in his direction. The page with the short article about the body of a woman found at the base of the cliffs. She knew it by heart already, the short, terse sentences sickening her, so ridiculously had they summed up Juliet's end.

According to the article, the body had been spotted by a young man out for an early-morning jog. The coastguards had been called but rescue from the top of the cliffs had had to be aborted. A search-and-rescue helicopter had gone in. There was even a photograph of a winch man steadying a stretcher suspended in mid-air. The name of the deceased was being withheld until close relatives had been informed. The Gardaí weren't looking for anyone else in connection with the incident, but they were appealing for witnesses, and anyone who might have seen anything unusual along the cliff path, from Friday evening onwards, was advised to contact them immediately.

She watched Matthew's face pale as he glanced at the newspaper before averting his eyes. He turned away and gazed out of the window at the back garden, where the morning breeze was riffling through clumps of daffodils that were artfully grouped around the lawn, made to look as though they had sprung up naturally.

'See?' Rose said, her voice shrill. 'Now tell me you can think of coffee.'

'I've already seen it, thank you. On the Internet. Long before you were even awake,' he said tiredly. 'I know you're extremely upset but—'

'I'll have to get a grip.'

'I didn't say that.'

'What do you think happened? How did she have such a stupid accident?'

'How should I know? I'm also finding it hard to believe. And I'm as saddened as you are.'

'Really, Matthew?'

'She was my friend, too, you know.'

'Was she, though?'

'Of course.'

'But she's no threat to you now, is she?' The words flew out of her mouth and quivered in the air between them.

Matthew became very still. Like an animal waiting to spring, as he stared out of the window, his head tilted slightly, as if checking for danger. He stayed like that for so long that something cold slithered down Rose's back.

'Matthew? Matthew, turn around and say something.'

'I might say something I'll regret.' His voice was tight.

'Like what?'

He wheeled around, his jaw clenched, his blue eyes full of anger. 'How could you think like that? How could you …' his voice broke '… at a time like this? Christ, Rose, what's got into you?'

'I don't know,' she cried, as she put her head into her hands. 'I don't want this to be real. I don't want Juliet to be dead. I can't bear it. I keep seeing her face, over and over. When she was young. I keep seeing her smile and hearing her laugh. But I can't help thinking this will change everything for you. She's out of your way now. And I wonder if I'm going mad again.' She burst into tears. She didn't know how she had any tears left. She'd already cried herself to sleep the night before, when they'd come home from Rebecca's, having called over to her after she'd eventually managed to contact them to break the shocking news.

'Juliet was never in my way,' Matthew insisted, in a quietly furious voice. 'Do you understand that? She was never a threat to me. Or to us.'

'What I can't believe is that my friend is dead and awful

thoughts are going through my mind. I must be a horrible person. I *am* a horrible person. Or else I'm going mad all over again.' More sobs shuddered through her and she fished in the pocket of her dressing-gown for a non-existent tissue.

Matthew silently tore off a few sheets of kitchen roll and handed them to her. 'You're far too upset to think straight. You've had a bad shock. Go back to bed and sleep some of it off. There's nothing you can do right now. Everything's on hold until Robert Jordan gets here.'

'What about James?' Rose asked, her throat sore. 'Are you going to tell him about Juliet? Rebecca's phoning Danielle this morning. He has to know but I can't bear to tell him.'

'I'll call him.'

'Do you think he'll come home for the funeral? He was very fond of Juliet. Oh, God, this is awful. I can't believe I'm actually talking about Juliet as though she's dead.'

She felt herself being lifted out of the chair, which prevented her from falling into a fresh storm of crying. 'Back to bed with you,' Matthew said, guiding her out of the room and towards the staircase. 'It might be best to stay there until Rebecca comes over this evening.'

'Rebecca's coming here?'

'You asked her for dinner.'

'Did I? I can't remember. I don't know why I asked her for dinner. How can we eat when Juliet is dead? None of us will have any appetite.'

'You might have by this evening. We can order in whatever you feel like.'

She stopped at the bottom of the stairs, under the Waterford crystal chandelier, and stared at him. 'Do you think Juliet fell on purpose or was it just a crazy accident?'

'Look, love …' Matthew sighed and shook his head. Wearing a plain grey jumper with black jeans, he looked more like the Matthew she'd known years ago and was comfortable with. She wanted to rewind time and go back to the start of their marriage when life had been innocent and full of promise. When they'd had no stair carpet for two years, and armchairs instead of a sofa. When they'd had to walk two miles to the nearest shop for bread and milk.

'It must have been an accident,' Matthew said. 'How else could it have happened? And Rebecca says the police aren't looking for anyone. So don't start imagining all sorts of things.'

'I can't stop thinking …' She stared at him, unable to move. It seemed as though her head had been hurting ever since Rebecca had broken the news to them. It had been hurting before that, since Matthew had told her he was interested in becoming a candidate in the presidential race. Nothing had been right since then. And now, with Juliet gone, it would never feel right again.

'This all started when you got ambitious ideas about yourself.'

'What all started?'

'My head. Feeling sore.'

Matthew looked as though his patience had been exhausted. She didn't care. At least he was paying as much attention to her as he did to his computer screen.

'Stop thinking,' he said. 'Just get some rest.'

'I don't know if I'll ever rest properly again.' She didn't wait for his reply. She walked up the thickly carpeted stairs, along the corridor and into the bedroom. She lay in the big wide bed with the Egyptian cotton sheets and Chantilly-lace-edged duvet and stared at the same spot on the Farrow & Ball-painted ceiling where Juliet's laughing face superimposed itself.

The face of the young girl whose sparkling eyes and big,

rebellious ideas had made her feel uncomfortable in her tightly ordered world, until she'd eventually found a grudging respect. It had been a respect tinged with envy, for Rose had never possessed a scrap of the careless insouciance that had been Juliet's trademark. She'd even been nervous about introducing her to Matthew, when they'd met for a meal all those years ago, terrified in case Matthew would find the bright, vivacious Juliet a more attractive proposition than the staid, rather safe Rose.

'Do you like her?' she'd asked Matthew afterwards, as they'd left the grill bar and strolled up O'Connell Street, the night somehow flat and colourless once they'd left Juliet and Rebecca behind. The girls were heading into a pub to meet friends for a drink, Juliet checking for her mints so her father wouldn't smell beer on her breath.

'Like her? Yeah, she's a bit of craic.'

'Am I a bit of craic?'

'Not in that way, thank God.' He'd tightened his grip on her hand. 'I'd hate you to turn into one of those women's libbers, always yelling for their rights. What's the betting she can't even boil an egg? Or iron a shirt? You're sweet and gentle, Rose, and that's why I love you.'

Later, he'd tried to go further with her than ever before, his kisses longer and deeper, his hands more forceful as he squeezed the swell of her breasts. She'd let him slip his fingers inside her bra, and he'd pressed her hand against the rather alarmingly long, hard bulge at his crotch. She couldn't imagine how it might feel, pushing all the way inside her on their wedding night.

Juliet, she'd thought, wouldn't be nervous of that. She'd welcome and enjoy it. And as soon as the ring was on her finger, and she was Matthew's wife, she couldn't afford to be nervous of it either. She'd have to welcome it.

Rose closed her eyes and waited for the pills to work. Sweet and gentle, Matthew had said, that long-ago night. He'd only been partly right, she thought, as she drifted into drug-induced sleep, for there were times when Rose Moore felt quite, quite savage.

THIRTY-FIVE

Stretched out on her sofa in front of the television, Liz tugged the soft velour rug closer around her. She had spent most of Sunday relaxing and watching her favourite feel-good DVDs, in which love, romance and happiness reigned. She'd originally planned to write up her diary column full of juicy gossip and sharply drawn innuendoes about Friday night's gala reception, but all of Saturday had been spent in the throes of hangover hell. Today, even though she felt marginally better, she hadn't got as far as checking Facebook or Twitter, never mind opening her laptop.

People would be wondering why she was off the radar, but she hadn't the energy to care.

Gavin hadn't contacted her since he'd marched out at lunchtime yesterday. It would be a while before she'd hear from him, if ever. He had looked totally pissed off with her, and she didn't blame him. Even she was pissed off with herself for rejecting his kindness and concern.

The closing credits of *Love, Actually* rolled up the screen, with everyone finding their happy-ever-after, something she sensed would always be elusive to her. She picked up the remote and flicked desultorily through the channels. She left on the main evening news because the newscaster's jacket was similar to one she'd recently tried on but rejected during a shopping trip to

London. Now she studied it critically, trying to judge if it would look cool and sexy on her.

Only for that, she might have missed the item about Juliet Jordan.

Professor Juliet Jordan had died suddenly at the weekend, the newscaster was saying. 'Vice chancellor of the Institute of Dublin University, Professor Jordan was renowned for her ground-breaking work as chairwoman of the European Equality Legislative Agency, her many publications and media appearances, and for her tireless contribution as founder and CEO of the Children's Dream Holiday charity. The professor died as a result of an accident near her home.'

As she spoke, file photos of Juliet flashed up on the screen: receiving a crystal bowl at an award ceremony in the Mansion House, being handed a bouquet of flowers at a dinner in Dublin Castle, and last, in Dublin airport, looking ridiculously young in jeans and a T-shirt, surrounded by an assortment of sick children, some wired up to portable drips.

'It is expected that Professor Jordan's funeral arrangements will be announced in the next couple of days,' the newscaster finished, before continuing with an item on the St Patrick's Day celebrations in New York.

Liz sat motionless, practically unblinking, and let the rest of the bulletin wash over her. After a while she lowered the volume, reached for her mobile, and called one of her news correspondent colleagues. 'Dave, hi.'

'Liz, what's up? Or should I ask who's going down this week under your sharp scalpel?'

'It could be you.'

'All my secrets are well out in the public domain, so there's nothing left for you to pillage. Although, knowing you, you'd find a needle in a haystack. Or a stray pubic hair on the wrong person's pillow.'

'Not always,' she said soberly. 'I've just been watching the news. Have you the inside track on Juliet Jordan?'

'What's it worth? And what are you doing sitting in on a Sunday, watching the news? You must be really ill if you're not out on the prowl.'

'It's worth a double tequila on the rocks, and I'm busy writing my copy.'

'Yeah, what's the betting you're recovering from an industrial-sized hangover?'

'Well, what's the news on Juliet?'

'Why are you interested?'

'I was hoping to feature her in my diary.'

'You were hardly putting Juliet Jordan under your dissecting knife?'

'None of your business. So, come on, what's the goss?'

'Very little, actually. She had some sort of accident off the cliffs at Howth on Friday night, I think, but her name was held back until her brother got home and informed the relatives. There will be a post-mortem tomorrow, but it's thought she missed her footing and fell. That's it. Seems an awful stupid tragedy for such a wonderful woman. And so bloody final. You won't be talking to her now. Maybe that's just as well. I wouldn't like to see you doing a hatchet job on her.'

'Thanks for your faith in me.'

'Unfortunately I have every faith in you, Liz, as well as your scandalous pen. Hey, how about meeting me for some hair of the dog? Or maybe some off-the-record scandalous sex? I enjoyed our last romp.'

'Shut up, Dave,' Liz said. She'd known him for a few years

and had fallen into his bed on a couple of occasions, the last time after she'd split with Gavin. They'd had a fun, no-strings night, prancing between his bed and his bath, but right now she didn't want a repeat.

They chatted some more, and when she ended the call, Liz went into the kitchen and put the kettle on to boil. She felt shaky and outside herself, funnily devoid of feeling, and she wondered if those were the final effects of her mega-binge. She took a mug out of the press and then, on second thoughts, replaced it and got out a glass instead. She switched off the kettle and picked up the bottle of vodka, splashed a generous amount into the glass, then topped it with cranberry juice. She took her drink into the sitting room and settled herself once more on the sofa.

One drink would be okay, maybe two, just to get over this weekend. It didn't mean she was going to end up like her mother, who had been an alcoholic for years. Her parents might have had plenty of money and lived in Upper Ballymalin Grove, but Liz would have swapped it all to have been born into a large, rough-and-tumble family with a more modest home in Lower Ballymalin Gardens. There, children sometimes slept three to a bed. She shivered in spite of the central heating. Growing up, she'd always felt cold. It had been a house that had echoed with bitter rows and icy silences between her parents, and where Liz had sometimes stolen through the rooms trying to avoid them and their angry words.

'If I'd given you sons, would it have made any difference?' she'd heard her mother cry. 'I know you desperately wanted a son to carry on your name.'

'Sometimes I feel like a failure, and not a real woman,' was another favourite lament.

'I've let you down, I know I have.' Over and over again.

The hard crack of a hand connecting with soft flesh. A muffled thump.

Then, sometimes, 'I hate myself. I hate you. Only for Elizabeth, I'd be long gone ...'

'And where would you go, woman?' her father had growled.

'That's the problem, isn't it? I'm stuck here. Because of Elizabeth. There's nowhere for women like me to go.'

Annie Monaghan had finally found her way out when she'd overdosed on vodka and pills just after Liz's sixteenth birthday.

The following year, as soon as she'd left school, Liz had fled to southside Dublin, a damp and noisy bedsit in Rathmines. She'd never looked back, leaving her father to his own sad devices much of the time. But her modelling career hadn't been the success she'd craved, even though she'd had the looks and the height, the deep blue eyes and the silky dark hair.

'You need to have more empathy with the camera,' they said. 'You need to mix a little vulnerability with that cool, calculating streak of yours.'

A load of crap, she'd thought. She was invulnerable. But when the modelling had led to a job helping on the fashion pages of a fortnightly magazine, she knew she'd found her niche. Her talent with words, combined with her stored-up anger and resentment, gave her a sometimes black but always pithy voice that got her noticed. Determined to make a go of it, she went on to study media and communications in her spare time, honing her craft, and shortened Elizabeth to Liz: it looked far punchier on a byline. And it had worked.

But love, marriage and the happiness thing had eluded her. Still, having witnessed her mother's misery in her marriage, Liz congratulated herself on cleverly avoiding that fate by ridding herself of Gavin at the first sign of trouble.

But she hadn't known the truth behind her mother's sense of failure until she'd emptied the house in Ballymalin and stumbled across documents that had changed everything. Liz took another gulp of her vodka and tried to stop shivering. In her shock, she'd left them behind, scattered on the floor. She needed to look at them again to make sense of what they had told her.

The truth might have made a difference.

Who was she kidding? It would have made all the difference in the world.

She went out to the kitchen to refill her glass. Even though her life had been pulled from under her, she wasn't going to follow her mother down the alcoholic trail, she told herself. Liz Monaghan was a voice to be reckoned with, every weekend in the society pages. Juliet Jordan might be beyond her reach now, but there were other people she could talk to. There were still some secrets to be unveiled no matter how deep their hiding place.

And, come hell or high water, Liz would find them …

THIRTY-SIX

'Rebecca?'

Liam. At last. Rebecca excused herself to take the call. She took a deep breath to steady herself. 'Hi, Liam, I'm in my sister's.' Her voice echoed around the vast, clinical space and she wished she was somewhere other than Rose's mammoth kitchen while she had this difficult conversation with Liam.

'You've seen the news? About Juliet?' he said, his voice strangled.

'I haven't watched it, but I'd been hoping you'd call,' she said. 'I wanted to avoid you getting a shock.'

'How long have you known?' It was almost an accusation.

'Since yesterday evening.'

There was a choking noise. 'God almighty.'

Her heart went out to him. 'Liam, I'm sorry you had to hear it on the news, but I'd no way of contacting you.'

'Of course. I know. Sorry, I'm just upset.'

'Juliet's brother arrived home this afternoon and, between us, we reached as many people as we could before the news was broadcast. If I'd had your number, I would have called you straight away.'

It had been an exhausting couple of hours. Robert had called her from his hotel room as soon as he'd arrived, and she'd begun contacting people who needed to know as soon as he was satisfied that immediate relatives had been informed. Thankfully, some of Juliet's colleagues had offered to pass on the sad news to their own circle of friends, thus sharing the burden with Rebecca.

'Dear God, I don't believe this.' There was another muffled sob, as though he was crying.

'Look …' She paused to gather her scattered thoughts. 'Do you want to come over? Rose wouldn't mind – she's so distressed that the whole army could march through her house and she wouldn't notice. Although …' she hesitated '… it might be best if you called over to my house. I can be home soon.'

'Yes, please.'

Rebecca gave him her address. 'Are you okay to drive?' she asked, conscious that he was in shock.

'Of course,' he said.

She made her excuses to Matthew and an inconsolable Rose, who hadn't touched a morsel of the beef dish Matthew had ordered in. 'We'll talk tomorrow,' she said, hugging her sister. Rose clung to her, and it was difficult to prise her away, until Matthew took his wife into his arms.

'She'll be fine,' he said to Rebecca, over Rose's head. 'I'll keep an eye on her.'

'Make sure you do,' Rebecca said, her tone light but meaningful. 'No starting down that campaign trail tonight or tomorrow. Rose needs you. What about James? Is he coming home?'

'In a couple of days.'

'God, it's an awful mess, isn't it?'

'Death is messy and rather awful at times,' Matthew said, looking at her steadily.

Just as Rebecca reached the door, Rose stirred in his arms and raised her tear-blotched face. 'At least Matthew has nothing to worry about any more where Juliet is concerned,' she said, in a slurred voice.

Rebecca threw her brother-in-law a startled glance. In the time she had been there Rose hadn't been drinking. She could only guess that her sister had taken one too many Xanax. 'Rose? Are you feeling all right?'

Matthew looked grim. 'Rose is … too upset to think straight,' he said, his arms wrapped securely around her.

'I *am* thinking straight,' Rose protested. 'It's all very clear to me. At least Juliet's out of Matthew's hair now.'

Matthew looked at Rebecca, his expression unreadable. 'Rose has this idea that Juliet was some kind of threat.'

'And you were the one who said we'd nothing to worry about,' Rose said, stepping back and staring up at him.

She was keeping well out of this, Rebecca decided. 'Stay where you are,' she said. 'I'll see myself out and, Rose, I'll call you tomorrow.'

৵৽

Shortly after Rebecca got home, Liam arrived in a taxi. He stood in her hall, looking like a haunted child.

'Did I say I was going to drive? I couldn't put the key into the ignition, let alone turn it,' he said.

A wave of dizziness washed over Rebecca. On impulse, she held out her arms and he went into them. They held each other for long moments. She found it strange to be in another man's arms, but needed some comfort and wanted to comfort him, and the heat of his body to warm her. Just for that moment it was good to be alive, breathing in and out, her heart pumping so that all her cells hummed, able to hold someone else and be held in return.

She brought him through to her plant-filled conservatory, with the bright, cheerful furnishings. The evening had fallen into night, and outside, garden lighting dispelled the darkness. She lit a white jasmine-scented candle, one that Juliet had given her and she'd been saving for a special occasion, and opened a bottle of Shiraz that Juliet had brought her from Stellenbosch. Then she sat beside him on the cane sofa and filled him in on everything that had happened since the police had called to her door.

She felt as though she was going through the motions on automatic pilot, that some weird adrenalin had kicked in to help her cope with the trauma of the next few days. Her grieving had to be carefully laid aside for now. People needed her: she had to talk to Robert about the funeral arrangements, possibly help with them, be there for mega-distressed Rose, prepare her spare room for Danielle tomorrow evening and comfort her, and now deal with Liam's shock.

But he had some inkling of how she must be feeling. 'If I feel as though I've been landed a sucker punch in the gut, how did you go through all that on your own?' he asked. 'Never mind the mortuary.'

'I did it for Juliet's sake,' she said, his concern warming her. 'Someone had to. No sense in Robert getting a heart-in-the-mouth flight home unless it was definitely his sister.'

'How did Juliet look?' He squeezed her hand.

She managed to smile. 'Rose didn't ask me that but, in fairness to her, she's very upset. It was okay, I suppose, as far as these things can be okay. I didn't know what to expect, and I was quaking. Juliet ...' She faltered as the image of her friend, pale and lifeless under the garish hospital lights, came back to her. Unreal. Surreal. Like Harry all over again: the searing pain was waiting behind a thin sheet of glass until the rituals were over, until weeks and months had passed and she missed Juliet more and more, the longer it was since she'd seen or talked to her. She lifted her chin a little, looked at the flickering candle flame and went on, 'Juliet looked like she was in a very deep sleep. She'd suffered internal traumas, and injuries to her legs and the back of her head. Still, I kept expecting her to wake up and laugh, and call out, "Gotcha!" or something silly like that.'

Liam's eyes were warm and they lifted her heart. 'You're a very courageous lady,' he said. 'I can see why Juliet is – was, God – proud to have you as a friend.'

Rebecca shook her head, tears gathering behind her eyes. She blinked several times. 'Don't talk like that, please. I can't bear it. Anyway, she was the trail-blazing lady of courage, not me. And my biggest regret, which will never go away, is that we had cross words the last time we were together.'

Liam put his arm around her shoulders. She was surprised by how good it felt. 'Hey, what are a few words compared to a lifetime's friendship? She forgave me for a lot worse. She would have forgiven you anything.'

'I still can't understand how it happened,' Rebecca went on, a little comforted by his words. She poured more wine, slipped off her shoes, swung her feet under her on the sofa and allowed herself to relax into the curve of his arm. 'Juliet told me she was going to spend the whole of Friday in her study because she had to put her head down and clear her reports.' She paused. 'God, Liam, you must have been one of the last to see her alive ...'

His face blanched. 'Don't say that.'

'What time were you there?'

'Around five o'clock. I didn't stay long.'

'You've no idea who else she was expecting?'

'No, she wouldn't say. She was joking about it. I started teasing her about her hair … It was kind of blonde with … um – I'm not sure what colour you'd call it. Oh, Christ, I can't believe I'm talking about the colour of her hair. This is awful.'

'It was a pink wash,' Rebecca said bleakly. 'She told me once she hated going grey – her hair was her one vanity.' She shivered, and Liam tightened his hold. 'I'll never get used to talking about her in the past tense. It feels so strange that it's like I'm sleepwalking.'

'Same here. Talk to me about her … Fill me in on the last couple of years … if you feel like it.'

She tilted her head so that she could look at him properly. He seemed genuinely interested and she gave him a grateful smile. 'That's exactly what I'd like to do. I could talk all night about her.'

He stretched out his legs. 'I'd love to listen.'

It grew late, and another bottle of wine was opened as they shared memories of Juliet, chatting about funny times and good times, Rebecca alternating between laughter and tears, as it passed midnight, and then one o'clock. Liam talked of calling a taxi. Rebecca worked out that almost two whole days had passed since Juliet was alive, so it was already days rather than hours since her friend had slipped from the world, and it was so sad that she didn't want to be alone in the darkened house. She knew the icy echo of dead silence in empty rooms, and she didn't want it tonight, while her warm, bubbly friend lay cold and stiff in a hospital mortuary.

'Rather than turf you out, I can put you up, if you like,' she suggested. 'I've three spare bedrooms and it means I won't be afraid if I hear a bump in the night. I even have a couple of spare toothbrushes.'

He looked pleased, and she felt unexpected warmth in her chest. 'Thanks, Rebecca. I'd like that. So long as you don't mind my rough face in the morning. If there's anything at all I can do, just ask, no matter what it is.'

'Rough faces are fine in the mornings,' she said, automatically glancing at his lean jaw line and lingering on his nice mouth. She slid her gaze away from it. 'I'll even stand you a cup of coffee.'

'How did you get through last night?' he asked, searching her face. 'It must have been torture. I can't believe we were joking and laughing about Juliet only yesterday morning.'

'Neither can I. I zoned out with the help of double-strength sleeping pills, but I was so befuddled this morning that I don't want to repeat that. Tomorrow will be busy, between talking to Robert about the funeral and Danielle coming home.'

She was comforted by his presence in the adjoining bedroom as she chased sleep, her mind on a constant loop from the moment the police car had driven slowly up the cul-de-sac to when she'd asked Liam to stay. What had happened to Juliet continued to haunt her. She tried not to see it re-enacting in front of her: Juliet setting out along the track in her usual jaunty manner, then the heart-stopping moment when she stumbled and pitched forward into the space between sea and sky …

How much had she been aware of? Had she lain unconscious all night? Or had she waited in vain for rescue, her body broken and battered, terror gripping her, and rescue, when it came, far too late?

They would never know.

Had anyone seen her out for her walk? Lots of people would have been walking along the headland. Had someone somewhere an idea of what had happened to her friend? She felt a howl of anguish building up inside her and tried to bite it back, but Liam must have heard a noise, a whimper, because he stood in the doorway against the landing light, still dressed.

'Are you okay?'

She sat up in bed, hugging herself. 'Yes. No. Oh, God, this is a nightmare.'

'Isn't it just? I still can't believe it.'

'Come here, Liam. Hold my hand, please,' she said. 'I can't bear lying awake in the dark.'

'Neither can I.'

Liam lay on top of the bed and held her hand, and she was glad he was there as the night darkened and deepened around them.

THIRTY-SEVEN

Sleep was elusive.

Friday night, it had been okay, the same for Saturday. But tonight the ghost started to appear. The ghost of Juliet. She could have been another presence pulsating in the room, her shimmering outline twisting and writhing, moving forwards and backwards, only now her eyes were as black as coal, her teeth yellow like fangs, her nails long and blood red.

It had been too easy.

Juliet had suggested the headland stroll. As they walked and talked in the gathering evening shadows, she had been defensive and on her guard, but still maintaining a calm kind of assurance that was infuriating. Then the angry words flowing into the air had become more barbed and heated, but Juliet had held on to that maddening composure, refusing to be rattled.

A glance along the temporarily deserted headland track, and the perfect solution presented itself. It hadn't taken a minute. Juliet hadn't even had time to cry out as she slipped over the edge and dropped like a stone, disturbing a flock of gulls that rose on beating wings circling and cawing into the calm evening air.

Now the room was pulsing with a giant image of Juliet's blanched face and terror-stricken eyes in the split second she'd realised what was about to happen.

It would never go away.

THIRTY-EIGHT

Rebecca found it almost impossible to face the new morning when the reality of Juliet scored itself freshly on her heart the minute she woke up. Weird, also, to see Liam Corrigan asleep on top of the duvet. No one had lain on that side of the bed since Harry. Rebecca picked up a throw and tucked it around him. She felt she was almost sleepwalking as she showered and dressed, then went downstairs to make coffee.

Liam joined her just as the doorbell rang.

It was the police. The same pair who had called to tell her of Juliet's death. Nausea rushed to her throat.

'May we come in?'

Wordlessly, she stepped back to allow them to enter. 'Liam, this is …' Her mind flailed as she tried in vain to recall their names. They stood awkwardly in the hall.

'Detective Inspector Callaghan and Detective Woods,' the policeman said.

Detectives! She hadn't realised. Their rank reinforced the gravity of it all.

'Liam Corrigan. I'm an old friend of Juliet's.'

'We need to have a few words with you about Juliet, if that's okay, Mrs Ryan,' Detective Woods began, in a sympathetic voice.

'Of course,' Rebecca said, leading the way into her front room.

For a moment the atmosphere was charged, Rebecca's mind whirling helplessly, the detectives looking as though they didn't know where to begin.

'Would anyone like coffee?' Liam asked.

The detectives shook their heads.

'We're trying to piece together what might have happened on Friday night, Mrs Ryan,' Detective Woods said.

Something cold slithered around Rebecca's gut. She was glad that Liam was sitting on the sofa beside her.

'We're keeping an open mind on everything,' Detective Inspector Callaghan said, 'but we need to conduct a fuller investigation into the circumstances around Ms Jordan's death and her movements on Friday evening.'

He was young, Rebecca realised. For all that, his eyes were sharp and keen, and slightly world weary, as though he'd seen it all before. She might have found him attractive had she been watching him on some detective programme. Juliet would have given him ten out of ten for those eyes.

They'd never watch television together again. Or go to the movies. Or out for a drink and a meal. Deep inside, she felt a huge reservoir of tears ready to burst through a dam. But not yet, please, not just yet.

'How can I help you?' she asked.

Detective Woods flipped open her notebook. 'According to Robert Jordan, you were Juliet's closest friend. Is that right?'

'Yes. We've been friends for a long time.'

'Since?'

'A lifetime ago.'

'So you'd know if anything had been bothering Ms Jordan?'

Rebecca felt the blood drain from her face. 'You don't think –
you can't mean—'

'We don't think anything at the moment,' Detective Inspector
Callaghan said. 'We're just trying to get as full a picture as
possible of Ms Jordan prior to Friday night. These are routine
enquiries.'

'She was much the same as ever,' Rebecca said. 'Busy in her
life, quite busy, actually. I know she intended to spend Friday
catching up on her paperwork …'

'When was the last time you spoke to her?'

Rebecca gulped.

*Maybe it's time a few things were out in the open … Maybe I'm
willing to take my chances … See what Fate has in store …*

'What is it, Mrs Ryan?' Detective Woods leaned forward. She
wasn't just a pretty face. She was as quietly alert as a cat waiting
for a mouse to come out of its hidey-hole.

'Nothing. I was just remembering something she said, the last
time I saw her.'

'Which was?'

Her mind sheered away from Juliet's words. 'I saw her last
Sunday, when we went for a walk around the headland.'

Detective Woods consulted her notes. 'We've obtained Ms
Jordan's spare set of keys from Mrs Breen, the elderly lady who
lives in the adjacent property. Mrs Breen says she has known
Juliet for most of her life. She was very surprised that Juliet might
have slipped and fallen. She said Ms Jordan knew the cliff walk
like the back of her hand. Would you agree with that?'

'Yes. She walked those cliffs most evenings. Sometimes when I
called in for a chat she dragged me along with her. She often did
that when friends or colleagues popped in.'

'It had rained earlier on Friday, so part of the track could have been damp and slippery,' Detective Woods said. 'But Mrs Breen says that Juliet was used to going out in all kinds of weather.'

'Had Ms Jordan any adversaries that you know of? Sorry we're intruding like this, but we have to eliminate all we can.' This was from Detective Inspector Callaghan.

Rebecca stared at him. 'Like what? What are you trying to eliminate?'

'Let's put it like this, Mrs Ryan,' Detective Woods said, 'We need to satisfy ourselves that Ms Jordan died by misadventure, accident or – or—'

'Whether we should be looking for someone else in connection with the incident,' Detective Inspector Callaghan said, his tone deferential but firm.

'Someone else?' Rebecca's voice shook. She was grateful that Liam immediately took her hand.

'All avenues have to be examined before they're excluded from our enquiries,' the detective continued.

'But who—' Rebecca couldn't continue.

'Ms Jordan was well known, with a very high profile. She could have been a target for someone she might have known or perhaps not. We have to consider everything.'

'Have you witnesses?' Rebecca asked. 'Did anybody see Juliet out on Friday evening?'

'We've nothing definite yet.'

'You might want to talk to me,' Liam said. 'I think I was one of the last to see Juliet alive.'

Both detectives sat up straighter, and Rebecca's stomach lurched as they began to question Liam in a manner of brisk efficiency that made her feel sick, jotting down his account of Friday night in their notebooks.

'You said you think she was expecting someone else, Mr Corrigan?' Detective Woods asked.

'Yes, we were in her kitchen and she threw an eye to the clock a couple of times. I joked and asked her if she had a hot date lined up.'

'And what was her reply?'

'She said it wouldn't be Friday night without a flaming hot date and I'd have to make myself scarce.'

'She didn't mention any names?'

'No, but it could have been anybody or nobody. That was the way Juliet went on.'

'Mrs Ryan, to your knowledge, was Ms Jordan in a relationship with anyone?'

'No,' Rebecca said immediately.

'And yet you were of the opinion that she intended to spend Friday catching up on her paperwork.'

'Yes, I was,' she said.

'So you weren't aware that Mr Corrigan would be calling to her.'

'No. I wouldn't always know the daily incidentals of Juliet's life,' Rebecca explained, 'but I'm positively sure she wasn't in a relationship.'

A small seed of doubt burst open in her head. Juliet could be very discreet, when the occasion demanded it. She saw her face on the cliff-top … *just as well you knew only half the story.* How much had she kept from Rebecca, then and now?

'Can you confirm that you met Mr Corrigan in the Seagrass Hotel afterwards?'

'Yes,' she said. 'I saw Liam in the lobby … it was after nine o'clock that evening, wasn't it, Liam? The news was still on the television. You hardly think—'

'We don't think anything at this stage,' Detective Woods said. 'As I said, we're keeping an open mind while we get a fuller picture. As you saw her on Friday evening, Mr Corrigan, we'll need you to come to the station in the next day or two to sign a statement. Could we have your contact details, please?'

'Fine by me,' Liam said, and gave them his mobile number.

'And, Mrs Ryan, we'll need your help with one further matter,' the policewoman said, her face full of empathy. 'Robert Jordan considers you're the best person to throw your eye around Juliet's home in case there's anything amiss.'

'Like what?' Rebecca asked, feeling chilled right through to her bones.

'Anything at all out of the ordinary. Any kind of disturbance. We still have the house sealed off, so we'd like to bring you across as soon as is convenient. Is that okay?'

'I can go with you now, if you'll give me a few minutes to have some coffee,' Rebecca said.

'I'll come too, if you like,' Liam said, squeezing her hand.

She shook her head. If she had to do this, she wanted to be alone, apart from the police.

'We just need Mrs Ryan,' Detective Woods said. 'If there's anything amiss, or evidence, we don't want to compromise it more than we have to.'

Evidence of what? Rebecca felt desolate. Still, she was the only person who could do this, for she was the one to whom Juliet had entrusted all her details in case of an accident: 'Someone has to know where I keep the keys to my safe and where I store all my important paperwork, my will and insurance and all those tiresome details we can't live without,' she'd said to Rebecca, soon after they'd both turned fifty. 'You're the person I'd trust the most to look after the pernickety stuff, should I get lost on a Himalayan adventure or in the South American jungle.'

'Don't talk like that.'

'I have to be practical. I don't have a spouse or partner, and Robert's in America. And it's much easier to sort out these matters while I'm still in rude health.'

'Knowing you, Juliet, you'll see us all down,' Rebecca had joked, and Juliet had gone on to tell her what kind of commemoration service she'd like.

There was no end, she thought. No end to the tunnel into which she'd pitched on Saturday evening.

&

She braced herself as they neared Verbena View, filled with sickening dread as she saw the police tape across the driveway flicking in the breeze and the officer standing in the porch. Rebecca's heart was in her mouth as she stepped across the threshold. She moved down the hallway and into the empty rooms, waiting to be assaulted with images of her friend, wondering if there would be any clues as to what had happened on Friday evening. Funnily enough, the house seemed peaceful and at ease. It was just as though Juliet had popped out to the shops and would be back at any moment.

Rebecca went into the study, half expecting Juliet to jump out of the deep leather armchair drawn up in front of the fireplace. She saw that the computer was logged off and the desk had been tidied, as though she'd completed her work before she'd left for her walk. She had a quick look through the papers on the desk, and in the drawer, but there was no sign of anything untoward. It was painful, however, to look at the framed certificates in the corner alcove and impossible to think that Juliet would never set foot in there again and sit at her desk with the glorious view of the sea.

'Nothing out of the ordinary here,' she said to Detective Woods.

The detective must have signalled something, for two officers moved in and began disconnecting the hard drive of the computer. Rebecca wanted to ask them to leave the room exactly as it was: she didn't want to see familiar parts of Juliet's life being fragmented.

Silly, really, when her life itself had been destroyed.

Into her bedroom, and Rebecca's heart squeezed, but all was neat and tidy, save for a pair of jeans and a pink cashmere sweater thrown on top of the laundry basket in the en-suite. The clothes she must have been wearing on Friday before she'd put on her tracksuit. She wanted to pick up the sweater and bury her face in it, to see if she could catch a lingering fragrance of her friend. She checked the walk-in wardrobe and Juliet's clothes were neatly arranged, along with her bags and shoes. The concealed door to her wall safe, which contained her jewellery and important papers, was still securely locked.

'This is fine also,' she said to Detective Woods.

Then Rebecca went into the kitchen, which had always been the beating heart of Juliet's home. She strangled a sob as she looked around the warm familiarity of it all and memories surged. Juliet popping the cork on yet another bottle of champagne: 'Just one more. Life is too short not to drink all the bubbly.'

Juliet in a funny Naked Chef apron, brandishing a wooden spoon coated in tomato sauce. 'Which brave soul wants to try some of my home-made lasagne?'

Juliet folding back the patio doors and opening the kitchen

to the outdoors. 'What a totally fabulous evening. Look at that ginormous sky. I could sit here and gaze at it all night …'

Juliet would never set foot in her kitchen again. A pulsebeat of pain ricocheted in Rebecca's head. She balled her hand into a fist and pressed it against her mouth. She felt Detective Woods place a hand on her arm.

'I know this is difficult,' the detective said, 'and you're doing great. Take your time, there's no rush. We just need to know if anything strikes you as odd.'

'Juliet—' Rebecca swallowed hard. 'She often wrote appointments into her calendar on the wall. Danielle gave it to her last Christmas, to help her plan ahead, as she was inclined to get so involved in her work that she forgot what was coming up.' She went over to the corkboard beside the fridge unit, but there were no entries in the box for the previous Friday.

And then: 'She must have left in a hurry,' Rebecca said, voicing her thoughts as she turned back and her eyes roved around the kitchen.

'Why is that?'

'Just … the only odd thing – the glasses on the counter … Normally Juliet would stick them into the dishwasher or at least rinse them. I can only guess that she was in a hurry to get going …'

'Did she always clear up before she went out?'

'Yes. She might have been a bit absent-minded now and again, but she was a tidy person and never left food, dirty dishes or glasses lying around, especially if she was going out.' Rebecca stared at the glasses.

Liam, with his bottle of wine? Whoever had visited after Liam? 'And there are two glasses,' she said, 'so Juliet had company before she left, although that doesn't mean anyone went with her. She usually invited you to tag along, you know, if she was heading out for her walk.'

Another nod from Detective Woods, and the glasses were photographed, then sealed in plastic bags and borne away.

'You're taking this very seriously,' Rebecca said. 'Do you think whoever was here—' She couldn't continue.

'It might mean nothing at all,' Detective Woods said. 'There could be a perfectly innocent explanation. But, in the circumstances, we're leaving no stone unturned.'

Rebecca's glance rested on the kitchen table, where the group of them had sat at Christmas before everything had gone crazy. Before Juliet had decided that a few things should come out into the open. Had she started down this road? Had she upset anyone? And something else had been nibbling at her subconscious since Sunday evening: *At least Matthew has nothing to worry about anymore where Juliet is concerned.* Just what had Rose meant by that? It seemed that Juliet's death was sending her sister spiralling back into the black void.

'We can leave now, Rebecca,' the policewoman said gently.

She didn't want to go. She wanted to sit in Juliet's kitchen and wait, in the hope that this was all a crazy mistake and any minute now Juliet might breeze through the door. Funnily enough, it was much harder walking back up the hall and out of the door than it had been to come in.

THIRTY-NINE

Funerals shouldn't be allowed to take place on warm, spring days, I decided. Especially the funeral of someone like Juliet.

All the way home from Rome I had been dreading this moment, and Mum, bless her, must have sensed it for she squeezed my hand and smiled at me as we drew up outside St Patrick's Cathedral for Juliet's commemoration service. I couldn't believe the size of the crowd gathered outside, although I hadn't expected anything less.

Earlier that morning, Juliet's coffin had been quietly brought to the cathedral directly from the funeral home, where her body had lain since it had been released on Monday evening. I didn't go to see her in the funeral parlour: I wanted to remember Juliet as she had been, full of laughter, full of love and full of life. I couldn't yet think of her as a body.

Rose and Matthew had accompanied us in the mourning car, and there was a flurry of interest as we stepped out, some photographers elbowing through the throng, cameras at the ready, anxious to get to us. Rose was dressed in designer black, from head to toe, oversized dark glasses hiding her eyes. Matthew was wearing charcoal grey and I felt he was more protective than usual of her. I couldn't help noticing, though, that rather than trying to avoid the reporters, as Mum and I did, my media-savvy uncle guided her in the general direction of the television crew, who were busy picking off the beautiful and important people.

Mum was wearing an elegant royal blue Joanne Hynes dress and coat, topped off with a jaunty hat. 'You look like you're off to a wedding,' I'd said to her, before we'd left our house, immediately sorry that I'd brought up the W-word. My abandoned wedding still hadn't been mentioned between us. We'd had little chance to talk alone: since I'd come home we'd been busy with endless phone calls and cups of tea, and people coming and going, including Robert Jordan, to arrange the service with Mum's help, and Liam Corrigan, who'd been hanging around like he didn't know what to do for the best. A far more subdued, reflective Liam compared to the flash poster-boy I'd remembered from the Celtic Tiger days. Then Rose had phoned, twice or three times, and I knew my aunt was crying from the way Mum tried to soothe her, and my cousin James had arrived home from the States and called over as well. So it was full on.

'A wedding?' She'd smiled easily, as though the word had no nasty connotations. 'That's exactly what Juliet would have wanted. And you look perfect yourself, darling. Juliet would have approved.'

'I hope so,' I said, smiling back. Our tacit understanding was that there would be no tears today: we would see Juliet off in the style she deserved. I was wearing a champagne knee-length dress embellished with black lace, and a matching tight black-lace jacket. I'd bought it in a boutique on the Via del Corso in Rome before I'd travelled to the airport, hardly able to believe I was buying an outfit for Juliet's commemoration service. My hair was swept to the side and secured with a diamanté clasp Juliet had given me.

We slipped through the throng of academics, politicians, television and radio personalities, and went into the cathedral. In contrast to the sunny morning, the interior was cool and dim, and filling up quickly. My eyes flew straight to the top of the main aisle, and my heart fluttered at the sight of Juliet's coffin, with the single spray of lilies on top. I told myself that the Juliet I knew and loved wasn't really there, in that shiny wooden box. Yet neither was she here with me and Mum, taking the piss with sharp comments about some of the jumped-up crowd milling around outside. The part of my life that she'd inhabited seemed cold and silent for now.

Mum and I went up the aisle and sat in the second row, leaving the front pew for Robert Jordan, his wife and sons. Behind us, I heard increased activity, as more and more of the crowd streamed in and took their places. Robert and his family arrived, shaking hands with Mum and me.

And then I sensed the person I loved most in the world arriving. My senses prickled and hummed, like stretched electric cable, but I kept my eyes focused on the stained-glass window over the altar.

Oh, Juliet, I cried silently, I've listened to my heart, but it's breaking in two and I've never been unhappier. Is this what you meant? And how could I even be indulging in thoughts like these when you're dead and gone from us all, and I'm alive and well, apart from my shattered love life? But no matter how hard I listened, in case some Juliet-type words of wisdom were floating in the sanctified air, I heard nothing but a resounding silence. If only I had entrusted her with my feelings, maybe called to see her at Verbena View, she might have been able to offer advice. Instead I'd hotfooted it out of Dublin, leaving Mum to pass on the news of my broken engagement to family and friends, and had only exchanged emails and an occasional phone call with Juliet. I thought back to our call last Thursday night, less than a week ago, when I'd put on my best happy voice and laughed along with her as though life was great. If she'd had time to come out to Rome, would I have confided in her? Hard to say, and all the wondering in the world was futile for I'd never know now.

The service started with the allegro from Bach's Brandenburg Concerto No. 1, and as the pure, joyous sound soared around the cathedral, I couldn't have thought of a more fitting tribute to Juliet's effervescent spirit. The service went by in a haze. Robert said a few words about his sister and her huge, unselfish capacity for striving to make the world a better place, her endless charity work, and thanked the large crowd for being there to celebrate her life. The chancellor of the university spoke about the pleasure of working alongside Juliet, the high regard in which she was held by the hundreds of students who had passed through her hands over the years, and he commended her absolute dedication to her job. There were more speakers, and finally Mum stood up and took the microphone. She stared at the congregation for a long moment, and then she spoke simply, in her husky voice, from the heart about the enriching value of friendship and love in all its forms, a lot of which she'd learned from Juliet. 'We go back a long way, Juliet and I, and I was privileged to share so much of my life with her …'

She finished by asking for a minute's silence. 'I want everyone to remember, just for one minute, something happy that you enjoyed about Juliet, perhaps it was something that made you laugh, smile or just want to be around her … and let us give thanks for our dear friend and send her off with a lift in our hearts.' She stood, for a full minute, alone at the front of the altar, with Juliet's coffin a few feet away, and then she led the

packed cathedral in a burst of applause, during which everyone
rose to their feet.

I swallowed tears and thought my mum had never seemed
braver or more beautiful. I know she annoyed me from time to
time, in the way she fussed around us all with no regard to herself,
but that was my mum. She was made of far more gracious stuff
than I was, and quite perfect in every way.

Then it was all over. We followed Robert and his family behind
the coffin up the aisle, as the music broke into Vivaldi's 'Spring'
from *The Four Seasons*. Out of the corner of my eye, I saw my
cousin James standing at the edge of a pew several rows up the
aisle. He gave me an encouraging wink as I passed, and then we
were spilling outside into the spring sunshine as the coffin was
placed in the hearse.

A queue of people had lined up to talk to Mum, more so than
to Robert, most of whom I didn't know, from elderly statesmen
to young college students. I stood quite close to her in support, as
they expressed their sadness. Some of the college students clung
to her and cried, and Mum took it all in her stride. I realised
belatedly that she didn't really need me. She was more than able
to take care of herself.

Except for one, who was pushing her way forward now to the
head of the queue.

I knew by Mum's face and the slight recoil of her body that
she didn't want to talk to Liz Monaghan, the jumped-up pseudo-
journalist who'd made herself a household name because she had
the bitchiest voice in tabloid newsprint.

'Have you any comment to make, Rebecca?' she asked, in
strident tones. 'We know the police investigation is still wide
open.'

'I have no comment,' my mother said calmly, moving slightly

away from her. Just as well she had filled me in on the whole rotten story and the questions the police had been asking. At least I'd been forewarned, but other mourners close by were startled.

'But you must have a theory of your own. You knew Juliet so well,' Liz cooed.

Mum refused to be drawn. 'I have nothing to say, if you'll excuse me,' she said, politely but dismissively.

Liz pressed closer to her, her eyes wide and calculating, 'Do you think Juliet had any secrets up her sleeve?'

Mum seemed a little alarmed but, to my surprise, Matthew came to the rescue. Standing close by, he had observed what was happening. Now he stared at Liz with a glint in his eye. 'Liz, we know your dedication to your job is paramount,' he said, in a silky voice, and drew her away from my mother. 'But surely you'll agree that there's an appropriate time and place for everything.'

'Well, hello, Mr Moore, it was worth it to get this close to you,' Liz said, in an equally silky voice, looking him up and down slowly and deliberately. 'You're on my hot list, you know. I've been hoping to do a no-holds-barred interview with you, and perhaps your lovely wife, but you keep ignoring my Twitter messages. I appreciate you're very busy at the moment.'

'Contact my PA,' he said. 'I'm sure you'll be able to ferret out her details. Or look up my new website.'

'So, is that a date?' She raised her eyebrows archly.

'Hardly, Ms Monaghan,' Matthew said. 'I usually do the running. It's never the other way around.'

'Can I quote you?'

'Feel free.'

'Your wife won't mind?'

'Why should she? The lovely Rose is the only woman I run after. And you can quote that too.' He turned away.

Good on you, Matthew. That put Liz in her place quite neatly. Although Liz wasn't one to let that bother her. I heard her shrill tones as she addressed no one in particular, confident that everyone within hearing distance was attuned to her. 'Oh, my God, is that Liam Corrigan? I'd heard he'd returned from exile but I'd never thought he'd have the neck to turn up here.' I hoped fervently that he was able to make himself scarce. I wasn't quite sure what to make of him, and was a little bemused by how friendly he was with my mother, but he didn't deserve to have Liz on his back.

Mum was talking now to a learned-looking gentlemen and his elegant wife. I was making my way across to her when a pair of arms came around me from behind.

'Hey, little cuz, how are you today?'

James.

I turned to face him. 'I'm good, considering. How are you?'

'Okay. Sort of. Mum's still in bits and Dad's doing his best to keep her upright, but I didn't realise how much I adore Rebecca until I saw her in action today. She played a blinder.'

'Yeah, she did. I'm very proud of her.'

The good thing about Ireland is that, by and large, famous people get to do their own thing, without too much interference or hassle. James Moore might have played a sell-out concert in Madison Square Garden a few nights ago, but today he was simply a mourner at the funeral of a dear family friend. Although we attracted lots of sidelong glances as we chatted, people gave him space and no one came rushing over to annoy him. Even Liz was busy chasing Liam.

'I didn't get a chance to ask you last night, but how are you now, after everything? And I don't mean Juliet.'

'So-so,' I said.

James was one of the few people I'd emailed about my crashed wedding in the immediate aftermath, conscious that The Name planned tour dates well in advance, so he'd have to know the band didn't need to be in the south of France on St Patrick's Day, after all. He'd called me immediately and had accepted that I didn't want to discuss it.

'Although …' I paused.

'Although what?' He tilted his head to one side and waited. 'Come on, spit it out, cuz.'

I decided it was safe enough to reveal the monster that had stalked my thoughts since Mum's horrific phone call. 'If things had gone ahead,' I said, 'Juliet would have been at my wedding and this wouldn't have happened.'

He bundled me against the front of his long navy overcoat. My head was stuck somewhere in his chest when he said, 'Danielle Ryan has managed to find a lovely stick to beat herself with. What time were you supposed to be getting married?'

'Five o'clock in the evening,' I said, my voice muffled.

'Right. Chances are, given how busy she was, Juliet would have planned to fly out that morning. And of all the conspiracy theories I've heard, that's pretty much the worst. Don't ever let me hear you repeat that, little cuz.'

He knew all about the police and the investigations from chatting to me and Mum last night and was just as bewildered as we were at the inexplicable circumstances surrounding Juliet's death.

'Right, big cuz.' We'd fallen into our nicknames for each other easily enough.

'Are you going with your mother to the crematorium?' he asked.

I shuddered at the thought of seeing Juliet's plain wooden

coffin sliding through the velvet curtains to what lay beyond. She'd told Mum, years ago, that she wanted her ashes scattered off the cliffs by Howth, and Mum was following her wish, even though we agreed how sadly absurd it seemed, given how she'd died. 'Yeah, I guess I'll have to go with her for company, although I don't think she needs me, and your parents are in the mourning car as well. How did you get out of that?'

'I'm staying in my apartment in the city centre and travelled from there.'

'Duh. Silly me, I'm not thinking straight.'

'How could you be? And I came in a specially borrowed car. I think Juliet would have approved.'

'I might have to approve it as well,' I said. 'If Mum doesn't mind, I'll take a lift with you.'

James tensed and looked over my head at someone beyond me.

'Somebody looks like he's anxious to talk to you. If you still want to come with me, I'll be waiting for you outside the side door.' He took his arms from around me and gave me a little push. Then I was face to face with Conor.

I'd hoped he'd leave quietly without talking to me, but he was too well mannered for that. A hysterical bubble rose in my throat – we should have been on our honeymoon. More poignantly, all the intimacy between us might as well have been sucked into a black hole, and I was like an awkward, self-conscious teenager.

I'd met Conor at Erin's thirtieth birthday party in the Odessa. I'd had a succession of unsatisfactory boyfriends and equally unsatisfactory relationships, and as soon as I was introduced to the software whiz, with the soft brown eyes, I'd thought it was the real thing. He seemed to feel the same about me.

Now his eyes were guarded. 'Danielle,' he said, taking my

hand as you would a stranger's, 'I'm so sorry about Juliet, I can't imagine how difficult this is for you but I know how much you loved her. I was very fond of her myself.' As his warm, familiar voice washed over me I thought I was going to cry. It wasn't quite three months since we had split up, and I had a sudden urge to throw myself into his arms and make it all right again, all the love and the laughter we'd shared. But nothing would ever make it right again.

'Thanks for coming,' I said, through the ocean of tears at the back of my throat.

'I couldn't not. How's your mother?'

'She's okay. It was a terrible shock, of course.'

'And not all that long after your father, either.'

'Six years,' I said softly, holding his gaze, recalling how he had comforted me during those terrible dark days.

'Wow, that long?'

It had been just before my father's death that we'd started going out, and all of a sudden I'd needed him so much it had cemented our relationship: the hospital dash that had been in vain, the funeral on a freezing cold and wet January day, the nights I couldn't sleep when he'd held me in his arms.

We both spoke at once.

'Time flies,' I said, so banal.

'You still have things left in—'

'I know.'

'They're safe, for whenever you want to collect.'

'Thanks.'

And just like that, we had exhausted the polite chit-chat suitable for funerals and there was nothing else to say. Nothing and everything, for it was all waiting to be thrashed out between us. What had gone wrong, how it had gone wrong, as well as the mundane details of breaking up our relationship and shared home, and on the other side of the huge chasm between us, there was a mountain of hurt and anger, but this wasn't the time or the place.

'We will have to talk, you know,' he said.

'Yes.'

'We can't just leave it in limbo.' He gave me a worried look.

'No.' I began to walk away, my legs trembling.

'Danielle?'

'Yes?' I half turned to glance back at him.

'Look after yourself, won't you?'

'I will, and you.'

I went in search of my mother, who had almost finished accepting condolences. People had started to drift away, and the hearse, the spray of lilies on the coffin, was ready to bring Juliet on her final journey. I told Mum I was getting a lift to the crematorium with James.

'That's fine,' she said. 'Did you see Conor?'

'I did.' I managed to keep my face neutral, though I could feel my mouth trembling.

'Good girl. See you later.' She gave me a warm smile – I'd held it together. She was thinking of me, instead of her own heartbreak. How had I ever felt irritable with her?

I slipped through the dispersing crowds back into the cathedral and out of the side door to where James was waiting, a gaggle of girls standing nearby laughing far too loudly and drawing as much attention to themselves as they could. When he saw me, he put on his shades and took my hand. Together we hurried around the side-streets to where his car was parked.

'Hey, little cuz, I thought we'd see Juliet off in style.'

It was a vintage soft-topped Triumph in classic red. He opened the passenger door with a flourish.

'Where did you get this?' I asked, amazed.

'I borrowed it from a friend just for today. Remind you of anything?'

'Of course,' I said, a lump in my throat. My earliest childhood memories of Juliet were of her coming to visit in her red Triumph, squealing to a halt outside the house, appearing very daring and glamorous as she hopped out of the car, with her short dark hair and leather trousers. She had sometimes brought me and James out for the day, to the sea, or the mountains, occasionally to Verbena View where I'd met her quiet, ladylike mother and tall, proud father, who had always slipped me and James crisp five-pound notes. Juliet used to pretend she'd kidnapped us and might never return us to our parents, and we had great fun going along with her game. She brought us to McDonald's, telling us it was a brilliant excuse for her to scoff their delicious stringy chips and cheeseburgers, and to pantomimes at Christmas, laughing as loudly as we did.

The engine roared, and James grinned as we pulled out on to the main road and joined the stream of cars behind the hearse. I began to cry then, silent tears that slipped down my cheeks and slid into my mouth. I heard myself sniff and rummaged furiously for my tissues. James said nothing, merely shoving his hand into the side compartment of the door and pulling out some Kleenex, which he handed to me. I was grateful for his silence and was composed when we reached the crematorium, as Juliet's coffin was lifted out of the hearse, the polished wood gleaming mockingly in the sunlight.

Then, after a short ceremony in a rather airless room, and to the sound of The Beatles' 'Here Comes The Sun', my beautiful Juliet was gone for ever and it was all over.

On the way back out through the porch, the final cadences

of the music were echoing in my ears, and the mourners were discussing the best way to get to the Merrion Hotel, where Robert Jordan had organised lunch. Something cold clutched my insides: we were leaving Juliet behind. Already life was moving on without her. On impulse I picked up the spray of lilies, which had been left in the porch. The final, flimsy link to my honorary mum.

'Are you hungry?' I asked James, carrying the flowers to the car, thinking how odd it was to be talking about food on a day like this.

'Not particularly, but I'm going to the Merrion anyway,' he said.

'Fancy making a detour?' I felt a little shaky as I said this, barely acknowledging to myself what I wanted to do.

James looked at the flowers in my hands, and his gaze travelled over my face, finally breaking into a smile. 'I think that's a great idea,' he said.

We drove back through the city centre, over the quays, then out to the north side and Howth Road. We swept up the hill close to Verbena View, where police tape still fluttered outside her house. James parked the car and opened the passenger door for me. I stepped out, the sea breeze so fresh and invigorating after the crematorium that it almost took my breath away. He held my hand as we walked, the spray of flowers tucked into my other arm.

Then the sparkling sea came into view.

I didn't know the spot where Juliet had fallen, and I was glad. I didn't know how long she'd lain injured, waiting for help, how much she'd known, how angry and terrified she might have been, but none of that mattered now, for it was over and she was beyond all pain. I took deep gulps of air, and felt strands of my hair escape from its clasp, whipping around my face as we absorbed the panorama. This was where I wanted to remember her for this was where her spirit danced and soared. This was all hers, the sea and the sky, the track around the headland. Her spiritual home, which she'd loved with every fibre of her being. When we were part of the way around, I buried my face in the spray of delicate flowers, inhaling the fragrance. Then I silently handed it to James. He reached out a long arm and sent it whirling as far as he could, so that it seemed to dance in the space between the sea and sky. I turned away as it began to fall. Then we held hands and walked back to the car.

FORTY

'Rebecca? How have you been?'

'I've seen better days,' Rebecca said, her hands tightening on her mobile as she stared out at the rain-washed garden. She had decided it was safe not to pretend with Liam. 'Danielle went back to Rome this morning and I dropped her out to the airport. It was good of her to stay on for a couple of days, but I miss her now.'

'Of course you do,' he said. 'It was lovely to see her. She's turned into a beautiful woman. You must feel very proud of her.'

'Yes, she is, and I do. That's why I was so gutted about her cancelled wedding. She deserves the best and I hate to see her upset. Not that we spoke about it.' She gave a half-laugh. 'It didn't get a look in because all our conversations revolved around Juliet.'

'Now that I've met her, Rebecca, I have to agree with what you said. If her fiancé broke it off with her, he doesn't deserve her and she's better off without him. If she cancelled her plans, she knew exactly what she was doing.'

'That's what's keeping me going. Why don't you come over for lunch?' she asked him. She hadn't seen him since the day of the funeral and it would be good to chat to him and reminisce about the day. By now, Sunday midday, it was already more than a week since Juliet had died. Rebecca knew, from Harry, how swiftly the weeks would fly by, how easily a loved one could slide into your past and their lives close over, unless you brought up happy memories of them with friends and family.

Rose had invited her to Belgrave Park that evening, as Matthew was hosting a drinks party for some of his inner circle, but it was the last place she wanted to be. Matthew would be trying to impress, and Rose … Rose had had such a look of desperation on her face on the day of the funeral, and she had sounded so edgy on the phone since then that, for once, Rebecca wanted to avoid her instead of jumping to the rescue. A case of healthy self-preservation.

'Thanks for the invite, but I don't think you'll want to see me for lunch,' Liam said ruefully.

'Why not? You're very welcome.'

'You haven't seen the tabloids this morning.'

'So?'

'Somebody thought it their duty to remind everyone about the heated exchange I had with Juliet before I legged it to Spain.' Liam sounded as if he was doing his best not to take it too seriously but his voice was tinged with annoyance.

'The heated exchange?' Rebecca was puzzled for a moment. Then, 'You're joking.'

'I'm not. Oh, it's all very carefully worded, not even a hint of libel, but the row we had has become a blazing quarrel, and it's also mentioned that I've just arrived back in Ireland, and the person with whom I had the altercation has had a most unfortunate accident.'

'Don't tell me, Liz fecking Monaghan,' Rebecca said, bile rising in her throat. 'What a perfectly horrible insinuation, with no regard to how you must be feeling about Juliet, never mind dishonouring her memory.'

'I don't care what she writes about me, I'm used to it, but I can't forgive her for dragging Juliet's name across her sordid page.'

In those halcyon days when Liam had been living the high life, he'd sometimes featured on Liz's society page as she regaled the nation with details of his lavish lifestyle.

'Liz Monaghan was always a bloody cow, but this is a new low,' Rebecca fumed. 'I don't know why she's decided to stick the knife into you. And I can't believe she featured Juliet like that. What the hell is she thinking of? She has no respect for Juliet, never mind her family or friends. No one with any decency will take any notice of what she's written.'

'How any editor had the gall to send it to print is beyond me.'

'Probably afraid of her tongue as well. She has no conscience.'

'About Juliet – have you heard anything from the police?'

'I haven't spoken to them since the day before the funeral.'

'So you don't know if there have been any further developments?'

'No, and I don't know how they operate, or what they do in these circumstances,' she said, feeling sad. 'There'll be an inquest, I expect.' There was a brief silence. Then Rebecca said, with forced cheer, 'Just relax, Liam, forget about Liz, and I insist you come for lunch. Better still, we should go out somewhere busy and public and be seen together. We'll stick our fingers up at Liz's grubby gossip.'

Liam laughed. 'Are you sure you want to be seen with me?'

'Don't you start believing the drivel that that poisonous pen wrote. Let's meet in the Shelbourne. The scene of the crime.'

'Are you serious?'

'Yes, I am. It'll show Liz we don't give a damn about her rubbishy column. I'll be there for two thirty. Meet you in the bar. Right? No excuses. I hope it's mad busy, that lots of people see us together and word gets back to that scheming bitch.'

Rebecca went upstairs to change out of her jeans into something a little smarter. Even though Danielle had stayed for less than a week, the house felt thick with the silence of empty rooms in which nothing but the light patter of rain on the windows disturbed the quiet. She felt a cold shiver as she went into her bedroom. All week, she'd been too busy and preoccupied to contemplate the huge gap that Juliet's death would leave in her life.

Far, far better to be meeting Liam than sitting here alone. That was the only reason she was meeting him for lunch, she told her reflection in the mirror. And if she had a sudden need to be around him, to relax in his company, to watch the warmth in his eyes as they talked, it had everything to do with staving off the emptiness of the day and the overwhelming sadness of loss.

❧❦

'You look great, Rebecca,' Liam said, when she arrived in the bar. He was sitting at a high table close to the window. He kissed her cheek, then pulled out a stool for her. 'Is three thirty okay for food?'

'It's perfect,' she said. The bar was humming with laughter and conversation, the iconic murals a splash of energy on the walls. Hard to believe life was still going on when Juliet was no longer around. She glanced outside. A constant stream of people passed the windows and taxis pulled in and out of the rank. Across the road on St Stephen's Green, the trees lining the perimeter of the park were frilled with baby green fuzz.

Spring. The renewal of life, whose cycle was fundamental and steadfast, no matter what else was happening in the world. She looked at Liam, took a deep breath and sank into the moment, feeling the tension that had gripped her all week dissolve. She was glad she was there: she was going to enjoy the afternoon, with this man as an antidote to the difficult week they'd had and the painful moments that lay ahead.

'However, Liam, I don't want a repeat of the last time I saw you in that restaurant,' she joked.

He looked startled, and then he smiled. 'Relax. I've ordered a bottle of champagne in honour of Juliet and I'm not going to waste a drop. Besides,' his voice softened a fraction, 'I'm not an angry bastard any more and I wouldn't dream of hurting you.'

'And, by the way, I asked you out,' Rebecca said, suddenly mindful of his financial constraints.

He shook his head. 'This is my treat, and please allow me.'

'In that case I will,' she said. 'I'll get you another time.'

'You'll probably have to. How've you been, really?'

'Too busy to think,' she told him. 'It hasn't hit me yet. I'm still numb and slightly stupefied by what's happened. I keep thinking of something I have to tell Juliet. Even today, when I was in the taxi coming here, I was about to text her to say I was meeting you …' Her voice trailed away.

'And what do you think she would have said?'

'If it was a text she would have replied either WTF or LOL. Or perhaps TAB.'

'What's TAB?'

'Totes Amazeballs.'

'Typical Juliet. I think it's safer to stick with LOL.' Liam laughed, an attractive and engaging sound, and she stared at him for a millisecond too long.

Liam looked at her with interest, as though he could read her thoughts. 'At the risk of putting my feet in it, I used to be jealous of your husband,' he said. 'Anytime I met you in Juliet's it was obvious you were still in love and very close to each other. You always seemed to be a warm, loving person and I wanted some of that.'

'Funny – I thought all the guys fancied Juliet.'

'She was my teenage crush, an exciting but empty kind of attraction. You, on the other hand—'

'Come off it, Liam.' Rebecca flapped her hand and ignored her quickening heartbeat. 'You were married yourself,' she pointed out.

'I was,' he admitted, 'and it was a mistake almost from the word go. I panicked, because I felt it was time I settled down with a wife and family. It's ancient history now. Then when Harry died … I didn't want to intrude at first, and later my head was somewhere else. Up my arse, to be precise.'

She burst out laughing. And then she recalled other times when Liam Corrigan had looked at her with interest, even years ago, when Harry was still alive and they'd met at Verbena View. Harry had been extra vigilant around her, but Liam had never overstepped the invisible boundary that Harry had silently marked out.

She wondered what Harry would say if he could see her now. They'd talked, of course, about what to do if the other went first, but just lightly, as though it was something that might happen in another century or two.

'If I go first, don't sit around moping,' Harry had said. 'You're allowed to grieve for a little while, and have a good cry, but after that, live your life, Rebecca. Go out there and live every day. Fill your life with good things and go on dates with men.'

'Dates with men? You mean sunbathing on the Riviera with

my French lover, or yachting with my Greek tycoon? Or what about touring South Africa with my toyboy?'

Harry had smiled. 'Of course, but only if they're good and kind.'

'Only if they're sexy and well hung, you mean,' she'd said, laughing. 'Like you.'

Little had they known how swiftly he'd be taken from her.

The champagne arrived and she touched her flute to his. 'To Juliet,' she said.

'Juliet,' Liam echoed. 'And to Harry.'

'Harry.' She smiled.

❧

'I know you don't feel up to it, but for my sake, can't you just pretend to be happy?' Matthew hissed, as they met in the hallway.

'Sometimes I feel I've been pretending most of my life,' Rose hissed back, momentarily shaken out of her usual restraint and gratified by his startled glance.

'This evening is important to me,' he said, his voice low and tight, mindful of the caterers taking over the kitchen and moving around with refreshments. 'You don't have to *do* anything, except smile. It's all being looked after.'

The doorbell chimed and he straightened his tie along with his shoulders as he went to open it. Rose saw him switch on a megawatt smile for the benefit of yet another political activist, who stood in the porch accompanied by his wife. A taxi was drawing away from the kerb. Rose wanted to ask the driver to take her somewhere. As the couple stepped inside, bearing flowers and wine, one of the hired waitresses moved forward with her tray of drinks, as composed as if she was the hostess. She looked barely twenty, and her slim figure was poured into a tight black dress. She had a beautiful Nordic face and a cascade of blonde hair. Another waitress, coming out of the kitchen, had short dark hair and red-glossed, pouty lips. She wondered if Matthew had hired them deliberately to sex up his campaign.

An informal evening, he'd said, when he'd suggested it just before Juliet's death. At home with the Moores. Drinks and nibbles for a few influential business friends. He'd hire caterers, and arrange for cleaners to do the necessary afterwards. Rose wouldn't have to lift a finger.

She had expected him to cancel the evening on account of Juliet's funeral earlier that week, but only yesterday he'd confirmed that it was going ahead. 'It's too late now to call it off,' he'd insisted.

'I just assumed …' She'd floundered.

Matthew had sighed impatiently. 'I understand you're still upset, but Juliet is the very person who'd tell us to go ahead with whatever plans we'd already made.'

'I feel as though my home and my life are being invaded when I least want it.'

'I don't have the luxury of time,' he'd snapped, looking distinctly hassled. 'Every day counts from now on. Every hour has to work for me. I'll make it up to you, Rose. I need you with me in this. I can't do it without you.' His blue eyes had been steadfast as they fastened on her.

She'd put on her Paul Costelloe silver sheath dress and white gold jewellery, then slid her feet into sparkly high heels and stared at herself in the mirror. She'd remembered for a fleeting moment a tartan A-line skirt she'd bought in Roches Stores that had once been her pride and joy and had cost the guts of two weeks' wages, never dreaming in those innocent days that, in time to come, she'd have an account at Brown Thomas, and a wardrobe chock full of designer clothes, courtesy of her successful husband.

Never dreamed, either, of the complex way their life together would become so entangled that she was being slowly suffocated.

She thought she'd looked the part as she greeted Matthew's guests, but some strain had shown in her face as she circulated around, hence Matthew's terse words.

Matthew escorted the political activist and his wife into the party, where more beautiful waitresses were gliding around with trays of canapés and sushi, and stuff Rose didn't recognise on cocktail sticks. The long, elegant room – they'd opened the interconnecting doors between drawing room and dining room – was filling with influential luminaries from business and political circles, milling about under the Waterford crystal chandeliers, against a backdrop of silk wallpaper and Irish paintings. Some were there because Matthew was keen to impress them, and others wanted to align themselves to his rising star, sensing the power struggle that was about to play out and hungry to be part of it.

After a while Rose slipped upstairs to cool her flushed cheeks, only to encounter a guest wandering along the landing. She tensed.

'Can I help you?' she said. 'There's a bathroom downstairs, if that's what you're looking for.'

The woman wheeled around, looking guilty, and Rose recognised her as Emma Brady, the wife of a prominent barrister.

'Rose! I've been caught trespassing. I'm terribly sorry,' she said sheepishly. 'I'm afraid my curiosity got the better of me. I was just sneaking a peek around the house of James Moore's parents. Sophie, my daughter, is a massive fan. She and I went to see The Name the last time they were in Croke Park.'

Rose felt dizzy with relief. She could manage this. 'Don't worry about it. Unfortunately James isn't here tonight. He went back to the States on Thursday after a flying visit. It was such a busy few days that I hardly saw him.'

He'd arrived and left in the space of three days, had disappeared with Danielle on the day of the funeral, both of them arriving in the Merrion Hotel just as people were starting to disperse. He'd been too busy with other engagements the following day to come over for lunch or dinner, merely calling in on the Thursday morning for coffee before his afternoon flight to New York. It had been just as well she hadn't seen very much of him, considering her dark frame of mind. All she could remember from Juliet's funeral service was the heart-rending image of James blinking back tears as he'd put his hand on the coffin.

'James never actually lived in this house,' she continued. 'He left home long before Matthew and I moved here.' The house had never resonated to the sound of his guitar in the way their earlier, more modest, homes had. Maybe that was partly why Belgrave Park felt so lonely and empty.

Delayed empty-nest syndrome had been one of the reasons trotted out for her breakdown. She'd nodded and watched the counsellor take note of it on her file, even though she knew it wasn't true. It was far preferable to having the counsellor probe deeper and deeper, no matter how non-threatening she had seemed in encouraging Rose to face a truth, for it was a truth Rose had no intention of confronting, even though it played havoc with her peace of mind.

Emma was talking. 'Of course, I don't know what I was thinking,' she said. 'I knew he was back in Dublin for Juliet Jordan's funeral. A terrible tragedy,' she went on. 'And you were a good friend of hers. It was incredibly sad.'

'Yes. Absolutely.'

Emma began to move back down the curved staircase towards the ground floor. 'And bitchy Liz Monaghan in that rag of a newspaper this morning didn't help matters.'

'I must have missed it,' Rose said, her pulse accelerating.

'A load of rubbish. She dragged up the row Juliet had with the property tycoon Liam Corrigan, or was it the other way around? She passed some cleverly worded but lethal comments about him arriving back in Ireland just as Juliet met with an accident.'

'But that's—' Rose stopped, her heart hammering, the staircase seeming to rise and fall in front of her eyes.

'Yes, verging on libel.' Emma paused on the stairs and looked up, her face a white blur to Rose. 'And from what I've heard on the grapevine, Liam Corrigan is a changed man. I think Liz would want to watch her step very closely indeed …' Emma's voice receded as she moved down the stairs so Rose missed her last words in the cadences of laughter and conversation floating up from the party.

On the landing, she gripped the mahogany banister and slowly let out her breath. She'd been about to speak when luckily Emma had interrupted her. She'd been about to blurt out something along the lines that it was silly to assume Liam had had anything to do with Juliet's accident when someone else had a far better reason for wanting her out of the way.

Someone like Matthew.

Or maybe even someone like Rose.

FORTY-ONE

Sometimes, during those first few days back in Rome, it was easy to forget I'd been home to Ireland for Juliet's funeral. The office was busy, we were now officially in summertime and the evenings had lengthened. At odd moments, dream-like snippets of it all would catch me off guard, sending the blood pounding through my head so that I felt dizzy. All the emotive images of those strange days were packed between Mum waiting in Arrivals on the Monday evening, with a brave smile, then pulling up outside Departures the following Sunday morning and jumping out of the car to give me a hug.

She'd dropped me at the airport many a time, and I'd usually said a hasty goodbye, my mind on the journey ahead, but for the first time, my concern was all for her as I steadied my case on the pavement and turned to say goodbye. All about us, cars were pulling in and disgorging travellers, and an Aer Lingus jet passed over our heads, engines screaming.

'Are you sure you'll be okay?' I searched her face and pictured her going back to the empty house, learning to live without her friend just as she'd learned to live without Dad all those years ago. Mum has a friendly face and a ready smile, and sometimes I thought she looked too soft and considerate, as though you might take advantage of her, but now I knew that her demeanour masked a core of steel.

'Of course, darling. I'll be fine. I'm going back to work on Monday, so that will keep me busy.'

'Let me know if you have any news about …' I couldn't bring myself to say 'about the cause of Juliet's death', but Mum knew what I meant.

'I will, straight away.'

'And wish Rose and Matthew the best of luck from me. Do you think it will actually happen? That he'll secure a nomination? James said—'

'What did James say?'

I knew my words wouldn't go any further. 'He said he's fully behind his father, but thinks he's being overly ambitious. He has the impression that, in spite of all his success, his father is still trying very hard to prove himself. Which he can't understand.'

'Very often, Danielle, we don't know what's truly going on behind the scenes. We can only accept people as they are and run with that.'

Once upon a time, in the days when I thought I knew everything, I would have commented that Mum was being her usual, ultra-tolerant self, but after the last few months I found myself in total agreement with her. Not even Mum knew what was going on behind the scenes in my life, and maybe this was her way of acknowledging that that was okay for both of us.

'Do you think you'll be seeing Liam now and then?'

'I don't know. Maybe. He's a friend from years back, and he's a link to both Harry and Juliet.'

'I won't feel too bad about going off if he's there to keep an eye on you. I don't think you can count on Rose for much support at the minute. All her energy will be going into Matthew's campaign.'

'And that's only right,' Mum said. We gave each other a final hug and she wished me safe travel. I wheeled my case across the pedestrian crossing, turning for a last wave before Mum drove away and I went inside the steel and glass monolith of Terminal Two.

Back in Rome, Erin was great. She didn't flutter around me with twenty questions. She seemed to know I was feeling subdued and had lots on my mind. She gave me time to settle back into the routine and find my own level. Even Gemma was more careful and considerate around me. But I couldn't slide back into the closed, defensive, uptight person I'd been when I'd first arrived in Rome. I don't know if it was because time had healed a little, or if a chink had opened in my shield after my trip back to Dublin. Or if the cold finality of Juliet's death had put things into perspective for me.

Things like, my heart wasn't going to break in two if I had to live without the man I loved. It could be done, on the physical and the emotional level. Things like, it was far more important that he was alive and well, laughing and talking and going about his normal day, and I could learn to accept that I would not feature as I wanted to in his life. My love for him didn't need to be spoken of, acknowledged or even acted upon to be legitimate. The reality that I loved him enough to let him go was validation in itself.

These were the lofty ideas that streamed through me as I sat at my desk inputting data on a spreadsheet, went for lunch with Erin and Gemma in quirky little restaurants, and dodged the traffic on the Piazza Venezia on the way home from work. I wasn't sure what had prompted them, beyond a changed perspective. And, despite my sadness over Juliet, I knew I would survive.

At least, I thought I would until I had an unexpected visitor.

FORTY-TWO

'Well, Dave, it's spill-the-beans time. What have you got for me on the Jordan case?' Liz asked. In Dave's bed, she propped herself on her elbow and scraped a red fingernail down his bare chest.

Dave grinned at her and looped an arm around her shoulders. 'I should have known you had an ulterior motive when you turned up here. You're not still banging on about our friend Juliet?'

She traced circles with her nail on his taut belly. 'I never said she was my friend and you should know if there have been any developments. Come on, dish the dirt.'

'You're hoping I'll say Liam Corrigan has been hauled in for questioning, especially after your hatchet job.'

Liz widened her eyes in mock-innocence. 'Why should I hope that? Liam is a friend of mine.' Her lips curved in a smile.

'He won't be after the way you kicked him in the bollocks last Sunday.'

'I never!' She slid her hand lower and cupped him.

'You as good as …'

She squeezed, until he gasped. 'For fear that I might meet similar treatment,' he said, lifting her hand and placing it outside the duvet, 'I can tell you that, according to my source, Liam had already called to the police station to give a statement. Even before Juliet's funeral. Apparently he'd dropped in to see her late that afternoon and left after a short while. So that's that.'

'So he's guilty as hell.'

It was his turn to sit up and fix a pillow behind his head. 'Guilty of what? Sorry, Liz, it was all perfectly innocent, and I hope I won't regret giving you that snippet of information.'

She lay back and cuddled into the duvet. 'So do I – hope you won't regret it, I mean.'

'You're dangerous, you know that?'

'So I've been told.' She giggled. 'But only by people who have something to hide.'

'What makes you think there's anything to hide in this case? Is that the only reason you came over and hopped on me? You think I have some insider knowledge?'

'I know you have your sources, and I have a suspicion that Juliet Jordan wasn't all she was cracked up to be.'

Dave threw her a puzzled look, alerted no doubt by her bitter tone. Liz reminded herself that she needed to stay in control.

It had been one thing to lose herself in Dave's arms. She'd been glad when he'd answered her call and told her he'd be happy to see her. Both of them had known without saying where it would lead. And she'd wasted no time. After a glass of wine, she'd sat on the sofa and begun to kiss him. She'd enjoyed their romp in bed – at the very least it had given her a physical release and obliterated the memory of the cruel way she rejected Gavin. It had been easy to close her eyes and pretend, just for a moment, that it was Gavin who was touching and stroking and bringing her to the brink before tipping her over the edge. For that moment it had felt so good, so right, so brilliant that she had revelled in it, only crashing back to earth when she opened her eyes and saw Dave's face above hers, his glazed look telling her he was about to come. She'd felt a shard of regret when she'd thought of what she could have had with Gavin, if things had been different.

If *she* had been different. If her life had been different, and she'd known a few truths.

Dave stroked her hair away from her face. 'I'm not sure what your agenda is, Liz,' he said, 'but, speaking as a friend, I think you should tread very carefully. Juliet was very highly thought of by most people, and now that she's met with an unfortunate accident, she'll be even more revered. Joe Public is very upset over her untimely death.'

'So the police are happy that it was an accident?'

'I didn't say that. Their investigation is still open. But if you start throwing mud in her direction it could boomerang and stick all over you. You barely escaped with it last Sunday. You were so close to the bone that even I almost choked on my breakfast.'

She fastened her eyes on him in what she hoped was a suitably seductive fashion. 'Oooh, we can't have that,' she murmured. She pushed the duvet off him, and gazed down at his naked body. 'I'll have to make that up to you,' she said, reaching out for him as she kicked the duvet off herself and straddled him.

'This is just for you, Dave,' she said, guiding him into her and moving down on him very slowly. She savoured the moment, clenched herself around him, and began to rock back and forth. 'Just for you,' she murmured. 'No strings whatsoever.'

'You're a witch, Liz,' he said, pulling her face to his.

'Believe me, I've been called far worse.'

∂∾⋌

It was later than she'd realised when Liz left Dave's inner-city apartment. Although pale blue light lingered in the western sky, banks of pewter clouds were gathering in the east. When she reached the traffic lights at Christchurch, she felt like going home and shutting the door on the world, but there were things to do and papers to check, so she took the turn for the north side of the city and soon she was sweeping into Upper Ballymalin Grove.

She parked her car on the gravel driveway and opened the complicated lock on the front door. The hall smelt musty and the chill hit her as soon as she stepped inside. Her footsteps echoed as she walked around, switching on lights and the central heating. Then she stood outside the living room and steeled herself before she went in.

It was almost two weeks since she'd sat on the floor of this room, sifting through the papers and documents that had turned her life upside-down. In that time she'd begun to wonder if she had misinterpreted what she'd seen, but everything was scattered across the carpet exactly as she'd left it in her haste to escape the brutal facts that were staring her in the face.

The same name leaped out at her now: *Juliet Jordan.*

She'd never be able to confirm the truth with Juliet. She got down on her knees, and her hands trembled as she gathered everything together and replaced the papers in the faded envelope she'd found at the back of the bureau, stuck between old photo albums she'd been emptying. Annie Monaghan had meant her to find this, Liz realised. She'd wanted her to know. This envelope had lain untouched since before she'd died, more than twenty-three years ago. But across that space and time, she had suddenly reached out to Liz.

Liz shivered uncontrollably and took several deep breaths. She tried to cry, but the tears wouldn't come through the wall of anger and confusion that wrapped around her. After a short while she got to her feet and picked up the crystal-framed photographs that had sat on top of the bureau for years of Liz on her Communion and Confirmation days, taken with her parents.

Her loving parents and their happy family. Not.

She picked up the Communion photograph and bashed the frame against the side of the bureau until the glass broke into smithereens and fell to the carpet in a hail of glitter. She pulled out the photograph and stared at it, Tom Monaghan, tall and dark, very good-looking in his day, his arm curled around Annie, his blonde, petite wife. Liz ripped it up, let the pieces fall to the carpet and ground them into the crystal shards. Then she did the same to her Confirmation photograph.

In the kitchen, she searched until she found an unopened bottle of whiskey. She rinsed a glass and sloshed some into it, topping it up with water. Her teeth chattered against the glass as she drank. When it was finished, she helped herself to more, knowing she couldn't drive home now. Then she poured enough whiskey down her throat to make sure she'd sleep. Later she turned off the central heating, but left all the lights on as she went into her childhood bedroom. She lay on the bed and fell into a deep sleep.

The following morning she locked the house, securing everything. This time she had with her the faded envelope as she went to her car. The morning was so grey and overcast that the shrubbery, lining the boundary of the garden, was a startling green against the drab background.

She pulled into the first service station she came to, and sat on a stool inside the plate-glass window sipping scalding coffee out of a cardboard cup and making an effort to nibble at a blueberry muffin. She stared out at the traffic surging by and wondered how she could get to the bottom of everything now that Juliet was gone.

Her mind flew back to the funeral service, just over a week ago. Outside the cathedral she'd spoken briefly to Matthew Moore, his aura of smooth confidence getting up her nose. His wife, Rose, however, was the opposite. Her eyes had darted nervously about and Liz wondered yet again what secrets she might be hiding. Someone with such a successful lifestyle and rich, handsome husband ought to be happy and contented. A thought struck her, like a blinding light: was Rose edgy around her because she knew something she thought Liz was unaware of? Something that perhaps her sister had told her?

There had been another person at the funeral, who surely knew all there was to know about Juliet. She'd spoken eloquently about friendship, and the importance of female kinship, her love for her friend apparent in her moving words.

'We go back a long way, Juliet and I …'

Surely if Juliet had confided in anyone it would have been her closest friend. The friend who was also a connection between Juliet and the Monaghans. Liz squeezed the cardboard cup of coffee so tightly that some of the hot liquid spilled on to her hand. She didn't notice it.

Rebecca.

FORTY-THREE

'Why didn't I do this before?' Liam said, as they crested the hill and the breadth and sweep of the Dublin mountains unrolled before them, a panorama of flinty grey granite and yellow gorse running through folds of green, indigo and purple. Springtime had cast a fuzz over the pockets of trees and shrubs that dotted the route, and sunshine licked the tender green shoots so that they were almost iridescent. Behind them, and far below the curve of the terrain, the city unfurled.

Rebecca paused beside him. 'I love coming up here at this time of the year. It's wonderful to see everything coming alive again after the long grey winter.' More importantly, it was a pilgrimage of renewal after the dark, upsetting days they'd just been through. She didn't need to say that: she knew from Liam's smile that he understood.

'Do you go hill walking often?'

'Once a month. I joined the group after Harry died. It's a great way of forgetting your worries and shifting your perspective, and this is my favourite time of year for it. Occasionally I brought Juliet up here, but mostly she dragged me around her cliffs,' Rebecca said easily. She hoped that, wherever Juliet was, she was as peaceful and serene as she herself felt.

It had been Rebecca's idea to go out for the afternoon. She'd returned to her job at Olivia Jayne the previous Monday but, much as she loved it, it had suddenly seemed so pointless. By midweek she'd been feeling hemmed in and even jittery, and the call from Detective Woods on Tuesday evening hadn't raised her low spirits.

'We've no further leads,' Detective Woods had said. 'If you think of anything, no matter how small or insignificant it may seem, please contact me straight away.'

'So there have been no developments at all?'

'No. We've had a big response from people who were out walking that evening but nothing we can pin down and no definite sighting of Juliet,' Detective Woods had said. 'The glasses we found in the house are being checked for DNA and fingerprints but I think they were too partial to be viable. We've examined the lie of the land above where Juliet was found and it's quite possible she could have slipped, particularly if the track was damp.'

'What's going to happen now?'

'In the absence of anything suspicious or questionable, the case will be wound down.'

It would be filed away, Rebecca had thought bleakly. Her friend's death would just be another statistic, a dusty file on a shelf. Juliet didn't deserve that.

Liam had called her later that evening, and she'd filled him in on what the detective had said. He was spending the week equally cooped up, but in his case it was with his accountants and solicitors, as he sifted through the financial wreckage he'd left behind.

'Any chance you could be free tomorrow afternoon?' she'd asked him.

'If it's for you, I am.'

Then she'd suggested hill walking. 'Nothing too strenuous,'

she'd said. 'I'll go easy on you the first time. I really need to get away from it all, even for one afternoon.'

'Count me in. I'd love that, thanks,' he'd said.

She'd picked him up outside his Rathmines apartment and driven up into the mountains, where she'd parked the car and taken one of the many walking trails that criss-crossed them. The afternoon was cool, but the morning's rain had died away and a pale sun peeped out occasionally from behind thin cloud.

'If you'd asked me to go hill walking a couple of years ago, I would have laughed,' Liam said. 'If it didn't include champagne, involve a flashy car or cost a fortune, I didn't want to know. Sometimes I can't help thinking what a fool I was.'

To Rebecca's surprise, she found herself stepping forward impulsively and putting a finger across his lips. 'Shush. You're not allowed to talk like that. What's done is done and it's in the past. And it doesn't suit you, Liam, to put yourself down.'

His mouth felt soft beneath her fingers. All of a sudden she could imagine kissing those lips. Kissing Liam Corrigan. Making up for some of his hurts. Letting him make up for some of hers. Time froze as they stared at each other, and then she dropped her hand as though it stung and took a quick step backwards.

'Don't tell me you preferred the old arrogant me?' he said, with a gleam in his eye.

'I'm not saying that,' she told him, a little waspishly, 'but I'd rather see you with some of your original spirit instead of this – this crappy self-disparagement. It doesn't solve anything. And I planned today as a day out, just for us, away from everything. Time out that we both need. It wasn't to have you beat yourself up because a while ago you couldn't see what was under your nose.'

He caught her hand and brought it to his lips again. Then he turned it over and watched her face as he kissed the palm. She felt as though he was kissing her on the mouth and her heart leaped.

'I like that, Rebecca,' he said. 'A day out, just for us. And I love the way you're not afraid to give me a boot in the right place, if I'm being self-indulgent. You look gorgeous when you're indignant.'

'Right then.' She grinned, ignoring the somersault in her chest. 'We've a bit of a way to go yet before we stop for food.'

'So there's food. All this and heaven too.'

'I was hardly going to starve you. Or myself. I have a lovely pub in mind where they do fabulous chowder and smoked salmon on brown bread.'

They fell into step once more, cresting the brow of another hill, where blue-green folds merged into one another, then took a path through the woods where the breeze whispered among the trees, and above their heads, patches of blue sky peeked down between the shifting canopy of branches. Rebecca let the healing power of her surroundings seep into her bones.

⊱⊰

The whitewashed pub boasted an aromatic turf fire and a vaulted timber ceiling. Trade was brisk, but they managed to nab a small table, with a view across the valley, just as some customers were leaving. They sat side by side and ordered seafood chowder and Dublin Bay prawn salad with homemade brown bread.

'I could sit here for ever,' Liam said afterwards, sipping his coffee.

'So could I,' Rebecca said.

'I feel like I'm playing truant from school. Rebecca, I …' He paused.

'Yes?'

He reached for her hand and held it gently. 'I know things won't be great with me for a while, and it's going to take time, especially for you, to come to terms with Juliet's death, but I meant what I said when we met in the hotel, about seeing each other. That's if you want to. On the other hand,' he grinned, 'you might just want to tell me to sling my hook and get out of your hair.'

'If I hear any more negative talk like that, I certainly will,' Rebecca said, with feeling. 'Look, Liam,' she went on gently, 'we both have history and complications in our lives, and at the moment things are topsy-turvy for both of us, but let's take it a day at a time. And let's make a pact.'

'Okay …'

'No matter what kind of crappy day we're having, you and I will try to be as positive as we can. Think happy thoughts. Even if we have to make an effort to turn something around, we'll do it.'

'And can we do happy things as well?'

'Of course. There are lots of days out around Dublin and activities that won't bore a hole your pocket …' As she met his eyes, her throat dried.

'Because I wish I could kiss you, Rebecca,' he said, his grip tightening on her hand. 'That would be a happy thing for me. I wanted to kiss you when I heard you speak at Juliet's funeral service and you asked everyone to remember something funny about her. It was perfect and you melted my heart. I wanted to kiss you the night we first met in the hotel, and you listened to me prattling on, even though you had worries of your own. I wanted to wrap you in my arms and kiss you when you told me about having to go and identify Juliet's body, and make up for such an ordeal. Harry was a very lucky man. Granted, his life was cut short, but the time he had was surely blessed. So, in the muddle all around me, you're the one honest, attractive and beautiful thing.'

Rebecca's face was hot. Sensations she'd long forgotten were chasing each other around her body. Her skin felt alive with anticipation. She stared out at the landscape, shimmering in the spring. She wondered what Juliet would say if she saw her now. *Go for it …*

And Harry? *Live your life …*

Liam was still talking: 'You must know I'm very fond of you, Rebecca. I love the way your face glows when you talk about your family. I'd love your face to glow like that when you talk about me. But I don't want to rush you and, as I said, I'm not exactly—'

'Hush.' She forestalled him. 'What did I just say? Only happy thoughts. Right?'

'Oh, I have some very happy thoughts,' he said, a smile playing on his lips. 'I just wish I wasn't sitting here now, in a busy bar.'

Something light-hearted freed itself from the dark tunnel of recent days and rose up inside Rebecca. She had the sense of being alive to something new, and not only revelling in the anticipation darting around her body but being grateful for it. 'I think it's perfect that we're sitting here. I hope some of Liz Monaghan's friends are around, if she has any left. This will tell her what I think of her nasty innuendoes.'

Then she moved into him and kissed him on the lips. It was brief, but it was warm and enticing enough to make her feel that everything about it was right.

❧❦

Later, she drove him back to Rathmines.

'I daren't ask you in just yet,' he said. 'The apartment is upside-down. Everywhere I look there's a sea of paper and forms that I'm still trying to organise.'

'No worries. I'm going home for a long soak in the bath,' she said, glad to be putting space between them: she wanted to get her head around the way he made her feel alive again to the endless possibilities of life.

'Don't be saying those suggestive things to me,' he said in a husky voice.

An unexpected wave of desire flashed through her. 'Just as well I'm going home,' she said.

'You might never talk to me again if you knew what I was thinking.'

A tiny pause, and he smiled at her, murmured her name and took her into his arms. This time they kissed tenderly and slowly. Her face was hot by the time they moved apart and she swayed against him.

'You're lovely, Rebecca, but far too tempting. I'd better get going while we're still friends,' he said, opening the door and climbing out.

She watched him as he mounted the steps, his long legs taking them two at a time. She was about to drive off, her foot poised on the accelerator, but something made her pause: a speck of glimmering sunlight peeping below a silvery rift in the clouds, the sound of birdsong flowing across the calm evening, the way Liam had looked at her as he told her she was beautiful? The feeling of his mouth on hers? Hope and expectation coursed through her veins. Life was precious and, oh, so transient. It was not only right but necessary to make the most of everything and to appreciate whatever gifts the universe saw fit to send your way.

FORTY-FOUR

By four o'clock on Friday I was in countdown mode for the weekend, dying to get away from the office and the endless spreadsheets. It was a bright afternoon in Rome, a thick band of sunlight streaming across the ochre-stone buildings opposite, reminding me of what spring looked like. It didn't seem right that the sun should be shining now that Juliet wasn't around to see it, that she was gone and we didn't know why or exactly how. I was staring at my screen but wondering how I was going to fill the hours until Monday. Everything seemed meaningless, especially on a Friday night.

Even Gemma was shooting me worried glances. She was chattering on about a new club she'd discovered in picturesque Trastevere, trying to round up a crowd to go there and telling me it might do me good to get out for the night, but I was sunk in a quagmire of sadness and anger.

More worryingly, all the noble ideas I'd had about the man I loved, which had helped keep me sane in the immediate aftermath of Juliet's death and my return to Rome, seemed irrelevant now that real life was rumbling on around me. It was one thing to acknowledge that I'd never be part of his life in the way I wanted, but as shock gave way to sadness, I just wanted to cry on his shoulder and be entwined in his arms.

I had just decided I was going to get pissed enough to blank out the whole weekend when my mobile bleeped with a new message. It was from James, short and to the point: *Hey lil cuz what time r u off at? J*

I texted back that I'd be in the office for another hour. I guessed he wanted to call me when I was free. We hadn't talked since Juliet's funeral: he'd returned to America almost straight away and was busy with tour dates in Boston, Chicago and Pittsburgh.

They're working u 2 hard! ☹
Some of us have to earn a living
And some of us are sipping G+T ...
Jealous.com
... in the St Michel

It took a minute for that to sink in. Then I was all fingers.

What??? Here?
Call over as soon as yur thru ☺

I took a deep breath, then another, as everything crashed through my head and the empty Friday night altered completely. James here in Rome? In the St Michel? I was gripped by a sudden wave of euphoria, until I reminded myself that I was stuck in the office until five. Not only that but I was in my office clothes of slim black trousers and a grey shirt. Hardly suitable to darken the illustrious door of that glitzy hotel, let alone cross the foyer.

Not glammed up enuf
Who cares? Lining up a cocktail 4 u

From across the work-station, Gemma had watched it all. 'Is everything okay, Danielle?'

'Yes, fine.'

It was and it wasn't. It was brilliant and fantastic and crap all at once. I didn't know why James was in Rome, or for how long, and wonderful as it would be to see him, if we were talking for any length of time, he was one person it would be difficult to fob off about my cancelled wedding. I'd got away with not talking about it in Dublin because we'd been wrapped up in Juliet and her funeral.

And it would be hard too, given our shared history with Juliet, to paper over the cracks of her absence.

'My cousin has arrived in Rome,' I said, 'so I'll be meeting him after work and won't be able to go clubbing after all.'

'Why don't you bring him too?'

'I don't know what his plans are,' I said, smothering a hysterical giggle.

Thankfully, she didn't know that James was an international star, fresh from a sell-out tour of the States, and would cause a major security incident if he happened to step into a nightclub in Rome. Erin knew of him, of course, and had met him in Dublin several times over the years, but she wasn't around so I didn't feel the need to explain anything to anybody.

At half past four, I went out to the Ladies and refreshed my makeup. Then on the dot of five, I left the office and headed for the St Michel. The pavements were crowded with workers streaming out of offices and the ever-present tourists, but the hotel was less than two miles from work and it was far quicker to walk than take a taxi through the congested traffic.

I hadn't realised quite how lonely I was in Rome, despite Erin, until James uncoiled himself from a deep armchair at the far end of the hotel foyer and stood up. He was wearing black jeans and a black shirt, and his wide mouth was curved in a big smile. He opened his arms and I flew into them, choked up at the warm familiarity of him, and the link he represented to home and Juliet. He ruffled my hair as I clung to him, the top of my head barely reaching his shoulder. I knew all the staff were watching covertly, even though they were keeping a respectful distance and pretending to be engrossed in their jobs, but at that moment I needed his hug so much that I didn't care.

'Hey, Dani – are you okay?'

I made a monumental effort to pull myself together, stepped away and sat down, balancing on the edge of one of the sofas. 'I'm fine.' I gave a shaky grin. 'It's just so lovely to see you. I've been feeling a bit upside-down.'

'Thought you might.' He sat down beside me, sinking right into the sofa and stretching out his legs. For a moment I thought he was a mirage.

'How come you're here?'

'We finished in the States on Tuesday night, and this weekend it's Croatia to shoot a video before we wind up the tour with a couple of East European dates. The rest of the guys are in Croatia now, but I got them to drop me off in Rome so that I could see for myself that my little cuz was okay after everything. Now I'm glad I came.' He put his head to one side and smiled.

'So, what's the plan? You're just in Rome for the evening? Nothing like having a private jet at your disposal.'

'It's handy for getting around, all right. I fly out in the morning. Here, I ordered this for you,' he said, handing me a Bellini. 'You look like you need it.'

I took a long slug of the cocktail. 'This is lovely, ta.'

'We could have a couple of drinks here and go for food. Or

else, if I put on a big pair of shades, do you think we could go out and mingle with the crowds? I flew in earlier today and crashed out for a couple of hours, but I'd love to stretch my legs. And I haven't seen much more of Rome since we gigged here than the inside of the stadium.'

I looked around the ornate, high-ceilinged foyer, at the gilt and marble décor, the sumptuous sofas. The elegant five-star hotel was shiny and beautiful, and then I thought of the sunlit evening outside, the lively, cheerful city.

'Let's go out as soon as I've finished this,' I said. 'But I can't guarantee you won't be papped.'

'I'll take that risk.'

'I'll probably be camouflage of some kind. I look far too mousy to be in the presence of greatness.' I said it lightly, tongue-in-cheek, and James gave me a sharp glance.

'I've a good mind to ground you for that crappy remark,' he said.

'Come on, I'm in my work clothes, and they're not exactly glam, are they? And grounding me would be a bit difficult,' I said, 'considering my apartment is on the other side of town.'

'You always were contrary, little cuz.'

'Ah, thanks,' I said. 'I'm the naughty little sister you never had.'

'So it seems,' he said, his face unreadable.

෨෪

When we'd finished our drinks, he brought me upstairs to his enormous, deluxe room and I nosed around, teasing him about the sumptuousness while he checked his email.

'I only get to see the inside of a five-star luxury suite when I bump into you on a tour somewhere,' I said, 'but this is the most decadent yet.'

'Is it?' He gave it a casual glance.

'Yes, you chump.'

'One hotel room looks like another to me.'

'What a waste.'

'Why? What do you think I could use it for, besides sleep?'

'Never mind.'

I helped myself to some of the freebie toiletries in the enormous bathroom.

'Are you that hard up?' he asked, picking up his jacket.

'No, but these are irresistible,' I said, showing him my hoard of designer soap and bath oil, comb and paper tissues before I threw them into my bag. 'Don't worry, there were three of everything so I've left some for you.'

I felt several pairs of eyes boring into my back as we crossed the foyer and walked out of the hotel. As we stepped into the sunny evening, the atmosphere at the heart of old-town Rome surrounded us: hectic, warm, almost carnival, the air redolent with the scent of olives under the traffic fumes; ancient palaces and dusty old churches side by side with dazzling graffiti. James whipped out a pair of wraparound sunglasses from the pocket of his leather jacket, but there was no disguising his wavy dark hair, which he had always worn shaggy. It stopped an inch or two above his shoulders. I knew that, as a teenager, he had grown it long to annoy his father, and when The Name had begun to establish themselves, his hair had stuck as one of their hallmarks.

We were a few streets away from Piazza Navona, where I thought it would be good to sit over some food and a drink, and we strolled along without attracting too much attention.

I sensed the ripple of is-it-really-him interest coming from an occasional group of tourists, who stopped in their tracks and raised their cameras, some more discreetly than others, but we weren't unduly bothered. I don't think they quite believed that James Moore of The Name was wandering through the back-streets of Rome with an ordinary girl in very ordinary clothes.

Even though James had been famous for years, I still found it funny that the cousin I'd grown up with and seen falling off his bike and crying over an injured kitten was now making heads turn and causing grown women to giggle and simper. That the guy I'd watched kangaroo-hopping Juliet's Triumph around the quiet roads of Howth as he learned to drive could impel an audience of eighty thousand to remain on their feet, waving lit mobile phones, in a dark stadium for three encores, right until the last notes of his guitar resonated into the night. Rob might be the lead singer, Gary the drummer, and Steve played lead guitar, but at six feet two James, with his long legs and lean hips, was the most striking figure on stage. It was no wonder I felt extra tiny as we walked to Piazza Navona, where we sat down at a table on the canvas-covered terrace of a restaurant.

By now, the shadows were lengthening, candlelight flickered on the table, and above us, tiny jewelled fairy lights threw a warm glow over our heads. There was a buzz in the atmosphere, the scents of herbs and spices mingling with perfume, laughter and chat rising above the chink of glasses and cutlery. Rome on a Friday evening.

James ordered a bottle of champagne without checking the drinks menu.

'So, how've you been, Dani?' he asked, leaning across the table towards me as soon as the waitress had hurried off in a ferment of excitement.

I knew he was in serious mode when he called me Dani. 'Really? It's crap,' I said, fiddling with the strap of my bag.

'I know.'

'I'm just finding everything so surreal,' I told him, over the lump in my throat. 'I can't believe I won't be visiting Juliet at Verbena View again.'

'Same here,' he admitted. 'I've never lost anyone I loved so much before, not that I wasn't fond of your dad.'

'You don't have to explain. Juliet was out on her own.'

'Holy shit.' He was staring into space. 'It's a bummer.'

'After losing Dad I know what to expect, not that it makes it any easier.'

'And what can I expect? You might as well tell me.'

'You really want to know?'

'Yes, little cuz, I do.'

I paused for a minute, arranging my thoughts. With my index finger I traced invisible doodles on the tablecloth as I spoke, giving me something else to focus on instead of his eyes. 'There's disbelief, such as now, mixed with a kind of unreality. Then there's anger, that she's gone and you're totally helpless to change it, gut-wrenching sadness that can take you by surprise when you least expect it, and there are moments,' I went on softly, my fingers running in circles and figures of eight, 'when you might feel you're going absolutely mad, crazy, but that's normal.'

I could have gone on – I can't sleep, I'm not eating properly, I'm drinking too much – but I wasn't going to admit to being such a total gibbering mess, especially when it wasn't only on account of Juliet.

For I wasn't only talking about Juliet. Or Dad. I was talking about the horrible sense of loss I felt, the howling anger and sadness, the utter helplessness that the love I wanted to share with all my heart, mind and body was impossible.

Our champagne arrived, and James poured it with a flourish, then handed me a fizzing glass. We waited until the waitress had left the table – she'd spent longer than necessary fixing a white cloth over the ice bucket.

'Sorry I wasn't around much when you were going through that after your dad,' James said.

'You were there when it mattered. I went back to work too, you know. It does get easier, in time. But you never stop missing them. Other people come and go in your life but there's always a space where they used to be. It's hard and jagged around the edges at first, then it begins to soften, but it never goes away.'

He picked up my left hand and looked at my ringless finger. 'Speaking of spaces, is there a big one in your life now that Conor's out of it? And I don't want the stock answer, Dani. We've never pretended to each other, have we?'

'No,' I lied, swallowing hard.

'You never got to tell me what really happened. Although I didn't help in that I was a few hundred miles away at the time.'

'I hardly spoke to anyone about it, James. Not even Mum.'

'Too sore?'

'Exactly.'

'So Conor hurt you badly?'

'Not exactly.'

'Hmm.' He gave me a long, searching look. 'I'd like to know if you need big cuz to go and beat the crap out of him, because if he hurt you, that's what I'd want to do.'

'You don't have to do that.'

'So if he didn't exactly hurt you badly, what did he do that there's no wedding? Last time I saw you guys together you were talking about your hen and stag parties, and we were working out the play list for the post-ceremony knees-up.'

'I know,' I said, remembering it all too well. Christmas, at Verbena View, the group of us gathered around the kitchen table, when all the tumblers had clicked into place in my head.

'Conor didn't do anything,' I said. I'd known I'd have to face this with James sooner or later, that he wouldn't rest until he got to the bald, honest truth, but it was even more difficult than I'd thought it would be.

James raised an eyebrow. 'No other woman? No deciding he suddenly had cold feet? All those reasons, by the way, are traitorous in my book if committed against you and they need to be punished.'

I gave a half-smile that somehow went wrong when my mouth trembled.

He spotted it immediately. His hand gripped mine. 'Hey, Dani – sorry if I'm upsetting you, big plonker that I am.'

'You're not a plonker,' I said. 'But there's no need to go dragging Conor down a back alley in search of retribution.' I took a deep breath and went on, 'You're the first person I've said this to, so, hey, you're privileged, but it was me.' I gulped. 'I'm the one who called off the wedding and gave Conor back his ring.'

His brows drew together in disbelief. 'You?'

'Yes, it was all my doing. I called off the wedding and broke up with Conor.' In spite of my sadness, I felt giddy and light-headed after this admission.

He looked at me for a long time. Then he picked up the bottle of champagne and topped up our glasses. He sat back, as though he was perfectly relaxed, and asked calmly, 'Well, little cuz, you must have had good reason. What went wrong?'

No way could I tell him the truth. No way could I be honest

and up front. And no way could I spill my heart out and tell him what was keeping me tossing and turning night after night, overshadowing my whole life.

I stared at him. My cousin James. The man I loved but could not have. I'm not sure what the legalities were, with first cousins, but conventional wisdom went against us having a relationship, never mind that he saw me purely as his little cuz, his honorary sister. I couldn't bear to think of his shock were I to admit my feelings, or how it would spoil our friendship for ever, never mind reverberate across our families.

It was a love that had crystallised inside me in the kitchen at Verbena View in the instant that I'd looked at him across the Christmassy table when we'd laughed about songs The Name could perform for the traditional first dance, the special moment when Conor Kennedy led me out on the floor as his wife. Something inside me had rebelled at the thought of James witnessing that significant moment. At the thought of having that significant dance with Conor. What did it mean for me and Conor? I'd laughed to cover my nerves, and said we'd really need to think about that one. Then, after the moment had passed, I couldn't look directly at James because a whirlwind of emotions sent everything I'd ever known up into the air, only to settle back again into a completely different pattern. Afraid in case he saw what was in my eyes, I looked to where he was reflected in the glass doors instead, and allowed my gaze to linger on him.

Then I caught Juliet watching me watching James.

Listen to your heart, Juliet had said, on an iridescent evening in Watsons Bay, her eyes imploring me not to have the kind of regrets she seemed to have.

I *had* listened to my heart. Later that night, in the quiet of the bedroom, long after Conor was asleep, I had paused the endless chatter of everyday life, where hundreds of impressions, assumptions and obligations, big and small, fudged together to constitute life's purpose and meaning. I had taken a deep breath and dived until I reached the very source of my heartbeat. And when I arrived there, all was light and clear and calm, and in the perfect stillness, the truth shone so blindingly that there was no denying it. My love for James had been there always, as much part of me as breath itself, privately unacknowledged and painfully ignored.

FORTY-FIVE

Somewhere in the vicinity a church bell chimed, the sound resonating across the air, bringing me back to the Eternal City, where evening shadows settled a mauve cloak over the terrace and gave a deeper glow to the fairy lights twinkling above our heads.

And bringing me back to where James sat opposite me.

'Well?' he repeated. 'What went wrong?'

'Nothing went wrong. I just fell out of love with him.' It was partly the truth. 'The spark was gone. I think it had been happening for a while, but I ignored it, what with all the wedding plans. I thought that maybe I was nervous, but when the wedding was weeks away rather than months, and panic set in, as opposed to happy anticipation, I knew I had to do something. I knew I didn't really love him.'

'So you called the whole thing off.'

'Yep.' I forced myself to meet his gaze. His eyes were kind.

'That took guts. It must have been difficult.'

'It wasn't,' I said, and this time I was speaking honestly. 'The hardest thing was facing the truth.' My voice cracked a little, but I continued: 'Once I'd accepted that, I was, like, God, I couldn't wait to get away from everything to do with the wedding, including Conor. It was hard telling him. We spent a whole weekend arguing and thrashing it out. It was a nightmare and

I'll never forget his face, but it was like something inside me had closed down and I was outside myself?' I ended on a questioning note. 'Does that make sense? It was as though I'd gone through so much of it in my head beforehand that I was full of a numbed resolve that stayed with me and almost sheltered me while I turned my back on it all.'

'And you came to Rome.'

'Yeah, typical flight syndrome. After I'd called the reception venue and the wedding planner, I had to get away. I'm not very proud of letting Conor down, or the way I left Dublin, and all that crap is running through me at another level, waiting for me to make some kind of resolution.' I gave a mirthless laugh. 'I mean, how do I even start to make it up to Conor? Sometimes I can't believe I actually did what I did. It's surreal. Between that and losing Juliet, I guess you could say I'm a right mess. I just feel totally adrift. I don't know where my life is going to go after this.' I stopped babbling, picked up my glass and drained my champagne.

'Ah, Dani,' he said, so softly I had to lean closer to hear him. 'If only …'

'If only what?' I asked, my voice suddenly thin.

We looked at each other for ages. My eyes roved over his face, his blue eyes, under dark brows, long nose and wide mouth. I knew that face as well as I knew my own. I would know it blindfolded. It had been there, laughing, teasing, sometimes sad, at all the stepping stones of my life.

He gave me a rueful grin. 'Nothing … More champagne?'

I put my finger on the bottom of my glass and slid it across the table. 'Yes, please.'

He ordered another bottle – the waitress almost swooned with delight at being called back to our table.

'I'll be pissed,' I said, the idea very attractive.

'You'll be fine. We'll get some soakage,' he said, passing me a menu, 'and then I'll see you home.'

And tomorrow morning you'll be going to the airport and heading off to your busy video shoot with the guys from the band, the crew of stylists and makeup people and creative directors, and it'll be a great laugh and a huge success, and I'll be alone in Rome with the whole of Saturday and Sunday to fill.

Self-pity will get you nowhere, Danielle Ryan.

Erin had said to call her any time, and that I was always welcome to drop in, but weekends were her precious time with Lorenzo and Aimee, and I wasn't going to hijack any of that. Neither did I want her feeling sorry for me – I'd rather spend the weekend alone than appear needy.

I didn't want to think about going home or to look any further than that minute, here and now: James sitting opposite me, his long, tapering fingers curled around the stem of his glass, chatter going on all around us. Except for the surreptitious glances of people sitting nearby, stabbing furiously at their mobile phones and looking as though they were having the time of their lives for James's benefit, we seemed to be marooned in a capsule of our own.

It was wonderful and crap all at once.

Then James sat back and said, 'Tell me about Conor. How did you know that the spark was gone? How could you put your finger on it? In what way were you sure enough to call off a wedding? I'm not trying to be picky here or delve into your intimate life, Dani, but just in general. Love changes as it grows and evolves. How did you know it wasn't just the first flush of passion settling into a different phase?'

'Why do you want to know?' I fielded the question.

'I'm curious.'

'They're rubbish questions,' I said, unwilling to answer. 'Hey, what's the betting you're trying to figure out if you're finally in love?' I said, darting him a glance. 'Who is she?'

It was a shot in the dark.

James had had a succession of girlfriends down the years, but he'd never hooked up with anyone for any length of time. He was too busy working and enjoying his life to be tied down, he'd said to me, when I'd pressed him on his lack of commitment. He had never met the right woman, had been another excuse. Some of his ex-girlfriends had gone running to the tabloids after their brief liaison crumbled, and there had been lurid headlines rating his performance as a lover, based primarily on the decibel levels emanating from a hotel bedroom and the number of times he was purported to have done it in one night. I think the record stood at nine. When I'd teased him about it, James had said it was made up. 'Anyway, it's quality, not quantity, that counts.' He'd laughed.

Now, for the first time, when the subject of his love life came out for an airing, James Moore looked embarrassed. Whatever I'd said had struck home, and my heart plummeted.

'Come on, there's someone, isn't there?' My voice was brittle and I hoped he wouldn't pick up on it.

'She ... I—' He slumped in his seat. 'I can't tell you.'

From James, this was totally out of character.

'Then you're not in love,' I said acerbically. 'For if you were, you'd be shouting it from the rooftops and telling me how wonderful she is.'

'I could tell you all that, and more. She's beautiful, talented and charming, but ...'

'But?' I could hardly breathe.

'Never mind, Dani.' He rubbed his face, looking suddenly tired, as though he hadn't slept enough recently. 'Sorry I started this conversation.'

'Hey, you can't leave it like that,' I said, picking up a coaster and scrunching it between my fingers.

'I'm not trying to figure out if I'm in love. I know I am,' he said quietly. 'I'm trying to figure out if it will go away of its own accord. If the spark will burn out.'

'What? James Moore, you really are the biggest commitment-phobe,' I said, lobbing the balled-up coaster at him.

'Yeah, well, maybe so.' He shrugged, his expression inscrutable. 'Time for food, I think.' He waved the menu in front of me. By now we were halfway through the second bottle of champagne and, to judge by the way the night-time piazza was becoming blurred and indistinct, coloured lights merging into a rainbow whirl, soakage was definitely called for.

'I'm not hungry,' I said.

'You have to eat.'

'No, I don't.'

'Come on, little cuz … What will Rebecca say if I don't look after you properly?'

'Rebecca?' I asked, seizing on this for necessary distraction. 'Is that why you're here? My mum sent you? To keep an eye on me?'

'No, hang on, you've got it wrong …'

'So she doesn't know you're here.'

'Well, she does, but I'm not here because of her.'

'Oh, yeah?' I felt icy cold inside and ready for a fight. I had tried to keep my emotions in check but it was impossible. Hurt and misery had been building inside me since James had started to talk about love, and described some other woman as wonderful, talented and beautiful. 'I thought you'd stopped off in Rome out of the goodness of your heart,' I said, my voice thick with childish resentment and hurt. 'I didn't know my mum had anything to do with it.'

'She didn't. I called her to see how she was and happened to mention I was planning on dropping in on you.'

'Well, when you report back to her tell her I'm fine, I'm great, I've never been better.'

I rose to my feet.

'Where are you going?'

'Home.'

'Dani, don't be like this.'

'I told you, I'm fine,' I said, pain shooting through me as I hooked my bag over my shoulder. A little devil inside me urged me to pick up the half-full bottle of champagne. 'No sense in leaving a hundred euro worth of bubbly behind.'

'You always were contrary, but this is as bold as it gets,' James said, taking out his wallet and flicking through some notes. 'Wait for me.'

I ignored him and marched away, barely conscious of him following me and the wave of interest that rippled after us, heads swaying like a field of wheat in a light breeze.

He caught up with me just as I passed the fountain. 'Where are you going?'

'I told you, I'm going home.'

'I said I'd see you home, didn't I?'

'Was that another of my mother's instructions?'

'Christ, Dani, you sound like a sulky teenager.'

'Maybe that's how I feel right now.'

We walked in silence through the night-time streets, me feeling secretly ridiculous as I grimly held the slippery bottle of champagne while we wove through the strolling crowds, my route home taking me along the Corso Vittorio Emanuele until we reached the Piazza Venezia.

Of all the squares in Rome, this, to me, was the most notorious for chaotic traffic and one of the most striking, with the lavishly decorated monument to King Vittorio Emanuele II, commanding a position right at the top of the Via del Corso.

'Holy shit, what's that?' James was looking across the piazza to the massive white marble structure that dominated the skyline. 'A wedding cake gone wrong?'

I couldn't help but laugh, which eased the tension between us. 'That's what a lot of the Romans call it,' I said. 'But it can be distracting, and this road is busy, so wait until we get across to the other side. Then you can gaze at it all you want.'

It took us a while to negotiate the careering cars and scooters, most of which took absolutely no notice of a red traffic light. James looked at the extravagant edifice in disbelief as we walked past it and turned down the side, coming alongside the Forum, with the Colosseum ahead.

'Some walk,' James said, whistling in appreciation. 'You get to see all the historic sights.'

'Cross here,' I said, leading the way across another junction, and marching up the street until I came to a McDonald's.

'You can't mean it … the sublime to the ridiculous.'

'I do, and I don't care. The walk made me peckish,' I said, forced to climb down off my high horse because I was weak with hunger. 'I'm getting a takeout as my apartment's not far from here. So if you want to hop into a taxi to bring you back to your posh hotel, that's fine.'

'You are joking?' He looked at me with a mixture of exasperation, impatience and a tinge of sadness. 'Look, Dani, I don't know how it all went wrong between us this evening, but this wasn't what I envisaged when I landed in Rome this morning.'

I knew the precise moment when things had gone wrong. I could pinpoint it exactly: when he'd told me about the girl who was beautiful, talented and charming, his talk of loving another woman twisting a knife inside me. Which was stupid. I had, in the depths of the nights before and after I had called off my wedding, reminded myself that I could never have James. I should have expected he'd fall in love with some wonderful woman. For, no matter how I felt about him, to James I would never be anything more than a contrary cousin, a sort of sister. I had a sudden memory of us sitting together on the floor of someone's house, and he was telling me I would be four years old the next day.

'And how old are you?' I'd asked.

'I'm eight,' he said. 'So I'm twice your age. I'm four years older than you. So, no matter what age you are, you'll always be my little cousin. You can be my sort of sister as well because I have none.'

Now, on the side-street in Rome, heartsick and forlorn, I said, 'This wasn't what I envisaged when I met you in the St Michel.'

'Hey, Dani, come here,' he said, clutching me to his jacket as he gave me a hug. 'It's silly for us to fall out. We both know that life's too short. And Juliet would kill us,' he finished, a smile in his voice.

When I moved away from him, I asked if he'd like some food. 'We went to McDonald's together for the first time with Juliet, remember?'

'Right, little cuz, you win. Let's get some fat-laden chips and quarter-pounders.'

I'd thought I'd be afraid of James's presence in my small, claustrophobic space. That he'd be overpowering, almost too much for me to handle, but instead I found it soothing, despite the stomach-churning knowledge that his heart was wrapped up with someone else. Having him there, in my space, was like a blessing, and he rid the apartment of all the bad vibes that had filled it since the day I'd heard about Juliet. So I soaked up the sight of him moving around my tiny kitchen and living area, his hands deft as he found plates and dished out the food. I hooked up my iPhone to speakers and tuned in to a radio station playing the hits of the eighties and nineties, including Duran Duran, Human League, Madonna, U2; all the music that had once formed the backdrop to our lives.

'I'm glad I brought this home,' I said, producing two glass tumblers and tipping the contents of the bottle of champagne into them.

'So am I, you bold thing,' he said, giving me a quirky grin.

And so we ended up in my tiny apartment, at my minuscule table, washing down chips and burgers with the last of a bottle of champagne, in the glow of a bargain-basement apricot-shaded lamp. Afterwards we stood for a while on my little balcony, listening to the thrum of the city as the cool, clear night settled around us. When we stepped back inside I opened a bottle of wine. We sipped it slowly and chatted about music and tour dates, carefully skirting any topic that might prove explosive, both of us knowing it might be a while before we saw each other again, and neither wanting to part on a bad note.

It was two o'clock in the morning and he was just about to

leave when he said, 'You never answered my question earlier tonight.'

'Didn't I?'

'Do you know which one I mean?'

I gave a half-laugh. I knew full well. 'Remind me.'

'How did you know it wasn't for keeps with Conor? Was it really just a missing spark?'

'That's a different question.'

'Okay, then, how did you know it was missing?'

I glanced round the apartment, wondering how to answer. 'James. It's late ...'

'Come on, cuz, this is me, remember? I'm probably one of your best friends.'

'I can't really explain. I just knew it was the wrong thing for me, marrying Conor. Juliet said—'

'Juliet said what?'

'Oh, hell. We were talking ... that time in Australia ... and she let slip that she had regrets in her life. I think it was because she didn't want me to have any. To learn from her mistakes. She said always to listen to my heart. And when I stopped long enough to ignore all the frivolous, meaningless crap and really listen to it, it told me not to go through with the wedding. I didn't love Conor enough. Does that answer your question?'

He smiled at me. 'I guess it'll do.'

I watched him move towards the door, wishing I could make him stay, knowing it was impossible. I wanted to squeeze my eyes shut so that I wouldn't see him leave. He gave me a hug and kissed my forehead, and then there was just a space where he'd been.

FORTY-SIX

When her landline pealed on Saturday morning, Rebecca snatched it up without checking caller identity.

'Could I speak to Rebecca, please?' It was a woman's voice, which she didn't immediately recognise.

'This is Rebecca. How can I help you?' she asked, wondering if it was the new part-time assistant at Olivia Jayne. Only friends and family had this number, and Amanda, her boss.

'You can help me lots, I hope.'

And just before she announced herself, Rebecca knew, for now there was no mistaking the strident tones: Liz Monaghan.

'It's Liz here, Liz Monaghan, and—'

'I've nothing to say to you,' Rebecca interrupted, outraged at the gall of the woman.

'I'm not sure how you got this number, but I'm ending the call now.'

'Afraid, are you? Of what I might be looking for?'

Rebecca shook with anger. 'I'm not afraid of you, Ms Monaghan, or your vituperative pen. But I'd rather not have anything to do with you.'

'We'll see about that. You were a good friend of Juliet's, weren't you?'

'That's got nothing to do with you,' Rebecca said sharply.

'And I'd be very careful, if I were you, of whatever scurrilous stories you intend to concoct in future.'

'I don't intend to concoct anything, Rebecca,' Liz said, in a smooth tone that grated on her. 'I'm putting together an article at the moment and I just wanted you to know that I might need your help. You may like the opportunity to confirm some of the facts before they go to print.'

'I've already said I'd rather not have anything to do with you.'

'You might change your mind. The facts are rather … ah, compromising. Have a think about it, and I'll contact you again early next week. And, by the way, I don't take kindly to my work being labelled scurrilous or vituperative. What I'll be writing about Ms Jordan will be nothing but the unvarnished truth.'

There was a soft click. She had hung up.

Rebecca stood staring into space, wondering what the hell that had been about. Once Liz Monaghan was involved, it could scarcely be good. She checked her phone but the number had been withheld, so there was no way she could call her back.

She went down to the kitchen and was sitting at the table with a cup of coffee when her mobile rang. She stared at it for long moments, not putting it past the woman to call her again on her mobile, just to throw her off balance. She snatched it up, ready to give her a piece of her mind.

But it wasn't Liz. It was the police, Detective Woods to be precise, and Rebecca had to ask her to repeat her words, because she couldn't grasp them at first.

'There's been a small development,' Detective Woods said. 'We've found Juliet's house key. Can you confirm where she usually put it on her person when she went walking?'

The room swayed around Rebecca. She saw Juliet laughing as she walked up the hall, tucking her mobile phone into her tracksuit pocket. Her key would be shoved into the other pocket as soon as she had double-locked the door. It was a ritual Rebecca had seen many a time. She took a few deep breaths.

'Rebecca – Mrs Ryan, are you there?'

'Yes,' Rebecca said, her voice faint. 'I just – sorry – lost it for a minute. Juliet usually tucked her key into her tracksuit pocket. Where did you find it?'

'That's the thing,' Detective Woods said. 'It was found on the cliff top, near to the spot where she must have fallen. It was hidden in some undergrowth so it wasn't found before now. It appears to have dropped out of her pocket before she fell.'

'*Before* she fell? What does that mean, exactly?'

'That it's possible there was an altercation on the cliff, which caused her key to be knocked out of her pocket and kicked into the undergrowth beside the track. If the key had slipped out as she was falling, more than likely it would never have been found.'

She closed her eyes. 'You're joking. Are you saying – do you think someone pushed her?'

'It's not at all clear what happened. As we said, Mrs Ryan, the inquiry is very much open and our investigation is continuing. So far we haven't located her mobile. We'll contact you and Ms Jordan's brother if there's anything else to report.'

After the call, Rebecca put her head into her hands. She was back there again, in the horrific spot she'd inhabited just after Juliet's death, only now the shock was wearing off and the pain was ready to attack her in large, unrelenting waves. How had this happened to Juliet? Had someone really been with her on the cliff top?

God, no. Who could have wanted to cause her darling Juliet any harm?

Rebecca felt a swell of sadness building inside her and

clutched at her stomach, as if to contain it. Eventually she picked up her phone and called Amanda. She was due at Olivia Jayne at midday, but no way could she be there today, smiling and greeting customers.

'No problem, Rebecca,' Amanda said. 'Take care of yourself, and I'll get someone to cover.'

Liam was next.

With her phone pressed to her ear, Rebecca stood up and went across to the conservatory window as she told him what had happened. It was a bright morning, with patches of blue sky visible above the shredded clouds, the trees glowing with feathery green tips that danced with careless grace in the light breeze.

Juliet had danced with careless grace, laughing as she twirled her body with such ease that Rebecca had always felt clumsy beside her. She took a few shallow breaths, trying to ignore the knife slicing into her heart.

'I don't believe it,' Liam said. 'No wonder you're so upset. Will I come over?'

'I'd rather just chill, Liam,' she said, feeling the urge to be alone in her familiar surroundings, like an animal hiding in its cave as it licked its wounds.

'Of course,' he said. 'Just look after yourself. And make sure you eat. We'll talk soon.'

When she called Rose, her sister was silent for so long that Rebecca decided she must have dropped the phone in her consternation.

Then she took her landline off the hook in case Liz Monaghan happened to call back. She was tempted to power off her mobile as she didn't want to talk to anyone else that day, but she left it on in case Danielle happened to call. She went out into the garden and tidied the straggling daffodil stalks. She mowed the grass, steadied a trellis under some ivy, and pulled weeds out of the flowerbed. Later, she took out her laptop and checked her emails, forgetting about the last email Juliet had sent until she saw it in her folder. As she stared at her friend's name and the opening line of her email, written in Juliet's usual enthusiastic tone, something cracked inside her. The tears finally came, falling swiftly, running down her face, trickling around her nose and dripping into her mouth. Her breath came in gasps as she struggled to fill her lungs. She heard a wail and realised it was her own.

It wasn't just Juliet, it was Harry, and the shock, long ago, of her parents. The loss of loved ones and the sheer transience of life.

Wallow in it, Liam had said. Don't block it. She fetched a box of tissues and blew her nose again and again, but made no attempt to stop the tears, and she put the television on purely to have some sound in the house besides her own sniffing and crying.

By early evening she was all cried out and the worst of the storm had passed. For now. There would be other moments, she knew, when raw grief would catch her unawares before she learned to adjust to it.

Later, when Liam arrived, juggling a bottle of wine, flowers and a takeaway meal, she was able to smile.

'I took a chance on you being home and maybe feeling a bit peckish. You can send me away, if you like ...'

'Come in,' she said, glad that he didn't give her red-rimmed eyes a second glance. 'I wouldn't have opened the door to anyone else.'

❧❧

'I can't believe we're going out for a meal with Celia Coffey and her husband of all people,' Rose said, as she sprayed herself with Chanel perfume and looked at Matthew's reflection in the bedroom mirror.

Matthew was too busy fixing his platinum cuff links to meet her eyes. 'Don't you know how influential Michael Coffey is? He's a respected economist who has contributed to the Forum, and his brother is a head honcho on the county council. It's unfortunate he was away in Marbella when we had our evening at home, because we really need the likes of him in our corner. And you don't normally get a table in Patrick Guilbaud's at short notice. I was lucky.'

Lucky? Celia Coffey was someone Rose usually tried to avoid. The other woman always grated on her, with her constant bitching and those supercilious eyebrows. You'd think she was the only mother who was trying to be hip with her teenage children. Oh, she smiled to your face, but you never knew what she was about to say behind your back. She always seemed to know what was going down, and the thought of an evening spent in her company was anathema to Rose. The meal in the restaurant with two Michelin stars would be wasted on her.

She tried to imagine what it would be like if it was just her and Matthew going out for a cosy Saturday-night dinner, a normal couple with a normal life, no talk of elections, campaigns or canvassing, or the infernal need to influence people, issues that had consumed their lives so much recently that she was beginning to wonder what they'd talked about before.

Some of their best nights out had been years ago, when they had gone to a local restaurant to save on the taxi fare home. Then Matthew had talked of his dreams, his vision carrying them away as he painted a picture of a lifestyle that both of them would enjoy. In time, his dreams had become their reality, but somewhere along the way Rose had got lost.

Or else, she thought, in a sudden moment of clarity, she had got real.

Real to the fact that their lives were built on secrets and bound by lies.

She stared at her reflection in the mirror, at the startled eyes of the elegant, mature woman about to put on her diamond necklace, and knew it was the dark corners of their life together, not her inability to cope with the pressure of Matthew's success, that had pushed her into a downward spiral. The dark corners that had become more frightening with Juliet's death, but couldn't be spoken of, even between them, because they weren't supposed to exist. Throwing a light on them would bring their lives crashing down around them.

'Darling, you look wonderful,' Matthew went on, his tone determinedly cheerful and upbeat. He stood behind her and squeezed her shoulders. 'Whatever you had done to your hair, it's fabulous. I know it's hard for you, going through the motions after Juliet and all of that. I know how devastated you must feel, but it's best to keep busy.'

'Busy,' she said. 'That's always been your solution, Matthew, your panacea to whatever problem you faced. Bury yourself in work, and make sure you're too busy to think.'

'Well, it got us where we are today, didn't it?'

She thought she caught the faintest glimmer of uncertainty beneath his smile and was tempted to speak. Instead she looked at the reflection of Matthew and Rose Moore in the mirror and felt like flinging her crystal perfume bottle at the glass so that the image would splinter and crack.

౾౿

Rose air-kissed Michael and Celia Coffey when they met in the Merrion Hotel, and Matthew ordered champagne to begin with, then insisted the Coffeys chose the wine to accompany the meal. Conversation was relaxed and friendly, the only sad note being the mention of Juliet's death, with Celia ferreting for details.

'We missed the whole thing because we were in Marbella,' Celia said, her eyes huge with drama. 'We flew out on the Sunday morning, and we heard the shocking news when we were having a drink in the Marbella Club. I kept thinking of you, Rose, and how we were only chatting about Juliet on the Friday night at the reception. I can't imagine how you must have felt. I had to have several brandies and I'll never be able to go to Marbs again without thinking of Juliet.'

To Rose's relief, Matthew steered the conversation towards holidays, and before long, Celia was in full swing, having moved on from there to boast about the varied exploits and accomplishments of their teenage children.

'They couldn't believe we were going for a meal with James Moore's parents tonight,' Michael said, as if conscious that his wife was dominating the conversation. 'All of a sudden it upped our currency. Big-time. It must be a good feeling to have a son who's followed his dream and worked hard enough to achieve such global success. We're still at the stage where we're at war with ours over their science homework.'

'I've worn that T-shirt,' Matthew said, with a good-natured, empathetic smile. 'But I think I lost that particular battle.'

'Just as well,' Michael said. 'It could have been a huge loss to us all if James had become a white-coated scientist.'

Rose heard herself laugh with Celia as though she hadn't a care in the world.

Before their dessert, Michael said he was going to stretch his legs in the garden outside the restaurant.

Celia laughed. 'Don't pretend, Michael, it doesn't suit you,' she said. 'He's off out for a sneaky cigar.'

'I'll come with you,' Matthew said. He grinned at Celia. 'And I'm only stretching my legs, honest.'

She flapped her hand. 'Oh, go on with you! It'll give me a chance to talk to Rose. We need some girly talk, don't we, Rose?' She turned to Rose, her eyes sparking with meaning.

Rose felt weak.

It didn't take Celia too long to produce her trump card: 'Tell me, Rose, how are you really coping with Juliet's death? It must have been terrible to lose such a good friend.'

'It was, of course, and it's hit Rebecca particularly hard. They were very close.'

'So maybe you should know …' Celia lowered her voice conspiratorially and her gaze swept around the restaurant as if she was making sure she wasn't being overheard.

'Know what?'

'Oh dear, it's all very dreadful, and I don't like to speak ill of the dead …'

'Celia, you must want to tell me or you'd scarcely have raised the subject,' Rose said, with unusual spirit.

'I'm afraid you may be sorry to hear the rumour circulating about Juliet.'

Rose kept her face straight, although her heart was hammering. 'I think I'd rather know.'

'Well, then …' Celia moved in so close that Rose caught the scent of her perfume. She looked delighted to be imparting the information. 'You see, Rose, being a good friend of Juliet's you ought to know that there's a whisper going around, just a tiny whisper, mind you, that she might have been embroiled in an affair. With a married man.'

She sat back, her sharp eyes observing Rose.

'That's ridiculous. Where did you hear this?' Rose's voice was thin.

'I think it was mentioned in my flagship salon on Wicklow Street. It's a mine of information, you know, all the stories that are revealed between Brazilian waxes and spray tans. Nothing like being stripped of your clothes and your dignity to loosen your tongue. Can you imagine if that got into the tabloids? Even if it's all totally innocent, Juliet's reputation would be tarnished for ever. Not to mention the man's.'

∂∾⊱

For the remainder of the night, Rose kept up a front with Michael and Celia, forcing herself to chat and smile, only lapsing into silence when she and Matthew were in a taxi on the way home. But as she sat in the television room, having a nightcap with him, she could contain it no longer.

'That was a very productive evening,' Matthew said. 'I had a good brainstorm with Michael in the garden and we're going golfing next week.'

'There's a rumour going around that Juliet had an affair with a married man,' Rose blurted. She watched him carefully, remembering that she'd wondered if Matthew had found Juliet irresistible, thinking of how they'd sparked off each other. But Matthew's hand was perfectly steady as he handed her a glass of wine and poured himself a whiskey from the decanter.

'Is that all? I was wondering why you were so quiet all the way home,' he said calmly. 'Don't let it worry you. I'm surprised something like that hasn't come up before now. Or that Juliet had lesbian sex, or seduced a couple of schoolboys behind the bike shed. Or that she was snorting coke. No matter how much of a humanitarian she was, Juliet lived a lot in the public eye and there's always going to be someone intent on stirring up mindless shite.'

'Which is exactly why I'd prefer it if we stayed as we are. I don't want to live the next few years in a goldfish bowl with the tabloids taking pot-shots. And supposing ...' her hand shook so badly that wine slopped over the rim of her glass '... just supposing someone decides to dig a little deeper. What then, Matthew?'

He sighed. 'I've told you before, and I'll say it again. We've nothing whatsoever to worry about.' He sat down beside her and squeezed her arm. 'I've no intention of letting any silly little rumour stand in my way. Not now I've come this far.'

She wanted to ask him what he proposed to do if a silly little rumour took on legs of its own and spread into their lives. She wanted to ask him how exactly he might stop things getting in his way. She thought of Juliet's key being found in the undergrowth, pointing to the possibility of a struggle at the top of the cliff, and wondered how soon the police might decide to investigate Juliet's friends for any possible motives.

After all, both she and Matthew had come home late that Friday night.

FORTY-SEVEN

It's getting worse. More and more difficult to pretend it never happened, and harder and harder to keep up a front.

Sometimes in the night Juliet stares down from the bedroom ceiling, her huge eyes reflecting that split second of terror, mouth wide open in a scream that never comes.

Sometimes she crawls out from under the bed, first her waving hands, clawlike and clutching, searching for a grip on the carpet, then her arms, pulling her broken torso behind her, and then her fractured legs, breaking away from her body so that they're severed at the hips.

Other times she steps through the wardrobe and floats about the room, sitting on the dressing-table or hanging off the curtain rail, her pale face glimmering with a ghostly sheen, coal black circles smudging her eyes.

She's even in the bed. Lying there cold and stiff, except for her eyelids, which snap open and closed on empty sockets. On those nights, sleep is impossible.

And she's starting to appear at the breakfast table, pale grey from head to toe, her eyes sad, her hair matted with dried blood.

It should never have happened. It had been a mistake, borne of a single flash of fury and resentment, like an electrical trip-switch hitting overload.

And horrifying to think what a split second of madness has done …

FORTY-EIGHT

'Mrs Ryan, may we come in?'

Rebecca blinked. It was Sunday morning and the radio was blaring in the kitchen, her toast browning nicely and eggs on the boil. She'd actually been singing along to Adele, a sudden burst of light-heartedness lifting her spirits and telling her that somehow she'd get through this dark tunnel and come out the other side.

The previous night, Liam had stayed until after midnight before getting a taxi home, and it had helped. She hadn't suggested he stay over in any of her spare beds or held her hand during the night. Much as she felt like having his arms around her, she knew it wasn't the right time. He seemed to sense that, taking her face in his hands and kissing her slowly and deeply before he left, stopping before they went further.

'Hey,' he'd said, their foreheads touching. 'Whatever that was about it was lovely.'

'Yes,' she'd said, drawing back so that their faces were inches apart.

'I'd better go.'

'Yes.'

Then he'd given her a quick hug and told her to look after herself.

Now Detective Inspector Callaghan and Detective Woods were standing in the porch once more, but his time, as she showed them into the front room, they seemed more distant and purposeful. Detective Woods was without her usual empathetic manner, as though the business of the day was more important than how Rebecca might be feeling.

'I presume this is about Juliet?' she said, fighting unease.

'Yes,' Detective Inspector Callaghan said. 'Our enquiries are still continuing, but we need to ask you a few questions.'

The pang of unease flexed and pulsed inside her. She sat on the edge of the sofa and tried to contain it. 'Sure,' she said, bracing herself for whatever might come.

'Mrs Ryan, how well do you know Liam Corrigan?'

Her face flushed. Well enough to want to go to bed with him, a little voice whispered. 'Has this anything to do with last Sunday's putrid article in—'

Detective Woods was shaking her head. 'Nothing whatsoever.'

'I've known Liam for a long time. He and my husband went to the same school. I ran into him several times over the years, in a purely social context, before he went to Spain,' Rebecca said. She tried not to think of how he'd been just before he went to Spain.

'And recently?'

'I hadn't seen him for quite a while until I bumped into him at a wedding in the Seagrass Hotel.'

'Were you at the wedding yourself, Mrs Ryan?'

'Yes. I'd been invited to the evening reception by the father of the groom who had known my late husband.'

'We need to verify some details. What time did you get to the hotel?'

Rebecca forced herself to sound patient as she recounted her movements, right up to the time she had seen Liam going into the hotel bar.

'Can you remember exactly what time this was?'

Rebecca shrugged. 'Around nine, I guess. I bumped into him later in the lobby as the television news was coming to an end.'

'And you were with him for the rest of the evening?'

'I went back to my room around half past nine and joined Liam for a drink soon after that. We were chatting for an hour, an hour and a half, I'd say. Why? What is this?'

'Did Liam Corrigan actually tell you he was at the wedding?'

She felt confused and tried to remember his exact words. 'From what he said, I understood he was. He's already been in to sign a statement, hasn't he? I'm sure he's told you all this. He dropped in to see Juliet before coming to the Seagrass, and he might have been the last person to see her alive.'

Detective Inspector Callaghan gave her a sharp, alert look. 'He might indeed, Mrs Ryan.'

'You see, Rebecca,' Detective Woods changed tack, 'we've intensified our enquiries in the light of recent developments. We've confirmed that Liam wasn't actually attending that wedding. He wasn't on the guest list, and he only made his hotel reservation at around ...' she consulted her notebook '... half past nine that evening.'

'Oh, gosh.' Rebecca felt all the air being sucked out of her.

'So if you've anything to add, or anything different to say, we'd like to hear it.'

She tried to breathe evenly. 'Hang on – sorry, what exactly are you getting at? I told you all I know. Have you talked to Liam?'

'Yes,' Detective Woods said. 'He has now stated that he didn't attend the wedding, but that's all he's prepared to say at the moment. We're putting out another appeal for information and will be checking CCTV in the area. Unfortunately Ms Jordan's system was malfunctioning, which is a pity, as it could have told us a lot.'

'Are you aware of the contents of Ms Jordan's will?' Detective Inspector Callaghan asked.

'Yes, I'm the executor of her estate,' Rebecca said, dread making her scalp prickle. 'I haven't even thought that far ahead yet. I'm still trying to get used to the idea that Juliet's ... no longer around. I know I'll have to contact her solicitor soon. And then talk to the beneficiaries and advise them of the contents.' That would be another day's work entirely.

Detective Inspector Callaghan studied his notebook. 'We've already been in touch with Ms Jordan's solicitor. You know she changed the terms of her will earlier this year?'

'Yes, I'm aware of that.' Rebecca felt faint, knowing what was coming next. There was no point in ducking it. 'Originally my sister Rose and I were her chief beneficiaries and there are some charitable bequests also.'

'What about her brother?'

'Juliet bought out his share of Verbena View years ago, but if there are paintings or furniture he'd like, he's to have them. Juliet hardly ever saw Robert,' Rebecca babbled. 'She didn't feel he was part of her life in the way we were. And he'd already made it clear to Juliet that he regarded Florida as his home.' She took a deep breath. 'But in February she drew up a new will, naming my daughter Danielle and Rose's son James as her chief beneficiaries instead of Rose and me.'

'Do you think Ms Jordan had any particular reason for changing her will in favour of them? Did she talk to you about it?'

'She told me she'd done it, but she didn't mention any reason in particular. She was very close to Danielle and James and always regarded them as the family she never had.'

'And had you any problems with this?'

'None whatsoever. And neither had my sister. Naturally enough we assumed this would all be happening at some distant time in the future. Even before she changed her will, we expected that Juliet's legacy would inevitably pass to Danielle and James through us.'

'Thanks, Mrs Ryan, that's all for now,' Detective Inspector Callaghan said, rising to his feet, and shoving his notebook into his jacket pocket.

'You've been very helpful.' Detective Woods's mask slipped as they went out into the hall and she gave Rebecca a sympathetic look.

As though what? Rebecca asked herself, as she stood in the hall and watched their figures recede into the distance until there was no sign of them through the glass door. As though Rebecca was someone to be pitied? Having been taken in by a bunch of lies?

What kind of a fool had she been to fall for Liam's sweet talk? And a bigger fool to have responded to his kisses. Humiliation scalded her at the way she'd been tempted to take him to bed, needing the comfort of his kisses and caresses.

And what else had Liam Corrigan lied about? Maybe there had been no reconciliation with Juliet. Maybe there had been no caller after him at Verbena View. She recalled his angry face in the dining room of the Shelbourne before he'd fled to Spain, and the way he'd admitted to once feeling savage towards Juliet. Could he have been angry enough to do something in the heat of the moment?

When her mobile rang and she saw his name, she snatched it up.

'Thanks, Liam,' she began, anger flaring inside her. 'How *dare* you lie to me like that? Have you any idea—'

'The police have talked to you.'

'Oh, yes,' she said, trembling. 'You weren't even invited to the wedding the night Juliet died. More fool me. How dare you lie to me? What kind of a fool do you think I am?'

'Rebecca, just hear me out,' he said, sounding so desperate that she was forced to listen. 'I would have come clean, but after Juliet died everything went belly-up—'

'Don't you dare use Juliet as an excuse. What else did you lie to me about?' Her voice was ragged. 'How do I know you made it up with her, you arrogant bastard?'

'I did,' he said quietly. 'You have my word. As soon as Juliet accepted my apology, I told her I wanted to talk to you. She told me you weren't around that evening as you'd be in the Seagrass. She suggested I drop into the hotel on the off-chance of seeing you, as it was less than thirty minutes' drive up the coast road. And she even told me—'

'What? Come on, I'm waiting.'

'She told me to say she'd sent you.'

'I don't believe you.'

'It's exactly what happened. Honestly, Rebecca. I was hesitant until Juliet laughed and she said she knew I'd always been attracted to you. She told me to go for it or I'd have her to answer to.'

'Keep talking,' Rebecca said, her heart sinking further and further. 'This is all very interesting.'

'When I saw you in the lobby, looking so lovely, I was afraid to scare you away,' he said. 'It was much easier to let on I was there for the wedding. When you went back to your room, I decided to book into the hotel for the night so that I could relax properly over drinks with you.'

'That sounds very romantic, but it's a heap of shit.'

He sighed. 'It's not, believe me.'

'It has to be,' Rebecca said wretchedly, feeling sick to her bones. 'You see, Juliet didn't know I was going anywhere, let alone to the Seagrass. I hadn't spoken to her all week. I can't believe you have the nerve to spin me a story that I can't even check with her.' Her voice wobbled. 'I don't know what your game is, but don't dare contact me again.'

She was hoarse with anger and fear by the time she ended the call. Anger that she'd allowed herself to be duped, and fear because she couldn't help wondering what exactly Liam had been doing at Verbena View or, to be precise, with Juliet.

After all, it was only a few short years ago that he'd threatened she'd pay for ruining him.

FORTY-NINE

After a weekend with nothing but her sore heart for company, there was something very soothing, Rebecca decided, about coming to work. The daily routine was almost calming in its pure normality, giving her something else to focus on besides the pain in her chest. It helped that she was spending that quiet Monday morning refreshing the spring-summer stock in the window of Olivia Jayne. She blanked her mind to everything except colour co-ordinating the display in shades of cobalt blue and lily white, smoothing materials over the mannequins, tucking and pinning, the drift of gossamer satin quite different but just as beautiful as the whispering silks and the frilly texture of lace.

She was alone in the shop except for Maria, one of the part-time assistants who lived locally. Then, at half past ten, Amanda bustled in with a selection of croissants. Although it was just a flying visit, she invited Rebecca into the tiny office at the back for a cup of coffee and a chat. 'How are you feeling?' she asked.

'I'm okay.' Their relationship was warm and friendly but business-like, which suited Rebecca. No matter how much she might be tempted to unburden herself, she couldn't take Amanda into her confidence about the unsettling police visits or the devastating fall-out with Liam. She hadn't even told Rose yet. Funnily enough, during a low moment on Sunday she'd found herself lifting her mobile to call Juliet – until the painful knowledge that she was gone hit Rebecca like a ton of bricks thudding into her chest.

'You don't look okay, Rebecca. You look as though you haven't slept all weekend. Losing your friend like that must have been a deep shock and it'll take time to adjust. If you need any more time off, it's no problem. I'll get cover for you.'

'Thanks, Amanda. I need a couple of days to pop over and see Danielle in Rome, whenever it suits you,' Rebecca said. Over the weekend, it had become very clear to her that she needed to talk to Danielle about Juliet's will and what it would mean for her. She had to be told before word leaked out from somewhere else. James needed to know as well. He was somewhere in eastern Europe at the moment so she'd let Rose and Matthew look after that.

Danielle had called her on Sunday evening, sounding lost and lonely, obviously missing Juliet. She'd try to persuade her to come home: hanging about in Rome wouldn't solve anything.

'Rebecca, go whenever you like,' Amanda said. 'Just look after yourself and take off whatever time you need. Once I have some advance notice it's fine by me.'

'Thanks, Amanda.'

Amanda arranged croissants and tiny pots of jam on a plate. 'It's the least I can do and no thanks are owed, except from me to you. I wouldn't be where I am today but for you. Don't even think about the shop. Just be good to yourself for a while. Starting with this,' Amanda said, proffering the plate.

Rebecca helped herself to a croissant, her eyes blurring. She'd thought she'd been good to herself by letting Liam into her life, and allowing herself to hope that love could come around once more. She'd even considered opening doorways to warm desires that had vanished with Harry. She remembered the way Liam's mouth had felt beneath her fingers, and the way she'd kissed him back on Saturday night, melting into his arms. Even, her throat swelled, the way she'd imagined going to bed with him.

What kind of a fool had she been? She had trusted him instinctively, but maybe she'd just clung to him because her heart had been frozen in those sad days after Juliet's death. Not that it mattered any more. He'd been spinning a very tall tale, and she still didn't know what the ending was going to be.

Rebecca spread jam on a croissant, and then she smiled at Amanda, trying to ignore the appalling image of Juliet and Liam quarrelling on the cliff. Of Liam's anger getting the better of him, then of him jumping into his car afterwards, blind rage causing him to flee up north County Dublin lanes towards the mansion he'd once lived in, only to realise he didn't live there any more and stop off in a nearby hotel.

Where he'd met Rebecca …

She told herself it sounded so appalling that it couldn't have happened. But why had he lied to her?

After lunch, she was in the shop window arranging a drift of scarves, classy shoes and soft leather bags when she felt a shadow falling across her, blocking out the light. She glanced up and started, almost stabbed herself with the thin stiletto heel of a glittering sandal.

Liz Monaghan was standing in front of the window, her face pressed to the glass as she stared in at Rebecca. Rebecca stepped back on to the shop floor. Thankfully, Maria was busy with a customer who was deciding between outfits for a wedding, so she didn't pay undue attention when Liz strolled in, looking as though she owned the boutique.

She'd forgotten how tall she was, Rebecca realised, bracing herself.

'Thought I might find you here,' Liz said.

'How can I help you?' Rebecca asked smoothly.

'You'd love to help me, I'm sure.'

'Liz, I'm sure you appreciate that I'm in work and busy. Why don't you just say what you've come to say and let me get on with my job?'

Liz smiled, cat-like. 'I'm getting on with my job as well. I want to know if you have any comment to make about the rumours that Juliet Jordan was having an affair with a married man.'

'That's a load of horse shit,' Rebecca said, in the pleasantest voice she could muster. 'And if you try to concoct anything false or defamatory about Juliet, you'll regret it because I'll be straight on to her solicitor.'

'Oh, it might well be scandalous, but it won't be false, I can assure you. I might run the piece by you later this week as I'm still trying to fill in some gaps. Then again, I might not. If you won't help me, I'll keep digging until I find what I'm looking for.'

'I don't know what's driving you, but I'm beginning to think you're one hell of a vindictive bitch,' Rebecca said, immediately sorry she'd allowed the woman to rattle her.

Liz paled. She stared at Rebecca for a long moment, then leaned in close to her and hissed, 'You'll regret those words when I blow Saint Juliet Jordan out of the water.'

Next minute she was gone, and when Rebecca looked out of the window, her hand still clenched around the stiletto heel, there was no sign of Liz's tall figure weaving through the afternoon shoppers. She had disappeared into the ether. Rebecca shivered and wondered for a moment if she'd imagined it. But she hadn't: even the air around her seemed to vibrate with Liz's naked venom.

FIFTY

In the days following James's visit to Rome, I went around on auto-pilot. Seeing him on the Friday night and having his presence seep into all the corners of my tiny apartment had me brimming over with so much quiet joy that it lingered in my heart long after he'd gone. I sat in the chair he'd sat in, and stood on my balcony in the same spot he had, as though it possessed a magic aura. However, as the days slipped past, I began to feel lonelier than ever before. I tried as hard as I could, but it was difficult to recapture those unselfish, high-flying ideas I'd had that at least the man I loved was alive and enjoying his life, when I wanted so much to be part of it.

But it wasn't going to happen, not in a million years.

And no matter how often I thought of the tender smile James had given me, or the way he'd looked at my face when he'd wished that if only – if only what? My mind flew off in a million different tangents. I told myself I was colouring everything like a woman possessed, that I was reading all sorts of fantastic things into ordinary moments and imbuing them with a meaning that didn't and couldn't exist. For he was in love with someone else.

I decided it was best to avoid James as much as I could. Even if it meant going to live far away from Ireland. My heart was battered every time I saw him.

If his visit had taught me one thing, though, it was that I needed to talk to Conor, to try in some way to make up for my disgraceful behaviour. I finally plucked up the courage to send him a long email, apologising once more from the bottom of my heart for all the upset I'd caused, and asking him how he'd been.

There was nearly a row in the office when Gemma found out the identity of my cousin. Erin let it slip when she joined us for coffee on Tuesday morning and asked about our weekend. The fantastic nightclub Gemma had discovered hadn't been so great after all, but few of the girls in the office had gone with her so her reputation as a raver was still intact.

'Did you go, Danielle?' Erin asked.

Gemma jumped in before I had a chance to answer: 'No, Danielle was too busy with her cousin. I thought she might have brought him along, but we weren't good enough,' she joked, in a half-mocking way.

'I don't blame her,' Erin laughed. 'Could you imagine James Moore let loose in a Rome nightclub? You'd have to call the *carabinieri*.'

Gemma's face went red. 'James *Moore*? You're joking. Not *the* James Moore? He's not your cousin, is he?' She looked at me almost furiously, as though I'd no right to have any claim to such celebrity.

Erin shot me a funny, questioning glance, then asked Gemma, 'Didn't she tell you?'

'I had a headache on Friday evening,' I said. It was partly the truth. My head had been swimming with thoughts of James. 'I wasn't much in the mood for talk.'

'Was he here for long?' Erin asked.

'Just Friday night. He was on his way to a video shoot in Croatia.'

'Jeez, Danielle, I can't believe you kept it to yourself,' Gemma said reproachfully. 'All that time you were texting him you never said a word. I'm a great fan of The Name. I've been following them for years and I'd've loved to meet James. Maybe I'd be the one to mend his broken heart. Maybe he's waiting for me to come into his life.'

'What broken heart?' I asked.

'It's obvious, isn't it? He's never married, despite all the gorgeous women who throw themselves at him. He's never been in a long-term relationship. Somewhere along the line he must have had his heart turned over.'

'Nonsense. He's too busy having fun,' I said, ignoring the pain in my chest.

I'd asked him before about his love life, and that had always been his stock answer.

'Yeah,' said Gemma, 'having fun while he's waiting for the right woman to come along and have his babies.'

My chest contracted at the thought of another woman having babies for James. I was a sad case. 'That's nonsense,' I said.

Gemma looked at me sharply. 'It's written all over his face, Danielle. I've watched him on stage and I have two of their concerts on DVD. Sometimes in the music he has this lost look in his eyes as though he's looking for love. Even in the extra material, where they show The Name relaxing with their families, James is playing with the other band members' kids. I'd say he's dying to be a dad when the right woman comes along.'

'I never heard anything more ridiculous,' I said, conscious that my voice was thick with resentment.

For the rest of the day, Gemma was offhand with me, as though I'd personally snubbed her by not introducing her to James. It was all I needed on top of my sore heart. And then, into that whirlpool of emotions, my mother called to say she'd decided to visit me. This coming weekend.

Perfect timing, I don't think.

I loved my mother. I was bursting with pride when I saw how she managed herself at Juliet's funeral. I just felt too raw and vulnerable right now to cope with having her attention focused on me. And I didn't know how long I could avoid talking about the reasons behind my busted wedding, especially when there would be no other distractions to hide behind.

'You can stay with me.' I felt obliged to offer when she began to make booking-a-hotel noises and the likelihood of there being one handy to my apartment.

'I don't want to disturb you,' she said, so lovingly that I was appalled by my reluctance to see her. 'But … well, it'll be just the two nights if you have room.'

'I have, of course,' I said, not bothering to explain that I'd have to sleep on the sofa and give her my bedroom, and that my bed was bigger than a single bed but smaller than a double.

The following day, Gemma relented enough to be pleasant and polite to me. I guess she figured that there was no point in scuppering her one and only minuscule chance of getting close to James Moore and The Name.

She asked me if I thought he'd be dropping in to Rome when his video shoot was over, and I felt a surge of power when I wafted a hand in a superior way and said nonchalantly that I hadn't a clue what part of the world the private jet was taking him to next.

FIFTY-ONE

Rose and Matthew joined the stream of theatre-goers spilling out of the heat of the auditorium into the wet Thursday night. As they moved away from the portico of the Gaiety, Rose looked up at the slanting rain in the light of a streetlamp and drew her scarf closer around her. She blinked, briefly unsure of where she was.

The opera was still swirling in her head, the purity of sound swooping into hidden corners and dark secrets, blowing away the dust with its true, shimmering notes, tugging at everything that was soft and vulnerable in her heart, and wrenching it into a fragile maelstrom.

A mistake, she thought, to have come tonight when she was already an emotional wreck, for now all the complicated layers of her life seemed to have been laid bare by the music.

'Rose.' Matthew's voice was close to her ear, as he put a hand on her arm.

She looked at his familiar profile, saw him smiling down at her it and whirled back in time to when he was the earnest young man she'd started dating all those years ago.

'Will we make a run for it?' he said.

'Yes, why not?' She grinned.

Together they hurried up the street to the taxi rank at the corner of St Stephen's Green, Matthew's arm around her shoulders. She gulped the fresh night air, felt the rain veiling her face and, in the energy of the moment, could have been nineteen again on her first date with him.

All the way home to Belgrave Park, as night-time Dublin flowed by the window, her head was filled with the music they had left behind. She felt raw and exposed. The odd sensation persisted as Matthew ushered her up the garden path and into the house, locking the door behind them. When she saw their reflections in the hall mirror she was even more disconcerted for it was a long, long time since she had been nineteen and innocent of what life would bring.

In the hallway Matthew looked at her. 'Rose, you're shattered. Straight to bed with you.'

'I don't think I can sleep,' she said.

'Didn't you like the opera?' He took off his coat and hung it in the hall closet. He began to slide hers off her shoulders, with her cream cashmere scarf. 'I thought you'd enjoy it. And the opening night is always special.'

She was tempted to ask if he'd brought her simply to secure more column inches – she could already see it in the newspaper: 'Matthew Moore and his elegant wife, Rose, were there, blah blah blah ...' But she let that go, allowing him to remove her coat and scarf and hang them up. She said, 'It was beautiful, so beautiful it made me cry and think of Juliet, and everything else ...' There was a lump in her throat.

He drew her close. 'Ah, Rose.'

She leaned against him, needing the solidity of his body to centre her. Then she moved back and gazed at his face. 'Matthew,' she said gently, 'we need to talk.'

His arms were still clasped round her. 'About what?'

'You know … Juliet's will – and James.'

'There's nothing to talk about.'

'Matthew, you might be the cleverest and most shrewd businessman, but we have to stop burying our heads in the sand.'

'My head isn't buried in any sand.'

'Yes, it is. Not once have we spoken of James or what Juliet's death means.'

His eyes were guarded. 'You're upset. Now is not the time. It'll all seem better in the morning.'

'I can't.' She felt as though she was going to shatter into tiny pieces.

'Can't what?' he asked, putting a finger under her chin.

'Can't stop the pictures going through my head … Juliet … everything …'

He sighed. 'Look, you'll have to take it easy and give yourself time … We've all had a shock.'

She continued as though he hadn't spoken, the words rushing out of their hiding place, the dark place in her heart that the wonderful music had reached: 'I can't stop seeing Juliet's coffin –' she halted for a moment and dropped her head into her hands, overcome with emotion, then forced herself to look into his eyes and make sure he understood where she was coming from '– and James coming up the cathedral and putting his hand on it.' Her voice broke.

A muscle jerked in Matthew's cheek. She thought she saw the glimmer of uncertainty in his eyes. 'If you're that upset about it, we'll talk in the morning.'

'You mean that? Promise?'

'Promise.'

Later, when he joined her in bed, they made love, almost feverishly, clinging to each other as though they needed to escape into a world where they were united, where there were no shadows and secrets, nothing but the physical closeness of deep, warm kisses, soft caresses and the long, hot moment of release.

Afterwards, when Matthew was asleep, Rose lay next to him, her mind still racing with the image of James putting his hand on Juliet's coffin, and all the dark corners of her life were illuminated, so that the memory pulsed, fresh and strong, the memory of when everything had changed for ever …

1973

That day, in the middle of March, was freezing cold, with heavy grey clouds that darkened the afternoon sky and promised snow. A cold wind whipped around the deserted roads of the housing estate. It wasn't the kind of day you expected your life to take on a whole new meaning or all your dreams to be handed to you on a plate.

Her housework had been finished by eleven o'clock. The Formica kitchen presses were shining, the net curtains starched whiter than white, the floor in the small front room gleaming with lavender polish. All the ironing was done. She'd even smoothed clean white sheets over the bed she shared with Matthew. The good sheets, edged with pink embroidery, had been a wedding present.

Matthew seemed happy with their love life, reaching for her three or four times a week. She hoped it was enough for him and that she was doing everything right. Sometimes she even reached for him, well used by now to the feel of him inside her and the ache it satisfied.

But the ache in her heart that longed for a baby of her own still hadn't been satisfied.

Rose put on the radio and listened to Gay Byrne's morning

programme to break the silence of the house and the empty hours that stretched boringly ahead until Rebecca's visit. Her sister had written to say she was taking a half-day off work and would be on the two o'clock bus out from town. Rose and Matthew had no phone. Nobody on the estate had one, as there was a three-year wait for a line to be installed.

Into this spotlessly clean house Rebecca arrived, full of vitality, the noise, chatter and gossip of the bustling typing pool still clinging to her. Rose made tea and set out her wedding-present tea service of cups, saucers and plates, as well as a glass stand with biscuits and small cakes.

Then Rebecca began to talk and Rose's heart swelled with the enormity of what she was saying.

∾

'What do you think, Matthew?' Rose asked, later that evening, her nerves stretched taut as she told him everything in a shaky voice. About Juliet falling pregnant. About her having a short fling with a married man. Naturally Juliet was weighed down with remorse and guilt, but she was also terrified of her father finding out. And she didn't want her baby to end up in some kind of industrial school or, if the baby was lucky enough to be adopted, to feel beholden to adoptive parents. She'd seen the chip it had placed on Liam Corrigan's shoulders. She was going to give the baby away and Rebecca had suggested Rose and Matthew, two people who would be the most loving parents, people she could trust to bring the baby up as their own in a safe and secure home.

'Rebecca knows I'm very unhappy because we've no baby of our own yet,' Rose said. 'And it has been nearly two years. But I blame myself for that,' she went on hurriedly, in case Matthew thought she was questioning his virility. 'I'm probably over-anxious about it, which doesn't help.'

Matthew's face was set as he considered what she'd said. Then, after a while, he smiled. 'Yes, I think it could work out,' he said slowly. 'If it makes you happy, then I'm happy. I know how much you've dreamed of becoming a mother, and I'm sorry it doesn't seem to be happening for us.'

'I'm just afraid it might go wrong later,' she said, surprised by his acquiescence – she'd been expecting him to put up more of an argument.

'How could it? With Juliet's plan, we'd be the registered parents. We're not doing anything morally wrong, just circumventing some red tape.'

'According to Rebecca, Juliet said it's the one sure way she can guarantee we'll have the child, and it means the little one won't grow up with the knowledge that it was adopted.'

'If she goes ahead with it, she can't change her mind later, ever,' Matthew said. 'Neither can she tell this married man, whoever he is, that she's had his baby. Ever.'

'She knows that,' Rose said. 'She says it's all over between them and she's already forgotten about it. And if she's afraid of her father finding out, she's never going to admit to having an illegitimate baby, let alone arranging to give it away outside the legal channels.'

At first Rose had lain awake at night, her mind whirling with the joy of having a child to call her own after so many long, barren months. Mixed with this was her surprise at Matthew's ready agreement to raise another man's child as his own. Occasionally, at night, she caught herself wondering if the baby was indeed another man's child, or if Matthew had finally been unable to resist the vivacious Juliet, something she'd privately feared might happen since the night they'd first met.

But as the weeks went on, it slotted into place so easily, as though it was meant to be.

She even didn't have to *do* anything beyond wait for the baby to arrive.

She and Matthew sold the first home on which she'd lavished such care and moved to the outskirts of Galway, where they lived very quietly with Juliet in the three months preceding the birth of her baby. Matthew found it easy enough to get a transfer to a Galway City branch of the bank. It was Juliet who had to be brave, wearing a wedding ring and passing herself off as Mrs Rose Moore when she visited a busy doctor's practice and got a referral to the equally busy maternity hospital in Galway.

Beyond Matthew going to work and Juliet to the hospital, the three barely ventured out, Rebecca coming down some weekends to see how things were, and bringing messages of love from Granddad Paddy who, with their friends and extended family, not to mention Matthew's ageing parents, thought Rose was having a difficult pregnancy and needed lots of bed rest.

When Juliet arrived home from the hospital and baby James was placed in Rose's arms, her aching heart flooded with love, and the joy of holding him outweighed all her fears. Juliet went home to Dublin, while Rose and Matthew settled into life in Galway with their brand new baby. By the time Matthew got a transfer back to Dublin, and they moved to another new house in a sprawling estate further out from the city centre, teeming with young families and stay-at-home mothers, James Moore was six months old and Rose, with her son, blended in easily.

From time to time, she looked at her baby's face, wondering

if there was any resemblance to Matthew. Like her husband, he had dark hair and blue eyes, but his eyes were a far deeper blue than Matthew's and, unlike Matthew, he was a quiet, sensitive child.

From time to time she wondered at the strained atmosphere between her friend and her husband. Eventually she plucked up the courage to raise it with Matthew. 'How come you and Juliet can't have a civil conversation without sparking off each other?' she'd asked.

He'd laughed. 'Our heated debates, you mean? They're just a bit of craic. Women like Juliet get on my nerves with all their equality shite. Thinking they're better than men. Thinking they can rule the country, never mind the world.'

In a sense they do, she'd felt like saying, for they give life to another human being, and what could be more brilliant, powerful or amazing than that? Something she hadn't been able to accomplish ...

By tacit agreement, she and Matthew never spoke of the circumstances of James's birth. Neither did Juliet. It was a silent intrigue that lurked between them and a subject they all avoided, as though it had never happened.

But Rose had never anticipated that what she and Matthew had brought about or, more importantly, how they had deceived James, as well as the stark terror of being found out, would explode in her consciousness now and again. It had nibbled away at her peace of mind, culminating years later in her breakdown. Still, she managed to paper over the cracks and glide along with the help of her pills.

It might have been okay if Matthew hadn't decided to blow the fragile peace apart with his plan to run for the presidency. Rose thought he was tempting Fate. As far as Matthew was concerned, there were no skeletons in their cupboard because they simply didn't exist.

And then Juliet had told Rebecca that she was having regrets, and didn't care if some secrets came out into the open. Naturally, Rebecca had told Rose, who had told Matthew, who had thought that Juliet was being her old rebellious self and simply trying to rattle him.

Juliet had plummeted down a cliff face less than a week later.

And after that it was never going to be okay.

FIFTY-TWO

'Don't forget I'll be late tonight,' Matthew said.

'You told me all about your busy day. I'm not to call you unless the house is on fire.'

'Too right.'

Rose lay in bed and watched him moving around the bedroom. It was barely seven o'clock on Friday morning and he'd already spent twenty minutes on the cross trainer in his den before he'd showered and dressed. Now he was off to Tory Technologies to put in a full day of wheeling and dealing, starting with a stand-up breakfast meeting. She imagined harried executives gulping coffee as they listened to his instructions, then scattering to do his will. He would have a working lunch, followed by an afternoon conference call with New York, and later, an exploratory meeting with his trusted advisers to begin mapping out the strategy for his presidential campaign. A day in the life of Matthew Moore.

'A hectic day with important people to meet,' he said, a lift of excitement in his voice, as though he couldn't wait to get started. 'I don't know how late I'll be so don't wait up.' She watched as he chose a tie, then looked at himself in the mirror and expertly knotted it so that it sat perfectly with his expensive grey suit. Then, with a flourish, he fastened his white-gold cuff links.

'Aren't you forgetting something?'

He paused by the door to his dressing room, alerted by the tone of her voice.

'You said we'd talk, Matthew. Last night? Remember? You promised.'

He came over to the bed and kissed her cheek, smelling of expensive cologne, looking handsome, trustworthy, the embodiment of honesty and integrity. 'Of course. We'll talk later. As soon as I'm home.'

'You told me not to wait up, that you might be late.'

'I know how you fret, darling, but just remember, you've nothing whatsoever to worry about. Everything is perfectly fine.'

He walked across to the door, his impatience to be gone flowing from every line in his body. He couldn't wait to get his teeth into the important challenges of his day, leaving her to her own frivolous devices.

Mrs Barry wasn't coming in that morning, and Rose had no appointments, no lunch dates, no charity work or anything else significant to do. It would be another long day when her fears and anxieties hung heavy in her head, when she took cat naps trying to make up for her sleepless nights.

All of a sudden, she couldn't stand it any more. She couldn't stand the thick silence between her and Matthew, the ease with which the day ahead had already absorbed his energy. Most of all she couldn't stand his naïve conviction that everything was fine when, in reality, it was far from it. Especially now that Juliet was gone and everything had changed.

Suddenly she could remain silent no longer. For someone who hadn't a rebellious bone in her body, she was surprised by the strength of the mutiny that bubbled up inside her. It broke free in her head, sparking around her temples, and she felt a moment's dizziness as she said, in a loud and determined voice, 'No, Matthew, it's not perfectly fine.'

Her husband froze. He turned very slowly and looked at her. 'What is it? You know I've a busy day ahead.'

'I don't care how busy it's going to be,' she said. 'We have to talk.'

'Now?'

'Yes, now.'

Something resolute in her face must have got through to him for he took his hand off the door handle and stood there, looking, she thought, unusually awkward.

'James …' She gulped. 'He didn't *know*, Matthew. He didn't know his real mother was dead. It's an image that's haunting me. I've been trying to ignore it, hoping it would go away, but it's getting worse and now I can't ignore it any longer. I can't get away from the image of James putting his hand on Juliet's coffin, not knowing she was his mother.' She gripped the duvet between her clenched hands and willed herself not to break down.

'Are you suggesting we tell him the truth?' Matthew asked, in a steely voice.

'How can we?' Rose said, her heart thumping. 'I looked at James standing there and knew he must never know, now that it had come this far. He'd hate us, and never talk to us again. Oh, Matthew, I feel overwhelmed because it's all so horribly sad.' She stared at him, dry-eyed.

Matthew glanced at his watch and walked over to sit on the bed. 'Look, I know you're upset, but think about it logically for a moment,' he said, taking her hand in his. 'Lots of adopted children never get to know who their birth mother is. And in the Ireland before the eighties, and God knows for how long afterwards, hundreds, if not thousands, of births were compromised in some way,' he continued, 'so there are hundreds, if not thousands, of grown men and women who are probably walking around quite happily unaware of their true birth circumstances. And that's without adding donor sperm or any modern interventions into the mix. The main thing is, they're walking around happily.'

'And does that make it right?' she countered.

'What is right?' Matthew gazed at her appealingly. She couldn't help wondering if he'd practised that look for the television cameras. 'We raised James as our son,' he said, in his warm, assured voice. 'Our names are on his birth certificate. We're the parents who loved him and took care of him from when he was a few days old.'

'Yes – but surely he has a right to know his true origins?'

'Why? What difference would it make? James has a fantastic and successful life. Why upset everything? Is it right to pull the rug from under him?'

'My head is telling me all this, and I know we daren't tell him the truth, but my heart is saying that it's different now that Juliet is dead.'

'Why is it different? If you feel so strongly that he should know his birth mother, surely it was more important when she was alive.'

'I couldn't think about it then. I was too afraid to. I didn't want James to hate me for what we did. Now if he finds out somehow, he'll hate me even more. Besides, while Juliet was alive I always thought in the back of my mind there would be time to put it right. Maybe when you'd retired … There was always the possibility that we'd find some way to resolve what we did.'

'And supposing it was all out in the open? Can you imagine how that might hurt James? How devastated he might be?' Matthew, the great debater, knowing what to target. 'I don't want James to hate me either. And I'm poised in front of the most challenging test of my life, Rose. We don't need this complication in our lives. And, believe me, neither does James. It would ruin everything.'

'I know what you're saying. It's everything I've said to myself, but I'm finding it impossible to live with at the moment. And whatever about James accidentally discovering the truth when Juliet was alive, it would be ten times worse now that she's gone.'

'I agree,' Matthew said. 'Apart from that, you must remember that what we did was illegal and unconstitutional. It might be similar to what went on in some Irish families, and it's a rather ordinary, everyday scandal compared to what passes for scandal nowadays, but because of who we are, including James, it would make front-page news and destroy our family, never mind every atom of my credibility. Neither of us can afford that to happen.'

'Don't remind me.' Rose buried her head in her hands. 'But just supposing someone got wind of it? I told you there are rumours flying around that Juliet had an affair.' She raised her head and looked at him closely, old insecurities rising to the surface, but nothing flickered across Matthew's composed face.

'Absolutely no one will find out, Rose. The only people who know about Juliet's link to James are you, me and Rebecca. There's no one else involved. Right? So unless one of us talks, which we won't, James is our son. Don't ever think anything otherwise. Don't let your fears get the better of you and we'll all be fine.'

He stood up and kissed her forehead. He was putting a useless sticking plaster on a raw, gaping wound, Rose thought.

❧❧

Rose watched Rebecca weave through the tables and across the restaurant to where she was seated in a booth at the back, looking so purposeful and vital that Rose was envious for a moment. It wasn't until her sister shrugged out of her leather jacket, and sat opposite, that she saw her face was pale and drawn.

'I'm glad you could meet me,' Rebecca said, putting her mobile on the table and her bag on the banquette beside her.

The hours since Matthew had left for the office had hung heavily on Rose's hands and she had felt a warm rush of gratitude when Rebecca had called, suggesting lunch in a city-centre hotel.

They ordered a fish starter, then lemon chicken, and a bottle of San Pellegrino.

'I wanted to see you before I headed off to Rome this evening,' Rebecca said quietly, fiddling with her napkin. 'You know I'll be telling Danielle about Juliet's will?'

'Yes.'

'And James needs to be told, too, sooner rather than later, before it gets splashed across the tabloids and he and Danielle are named as prime suspects in causing her death.'

Rose put down her glass of water. 'Don't joke about things like that.'

'Well, be warned. I had Liz Monaghan in the shop earlier this week. She's concocting some piece on Juliet and I shudder to think what's in it. She's already asked me if I knew Juliet was having an affair. I don't know what she's trying to get at.'

'Not Liz as well?'

Rebecca looked at her sharply. 'Why? Did you hear it too?'

'Matthew and I were out with the Coffeys on Saturday night, and when Celia got me to herself she said much the same thing. Apparently it was going around the beauty salon.'

'And what did you say?'

'What do you think? Should I have said Juliet had loads of affairs? Or left a trail of broken hearts behind her? I told her it was a ridiculous idea. Problem is, once something like that starts circulating, it's hard to rein it in. Oh, Rebecca, where is all this going to end?'

'I don't know,' Rebecca said soberly. 'It's a nightmare that Juliet's gone in such a mindless way, and we're left with whispers and rumours, and my gut feeling that her death couldn't have been an accident.'

Rose's heartbeat accelerated. 'You scarcely think that Juliet herself ...'

'No, definitely not,' Rebecca said stoutly. 'But something happened, something went wrong. And whether it was a person she knew or whatever ...' She let out a slow breath and looked totally dejected. 'And I still have to tell you about Liam Corrigan.'

Rose listened silently as Rebecca filled her in. 'No wonder you look so cut up.'

'Do I? Thanks,' Rebecca said drily. 'I don't understand all the lies. God knows what he's covering up, and I can't help remembering that time in the Shelbourne when he threatened to make Juliet pay.'

'Don't laugh, but if anyone needed Juliet out of the way it was Matthew. And me. If anyone starts digging too deeply, we'll both be in trouble.'

'Rose!'

It was a relief to unburden herself to some degree. 'That's how spooked I'm getting,' Rose said. 'I'm just ... feeling as though things are slowly falling apart. As though I'm falling apart. You see, Matthew was home later than me that Friday night, even though we had an important reception. He barely had enough time to get ready. And he was very agitated. Later on, I had a look at his mobile and he'd been texting Juliet, wanting to see her. And, let's face it, he has a huge motive because Juliet was an obstacle to his dreams in more ways than one.'

Rebecca leaned across the table. 'Rose, hang on. You're talking about your *husband*, for God's sake. No matter how ambitious Matthew is, you hardly think he's capable of cold-blooded murder?'

'No, I don't, any more than anyone else is. But supposing … supposing he didn't mean it? That it was an accident that just happened. Juliet used to get up his nose sometimes. Supposing he got very angry with her …'

Rebecca smiled sympathetically. 'You've really worried about this, haven't you?'

'Supposing they went for a walk along the cliff,' Rose said, unable to contain herself. She twisted her wedding ring around and around as she spoke, her voice low. 'She often invited her friends to do that. And if they had a quarrel halfway around? I know Juliet could be maddening at times. What if she riled Matthew so much that he became incensed and hit out at her?'

Rebecca shook her head. 'I know Matthew gets fired up at times, but I can't see him being angry enough to strike any woman.'

'Yes, but supposing Juliet totally enraged him and he had a mad, senseless moment? She could have destroyed his credibility along with his dream if she'd lived long enough to take the skeletons out of her cupboard. We don't know what people are capable of, when pushed to the limit, do we? God, Rebecca, I know all this sounds awful but my brain feels so scrambled at the moment that I can't think straight.'

'Neither can I. Once or twice I had ridiculous images of Liam doing much the same.'

'Oh, God, what are we like?' Rose felt the prick of tears at the back of her eyes.

'We're both gutted over Juliet,' Rebecca said, clasping her hand. 'We're both crazy with grief, underneath it all. Sometimes I forget she's not around any more, and then it overwhelms me like a black tide.'

'Same here. Matthew and I had a talk this morning,' Rose said. 'What's really upsetting me is James …'

Rebecca gave her a sharp look. 'James? As in …'

Rose toyed with her chicken. 'I was very upset last night after we'd got home from the opera. I can't believe I didn't realise how badly I'd feel about him not knowing … anything. It's tearing me apart. And now it's impossible to tell him the truth.'

Rebecca's eyes were wide with alarm. 'In all these years, that's the first time you've ever brought it up. You must be very badly shaken. I'm really sorry and wish there was some way I could help you and make it better.'

'It's not your problem. It's mine and Matthew's.'

'Yes, but I can't help feeling partly responsible.'

'It was me and Matthew who made the decision to raise James as our son,' Rose said. 'You weren't responsible for our actions. We were. Sometimes, Rebecca, you assume too much.'

'What do you mean?'

'I know you like to be helpful, but sometimes you forget that other people are grown adults, in charge of their own lives. There's a fine line between … God.' She stared at Rebecca's set face. 'I know this is coming out wrong.'

'It's not. I think I get the picture. Keep your nose out of our business, Rebecca. Get a life of your own. You only know the half of it.'

Rose was mystified. 'Did I say that?'

'No. Juliet did,' Rebecca said, looking haunted. 'I'm still trying to figure out what she meant. I'll probably never know now.'

'I'm sorry,' Rose said. 'I wouldn't hurt you for the world.'

'I butt in too much, don't I? I just want the people I love to be happy.'

Rose bit her lip. 'I know you do, but I wish you weren't so naïve at times. Sometimes that just isn't possible. People have to make their own mistakes, then live with them as best they can. There's no such thing as happy ever after.'

Rebecca stayed silent until the waiter had cleared their plates. Then she laughed a mirthless laugh. 'Well, if the last two weeks have taught me anything it's that. Do you think you made a mistake all those years ago?'

Rose stared into space for a moment. 'No, I don't, and at the time we had to go by Juliet's wishes, but looking at the nightmare situation we're in now, I think I would have handled it differently.'

Their coffees arrived. Rose stared at hers, feeling she'd had enough coffee over the last fortnight to last her a lifetime.

'James has to know about her will,' Rebecca said.

'I know.' She sighed heavily. 'He'll be back in Dublin early next week.'

'I'll see how I get on with Danielle,' Rebecca said, 'and we'll talk some more. But whatever you do, keep away from Liz Monaghan while you're feeling upset,' she cautioned. 'I don't know where she's coming from, or what her problem is, but with the mood she's in at the moment, her tongue would tear you to pieces.'

FIFTY-THREE

It was late on Friday evening when Mum arrived. She called my mobile as soon as she was outside the apartment building, having got a taxi from the airport. I went down to let her in and bring her up to my second-floor apartment. As soon as I saw her, I realised how selfish and wrong my assumptions had been.

For this wasn't about me: Mum hadn't come over to Rome just to lavish love and undivided attention on her only daughter, or to offer consolation in the aftermath of my busted wedding and mend the cracks in my shattered life. She was tired and sad, with military-sized shadows under her eyes, and I could have kicked myself for losing sight of the fact that she was grieving for her best friend, a sad journey she was only beginning. Maybe, I thought soberly, as I hugged her and picked up her weekend case, it was my turn to lavish a little attention on her.

But some things hadn't changed. Because it was mine, she thought my dog box of an apartment was fabulously chic, even down to the mismatched cushions and fake lavender in the blue jug. It wasn't, by any stretch of the imagination. She was nonplussed when she noticed there was only one bedroom.

'You're in here, Mum,' I said to her, putting her case on the floor.

'And where are you?' Her eyes cast about as though another

room was going to manifest itself. 'Ah, no, Danielle, I can't let you do that.'

'Do what?'

'Give me your lovely bedroom. Where will you sleep?'

'I've a perfectly good sofa, with a soft, patchwork quilt, and it's only two nights. No arguments, right?' I said, in a jokey voice.

To my surprise, she acquiesced a lot more readily than I would have thought. Another sign that she wasn't herself.

'Do you want a rest after your journey, Mum?' I asked solicitously. 'If you don't feel up to going out, we could have a drink here.'

'A rest? I'm not decrepit yet,' she said, a little smartly. 'I wouldn't say no to going out and having a few decent glasses of chilled Sauvignon Blanc.'

'There's a bar on the corner, and if they like the look of you they'll put out nibbles on the house,' I said. 'Or we can hit the town,' I continued, trying to sound cheery.

'Hit the town,' said Mum. 'It's a while since I lived it up in Rome.'

I knew from the faraway look in her eyes that the last time she'd been here she was with Juliet.

Mum had a quick shower, emerging in a waft of Jo Malone and declaring she was fresh and ready for action. She wasn't, not really, for her face was strained and pinched. When I suggested we start with the bar on the corner she sounded relieved. It was very modern and cosmopolitan, and we sat side by side in a booth by the window, watching the swirl of cars, scooters and people going by outside while we lashed back chilled white wine and chomped at a large bowl of crisps.

Another Friday night in Rome. The first three months I'd been here, I'd seen no one. And now, for the second week in a row, I had a visitor. The background music was coming from a pop station playing English love ballads, and my heart ached with a mixture of homesickness, unrequited love, empathy for my mother and the loss of Juliet. I wished that, for one moment, I could transport us back to Juliet's kitchen at Verbena View with the warm welcome, the big table and the doors folded back to the sea and sky. I wanted one more chance to hug Juliet really tightly and tell her how much I loved her, the way I'd meant to time and time again; the way I should have before she was gone and it was too late.

I still couldn't believe I'd never see her again. Ever.

After a while we'd exhausted safe topics such as the weather, my job, Rome traffic, her flight, and there was no mention of moving on to another bar. I knew something was seriously wrong when Mum said, 'I don't know where to start.'

'I thought we'd already started,' I said inanely, unease prickling under my skin.

'Ah, Danielle, if only …'

'If only what?' I asked, my heart contracting: the same words had been spoken to me just last weekend.

'If only I was just here for a social visit.'

'What is it, Mum? What are you trying to tell me?'

She stared out of the window for so long that I grew alarmed. Then she gave me a piercingly sad look and said, 'It's about Juliet. And I'd prefer to get the unsavoury news out of the way first.'

She told me then, in a voice drained of emotion. I listened in growing disbelief and dismay about the police call to the house, the ongoing investigation and the possibility that Juliet had been involved in a struggle at the top of the cliff. 'We still don't know what happened,' Mum said. 'I don't know if we ever will for sure.

I feel as though my head is going to burst with the craziness of it all. Rose and I are at our wits' end. Rose, even,' she gave a harsh laugh, 'was wondering if Matthew pushed her in a fit of anger.'

'*Matthew?*' I couldn't keep the shock out of my voice. 'Why would Rose think that?'

I remembered then that Rose had had some kind of a breakdown a few years ago. The stress of Juliet's death must have unhinged her slightly.

Mum blinked, then looked at me as though she was coming back from somewhere far away. 'That's how mad it's all becoming,' she said, her voice a little shaky. 'I was even imagining Liam Corrigan having a fight with Juliet and maybe …'

'That's a turnaround. I thought you guys were getting on,' I said, sad that something had gone pear-shaped with her and Liam, just when she could have done with a big, strong shoulder to lean on.

'We were.' Mum gave another gruff laugh and, to my horror, a tear slid down her cheek.

I'd seen her cry before, when Dad had died, but that didn't make it any easier to see her struggle to hold back tears now, as all about us the bar was filling with laughing people and Friday night revved up a gear.

I let her pull herself together. Then I said, very gently, 'What happened with Liam?'

'I found out he wasn't to be trusted,' she said, and told me about yet another police visit to the house.

No wonder they were all finding it difficult to cope back in Dublin. My head was spinning with supersized images of Detective Woods and Detective Inspector Callaghan taking up all the space in our front room and upsetting my mother not once but twice and then again. On top of which her best friend had died. In fact, my head was spinning so much that I missed some of the details, the gist eventually trickling through to me.

'Hang on a minute, Mum,' I said. 'You think Liam didn't know you were going to be in the Seagrass? That he was telling lies about wanting to see you?'

'How could he have known I was there? He said Juliet told him, but I hadn't spoken to her all week.'

I found it surprising that Mum hadn't talked to Juliet all week, but I ignored that for now. Something else was flowing through the synapses of my brain, like a crystal stream: the knowledge that I could, with a few words, make up for some of Mum's desperate unhappiness.

'Actually, she did know,' I said softly.

Mum frowned at me. 'Please don't talk in riddles, Danielle. I can't take any more.'

'I'm not. I was talking to Juliet on Thursday evening, remember? The night before she … the accident … She was talking about coming to see me in Rome. And,' I smiled, 'she said she was sorry she wasn't going to be around for you that weekend on account of her commitments, and I told her you'd just decided …' I was unable to stop the smile spreading across my face as I watched her grappling with the meaning of my words.

'You told her I was going to the wedding in the Seagrass,' Mum said flatly. 'And when Liam called to see Juliet, she told him.'

'There you are,' I said. 'He wasn't making it up.'

'God.' She closed her eyes and sat back against the banquette. She stayed silent for ages, as though she was trying to absorb it all. Then she opened her eyes and looked at me in consternation. 'What have I done? I bawled him out of it, Danielle.'

'Yes, Mum,' I grinned, not believing her for a minute. 'I'd love to see you bawling someone out of it.'

'I did. I was so angry. You should have heard me. I told him he was never to contact me again.'

'So? Think how delighted he'll be when you call him. If he has any sense, he'll know you were under terrible strain. And if he doesn't understand, he's not worth bothering with.'

Mum gave me a tiny smile. 'You wouldn't find it a problem if I was seeing him?'

I flashed her a stern glance. 'What have I said to you time and time again? Get a life for yourself. Look, Mum, who knows what will happen tomorrow? If you have a chance of happiness you seize it with both hands.'

'That has come home to me more than ever over the past couple of weeks.'

'And the other thing is,' I went on, amazed that I was meting out advice to Mum, 'whatever did happen to Juliet, you can't change things now, nor could you have prevented it. Juliet would disown you if you didn't live your life and make the most of it.'

'I hope to God I had no hand in what happened to her,' she said, mystifying me completely.

'Of course you didn't,' I said stoutly. 'Any more than you could have prevented what happened to Dad. Unfortunately, Mum, you don't have a magic wand to prevent all bad things from happening. Neither do you rule the world.'

Once more she stared out of the window, deep in thought, for so long that I had to wave my hand in front of her. 'Are you there?'

She seemed to snap back to attention, as though she was throwing a mental switch inside her head. Whatever was flickering in her eyes disappeared behind a shutter as she put on a smile, and said, 'I'm here, Danielle, and now I want to get fresh drinks and talk to you about the good news.'

'So there's good news?'

'Yes,' she said, smiling as she summoned the barman, who promptly refreshed our drinks and gave us a dish of assorted nuts, as well as refilling the bowl of crisps. When he had left our table, she twirled the stem of her glass, and said, 'You know I'm the executor of Juliet's estate?'

'Yes?'

'Well, darling, I have some rather surprising news for you. Juliet changed her will in February and she named you as one of her chief beneficiaries.'

She sat back, clearly waiting for me to react with some level of enthusiasm, but I couldn't. Shock mingled with foreboding snagged my breath. 'What does that mean exactly?' I asked, as though there were jagged boulders in my mouth.

'Juliet's will includes some charitable bequests, and Robert Jordan can have whatever furniture or paintings he wants. After that, Juliet had savings and investments, and those, with Verbena View, make up the bulk of her estate, which she has willed equally to both you and James.'

Something punched me in the solar plexus and I gasped. All the fragmented pieces that had made up my life in the last few months exploded in front of me: the Christmas table at Verbena View, me catching Juliet watching me in the reflection of us all in the darkened window, me calling off my wedding, and Juliet changing her will soon after. Fast forward a few weeks and she'd wanted to come out to Rome to see me, to talk to me, but before she'd had a chance she'd had a fatal accident.

James's eyes when he'd said, 'If only …'

The unconnected pieces twirled in front of me, making me giddy and nauseous.

'Danielle?'

I made a huge effort to anchor myself in the present. My mother was waiting patiently, a smile on her face, anticipating my joy at the life-altering news.

'You're not serious,' I said.

'I am, darling.' Mum gave my shoulder a squeeze. 'It means you won't have any money worries for a long time, if ever.'

When I fell back into silence, she went on, 'Now I'm going to give you some of your own advice. I know it's a little bittersweet, that you're receiving Juliet's legacy because she's gone, but …'

I put up my hand. 'Please don't say it.' Don't tell me to enjoy the benefit and live my life to the fullest.

'I can see it's upset you.' Mum was stroking my arm. 'And that's the last thing Juliet would want. She'd want you to be happy, Danielle.'

Poor Mum! She hadn't a clue why I was so upset, and thought it was because I was distressed at benefiting from Juliet's death. That, too, was going on in the background. The prospect of owning the wonderful Verbena View was something I couldn't quite grasp. But most devastating of all was that Juliet had bequeathed the bulk of her estate to me and James.

James! The person I most needed to avoid. Now we would be thrown together. No way would I emerge unscathed.

'Why me and James?' I managed to ask, my voice reduced to a high-pitched squeak.

'She always regarded you two as the family she never had,' Mum said.

I'd known that much because Juliet had told me several times that I was her honorary daughter. It had made me feel special.

'And did she give you any reason for changing her will?' The million-dollar question. Had she seen something in my eyes? If so, how did she think that throwing us together as we sorted out the legalities, never mind the emotional trauma of going through her effects, would solve anything? It would scald my heart.

'No, Danielle, she didn't. She only told me when it was done and dusted. Originally Rose and I were her beneficiaries, so chances were, her legacy would have filtered through to you and James anyway.'

'This is why you came to Rome, isn't it? To tell me.'

Mum nodded.

'Does James know?'

'Not yet,' she said. 'If Rose won't talk to him I guess I'll have to.'

I focused on this because it was easier than imagining James's reaction to the news. 'Why wouldn't Rose tell him?'

'No particular reason. She's still gutted about Juliet.'

'So are you,' I said, emerging from my shell shock for long enough to touch her arm. 'You're obviously made of sterner stuff. And now I know why Rose thought Matthew might have had a motive for fighting with Juliet.'

My mother spluttered as her wine went down the wrong way. It took her several moments to recover her breath. 'Like what?' she asked me, in a strangled voice.

'Matthew was probably raging that he'd lost the chance for him and Rose to get a claim on Verbena View.'

'Danielle! No way. They're so comfortable it wouldn't make much of a difference to them.'

'Yes, but it was Juliet's house, and Matthew's always been a little jealous of her. He'd love the idea of lording it in her home and sitting at her antique desk. He'd probably take great pleasure in dumping all her certificates in the bin,' I added, in a fit of petulance, still overwhelmed by the twist of fate that would throw me head to head with James.

'Darling, you don't mean that.'

'Come on, Mum, you know he was always defensive around her. You've heard him trying to outdo her at dinner-table debates and dishing out faint praise on her successes. Maybe she made him feel a little inferior, with her education and background, because he could never compete with that, and life, to him, is a competition.'

'I don't know … I suppose that's one way of looking at it.' Mum's brow furrowed. Then she brightened, in typical Mum fashion, looking for the best in something, trying to make me happy. 'What's done is done, Danielle, and I'm glad you'll have the comfort of that financial cushion, even though it's hard to accept the hows and whys of it, and it'll be difficult sorting through the red tape. But Rose and I will help with the house and Juliet's personal effects. Robert Jordan has already asked me for help as he wouldn't have a clue.'

'Yes,' I said, still feeling faint, knowing that I had the hardest struggle in my life ahead of me. And there was absolutely nothing Mum or anyone else could do to ease the pain of it.

FIFTY-FOUR

Rose smiled and remembered to put her weight on one foot as Juliet had advised when she posed to have her photo taken for the diary pages in a glossy magazine. She looked the part in her softly draping jersey sheath and L.K. Bennett peep-toe shoes, with her hair freshly blow-dried. But she shouldn't have had that second glass of wine. Not mixed with her little white pill. And not in the middle of Saturday afternoon, at the fundraising fashion show in the D4 Berkeley Hotel. Especially when there were so many press around. She'd seen Liz Monaghan slithering through the crowd at the back of the hall earlier and prayed she'd manage to avoid her.

She shouldn't even be here in her fraught frame of mind, but Matthew had insisted.

'I think I'll give it a miss,' she'd said to him, during breakfast that morning, when he'd asked her what time she was leaving. 'I don't feel up to all that happy socialising.'

'You have to be there, Rose,' he'd said, pouring more coffee. 'That fundraiser is going to get a lot of media coverage and it'll be valuable exposure for you.'

'Exposure!' She'd laughed. 'That's exactly what I'm afraid of. We're frauds, Matthew, you and I, pretending to be above reproach, people of honour and integrity. Supposing our little secret got into the wrong hands? What then?'

'It had better not,' he said curtly. 'And I wish you'd stop obsessing about it. You have to pull yourself together and forget it ever happened. Maybe we ignored some red tape, but we did what we thought was best. That's all you have to remember. Forget the rest. If word leaked out now, it would be explosive.'

'Do you feel at all relieved that the threat of Juliet letting the cat out of the bag is gone?' she asked, watching him closely.

'What kind of a question is that?' He rose from the table and picked up his mug of coffee. She could see him moving into work mode, his mind ticking off what had to be done, like a well-oiled machine. 'I've calls to make,' he said, 'and I've meetings with potential advisers later this morning. It's going to be another busy day. Let me know what time you're leaving and I'll call a taxi for you. And, darling,' he paused by the door and smiled reassuringly at her, 'just relax about everything. The sky is not about to fall in.'

Oh yes it was, Rose decided, remembering his words as she gripped the stem of her wine glass and watched Liz Monaghan plunge through the crowds, homing in on her like a shark having scented its prey.

'Rose! I thought you might be here! Great to see so many people turning out to support the charity, isn't it? And amazing that so many A-list models and celebs are giving their time. Still, it's a great cause. Juliet would have been thrilled.' Liz fixed her with a laser-like stare. 'She was one of the patrons of this charity, wasn't she,' Liz went on, 'along with her own foundation? She was a busy lady on the fundraising circuit. I wonder what will happen to that now?'

Rose found her voice. 'I've no idea. If you'll excuse me ...' She darted a look towards the exit, which Liz intercepted. There was a swathe of designer-clad people milling around between her and the double doors to the hotel lobby and her ultimate escape. She wished there was someone to come to her rescue. She couldn't handle Liz by herself. Not today.

Liz put a hand on her arm and Rose flinched.

'Before you go,' the gossip columnist said, 'did you hear the rumour going around about Juliet? That she had an affair? If anyone should know the truth it's you and your sister. But Rebecca won't talk to me. I went by that little boutique she hangs out in yesterday and again this morning but she wasn't there. Do you think she's trying to avoid me? She told me she thinks I'm a vindictive bitch. What do you think, Rose?'

'Whatever Juliet did or didn't do, it had nothing to do with my family or Rebecca,' Rose said, her voice tight.

'Your *family*? What happened in your family?' Liz asked, her eyes alight with curiosity as she pounced on Rose's words.

'Nothing,' Rose said, hot colour sweeping across her face.

'Nothing?' The twin arches of Liz's eyebrows lifted in perfect unison. 'I was only asking if you knew about Juliet's affair with a married man. Seeing as you were such good friends with her, I thought you'd know. I certainly wasn't asking about your family. Or your drop-dead gorgeous husband. There's hardly any connection, is there?' she asked silkily.

'You'll have to excuse me,' Rose said, sidling away.

As Rose put her glass down on a table and moved in the direction of the door, Liz followed her. 'Oh, gosh, you are edgy, aren't you?' she said. 'What could you have to hide, Rose?'

Rose passed Celia Coffey chatting to her cronies, Rachel and

Megan. Feeling ridiculous, and hotly embarrassed, she smiled brightly as though nothing was amiss, even though it was obvious that Liz was stalking her.

Never again, she decided grimly. No matter what Matthew said, she was never again attending any function on her own.

'Rose? Did I hit a nerve? I can see you're upset.'

Then, 'Rose! What's up? Why won't you stop and talk to me?'

When they reached the doorway, with the lobby ahead and the taxis lined up outside the entrance, waiting to whisk her away, Rose finally turned to face her.

'I've nothing to say to you, Liz. Nothing at all.'

'What are you afraid of?'

'I'm not afraid of anything.'

'Like hell you're not.' Liz's mouth curved in an empty smile. 'And why won't your husband reply to my emails? What's going on there? Or is he afraid of something too?'

'Rebecca was right. You are vindictive.' Rose grabbed at the words and flung them out like daggers, trying to stop Liz in her tracks.

'You may be sorry you said that,' Liz said, 'when I get to the bottom of whatever is going on between you, Rebecca and Juliet.'

'Why don't you fuck off?' Rose said, her legs shaking. She hurried towards the lobby and the safety of the waiting taxis beyond. She gave the driver her address, sank back into the soft leather, and wondered how much longer she'd be able to stop her life totally unravelling. Her tenuous hold on her emotions was slipping.

FIFTY-FIVE

I watched Mum close her eyes behind her shades as she tilted her head to the sun, and the contours of her face relaxed, as though she was finally unwinding and grateful to be here. We were sitting with what seemed like a million chattering tourists by the fountain at the bottom of the Spanish Steps. Saturday afternoon was sunny, but cool enough to wear a jacket. Ahead of us stretched the Via Condotti, and the narrow street of designer shops was heaving with weekend shoppers.

Even though she'd visited years ago, I'd spent the morning bringing Mum on a whistle-stop tour of the main sights in the historic centre of Rome, which, thankfully, allowed us little time to talk. We'd had toasted panini for lunch in a small café on a narrow street near the Trevi fountain. Then we'd strolled to the church at the top of the Spanish Steps, where we'd stood and looked at the vista of the city, the elegant buildings washed in pale apricot and yellow, the green-grey domes and steeples of the churches and, hugging the horizon, the undulating green of the hills. It had seemed so peaceful from that perspective, and it had obviously relaxed Mum, but I'd felt detached from reality since she had dropped her bombshell about Juliet's legacy.

'Are you feeling any better about things today, Danielle?' she asked, as we sat by the fountain, raising the topic we'd avoided all morning.

'Sort of,' I said lamely.

She took off her sunglasses. 'I wish you'd come home,' she said.

'Is that another reason why you came out to see me?'

'Yes,' she said. 'If you were here for the pleasure of it, I could live with that. But you're not. You came here to run away from a bad situation and that's fine for a while, sometimes we need a hidey-hole, but it's not going to fix anything. The longer you leave things unresolved between you and Conor, the more difficult it's going to get.'

'Who said anything was unresolved?'

'Danielle, I can see by your face that you're deeply unhappy, and something is eating you up. You've lost weight as well. I don't want to interfere, but I don't like seeing people I love unhappy.' Then Mum gave an embarrassed laugh. 'There I go again. You can tell me to take a hike and get my own life, but I'm concerned about you.'

'It's okay, Mum, I know you are, and it's nice,' I said, feeling so rotten inside that for once I welcomed her attention.

Mum positively beamed.

'And while we're on the subject,' I continued, watching a small dark-haired girl skip happily around the fountain, 'I emailed Conor earlier this week and he replied the other night. So we're talking now, and we've a lot of stuff to work through but it's well and truly over. And, Mum,' I took a quick breath, 'I was the one who cancelled the wedding, not Conor. I decided I couldn't go through with it as I didn't love him enough.'

I waited for remonstrations: Conor was wonderful; I wasn't getting any younger; how about our lovely home, that fabulous wedding dress and the honeymoon? But those were the arguments that I'd imagined in those fraught nights before I'd called the whole thing off. I hadn't given enough credit to my mother.

'Oh, darling,' she said, her face soft with affection, 'I'm sorry to hear that, but you were very brave to do what you did and perfectly right. The world would be a much happier place if people stopped doing what they felt they should do, and just listened to their own instincts, no matter how difficult it seems at the time.'

'In other words, listen to your heart,' I said, loving her and feeling a little choked because what she was saying was so similar to what Juliet had told me. I had a sense of them forging a path through life from their teenage years, learning from their knocks along the way, and swapping gossip as well as advice.

'Exactly.' Mum smiled, as she patted my knee. 'It won't lead you astray.'

But it already has, I felt like weeping. It's made me fall in love with my cousin. I held back my urge to throw myself into her arms and suggested we take the Via Condotti by storm. Mum laughed and stood up. She hoisted her canvas shoulder bag and, perching her sunglasses on the top of her head, she asked which I'd like to hit first: YSL, Prada or Hermès.

'Let's pick up a few Armani bags,' I joked.

Neither Mum nor I had any truck with designer labels for the sake of it. Okay, if you wanted to look groomed, a little splurge was sometimes necessary, more so at Mum's age than mine. But I couldn't understand women who joined waiting lists to pay the guts of a king's ransom for a bag. Surely you'd get tired of it after a few seasons.

I pretended to enjoy running in and out of the horribly expensive shops, nosing around the opulent accessories

departments, comparing hugely expensive shoes and bags we'd
no intention of buying. Mum seemed to enjoy it, and was a
lot more relaxed than when she'd first arrived. She was clearly
relieved to hear I'd called off the wedding and she was also
buoyed up by the realisation that Liam hadn't been telling her
a load of fibs after all. He *had* been interested in seeing her;
furthermore, he'd been sent to her with Juliet's blessing. I just
didn't know what kind of blessing Juliet had been invoking
when she'd changed her will and set me up against James.

And afterwards, most unfortunately for me and my mother's
sensitive ears, it all came flooding out.

࿔࿇

Later that evening, we sat in a restaurant off the Via del Corso
sipping Prosecco and nibbling pan-fried sea bass. The restaurant
was chic, with whitewashed walls, wooden ceilings and flickering
candlelight in coloured glasses dotted around the tables. A few
hardy souls were sitting outside on the terrace, watching the
world go by, but we had opted for a table inside.

'I'm so glad we had this weekend together,' Mum said.

'Yeah, it was good,' I said, realising too late that I sounded
totally pissed off.

'But, Danielle, I don't understand.' My mother looked at me
shrewdly. 'How come you still look so – I dunno – woebegone,
three months down the line, if it was you who called off the
wedding? And why couldn't you tell me at the time? Am I that
much of a monster? Or are you having big regrets?'

I sighed and bit my lip. 'No regrets, Mum, but it's a long
story.'

It wasn't that I looked woebegone, not literally. It was more that my state of mind was at an all-time low. The hopelessness of my situation had been running through my veins, faster and faster, building up inside me ever since I'd seen James in the St Michel. That weekend had been the first occasion I'd spent any length of time with him since I'd realised how I felt. I didn't count the day of Juliet's funeral – that had been a fragment of time out of step with everything else. And I was beginning to realise that it wasn't just a case of learning to live with unrequited love, or unfulfilled desires: it went deeper than that, as though everything that defined me, both physically and spiritually, had utterly changed.

No matter how hard I tried to reach back to the me who had been chugging along, putting down a growing dissatisfaction with my life and impending wedding to pre-nuptial jitters, or to the me who'd been putting up a false front for Erin and Gemma, that Danielle was gone for ever. The new me's nerve endings were exposed like frayed threads, and even my heart felt raw and tender, as though all the protective layers had been removed. How I was going to stay sane as I went through the ordeal of talking about Verbena View with James, I did not know.

And now that Mum was feeling a lot more on top of things than she'd been when she'd first arrived in Rome, her problem-seeking antennae had zoned in on that. She was obviously scared of putting her feet in it because she merely said, 'I'm glad you have no regrets, and I won't probe, darling. I'm sorry if I've upset you.'

'No worries,' I said, attempting to eat some lettuce that tasted like rubber as depression settled like a heavy cloak on my shoulders.

'Well, this is nice, isn't it?' Mum said, with forced cheer, as she glanced around the restaurant, determined to look on the bright side. Her mouth curved in a wide smile, but it was totally at odds with the pained look in her eyes as she glanced tentatively at me.

That look tipped me over the edge. My face collapsed and I burst into tears.

I don't know who was more horrified, me or Mum. I stared at her wildly and caught my breath, but instead of managing to compose myself, it was as though something had been breached inside me and the floodgates opened. I picked up my bag and dashed for the Ladies.

I thought I was never going to stop crying. Even my stomach was heaving. I pictured Mum sitting alone outside, agonising about her choice of words as she tried to figure out what she'd said to send me into a meltdown. After a short while the outer door opened and I heard her voice.

'Danielle, I'm outside,' she said calmly. 'Take your time, darling, and whenever you're ready we'll head off, okay?'

'Okay,' I said thickly.

It was another full five minutes before I was composed enough to open the door of the cubicle and go to the washbasins. Mum was sitting on a chair. She jumped to her feet and wordlessly gave me a hug. I fixed my face as best I could, tidied up the mascara running down my cheeks and patted my hot, damp skin.

'I think I'm ready now,' I said, giving her a watery grin.

She smiled. 'Right so.' Head high, she led the way out of the restaurant, as though she was shepherding the Queen on a walkabout. I followed her, bravely ignoring the curious glances. Outside, I drew in gulps of the chilly night air. It slid across my hot face, cooling and soothing. I had a peculiar blank feeling, as though I was totally drained inside. We said very little as we walked home, along the same route I'd taken with James just over a week before.

Then I found my voice. 'The reason I broke up with Conor …' I began.

'Danielle – honestly, love, you don't have to tell me if you don't want to.'

I ignored her. 'It was because I knew I didn't love him, not properly, because, you see, I realised I loved someone else.'

'Oh, God. Then of course you'd no choice but to call off the wedding.'

'I know.'

We reached the big intersection in front of the monument to Vittorio Emanuele II. I felt dizzy, remembering the feel of James's hand on my arm last week as we crossed the busy road. I could almost pretend he was there now, could feel his tall frame moving alongside me, that I just had to tilt my face to see him silhouetted against the street-light.

I blinked. Of course he wasn't there. And I missed him so much that the ache swelled inside me, like a cold, sharp wave.

'This other man. The one you love, is he here in Rome?' Mum asked, as we waited for a safe moment to cross.

'No, Mum. He doesn't even know how I feel about him and he can't find out. So it's a hopeless situation.'

She digested this in silence as we concentrated on getting across the intersection. There was a slight break in the traffic and we ventured into the road, Mum doing her best impression of a traffic warden as she raised a forbidding hand against a motorcyclist, lest he dare pass within a few feet of me and harm a hair of my head.

When we got to the other side and headed in the direction of my apartment, she said, 'That's too bad, Danielle. I'd imagine any man would be delighted to know you love him.'

Ahead of us lay the Forum. The remnants of temples and

basilicas lay eerily still in the night air, a lot of the magnificence now reduced to rubble, tumbled walls and redundant columns rising a ghostly grey into the sky. On the road, scooters buzzed and cars honked.

'Look at that landscape,' Mum said, pausing in her stride. 'The heart and soul of ancient, civilised Rome. So many historic ruins. It makes you think, doesn't it?'

'Think what?' I asked, a little annoyed that she'd changed the subject so easily, when I'd just revealed what was in my innermost heart.

'About all the thousands of spirits that have passed through here for generations, living and loving. Our ancestors. All gone now and most of them forgotten.'

'Yeah, we're just insignificant dots in the great scheme of the universe, aren't we?' I guessed where she was coming from: it was typical Mum-speak for putting your problems into perspective.

'That's not what I was trying to say, Danielle,' she said, turning to face me. 'I guess I'm a bit emotional right now, thinking of Juliet, your dad too, but the gift of your life, *your* life, is very significant and beyond price. It's worth everything. You're very precious to me, to your family and your friends. And the love you have for someone, even if it can't be reciprocated, is a very special gift. Juliet loved you, and that's still there, in your heart, even though she's not around. Don't ever think love is hopeless or put yourself down for feeling it. Love is never, ever wasted and it's always positive.'

'Yes, but supposing … supposing you love the person so much that you want to be with them and you can't, and it makes you sad?'

'Ah, that happens,' she said, smiling at me. 'I didn't say loving someone was easy. It brings its own costs, like anything else worthwhile. I was in great pain after Harry died and he was gone from my life. Now I'm grateful for what we had, and it's still in my heart. Have you even tried telling him you love him? Or, better again, something more important, have you shown him by your actions that he means so much to you? Just in case?'

'No way,' I said. 'That would cause all sorts of problems. Even your best magic wand, Mum, can't sort this out for me.'

'Of course not, Danielle. I know that. I can't make everyone happy, much as I'd like to. I'm just giving you something to think about. Imagine for one moment if Juliet was in your situation, what do you think she'd do? Would she take a chance? Risk all for love?'

I started to cry again. For a moment I felt Juliet putting her arms around me, full of warmth and love, then smiling at me in that jokey way she had. I heard her telling me to listen to my heart. I saw her watching my face in the reflection of the glass at Verbena View and intercepting the way I was gazing at James.

Mum didn't know what to make of me as, once more, I sniffed and choked and bawled into a wad of tissues.

'I'm sorry, I shouldn't have mentioned Juliet,' she said, her hand creeping around my shoulders. 'It's still so raw and sore.'

And then the words gushed out of me, as though a plug had become undone.

'I think Juliet knew,' I gasped through my tears.

Mum was puzzled. 'Knew what?'

'Knew that I was in love …'

'What makes you say that?'

'She saw. She saw me looking at him,' I babbled, my whole body shaking. 'In Verbena View. At Christmas. And then she went and complicated everything. And now she's gone I can't even ask her what the hell she was thinking …'

'Danielle, calm down. Just breathe slowly. In and out. Who did Juliet see you looking at?' Even though her face looked swimmy through my tears I saw that her eyes were huge with apprehension and I think she knew what I was going to say before the words shot out of my mouth.

'James. My cousin. See?' I glared at her. 'And it's all a big fat crappy mess.' I promptly leaned into her and burst into more tears.

FIFTY-SIX

There was a lot to be said, Rebecca decided, for being enclosed in a capsule speeding thousands of feet above the ground, looking down at fuzzy cotton-wool clouds and, between the gaps, the sugar-dusted slate grey peaks of the Alps. Detached like this from ordinary life, with a stranger sitting beside you, there wasn't much you could do and no one was able to contact or expect anything of you. A welcome respite between the trauma of Danielle in Rome and whatever difficulties lay ahead when she got back to Dublin.

If only she could stay like this for a little longer. Because, for once in her life, Rebecca knew that there was no easy way out of this dilemma. No matter what she did or didn't do, she was caught between her daughter and her sister, and one of them was going to be hurt. The hardest part of love, she decided, was standing back while others got hurt, and all you could do was to pick up the pieces.

'Don't tell a single soul, Mum,' Danielle had urged, the previous night, when they were back in her apartment and she was a little calmer. 'Whatever I said, please keep it to yourself.'

'I will, if that's what you want,' Rebecca had answered, her heart heavy. 'Whatever happens, I love you, Danielle. I just want you to be happy.'

Long after she'd gone to bed in Danielle's tiny bedroom, Rebecca had lain awake, tossing and turning. How could she tell Danielle the truth about James? If she remained silent, was there any chance Danielle might patch up her sore heart and get on with life as best she could? If she told her the truth, all hell would break loose. Danielle couldn't be expected to keep something so shattering to herself. James would find out sooner rather than later. Rose would never speak to her again. And she hadn't even started to think of Matthew, hell bent on his latest challenge.

They couldn't even keep it within the family, because if Danielle and James did get together, the news and gossip would explode across the media stratosphere and the likes of Liz Monaghan would have a field day.

If they got together.

For, as Danielle had told her when they had chatted late into the night, even with all conventions laid aside, James still regarded her as a sort of sister. Yet, Rebecca told herself, Juliet, in changing her will, had set them up for some kind of showdown. And she'd spoken of setting the past to rights just before she'd died. She might have retained some of her youthful rebellious streak, but no way would she have set out to hurt either Danielle or James.

It had been almost light by the time Rebecca had nodded off, managing to snatch a couple of hours' sleep before she had to get up, grab a quick breakfast and head to the airport. Once she'd been through security checks and Passport Control, she'd sat down with a large cappuccino and an apple croissant, taken a deep breath and texted Liam, apologising for the misunderstanding.

Liam had replied just before she boarded her flight:

Would love to c u right now to clear this up in person x
Difficult! I'm in Rome about to board a flight home xx
Hope to c u later xxx

All too soon, they landed in Dublin airport, and Rebecca's heart was heavy as she disembarked, thinking of the difficult predicament she faced.

To her pleasure, Liam was waiting for her when she came through Arrivals. He was looking elsewhere, his attention caught by three small children hurling themselves at their waiting grandparents, and it gave her time to study him unobserved. He was smiling at them, his eyes kind, his face soft. He looked like the sort of man she'd want to spend time with and get to know a whole lot better. And maybe have him at her back if things got too crazy.

The kind of man Harry would have approved of.

The man Juliet had nudged in her direction.

Her heart lifted a little. She moved towards him, feeling a little giddy. Then he looked at her and his face changed as something like gratitude broke across it. They came together in the middle of the hall, and she inhaled his lime scent as his arms went around her.

'Thank you,' she said, her voice muffled against the curve of his neck. She leaned back to look at his face.

'I haven't done anything yet,' he said.

'You're here. You've forgiven me for being so horrible to you.'

'Oh, have I?' His eyes teased. 'I could be working out an appropriate, equally horrible revenge.'

'Like what?'

'Let me see …' He linked his hands around the small of her back, holding her securely. 'This for starters,' he said, bending his head so that his mouth was inches from hers. She waited, leaned into him more and gave a little sigh. At last he began to kiss her, very thoroughly, heedless of everyone else. She clung to him and kissed him back, equally heedless because, she reasoned, the airport was one place you could kiss in front of crowds of people and get away with it.

∽∾

She'd never liked Sunday afternoons. They reminded her of tedious Sunday afternoons in Ballymalin when the stale air permeating the house seemed weighted with her mother's abject unhappiness. Not to mention the Sunday afternoon when Annie Monaghan had decided that enough was enough and taken leave of a life that had brought her heartbreak, heedless of the fact that her sixteen-year-old daughter would find her.

Now the walls of her house in Harold's Cross were crowding in on Liz, the solitude crushing her spirits, and she couldn't rest easy. On impulse, she put on some mascara and lip gloss, tied her hair back in a ponytail, fetched her Polaroid sunglasses and a jacket, and left the house. She hailed a passing taxi and went to Grafton Street. Better to mingle with the cheery noise and life of city-centre crowds on a Sunday afternoon than sit moping alone at home.

The street was thrumming with life and colour, thanks to the mêlée of flower sellers, buskers, tourists and shoppers, but as she drifted through it all, observing the vitality around her, she felt eerily detached from everything. She stood outside Brown

Thomas, staring in at the busy cosmetics counters, but couldn't bring herself to venture in. She was barely able even to recognise her reflection, thrown back at her from the large mirrors inside.

As luck would have it, on the one day she was hoping not to run into anyone she knew, she bumped into Gavin as she turned away dejectedly from the window. He was marching purposefully down Wicklow Street. At the last minute he saw her and stopped abruptly.

'Liz! What happened to you?'

She stared at him, her heart sinking. 'What do you mean?'

He was clearly flummoxed. 'It's just … you look different …'

She took off her sunglasses and narrowed her eyes, meeting his gaze. 'You mean I'm not all glammed up.'

'That's probably it, yeah, right,' he said. He seemed embarrassed, yet he went on to ask her solicitously, 'You're a bit pale. Are you feeling all right?'

'Why wouldn't I be?'

'Everything okay?'

'Yes, of course.'

'I didn't see your diary slot this weekend.'

She shrugged. 'Just taking a break.' She was unwilling to admit that she'd been too low and depressed to summon any enthusiasm for her usual outrageous commentary.

There was another silence between them and, to her horror, he put out a hand and smoothed back tendrils of her hair that had escaped from her hasty ponytail.

'I still think we could have made a go of it, you and I.'

She felt sudden tears at the back of her eyes and ordered them to stay there. He was right. He'd been right all along when he'd sussed out the problems in their relationship. She knew that now. And if she'd known earlier that she hadn't, after all, been responsible for her mother's unhappiness, she might have had the guts to make a go of her own marriage.

But it had come too late to rescue her.

'We might have, once upon a time,' she said, 'but too much has gone wrong.'

'Has it really, Liz?' He looked at her intently, and her heart leaped with the hope she saw in his face. And then it crashed back to earth.

'It's too late for us, Gavin. Too late for me.' She laughed dismissively. 'But thanks anyway.'

She swung through the door into the big department store, trying to get away from him, conscious of him staring at her through the window as she went through the cosmetics department until she was satisfied she was out of his sight. Then she headed for another exit.

Back home, she sat at the kitchen table and poured herself a vodka. She opened the envelope she'd brought up from Ballymalin and spread the documents across the table, examining them closely: the bills from a psychiatric hospital, where her mother had been a patient not once but *three* times. One of those times had been soon after her parents' wedding. Two receipts from a hotel, just one night each, so faded they were almost indecipherable; she made out that one was dated several months before she was born. Then, tying the whole lot together, the small, square, borderless photograph with the name 'Juliet Jordan' written in pencil on the back. She wouldn't have recognised the girl with the short black hair wearing the yellow-rimmed sunglasses but for that. The photograph, also, was faded. She knew from its condition that it had been taken many years ago.

Separately, they could have meant anything. Her mother ill, yeah, right. Thanks to her alcoholism, she'd been ill throughout

Liz's life. That was no secret. Hotel bills? Her father might have been on a business trip. But a photo of someone she hardly knew, with all of these, was another matter. Especially when they had been carefully placed together in an envelope for her to find.

Together they spelled out the sordid little secret behind her mother's ill health and alcoholism. She wanted to cry for that bewildered child, and even more devastated teenager, who'd felt somehow responsible for her mother's unhappy life, never mind her tragic death. But she couldn't allow herself the luxury of tears just yet.

Rose and Rebecca, Juliet's friends, must have known something. Coming from Ballymalin, they were the only obvious link between Juliet and Liz's father. Without them, it was very doubtful that their paths would have crossed. She'd enjoyed spooking Rebecca who, naturally enough, wasn't going to admit that her friend had had an affair, but the anxiety sparking in her eyes had told Liz that she was on the right track. She'd enjoyed spooking the terrified Rose even more: she had looked so full of guilt and for some reason seemed to think her whole family was under threat.

There was another story there, she sensed. Something deep and dark was troubling Rose. But that was for another day. Right now it was time to find out which of those bitches had been responsible for bringing Juliet and Tom Monaghan together. Because it was perfectly clear to her that his affair with Juliet had caused her mother heartbreak, destroyed her marriage and led her down the road to a psychiatric hospital, followed by alcoholism and a tragic death.

And ultimately ruined Liz's life too.

FIFTY-SEVEN

'I'm incredibly nervous,' Rebecca said.

'Me too.' Liam smiled at her.

'I haven't … since …'

'And I've waited a long time for this.'

'Really?'

'You look beautiful when you blush like that.'

'Do I?'

His hand reached out and curved around her hot cheek. 'Yes, Rebecca, you do.'

She'd known this was about to happen since she'd seen him waiting for her in the airport. She wanted it to happen. She wanted to forget, for an afternoon, her dilemma: she had to choose between the happiness of her sister and that of her daughter.

Although it was no real dilemma: Danielle would always come first.

But, no matter what happened, this was her life too, and she wanted to live the rest of it to the max, to feel desire fulfilled and the heat of a lover's caress, as well as the warm comfort of a cuddle. She wasn't going to waste a single moment, or pass up any capacity she had to give or receive love.

Liam had driven her home after he'd collected her at the airport, and she'd felt full of edgy anticipation as she'd hurried upstairs and changed out of her travel clothes. Her hands had been shaking as she'd riffled through her wardrobe, picking out a scarlet shirt, black trousers and thin stiletto heels. They went for a late Sunday lunch in Dawson Street. Now it was the early evening and they were sharing a bottle of wine in his apartment. It was basic but modern, and had everything a person could need. Outside the window, the evening sky was serrated with herringbone clouds, and the muted rumble of passing traffic mingled with the cries of the seagulls along the nearby canal.

Sitting on the sofa, she said, 'Seeing as you've waited a long time, and I'm so nervous that I'm trembling, I think we should get this over with as quickly as possible.'

His eyebrows shot up. 'Get it over with? My dear Rebecca, I want to take my time and enjoy every inch of you. Slowly and leisurely.'

Her face flooded with more heat. 'I meant the, um, undressing part. I'm not exactly in my prime. The quicker I get between the sheets …'

'I've no intention of hiding you under the sheets,' he said gently, 'and you are fabulously beautiful, every part of you. But, yes, the sooner we get started the better.'

Before she knew it, Liam had lowered the blind on the window, and swung her around so that she was lying along the sofa. Her heart tripped alarmingly as he took off her shoes and kissed her feet. Her throat tightened as he began to undo the buttons of her shirt, his eyes widening as he took in the scarlet lacy bra she was wearing underneath.

'Wow,' he said, smiling at her, the spark in his eyes melting away all her fears.

She didn't tell him that Harry had bought it for her, on holiday in Spain one year, but he had passed away before she'd had the chance to wear it for him, and she'd stored it in its tissue paper. Until now. She didn't tell him that under her black trousers she was wearing matching scarlet briefs. She'd let him find that out for himself. Which he did, flashing her another look: it was thick with desire and melted her insides.

Soon the room was filled with the sounds of love: laughter and long, deep sighs, of Rebecca's sharp intake of breath and low moans, of helpless giggles when one side of the sofa suddenly jerked backwards so that they had to abandon it for the accommodating width of the bed, pattering hurriedly across the wooden floor in bare feet, their giggles quietening down once more to soft murmurs and cries of pleasure.

And finally, long afterwards, the sound of sleep as night fell and they cuddled under the duvet.

⇝⇜

Rebecca waited until Monday evening before she made the difficult call to Rose: she wanted to prolong the lovely glow that surrounded her after her night with Liam. She clung to it like a safety net, letting it warm her as she speed-dialled her sister.

'How were Rome and Danielle?' Rose asked.

'So-so,' Rebecca said, and chatted about her flights, shopping and Danielle's apartment before she came to the point. 'Danielle was very surprised when I told her about Juliet's will. I don't think it really sank in. Have you given any thought to what you might say to James?'

'No …' Rose sounded hesitant. 'I was half hoping you might talk to him, you being the executor of the will.'

'Yes, but he'd think it strange that his own parents hadn't mentioned it to him.'

There was a short silence and then Rose admitted, 'I'm terrified of somehow saying the wrong thing. Even Liz Monaghan—'

'What about her?' Rebecca asked, feeling her hackles rise.

'She was chasing me for a comment on Saturday at the charity fundraiser. I didn't want to go but Matthew insisted, and she managed to snare me. Anyway, I lost the plot and told her – God, Rebecca, I went and told her to fuck off.'

'*You?*'

'Yes. I was so shaken by her. She says she's determined to get to the bottom of whatever's going on between us. Oh, Christ, I'm falling apart. I don't know what else might come shooting out of my mouth.'

'You're not falling apart. But I was thinking of what you said about everything changing now that Juliet is gone. And maybe,' Rebecca went on ultra-carefully, 'just supposing you were to tell James the truth, in a quiet way?'

'Are you *mad*? I can't do that.'

'You said it yourself, Rose, that you felt badly about James not knowing his mother was dead. And supposing Liz does manage to stumble on something … or if you let something slip … It could be a whole lot worse.'

'I wish you wouldn't scare me like this.'

'I'm not trying to scare you. I'm just suggesting that if somehow James was to discover the truth, it would be far better coming from you than for him to find it headlined in Liz Monaghan's tabloid column. Think about it.'

'It's totally and unbelievably out of the question,' Rose said, her voice shaking.

'Is it? I'm sure it could be sorted out quietly, somehow, without getting blasted across the national press. Where is James now?'

'He's home since this morning. So, please, would you talk to him? And forget all this other nonsense.'

'God knows what I might say to him.'

'Don't be like that, please, Rebecca. You know I trust you.'

And so does Danielle, Rebecca thought bleakly.

After the call, Rebecca went into the conservatory and tried to recapture the magic of the previous night with Liam. She'd be seeing him tomorrow evening and, all of a sudden, it couldn't come quickly enough. Yet her head was filled with Rose and Danielle and she kept coming back to the moment on the cliff when Juliet had talked about the truth coming out, telling Rebecca she didn't know the half of it. What had she meant? Had Juliet known something about James that had made her feel it was time to come clean? Changing her will didn't mean all that much: chances were, Juliet had expected to live a long and happy life. It might have been another thirty years before Danielle and James were thrown together in the melting pot of her legacy.

Unless it had been just the start of Juliet allowing things to come out into the open.

It was all so terribly messy. Rebecca was caught between her daughter's happiness and her sister's peace of mind, and for someone who liked everyone to be content, it was an impossible place to be.

FIFTY-EIGHT

'Rose? What's the matter?' Matthew asked, stepping into the kitchen where she was sitting at the table with a glass of wine. He was in his shirtsleeves as he took a glass from the press and filled it with filtered water and ice.

In other words, he was still working, even if she was relaxing to the point of getting quietly drunk.

'Oh, nothing,' Rose said. 'As if Liz Monaghan wasn't bad enough in her mission to dig up some dirt, now Rebecca's trying to scare me half to death.'

'What is it?' He looked impatient. Impatient, but resigned to the prospect of talking his wife through yet another mini-meltdown.

'Nothing you need worry about,' she said. 'I daren't keep you from your busy mobile or your all-important blog.'

'Right so,' he said. 'I won't ask you what you're doing drinking in here on your own.' He walked back to the kitchen door.

'You might be free of Juliet's threat,' she said, halting him in his tracks, 'but you could have a problem with Rebecca.'

He wheeled around. 'Don't tell me we're back to this again! I told you, Juliet was no threat.'

'I always wondered why you were so sure of that,' she said. 'You know, Matthew, you never told me you were texting Juliet. The day she died.'

'What are you on about now?'

'I know you sent Juliet a text that day.'

'So? I would have sent her a few texts. We sometimes compared notes and I checked points of business law with her.'

'Wanting to meet up at her place doesn't sound like a business call to me. "We have to talk. Your place."' The words that had imprinted themselves on her brain flowed all too easily, considering how choked up she felt.

There was a tiny pause. Then, 'For God's sake, Rose, okay, maybe I wanted to talk to her to make sure she wasn't going to do anything stupid, anything that might hurt you or me, but she never replied.'

'So you weren't having an affair?'

She hated the way he looked at her, as though she was stark, raving mad.

'I don't know what's got into you tonight,' he said evenly, 'but I've work to be getting on with.'

'You didn't answer my question. So. You. Weren't. Having. An. Affair. With. Juliet?'

'Of course not. What's brought this on?'

'But you were concerned about the can of worms she might have opened after all, even though you told me not to worry.'

He gave a small shrug. 'It doesn't matter now, does it? I didn't get a chance to talk to her.'

'Didn't you? I've had nightmares, Matthew. I've been having them for years, but they've got much worse since Juliet died. I even had a nightmare that you could have been with her on that cliff just before she fell. Because she could have pulled the plug on your ultimate dream.'

He looked disbelieving. 'For God's sake, Rose, how many bottles of wine have you drunk?'

'It doesn't matter. It's not the wine. I just can't hold it together any more,' Rose said, trying to make sense of the formless panic that had swept through her during Rebecca's phone call and stayed. 'I've had the feeling that my life was about to unravel and I think this is it. I've lost the plot. So I'm just getting some stuff off my chest, stuff I was afraid to say before. But now I don't give a damn. Nothing matters.'

'You'd better pull yourself together in time for tomorrow night,' Matthew said. 'We've a reception to go to. And I don't know where you got the crazy notion that I was having an affair with Juliet.' He seemed mildly insulted as he headed for the door.

And once more Rose stopped him: all her pent-up insecurities and fears were finally getting the better of her. 'You see, I sometimes wondered if James was actually yours,' she said. 'I even thought you might have been the married man Juliet had the affair with. I was amazed you agreed to take him on as your son.'

'I wanted to make you happy, Rose. I knew how desperate you were for a family. And it was the least I could do.'

In the distance, from his study, there came the tinny sound of his mobile.

'What do you mean, the least you could do?' she asked.

Matthew went to the door. 'I have to get that.'

She got up and followed him along the corridor, the mobile increasing in volume. 'You didn't answer me, Matthew. The least you could do for Juliet, having made her pregnant?'

Just as Matthew reached his desk, his mobile stopped ringing. He picked it up and checked the caller display, exasperation darkening his face. 'I don't know who that was,' he fumed. 'And I'm expecting an important call.' He tossed his mobile on to the desk and gripped the back of his chair. 'I told you I wasn't having

an affair, God damn it.' His voice was raised. 'Neither did I push
Juliet off a cliff. And I wish you'd pull yourself together. I did it
for you, Rose, to give you the baby you desperately wanted.'

She stared at him, something astounding shimmering at the
edge of her mind. When her voice came out it didn't sound like
hers. 'Did you not think, Matthew, that we might have had one
of our own?'

His easy confidence faltered. 'Well, we weren't, were we?'

She felt a coldness crawling up her spine. In spite of the fuzz
of the wine, she saw a guarded apprehension in her husband's
face that alerted her. 'You seem very sure of that, Matthew,' she
said, her voice soft. 'Did you know for definite we weren't having
any ourselves?' Then she raised her voice: 'Did you?'

'It scarcely matters now, in the overall scheme of things,'
he said, his eyes flickering to his laptop screen. 'It was another
lifetime ago.'

'What scarcely matters? Why did you accept Juliet's baby so
readily?' she pressed.

'I told you, I was only too happy to make sure you had your
dream of motherhood.'

'Because you couldn't give it to me,' she said, taking a wild
leap into the very worst of her dark corners. 'You couldn't give
me a baby.'

'Well … I didn't know for sure …' He stared at his mobile, as
though he was willing it to ring.

Her head felt light. For a minute she couldn't breathe. Her
voice, when she managed to speak, was thin and whispery. 'Is
this – are you telling me— What do you mean, Matthew?' She
found it impossible to grasp what he was saying.

'Look,' he snapped, 'if you really have to know, I'll spell it
out, will I? There was no affair with Juliet, and James is not my

biological son. I had a rather bad case of mumps the year before we married.'

She shook her head. 'I don't remember that.'

'I told you it was tonsillitis.'

'*What?* Why did you lie to me, Matthew?'

'Because I had to. Because I was told there was a good possibility that I couldn't father a child. But it worked out all right, didn't it? You had your baby.'

Unable to believe what she was hearing, she scrabbled for words. 'You mean you knew, when you married me, that there was a good chance we'd never have a family?'

'Not for definite. But when nothing happened after we'd been trying for more than a year, I – um – guessed it was my fault.'

She was sinking into icy water. It was closing around her, so cold she could hardly breathe. 'But how – how could you have married me, knowing that? Knowing how much I wanted children?'

'I told you, I didn't know for certain. I thought you loved me for myself and not for my capacity to give you kids.'

'Yes, but we talked about having a family.' Her breathing was laboured. 'You knew how I felt about that and you said *nothing*?'

'Rose, it was years ago,' he entreated. 'Look how far we've come. I took you away from that crappy job and working-class Ballymalin. I gave you everything you could wish for. Stop looking at me as though I'm the devil himself. It scarcely matters any more, does it?'

She felt faint. 'I can't believe this. I gave up my job … my *life* … to marry you and have your children.'

'I'm sorry if it's a shock,' Matthew said, uncertainty in his eyes, 'but everything turned out fine, didn't it? We have our son, even if it wasn't quite how we expected to. I've spent my life making up for it, giving you everything I could.'

'I can't believe your arrogance. Why did you marry me? *Why?*'

'I loved you. I still do.'

Something snapped inside Rose. She was still trapped in that freezing water, but now she struggled to free herself instead of allowing it to overpower her. 'No, you don't. You didn't,' she said, her voice quivering. 'If you'd really loved me, you'd have told me the truth. You married me because you thought I'd be a good, placid wife, happy to cook and clean and iron your shirts, there in the background of your life, nothing better than an unpaid skivvy and an unpaid prostitute. Someone who thought it was *her* fault when no children arrived ... someone who wouldn't dare question the virility of ambitious, egotistical, fucking brilliant Mr Matthew Moore.'

'Jesus, Rose, that's a bit over the top.'

'I haven't even started,' she stormed. Trembling with shock and rage, she continued, her voice hoarse, 'I used to wonder, Matthew, what was driving you onwards and upwards. Why you weren't content with your lot. I used to wonder why you clashed with Juliet at times. I thought it was some kind of unfulfilled passion running between you. Now I know it was envy on your part. Because she did something you could never do. She'd had a child of her own. You owed her big-time for getting you out of a stinking big hole, and you resented that because you didn't like being beholden to her. It all makes perfect sense to me now.'

'You're talking rubbish.'

His mobile rang.

'Leave it,' she barked.

His hand reached out, but she was too quick for him. She grabbed his shrieking phone and lifted her arm.

'Rose. Don't.'

'Don't what?' For someone who'd been drowning a moment ago, she felt an amazing surge of power.

'Put that down.'

'It's payback time, Matthew.'

'For what? I gave you what you wanted.'

'No. You gave me what suited *you*. You deceived me. You married me under false pretences. You lied to me by omission.' She brought down his mobile with such force that it crashed against the keys of his laptop and was instantly silenced. 'And that's just for starters.'

'For fuck's sake, Rose, are you mad?'

'Yes, I am, I'm as mad as hell – and do you know something? It feels bloody great! It feels brilliant!' The words tumbled out, like a volcano spewing lava. 'All these years I felt guilty for not giving you a family. I thought *I* was to blame. That I was doing something wrong, or wasn't good enough to have a child of my own. All these years I've lived with the fear of being found out over James. Sometimes it made me feel savage inside. And it got much worse in the last few weeks. But guess what, Matthew? I feel liberated at last. I'm not afraid of anything any more.' Her eyes darted about his desk and she picked up his laptop so swiftly that the power cord was yanked out. Then she hurled it across the room so that it hit the glass doors of the antique bookcase, shattering them.

He stared at her, his face pale. 'You've gone too far this time.'

'You're the one who went too far, Matthew. You've forgotten who you are – that's if you were ever anyone to begin with. And don't let me get started on your integrity bullshit, or God knows what damage I might do to that monstrosity of a kitchen.'

She knew from the shock in his eyes that he had finally grasped the depth of her rage.

'You have to calm down,' he urged. 'We can talk about this, work it out.'

'Don't you get it? It's too late,' she cried. 'I've been living on a fault line for years. Now I've finally fallen through the crack, right to the bottom, and guess what, I'm still alive. At last I'm making sense of me. Nothing worse can happen.'

'Yes, it can,' he said, his jaw tight.

'Oh? And what might that be?'

'You'd want to be very careful.' He spoke to her as though he was dealing with a particularly fractious child. He started to move around the table towards her. 'You'd want to calm down, chill out, maybe go away for a few days to a relaxing spa. You'd like that, wouldn't you? If you don't cool down you might say something you regret and, who knows, word might get back to James.'

'Ah, yes.' She smiled, standing her ground. 'James. I was wondering when we'd get around to him.'

FIFTY-NINE

'It's fine, honestly,' Rebecca said to Maria. 'You go ahead and I'll lock up.'

Tuesday afternoon at Olivia Jayne had been quiet, and it was just coming up to a quarter to six when Rebecca told Maria to go home.

'Are you sure?' said Maria. 'You know Amanda likes two of us to be here at a time.'

'Yes, but it's not as if we're going to be deluged with last-minute customers,' Rebecca said. 'I'll be after you shortly.'

After Maria had left, Rebecca refreshed the Mimosa fragrance diffuser and checked the bargain rail. The occasional customer had the happy knack of placing a full-priced dress or shirt on it, then looking for a discount. Outside, the skies were low and grey and the car park in the small shopping complex was slowly emptying. The bookshop next door had already closed for the evening and the chemist would be next. The wine shop on the corner would be open until ten o'clock, and as soon as she locked up the boutique, Rebecca was going to pop in to pick up a couple of bottles of her favourite rioja reserve and some nibbles.

Liam was calling over at seven, and bringing an Indian takeaway. They both knew he would be staying the night, in one of the spare rooms, with Rebecca. She wasn't quite ready yet to take him into the bed she'd shared with Harry, but she couldn't wait to spend the night with him and feel his arms around her.

She'd had the weird feeling all day that she was moving about in the eye of a storm. There had been silence from Rose after her call the previous evening. Funnily enough, she'd half expected to hear from Matthew, angry with her for upsetting his wife. And she hadn't dared to contact Danielle, beyond a couple of texts, afraid of what she might be tempted into saying over the phone.

A few short weeks ago, she would have asked herself what right she had to find happiness in Liam's arms, given the mess that her sister and daughter were caught up in. Now, as she fastened buttons on silk shirts and hung dresses tidily in size order, she felt curiously disengaged from their problems, as though she and Liam existed in their own private bubble, away from whatever was going on around them.

Sometimes she'd felt like this with Harry, that they drew strength from each other against the world.

At five to six, she checked that the back of the shop was locked up, the cash and receipts secured in the safe. She went out into the blustery evening and pulled the shutter across the window, locking it in place. Then she pulled the door shutter halfway down and ducked back inside to fetch her bag, switch on the alarm and turn off the lights.

She was turning off the lights in the small storeroom when she heard the shutter over the door being pushed up, then yanked down again.

'I'm sorry, we're just …' The rest of the sentence dried in her mouth as she turned around and came face to face with Liz Monaghan.

'Liz?' she said. 'Are you okay?'

❧

Rose stepped out of the taxi at Spencer Dock and shivered in the blustery wind blowing off the Liffey. For once she didn't have to put on a false mask in front of a camera lens or pretend to be someone she wasn't. The river was running at full tide, the choppy surface mirroring the slate grey sky, against which the arches of the Samuel Beckett Bridge gleamed like bleached bones. She took a deep breath of the salt-laden breeze.

She was amazingly calm as she straightened her shoulders and wove through the oncoming pedestrians, guessing from the high-spirited groups of jeans-clad twenty-somethings making their way down the quays that there was a gig on tonight in the O_2.

Oh, to be young, carefree and heading off to a pop concert. She'd never had that freedom. She'd never travelled the world, or even backpacked around Europe. She'd never watched the sun rise in Paris or the sun set off a Greek island. She'd never spent a gap year in Australia, gone up in a hot-air balloon or risked a parachute jump. At sixteen, she'd gone straight from school into the civil service, and a few years later into marriage with Matthew. Another form of servitude. There had been no such thing as the luxury of finding herself. She'd thought her marriage had been bound by lies, little realising she'd been oblivious to the biggest lie of all: Matthew's false promises.

'You're not going to do anything foolish, are you, Rose?' Matthew had said, the previous night, as she'd marched out of his study and up to their bedroom. She'd ignored him, taking her small travel case out of her dressing room, her hands remarkably steady as she'd folded in clothes and underwear.

'We're in this together,' he'd said. 'You don't want James to hate you, do you?' He was moving around the bedroom, towards her. If he put his arms around her she'd scream.

'All of a sudden that doesn't matter,' she'd said, surprised by how free she felt, how clear it all was, so simple and yet so right. 'The most important thing is that I'll never stop loving him. That won't change, no matter what happens. But now I love him enough to tell him the truth, whatever it costs me.'

She'd walked out of the gilded bedroom and he'd followed her down the stairs.

'This has gone far enough,' he'd said, standing between her and the door, but not laying a finger on her, as though he knew she'd explode. 'Come on, Rose, cut the crap.'

She'd smiled at him. 'That's exactly what I'm doing, Matthew. I'm cutting the crap out of my life. If there's one thing I've realised, with Juliet gone, it's that life is far too short. It only happens once and there are no second chances. For me, this is it.'

As she'd walked out of the door at Belgrave Park, Matthew had stood in the porch, looking as though he expected her to turn tail and come back, but she didn't. Legs shaking, she'd walked up to the junction and hailed a taxi, asking the driver to take her to a business hotel on the outskirts of the city where it was unlikely she'd be recognised.

Without Matthew, nobody had given her a second glance. The receptionist had barely looked at her as she'd asked if Rose had a reservation.

'I don't,' Rose had said.

The receptionist had checked her computer terminal as she ran her fingers over her keyboard. 'We have availability.' She'd smiled a polite smile. 'What's the name?'

'Rose O'Malley.'

It was a long time since she'd been Rose O'Malley and it would take a while to find her again, get to know her. As she'd stood by the desk, something had shimmered in front of her eyes.

The rest of her life.

Now she hurried towards the entrance to the apartment block on Spencer Dock, where James's luxury penthouse took up the top floor.

ᏬᏇᎦ

'Hey, lil cuz.'

My heart warmed at the sound of James's voice on the phone. 'Hey, yourself. And what fabulous hotel room in what fabulous part of the world are you calling from now?'

'Would you believe I'm holed up in some crummy flat in Dublin, down by the Liffey?' He laughed.

'You're back,' I said, a wave of homesickness sweeping over me.

'Yeah, I got home yesterday morning, and it's good,' he said.

'I think I'd call a five-star signature penthouse pretty good. You'd have to bolt down your toiletries if I happened to visit.'

'I'd give them to you for free if you happened to visit.'

His words echoed in my heart and I told myself not to make too much of them. It was just James talking to his sort-of little sister.

'I think it'll be a while before I'm home,' I said lightly.

'Pity. I could do with having you around.'

'What for?' My voice cracked.

There was a beat of silence, and then he said, 'It feels weird this time. No Juliet to laugh with, and I don't think I've any idea yet how much I'm going to miss her.'

'I know.'

'You didn't hear any more from your mum, I suppose, about how Juliet died?'

'The investigation's still going on,' I said. 'The last I heard from Mum is that the police are still not sure if she fell or was pushed.'

'Jesus. Pretty rough for Rebecca and my mum. Never mind Juliet. Who the hell would— Christ, if I thought anyone had touched a hair on her head, I'd strangle them myself with my bare hands. Mum's calling over to see me this evening so I'll get the latest from her.'

Suddenly my heart was hammering.

'She said she needs to talk to me,' he went on. 'I'll ask her if The Name can keep up the promo for Juliet's children's charity. It's the least we can do. What's happening to that, do you know?'

'I'm not sure,' I said slowly. 'It'll be a while before her affairs are sorted.'

'Seems a shame to let that slide. There's a job for you, if you ever come home. You could put your marketing skills to work. Anyway, my door buzzer's going so Mum's here. Earlier than I'd expected. I'll catch you later, lil cuz.'

'Thanks, James.'

I looked at his name disappearing off my mobile display as the call ended and something like desolation swept over me.

❧

'I'm sorry, Liz, we're closed,' Rebecca said, as the other woman advanced into the boutique, her feline eyes darting about.

'I'm not interested in any of your crappy clothes,' she sneered.

'What do you want?' Rebecca asked, suddenly alert, her skin prickling.

'I want to find out which bitch introduced Juliet Jordan to my father. You or Rose?'

'Your *father*?' Rebecca was perplexed. 'Tom Monaghan?' An image of the tall, attractive doctor who'd lived on the affluent side of Ballymalin popped into her head. He'd been a few years older than her and she'd hardly known him because their paths had rarely crossed. She did remember, though, the hushed gossip when he'd married Annie: people were astonished that kind-hearted Tom had lumbered himself with such a troublesome, vexatious woman.

'Yes, my father. The great Tom Monaghan. Only he wasn't so great after all when he went and had a dirty little affair with that slut Juliet, ruining my mother's life. *And* mine.'

'I don't know what you're talking about.'

'Yes, you do. You must have introduced them. Either you or your sister. How else would they have met?'

'Sorry, Liz, I haven't a clue what you're on about.' Rebecca wondered how quickly she could get rid of her.

'Like hell you don't. I know for a fact that Juliet had an affair with my father. The stress of it landed my mother in a psychiatric hospital.'

'Your mother? But she passed away years ago. Besides …' Rebecca fell silent, deciding it was best not to say that Liz's mother had been well known in Ballymalin for having so-called delicate nerves long before she'd married Tom.

'I *am* talking about years ago,' Liz said. 'I knew my mother was unhappy with her life, and I thought I was somehow to blame. Because of me she was stuck fast in a marriage she couldn't escape from. See?'

She didn't see at all, but Rebecca nodded. Maybe Liz just needed to get something off her chest.

'All along I thought I'd done something wrong by being born.' Suddenly she poked at Rebecca's shoulder with her index finger and Rebecca backed away. 'But when I was emptying the house I found it.'

'Found what?'

'An old photograph of Juliet in an envelope.'

'That doesn't mean anything,' Rebecca said, her head whirling as she tried to make sense of this.

'Not by itself, no,' Liz said, her hand now clenched around the bargain rail so that the knuckles were white. 'But it was in an envelope, hidden in a press, with old hotel bills and bills from a psychiatric hospital … It all adds up. Juliet had an affair with my father. And it broke my mother's heart.'

'I don't know anything about this,' Rebecca said, feeling faint. 'And if the photograph is old, how do you know it's Juliet?'

'What about this?' With a flourish, Liz pulled a small photograph out of her jacket pocket and held it so that Rebecca could see the name pencilled on the back. She turned it around, and Rebecca saw her friend smiling at her against a background of a bright blue sky. The way she'd smiled at her years ago. On the beach in Benidorm. She even recalled Juliet haggling over the cheap yellow sunglasses in a local souvenir shop. How the hell had a picture of her in Benidorm ended up in Liz Monaghan's parents' house?

'Where did you get that?' she asked Liz.

'I told you, it was hidden away by my mother. She knew I'd find it in years to come, when I'd be clearing out the house. She must have discovered it in my father's office some time before she died.'

Then everything clicked into place.

They'd met at the airport. In the long check-in queue. He'd been in a group of four, all people Rebecca knew, all on the same flight, heading for the same resort.

'I didn't think half of Ballymalin would be on our flight,' she'd grumbled.

'He's a bit of all right,' Juliet had said, eyeing a tall, attractive man.

'Yes, he's lovely,' Rebecca had said, 'but he's married and his wife is very odd. I hope they're not going to the same resort as us.'

'You might as well introduce us.'

'Okay, but after that I'm keeping away from them as I don't want to speak to a single Irish person for the next two weeks …'

You knew only half the story, Juliet had said. It had been an affair with a married man, all right, but not a far-flung anonymous cousin of her old boyfriend – Rebecca couldn't even recall his name. It had been someone far closer to home. It had been the unhappily married, good-natured, attractive Tom Monaghan, who had died soon after Christmas, after a long spell in a nursing home.

And all those years ago Rebecca had introduced them. She could easily see how Tom had fallen for the bright, effervescent Juliet and vice versa. She could imagine the sparks flying between them. No wonder Juliet had withheld the truth from her. She'd known her friend would have felt partly responsible for Juliet's predicament in having introduced them, and it would have made the arrangements for the baby a lot more difficult.

James! Was Liz his half-sister? Rebecca couldn't even begin to work out what it meant for him. 'Holy shite.' The words escaped her lips.

'So you did know.' Liz's eyes glittered.

'I didn't,' Rebecca said. 'I don't know anything about this at all.'

Liz leaned in close to her, her eyes blazing. 'You're just as infuriating as she was.'

'What do you mean?' Rebecca asked, a sliver of foreboding creeping up her spine.

'Juliet. When I asked her.'

'When did you talk to her?'

Was this why Juliet had talked of regrets? Had Liz snagged at her uneasy conscience? Rebecca fervently hoped it was, rather than the terrifying thought that hovered in the air. She was aware of how defenceless she was against the height and strength of an angry Liz, almost as defenceless as Juliet would have been on the cliff. She was alone in the shop with her, and no one could see in through the shutters. Her bag, with her mobile tucked away, was down by the far side of the counter. Liz was standing rather threateningly between her and the doorway.

'When were you talking to Juliet?' Rebecca asked once more, blood turning to ice in her veins.

Liz's eyes were suddenly guarded, and Rebecca realised she was doing this all wrong. 'Why don't we go out for a coffee, or a glass of wine, and have a proper chat about it?' she suggested, in the pleasantest voice she could muster. 'I can see how this must have been upsetting for you, Liz. I'm sure there's a rational explanation.'

'That's exactly what she said,' Liz replied, leaning towards her. 'She got the surprise of her life. But she still wouldn't admit anything.'

'When was this? Tell me about it, Liz,' she asked softly, quietly amazed at herself.

'I called her and told her I wanted to do a profile of her, seeing that there was talk of her running for the presidency. She said she was busy and I should make an appointment. Then I said I was keen to prove myself as a serious journalist. I told her I'd love to publicise her charity efforts. Just five minutes? That was clever of me, because she said she hoped to go out for her walk later that evening, so if I could join her then, it was the only free time she had to chat. But when I called to the house I was too early so she even poured me a glass of wine ...' Liz's eyes had a faraway look in them that chilled Rebecca to the bone. 'I insisted that she have one as well, and I said a walk would be lovely – I could get to know the real Juliet that way. But that was only a ruse, of course. We hadn't gone too far around the cliff top when I told her I knew about her and my father. But she wouldn't admit it. She wouldn't admit *anything*. She even got cross with me for pretending I wanted an interview. How was I supposed to feel?' Once again, Liz poked Rebecca's shoulder, and continued until she was pinned against the wall.

'I don't think Juliet meant to get cross with you,' Rebecca said, willing herself to remain calm.

'Yes, she did. The slut! She didn't care about my mother, or the crappy childhood I'd had.'

Rebecca found herself rising to her friend's defence: 'Your mother was sick, Liz, even before she married your father. Everyone in Ballymalin knew it. I think your father thought he'd cure her but he couldn't. It wasn't Juliet's fault she landed in a psychiatric hospital. Look, let's go somewhere and talk properly about this.'

'That's exactly what *she* said, about my mother being sick. But it's a lie. I got so angry that I shouted at her. But she still didn't say she was sorry.'

Rebecca's throat almost closed with fear. Every cell in her body turned to water. 'I can understand how angry you must have felt,' she said.

'My mother was a very angry person. Do you know what she used to do to my father? And sometimes me?'

Rebecca shook her head.

'This,' said Liz, drawing back her arm and striking Rebecca hard across the face. 'She hated being stuck in her marriage,' she shouted. She swung her arm the other way and struck her again, harder this time.

'You're a fucked-up bitch,' Rebecca said, through gritted teeth.

'And guess who caused it,' Liz roared, lunging at her.

All of a sudden Rebecca was fighting for her life. She tried to get away from Liz, but she was no match for the taller woman. Liz caught hold of her from behind, one hand gripping her hair, the other her shoulder, and pushed her hard against the end of the bargain rail so her neck was squeezed against the chrome. Rebecca was winded and dazed. Her arms flailed uselessly into the row of clothes, the hangers jangling. She aimed feeble kicks at Liz's shins. Liz pulled her back, almost lifting her off her feet, handling her as though she was a rag doll.

'See? You can't even cry, can you? Juliet had no time to cry out. I don't think she even knew what was happening.' Once again, she shoved Rebecca's neck hard against the chrome rail. Rebecca was so dazed she might have collapsed, except that Liz was holding her. Once again she dragged her back from the brink of unconsciousness. Rebecca dimly noticed she was pulling her further back to propel her even harder against the end of the chrome rail. Through half-closed eyes, she watched the hazy jumble of chrome and clothes rushing towards her, but this time she burrowed her arms into the clothes, clawing at them, her fingers working furiously and instinctively until she'd freed a hanger. As she slumped against the rail, she slid the hanger down between the clothes until she was grasping it with both hands. The minute she felt Liz draw her back again, she lifted the hanger and pushed it back as hard as she could over her head, in the direction of Liz's face, until she felt it connect.

Liz let go of her, which gave Rebecca one split second. One second to make a dash to the doorway, half running, half crawling, to push up the shutter enough to crawl out, feeling Liz's hand snaking around her ankle. Supporting herself on her hands, she aimed a kick with her free leg, and then she was gulping cold, fresh air, her heart thumping as she crawled on to the pavement, lurched to her feet and staggered to the safety of the chemist.

The girls in the shop sat her down and phoned the police. But when they went up to the boutique, all three of them, to fetch Rebecca's bag and her mobile so she could call Amanda and Liam, the shop was empty.

SIXTY

Liz took another slug of neat vodka. It burned her throat and helped another layer of comforting fuzz to settle around her. She was in the front room of the house in Ballymalin, half sitting, half slumped on the sofa. Outside, the bushes were rattling in the breeze and it was getting dark. Inside, the house was full of shadows and silence. She hadn't bothered to switch on the lamps, the light slanting in from the hall more than enough for her. She had plenty of tablets and plenty of vodka. She wondered if she'd pass out from too much drink before she managed to complete the job.

There was no point in anything any more.

She couldn't sleep and she couldn't eat. Every time she closed her eyes she saw Juliet in the moment before she fell. The look in the other woman's eyes haunted her. She hadn't meant to push her. She certainly hadn't meant to kill her. Afterwards, she'd tried to blank it out, convince herself it hadn't happened. But Juliet's eyes hadn't allowed for that.

That was why she'd made sure Rebecca Ryan was facing away from her as she'd bashed her against the clothes rail. Somehow that had gone wrong, too. She hadn't meant to hurt Rebecca any more than she'd intended to hurt Juliet, but they'd fired up her temper so much that she'd lost control.

Who did they think she was that they couldn't just admit the truth? Why had they been so dismissive of her? What had they been afraid of?

Juliet had ended up plunging down a cliff, making things messier than ever, and Rebecca had almost broken Liz's nose. After Rebecca had escaped and run for help, Liz had rushed out to her car and driven on instinct to Ballymalin.

She wondered how long it would take the police to figure out she wasn't in Harold's Cross. She hoped she'd be unconscious before they arrived here. She'd never realised she'd feel quite so sad and lonely near the end. Had her mother felt like this before she'd lost consciousness? Had Juliet? Then again, she'd had good friends, friends who clearly loved her.

Her father must have loved Juliet to risk an affair with her, given how angry her mother could be.

Her father. He'd never got over her mother's death and Liz had turned her back on him in the aftermath, as if blaming him in some odd way.

But there was someone who would have loved her, Liz realised, if she'd allowed him to. If things had been different. Her mobile sat on the table in front of her. It would take a minute to press a couple of buttons and bring up her emergency contact number. But she couldn't do it. How could she drag Gavin into all this? It was far, far too late, now that she had murder on her conscience, no matter how much he said he loved her.

And no one would believe she hadn't meant it to happen.

She took another tablet and lifted the vodka to her lips, tilting her head to take a decent long slug. One more should do the trick. Maybe two.

And then she saw it, shimmering against the dark shadows in the corner of the room. It was the figure of a woman, not grey or frightening, not bloodied or terrifying. She looked ethereally beautiful. And her eyes were smiling.

Liz froze. She was still sitting there, the bottle poised against her mouth, when from outside the flash of revolving blue lights lit up the room, scattering the shadows and anything within them. She waited quietly, ignoring the lone tear that trickled down her face.

SIXTY-ONE

As luck would have it, the Friday-evening flight from Rome to Dublin was delayed and I had to sit, my irritation rising, with at least a hundred impatient travellers in the holding area beside the boarding gates for more than half an hour. Mum's call had been mystifying, and I was dying to get home to find out what was really going on.

'I'll pay for your flight,' she'd said hoarsely, when she'd called me on Wednesday evening. 'I know it'll be expensive as you're booking it at the last minute, but just get home this weekend. I have to see you.'

She'd sounded as if she'd spent at least three weeks crying.

'I'm not that hard up,' I'd said. 'Aren't you going to tell me what's wrong?'

Mum gave a heavy sigh. 'There's a lot going on, Danielle, and I have bad news that I'd rather tell you face to face than have you come across it online.' She paused.

'What is it?'

'It seems Juliet *was* pushed off that cliff,' she said. 'For some reason Liz Monaghan, the gossip-column woman, was with Juliet that evening. She was hoping to write a piece about her but freaked out when they were walking around the headland. Next thing …'

The hairs rose on the back of my neck. '*What?* I don't believe you.'

Mum was silent. After a while she said, 'It's a long story, and I want to see you and talk to you about it. So far it hasn't got into the papers as the police have a lid on it while they investigate further, but it's only a matter of time before it reaches the networks. Has … has James been on to you?'

'No, he was supposed to call me back the other evening but he didn't.' I'd sounded defensive – I was nervous of her mentioning his name, knowing what she knew.

'I see.' Another silence.

'Does he know what happened?'

'Look, Danielle, I'll see you on Friday night.'

The minute Mum had ended the call I'd tried James's mobile, but he seemed to have disconnected it as it didn't even go to voicemail. Now I felt even more uneasy. I'd tried to call him again on Thursday and the same thing happened. When I'd texted Mum my flight details, I made myself ask if he was okay. She texted back that he was fine. At least he was alive and well, but something big was definitely amiss. My impatience was spilling over as I joined the queue shuffling down the grey tunnel to the plane.

And I knew for sure something was wrong when Liam Corrigan was waiting for me in the arrivals hall at Dublin airport. Without Mum.

'What's going on, Liam? Where's Mum?' I asked, alarm mounting inside me when he picked up my weekend case and led the way not to the car park but to the coffee shops and sitting area.

'She's fine. Take a seat and I'll explain in a minute.' He smiled at me and went to the counter to order two coffees. I had no choice but to wait until he returned.

'Your mother is taking it easy at home for a few days,' he said. 'She asked me to collect you, just to put you in the picture. She doesn't want you to get too much of a shock when you see her. You see, Danielle, she was attacked in the shop by Liz Monaghan on Tuesday evening, but she's fine now.'

'*What?*' I spluttered into my coffee and pushed the cup away.

He told me then, glossing over the details, about the attack, then Mum managing to break free and running to the chemist. The assistants had called the police, and when they went to Olivia Jayne, no one was there and nothing had been disturbed. Then Mum had called Liam and Amanda, both of whom rushed over. As far as Amanda and the girls in the chemist were concerned, an intruder had broken in as Mum was closing up. But Mum had told the police about Liz, and what she'd said to her, and they had called the detectives involved in Juliet's case. Mum had had her injuries checked out, and afterwards had given a full statement to the detectives.

I was numb with shock, but I knew my questions would have to wait, for right then my main concern was Mum.

'Rebecca has bruising to her neck, and a black eye, but she'll make a perfect recovery,' Liam said.

I could see anxiety flickering in his eyes. 'I hope you've been taking good care of her,' I said.

'I have, and I'm going to keep on taking care of her, if she lets me. I hope you don't have a problem with that?'

I met his gaze head on. 'I'll only have a problem if you don't look after her properly. I want Mum to be happy.'

'You're your mother's daughter.' He smiled.

A few weeks ago I would have dissed that remark. Now I glowed with it. 'She's very special,' I said, 'and I love her to bits.'

'So do I.'

'Make sure you tell her that,' I said.

⋙⋘

Even though I'd been prepared, it was hard to hide my shock when I saw my beautiful mum with so many bruises discolouring her jaw and neck, never mind the black eye. I flew into her arms, careful not to hurt her.

'You should see the other guy,' she joked, sitting on the sofa in the conservatory, surrounded by a forest of flowers and magazines.

'Where's Liz?' I asked.

'She's still in hospital. In the psychiatric unit. She tried to … to take her own life, but they caught her in time.'

'What a pity,' I fumed. 'I can't believe what she did, Mum. She must have been crazy. I hope she'll be locked up for life. I presume she's been arrested?'

'She will be. And now, Liam,' she gave him a meaningful look, 'thanks a million for collecting Danielle, but I'll let you head off and see you tomorrow.'

Liam gave her a kiss and a hug, and he hugged me, too, before he left, then gave me a warm smile that put me on guard. He knew whatever there was to know, I guessed. And I was going to find out pretty soon.

I braced myself when Mum asked me to get a bottle of wine and two glasses, then patted the sofa beside her and asked me to sit down. 'I need to tell you exactly why Liz Monaghan did what she did.'

'I always knew she had a screw loose,' I said flippantly – the grave look in Mum's eyes had told me I was going to be well and truly shocked.

'She has big problems, all right,' Mum said. 'She's had an unhappy life and she lost her own mother tragically when she was only sixteen.'

'As if that makes it okay.'

'Anyway, Danielle, I need to start at the beginning, so you'll understand everything. All this goes back years ... back to the time, I guess, when Rose and I met Juliet on the train and we picked up the threads of our friendship.'

'Are we back to that story?'

'Yes,' Mum said gently. 'But this time I want to tell you the other side of it. And, please, don't hate any of us for what we did.'

I laughed. 'Of course not. How could I?'

It was the last time I laughed. It was after midnight before Mum got to the end of the story, about Juliet, James, Liz, and what had happened between Rose and Matthew, then Rose calling over to James's apartment to tell him the truth after her row with Matthew.

James had gone ballistic. It was just after he'd been talking to me. And I knew then why I hadn't been able to reach him on his mobile.

That was the moment I put my head in my hands and begged Mum not to tell me any more.

I don't know how my legs carried me up the stairs to my bedroom. I felt so fragile I thought I was going to disappear. My hands seemed transparent and my legs felt like water. I only knew I was still alive by the breath coming in and out of me, and the thump of my heart. It was mad, I thought, how the physical body continued to exist after the rest of you was smashed up. I was still awake at three o'clock in the morning, trying to make sense of the way every single part of my life had been torn asunder and flattened into microscopic dust.

I must have slept eventually because when I woke up and reached for my mobile, it was eleven o'clock the following day. I got out of bed automatically. This is how a robot must feel, I decided, as I showered and dressed. Then I saw how ridiculous that idea was: robots had no feelings because they were mechanical objects. I wondered if I'd go through the rest of my life like an unfeeling machine.

But when I caught the scent of coffee coming from the kitchen, my mouth watered. I went downstairs to find Mum at the table with a light scarf wrapped around her neck, and her black eye all the colours of the rainbow.

She gave me a tentative smile. 'I'm glad you're still here,' she said.

'I am, just about,' I said, unable to return her smile. I poured a mug of coffee and sat down opposite her. 'I don't hate you, Mum,' I said, 'but I'm all over the place and I need to get my head straight.'

'Of course.'

'Where's Rose now?' I asked, still piecing stuff together.

'She's staying in a hotel while she decides what do to. She called over on Wednesday and we had a long chat.'

I took a few sips of coffee. 'I can't believe she's walked out on Matthew, never mind had the guts to come clean with James.'

'She says she found the courage from somewhere inside her. She said that James deserved to know the truth and she loved him enough to risk his anger.'

I sipped more coffee and silently applauded my aunt.

'She's upset, of course, that he went mad, but she's still glad she told him,' Mum continued. 'She's not going to rush into anything, and for the first time in years she feels free of the burden that was eating her up inside.'

'Do you think she'll go back to Matthew?' I asked, helping myself to a croissant.

'I honestly don't know, Danielle. If she does, it'll be on her terms.'

'I suppose his campaign has gone down the tubes.'

'I'm not sure about that either, but it hadn't really started. I haven't been talking to him, but I gather from Rose that he's devastated she's walked out and he's more concerned with saving his marriage, if there's anything left to save.'

'Good. I guess he does love her, then.'

'I don't know what kind of media fallout we can expect, but none of us will be talking to the press.'

'No.'

We fell silent, while I finished the croissant and toyed with the burning questions I was terrified of asking. And, full credit to my mum, she guessed what I needed to know but was afraid to voice.

'James is over at Verbena View,' she said.

'Oh?'

'Yes. He called in to see me on Thursday for a chat. He wanted to hear the story again from my point of view. Unfortunately I had more shocks in store for him as he didn't know I'd been hurt. Neither did he know about Liz Monaghan and that connection … I didn't breathe a word of our conversation, Danielle. He's …'
She paused.

'He's what, Mum?'

'He's very upset and confused. In shock, I suppose. He told me he's never talking to Rose or Matthew again. He understands what they did, years ago, even if they did ignore the law, but he can't believe that they hadn't the guts to tell him the truth before now. He's even more broken-hearted now that Juliet's gone.'

'In that case,' I asked, my voice shaking a little, 'what's he doing at Verbena View?'

'I gave him the spare keys,' Mum said. 'The police finished with the house on Wednesday and handed them back to me. It's still as Juliet left it, full of her presence. I suggested he spend a couple of days there, among her things, remembering the good times he had with her. I thought it might help him to feel close to her and come to terms with her in this new light, to cherish her memory and appreciate her love. It may give him some kind of consolation, if that's possible.'

I was crying by the time she'd finished talking. 'I have to see him,' I said, my voice thin and jittery.

Mum's hand came across the table and covered mine. 'Of course you do,' she said. 'Take my key in case he won't answer the door.'

We sat in silence for a while as her hand rested on mine, all the energy and warmth of her love flowing into me.

I wondered if I could do the same for James.

SIXTY-TWO

A torn remnant of police tape, still caught in the gates to Juliet's house, fluttered in the breeze. I parked in a corner of the driveway beside James's car. The front windows of the house glinted with pale sunshine, the sky was a faint blue, scored with jet trails, and the air tasted fresh and tangy.

I'd already texted James to say I was on the way, but I didn't know if he was checking his mobile. I wasn't surprised when he didn't answer the door, but I pressed the bell and called through the letterbox to warn him that I was there. Then my shaky fingers fitted the key into the lock and I went in, my blood pounding in my ears.

Mum was right. The house echoed with Juliet's spirit, and it was as warm and inviting as ever, not in the least bit spooky. I wouldn't have been afraid to be there on my own. I passed down the hall, echoes of her laughter wrapping around me, and in the kitchen her smiling face was everywhere.

My throat closed when I saw the calendar pinned to the corkboard, the one I'd given her last Christmas. It still displayed the month of March, and the picture was one James had taken of Juliet and me against a backdrop of the Blue Mountains in Sydney. I'd even had my wedding printed in the box for 17 March.

Beyond the table, the patio doors were folded back, and I

could see the top of James's head as he sat in one of Juliet's patio chairs, facing the back garden and the crystalline light of the sea beyond.

Something was knocking on the wall of my chest. After a minute I realised it was my heart.

'James, it's me,' I said.

He remained motionless. I walked out on to the patio. He was slumped in the chair, legs stretched out, eyes fastened on the blue-grey infinity, while a muscle flexed in his unshaven jaw. He ignored me as I pulled out a seat and sat alongside him.

'James, your little cuz wants to talk to you,' I said, not knowing how I managed to speak.

No reaction whatsoever.

'I know you're shocked and upset. I understand.'

Still a stony silence.

'I'm here to help.'

I waited. He continued to ignore me. I tried a different approach. 'James? What kind of crap is this? You can't just pretend I'm not here.' I was hoping to jolt him out of his silence.

It didn't work. I racked my brains, wondering how to get through to him.

'Juliet loved you very much,' I began, stumbling over my words. 'Remember we were talking, when you visited me in Rome, about the long conversation I had with Juliet in Sydney? When she said she had big regrets? She told me there was someone she loved very much but she wasn't in a position to tell him. I thought at the time she might have been involved with a man, but looking back on our conversation now, I realise she was talking about you.'

I stole a look at him. Nothing about his face had changed. I stared beyond the light of the sea to the folds of the Dublin mountains, shimmering on the far-off horizon, and wondered what to say for the best.

'Juliet told me she didn't have the courage to listen to her heart at an important time in her life,' I went on. 'And in case you were too shocked to take on board anything my mum said to you on Thursday, Juliet was talking to her in the week before she died about putting the past to some kind of rights. Unfortunately,' my voice softened, 'she ran out of time. I'm glad to say I've plenty of time. I have the whole evening just to sit here talking to you.'

There was still no response from the man sitting beside me and my courage was faltering.

'I know you're very angry with Rose and Matthew,' I said. 'I don't know what to say except they loved you as best they could. No way would Juliet have given you to them, to love and cherish and take care of, unless she was pretty sure she could trust them to do a damn good job. Which they did.'

He was still silent.

'As time went on it must have seemed impossible to tell you the truth. I'm not surprised Rose ended up having a nervous breakdown. This is exactly the kind of situation that she and Matthew were terrified of. You, their cherished son, refusing to talk to them, ever again.'

My heart quickened when James ran a hand over his stubbly chin and closed his eyes. I didn't know what kind of pictures he was seeing. I wondered about the girl in his life, the beautiful, talented and charming girl he'd told me about in Rome. The spark he'd hoped would burn out. But I was going to tell him what Juliet hadn't had time for. I was going to risk all for love. And it was easier to speak when he had his eyes closed.

'It was my fault that Juliet changed her will in favour of us,' I began tentatively. 'She saw me, at Christmas, when …' The rest of the sentence died in my throat, because he finally opened his eyes. My heart lurched when I saw the tenderness in them.

'How could it have been your fault?' he asked.

I took a deep breath. 'Juliet caught me looking at you, just after we were joking about the wedding music.'

'So?'

I wasn't sure how to do this. I heard the echo of Juliet telling me to make every moment of my life count, and this, surely, was as important as it would get. 'It was the way she saw me looking at you. Like this …' Suddenly I had the courage to face him head on, and I gazed at him, my eyes roving slowly across every contour in his face as though it meant the world to me. I absorbed every part of it, the slight grooves in his wide forehead, and his suddenly guarded deep blue eyes. I let my gaze linger on his soft mouth, then down to his square chin, my own eyes full of longing, full of desire, and then at last I spoke the words that Juliet had never been able to, the words I had thought I could never voice.

'I want you to know that I love you, James,' I said. 'You're the reason I called off my wedding. I knew here, at Christmas, that I couldn't marry Conor because of how I felt about you. And I love you enough to risk making the biggest fool of myself. I don't care if you think I'm mad, or speaking out of turn, but I'm not going to have the same kind of regrets that Juliet had. I know you just think of me as your honorary sister, your nuisance of a cousin, but—'

'I don't,' he said, looking at me.

My eyes locked with his. There was a moment of silence when nothing else existed, not even the running of the sea, because of the way James was looking at me. As though I was beautiful, talented and charming. As though he loved and desired me. As the world slowly moved again, I scented the salty breeze riffling through the bushes, I felt the light coming off the sea on my face and I blinked. I heard two gulls call as they wheeled into the air. And all my raw, spiky nerve endings healed so that they glowed and sparked, and my heart rose into my throat.

'When … when did this happen?' I asked.

'I've always loved you, Dani,' he said. 'Didn't you know? You mean the world to me. You always have. I think Juliet guessed how I felt because she would have caught me looking at you. But from the time you were sixteen, there was always some guy in your life. You had a right procession of them, all dancing attendance on you, and then you went and hooked up with Conor … and, anyway, it would have been a little messy between us, to say the least.'

'Those guys? James, you've come between me and every man I've ever known. I tried really hard to make a go of it with Conor because I thought I couldn't have you. Then I realised that marrying him would be wrong. But it's not messy any more,' I said, rising to my feet and going across to where he was sitting.

Juliet's tall and beautiful son.

Mr Justice Henry Jordan's beautiful grandson.

The man I loved.

I put my arms around his shoulders and kissed the side of his face, my heartbeat thrumming in my ears.

He put his hand up, caught my arm and said, 'I've wanted you for ever, but I'm not in a good place right now, Dani. I feel too dark and down to impose myself on you. You deserve better than this.'

'Better than this?' I asked, moving around in front of him, putting my cheek close to his, feeling his breath on my face, his skin against mine. 'I'm in the most perfect spot in the world with the man I love. What more could I want? Juliet can't tell you she loves you, but I will, over and over. Every day, for the rest of my life.'

I drew back slightly, touched his mouth with my fingertips, and something rippled across his face. His eyes filled with tears. Then he turned his head so that his face was cradled in my hand and the tears slipped through my fingers.

'Whatever place you're in, I'm with you,' I said, just before I kissed his mouth.